BRUTAL BULLY

A DARK HIGH SCHOOL BULLY ROMANCE

LOGAN FOX

AUTHOR NOTE

This book contains mature content and subjects some readers may find triggering.
For a full list of triggers, please visit my website at https://authorloganfox.com/triggers.

Please note that this book was previously published as Brutal Prince.

JOIN THE FOX DEN

Can I send you my secret dark romance novella that's never been published…?
Join my VIP newsletter and you'll receive your own exclusive copy of My Darling, and I'll keep you up to date with my new releases and promos!
https://authorloganfox.com/my-darling-signup

PLAYLIST

French 75 — Cane Hill
Cage — Blackshots
Who's Gonna Stop Me — Tommee Profitt, Jung Youth
lovely — Billie Eilish, Khalid
Forgive Me — The Plot In You
My Body Is a Cage — Monarchy
DRIP — Crywolf
when the party's over — Billie Eilish
Your Love is Like a Car Crash — Blue October
Stop a Bullet — Black Light Burns
Heaven — Julia Michaels

To view this playlist, please visit my website at https:// authorloganfox.com/playlists.

PROLOGUE

Life isn't fair.

Life is fucking cruel.

But we only get this one, so we have to make it count. You can't dwell on the past. You have to look ahead, count your blessings, and make plans for the future.

That's what my mother used to tell me, when I was sad because my best friend moved out of town. When I had to have surgery to remove my tonsils. Then, a year later, my appendix.

She'd always have faith that a better day was just behind the horizon.

Go to sleep, my girl.

Have pleasant dreams.

Tomorrow is a new day.

My mother was raped, tortured, and murdered last week during a home invasion. The sadistic criminal who did it then set fire to our home.

Where was I?

At a party, getting drunk and trying to lose my virginity.

It's been eight days, fourteen hours since my mother's

beautiful soul left this earth. Life should have been easier by now, but it's not.

See…Mom lied.

It doesn't matter how many times I go to sleep, I don't have pleasant dreams anymore.

When I try to count my blessings, I come up short.

My plans for the future?

I don't have any.

When I look ahead, all I see is darkness.

I'm waiting for that bright new day you promised me, mom.

Because tomorrow still hasn't come.

CHAPTER ONE

INDI

I don't remember Lavish being this travel-brochure perfect town nestled against the gentle slope of a mountain. Somehow, it's impossible for me to picture myself ever having lived here. I travelled through Mallhaven—Lavish's sister town— to get here. The towns share sinister-looking black peaks, as if they were split down the middle when those spires rose up out of hell.

When I drove through Mallhaven, the town was already cast in shadow. Lavish, on the other hand, dazzles in the remaining hour of sunlight.

My GPS sends me straight through town, where my path winds up one of the roads leading higher into the mountains. There are tons of pines here; so many that twilight's shadow falls around me as I stop outside a fanciful wrought-iron gate. I can't see a house from here. Instead, I'm surrounded by more firs and the dark, distant peaks of the Devil's Spine.

Getting out of the junker Mom's insurance company passed off as a rental car, I head over to the gate and grab hold of one of the iron flourishes.

The metal is ice-cold, slightly damp.

There's an intercom to one side. I press its button, and seconds later a voice warbles out through the speaker.

"Yes?"

"It's Indi."

"Excuse me?"

I grind my teeth as I bend at the waist to put my mouth closer to the slotted microphone. "Indigo. Virgo. Your granddaughter?"

"I was expecting you several hours ago."

I straighten, thinning my lips and hoping to all hell the voice on the other side of the line isn't expecting a reply. It was a five-hour drive through states and counties I've never been. What the hell was she expecting?

Slamming my car door, I rev the engine and tear through the gates as soon as they're just wide enough for me to pass.

As much as I would have liked to knock those majestic gates off-kilter, the last thing I need is Mom's insurance company billing me for damage to their car.

It's super hard to stay angry. I mean, I'm *trying*, but this place is just so fucking beautiful. The air is fresh and piney. A chill promises a cool night.

Lakeview—which I still insist should have been named Swampview—was always so hot and sticky. Even in winter, the nights were hot. We had air conditioning at our lake house, of course, but I've always been the outdoors type. I hated being cooped up in my room. Mom used to—

The road curves, and I almost don't make the unexpected turn. My wheels go off the side of the paved road, digging into soft grass and spitting it out behind me before I can steer back onto solid ground.

"Fuck."

I slow down the car, and then stop. As I wait for my heartbeat to drop back to normal, I peer out my windows to take in the towering pines and the dark, distant peaks.

They're prettier on this side. Not as sharp, not as jagged.

Hiding their true form.

It takes me a good few minutes to reach my new home.

I was expecting a mansion, but gran's place is just a big house. Double story, with a loft or attic on top. Big wrap-around porch. Immaculate lawn. No fences either—the lawn ends several yards away from the house.

Right where the now-black forest begins.

There's a woman standing by the front door. She looks like those old, rich ladies who wear pearls to breakfast and have a butler whose name is undoubtedly James. But contrasted against a house that needs a new coat of paint and some replacement roof tiles, Grandma Marigold looks out of place.

I stop my car in the drive, get out, and wave at her.

She's wearing a dress-suit and standing tall and proper, with her lips pursed and red as a raspberry. She shifts her shoulders a bit, purse intensifying the closer I get.

It's been years since I've seen her last. Close to two decades, in fact. That was right about the time Mom and I moved to Lakeview.

She's not anything like I remember, except if what I have in my head are manufactured memories from a toddler. *My* gran had rosy cheeks, a chubby body perfect for hugs, and a smile that could light up the room.

Just like my mother.

I force a smile. "Hey, Granny—"

"You shall call me Marigold," she cuts in. Her eyes rake over me, and don't I feel every inch of a pile of brittle yellow autumn leaves right now?

"You look just like your mother." It should have been a compliment—Mom was the epitome of grace and beauty—but in that tone of voice, it becomes an insult.

Eyes the color of flint dismiss me. "And you're late, just like she always was."

"Yeah, I do take after her," I murmur to myself as Marigold pivots on her mules and struts inside.

I glance out at Lavish before following. I'm starting to wish I'd had a flat on the way and had to sleep in my car instead of washing up here.

Not that I have a choice, of course. I still have a few months to go before my eighteenth birthday, which means I'm still a minor.

Someone, apparently, has to take care of me until then.

Somehow, whoever gave Marigold that responsibility, has never met the witch in person.

"Dining room," Marigold states, flipping a hand in the direction of a glaringly sober teak dining room set sporting silver tableware.

"Living room." Another flip of her hand points at a room that hasn't seen any living in a fuck-long time.

She doesn't even have a television in there.

"Your room is upstairs, first door on the left."

"Thanks," I murmur.

Marigold stops, twists to face me, and studies her watch with lifted brows. "Dinner was ready an hour ago." Her mouth twitches as she lets out a labored sigh. "But I guess I can reheat everything. Wash up and be ready in fifteen minutes."

With that, she strides away.

I take the stairs two at a time, shaking my head and grinding my fucking teeth. I toss my backpack into my room which—no surprise—looks even less hospitable than the living room, and immediately begin exploring the house my mother grew up in. In fact, I grew up here too. For a year or two, anyway.

Which room was hers?

The next door opens to a second room that looks as much a guest room as mine. I don't even bother going inside.

There's a bathroom, a study, and then another bedroom on the other side of the hall.

Another guest room.

And, of course, the last room must belong to Marigold. I don't bother going to look—I'm pretty sure it's as devoid of personality as the rest of the place.

My shoulders droop as I thump my way downstairs.

I'd really hoped some trace of Mom remained in this place. A family photo, some toys; heck, even just one of her earlier paintings.

Guess Mom wasn't kidding when she said she and gran weren't on good terms. It all had to do with Dad, of course. Mom was a hopeless romantic, and as soon as she met her husband, she turned her back on the Davis family and became a Virgo instead. She lived in Lavish for a year or two after I was born, but then we all moved to Lakeview.

That was the last time I ever saw any of my family from Fool's Gold county. Honestly, I didn't miss them. My mom and my dad were the only family I ever needed.

I'm halfway down the stairs before I remember Marigold's stern instructions. And she's probably the kind of woman who'll insist on seeing my fingernails before I can sit at the dinner table.

I wash my hands in the bathroom sink and catch sight of myself in the mirror when I'm looking for the towel.

I look every inch the orphan I am. Shadows under my green eyes, my dark hair is mousy and unkempt, skin sallow.

Dinner is served on white china, with silver cutlery. Mashed potatoes, pale pork bangers, and a heap of pale peas.

I guess if anyone could suck the life from a bunch of peas, it would be Marigold.

And yeah, she does check my nails. I keep them short these days, no polish. I mean, what would be the point?

"I trust your trip was a pleasant one?" she asks, startling me out of the trance I put myself in trying to pin down a slippery pea.

"Huh?"

Her eyes narrow. "I do hope you don't plan on slouching like that at your new school, young *lady*."

Yup, there it is.

Guess gran was expecting a younger version of Mom. All radiant debutant and perfectly honed social skills. I used to love playing dress-up with her elegant cocktail dresses and expensive jewelry.

But ever since the home invasion—

"Sorry," I mutter, resuming my pea-chasing adventures in the land of white china and colorless silverware. "I left my ball gown behind in the blackened shell that used to be my house."

When I look up—because Marigold's gone all quiet—I regret the comment. Her face is as bone-white as the china. Even her red lips have paled.

"I'll see myself out," I mutter, shoving away my plate and storming from the dining room.

"Where do you think you're going?" Grandma's reedy voice calls out behind me.

"Out!"

"You can't drive on these roads after dark. It's too dangerous."

"Then I'll walk!"

"Don't go far."

Thankfully, the front door isn't locked—guess Lavish is one of those awesomely safe small towns where everyone's so rich, no one has to steal each other's stuff—so I head straight out and stand in what's left of twilight.

There's a buzz in my ears, and I don't like it one bit. It's usually the precursor to a binge. Like the one I was on the night my mother was murdered.

I glance behind me at the slightly dilapidated house and picture the prim and proper woman probably still seated at the dining room table, taking one tiny bite of food before putting her knife and fork down again.

Zipping my hoody up to my throat and whipping the hood over my head, I fast-walk straight for the fringe of pine trees suffocating Marigold's pathetic house.

How long until that bright new day, Mom? 'Cos all I'm seeing on the horizon are goddamn thunder clouds.

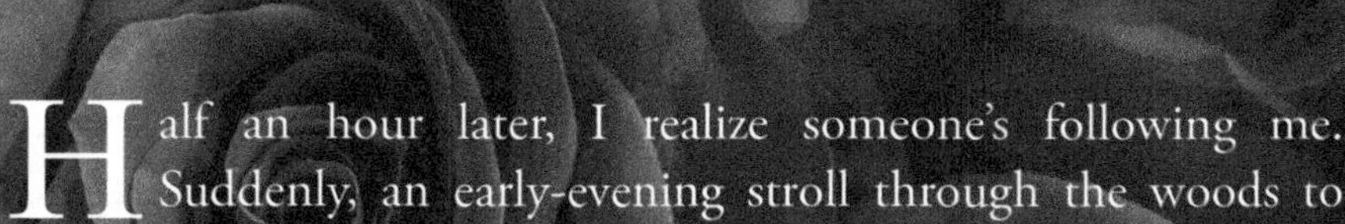

Half an hour later, I realize someone's following me. Suddenly, an early-evening stroll through the woods to clear my head doesn't seem like such a good idea anymore.

I know I should hurry back to Marigold's house as if the Big Bad Wolf himself is after me, except…

I'm lost.

Yeah, I love the outdoors, but that doesn't mean I know how to navigate using the stars and shit. And the woods in and around Lakeview don't have shit on this place. I'd been following a path that became fainter and fainter, until I wasn't following anything anymore except my desperate need for space.

I glance around, but see nothing. I tug my hood up a little higher, wishing it was black and not beige. At least that way I could slip away into the shadows.

I break into a trot.

A second later, so does the person following me.

My trot turns into a slow run.

My pursuer speeds up.

I begin sprinting.

I dart between the trees, and barely avoid falling flat on my face when a root snags my sneaker. Catching myself against a tree trunk, I pause for all of one breath before I hear foliage snapping and breaking behind me.

I shove away from the tree and break into a run.

My breath comes hot and fast, my lungs screaming for me to stop. But if I do, I'm dead. I mean, why the hell else would some random guy be chasing me if he doesn't want to slit my throat? It's not as if I dropped my wallet or something.

I bat branches and leaves out of my way, forcing myself not to look back, knowing the second I do, I'll trip, fall, be gutted to death.

Instead, I squint forward. Finally, a dark shape looms up ahead. I skid to a halt as I gape at the remains of a church. The roof and two of the walls are caved in. Brambles have reclaimed much of the structure, leaves and drifts of dirt the rest. But there's no mistaking the cross that used to be on the tower, even if it's stuck upside down in a hillock of soil that's grown moss and small shrubs all over it.

And here I was trying to find my way back to my gran's house.

I want to laugh, but I'm too busy panting. Thundering footsteps push me out of my trance, and I dart into the midnight depths of the church. My heart thumps too hard, too loud, as I hunt around furiously for somewhere to hide.

BRIAR

I slow down to a walk, allowing my breathing to return to normal after the first leg of my evening run. I love these woods on a Sunday night. So quiet. Nothing but me and the trees. Early evening is best, of course, when there's just enough ambient light to make out the well-worn path between my house and the church.

Back in the day, I played cops and robbers in these woods with my best friend, Marcus. The church would always end up being the site of our inevitable Mexican standoffs. But fuck, that was more than eight years ago now. I don't even go inside the building I just use it as a landmark during my evening run. Halfway.

It's a challenging run; largely on an incline, and veering around the tangled foliage and the wicked thorns that give these woods their name. I've torn plenty of my clothes up here, and even had some scars added to my existing ones. The church itself is still a ways off, but I know this path so well I could walk it blindfolded.

I heave in a huge breath, mentally readying myself for another sprint, before a faint snapping of twigs reaches me. I let out a slow breath, straining to hear over the rush of blood in my ears.

I'm not alone anymore.

Wolves have been spotted here before. It's one of the reasons we were told never to play here when we were kids. Not that me and Marcus ever fucking cared.

As I listen, the sounds transform into footsteps.

Who the fuck dares to walk in my woods?

I bunch my jaw and change direction, angling toward the intruder.

By the time I get close enough to spot the idiot, it's so dark I can barely make them out.

If they hadn't been wearing a pale hoody, it would have been near impossible to track them.

I try to keep my footsteps as quiet as possible, but I'm tall and my shoulders are wide—I can either lose them or let them know I'm here.

Whoever it is, they're definitely on to me. That pale, baggy hoody keeps glancing left and right as their pace picks up.

Who the hell is this guy? He wears baggy clothing as if to disguise the fact that he's both short and slight.

Lavish is a small town—I would have heard of someone new arriving. Which means this guy's up to no good. Could be a vagrant from Mallhaven, or someone who got on the wrong bus and then decided to stay. We get them sometimes—people who come here lured by the promise of wealth just like my forefathers back in the day.

The guy in the hoody breaks into a jog.

I speed up, a faint smile touching my mouth.

They think they can outrun me? I'm Lavish Prep's best receiver.

But I guess they don't know that, do they?

INDI

I wedge myself behind the charcoal shell of a half-burned pew, my arm brushing against a vicious looking bramble clambering through a hole in the nearby wall.

The sound of running footsteps slow, slow, stop.

I clap both hands over my mouth, and consider the risk of

closing off my nose too, but I'm so out of breath, I'd probably pass out if I tried.

I hug my legs to my chest and burrow my head into them, desperate to quieten my panting. Carefully, so as not to make a sound, I lever the switchblade from my belt.

It's only a week old, but it already feels like an appendage. Now that it's in my hand, it feels heavy and cold. I pull out the blade, but I don't lock it in case that tiny sound gives away my location.

The police report stated that they suspected there was only one unsub responsible for what happened to my mother. They found only one pair of footprints, only one set of prints. Someone who wasn't in the system. Yet. I was informed invasions were a fact of life, even though I'd never heard of one happening in Lakeview before. The police told me it was probably a robbery, but that Mom surprised the thief when she came home early from her art exhibit.

If she hadn't come home early…

If dad had still been alive…

If she'd had something to defend herself…

So many ifs, and no one mentioned the one that mattered most.

If only I hadn't slipped out that night. Yes, it would most likely have been me surprising the thief while coming downstairs for a snack.

But then Mom would still be alive. And that's all that matters.

Dry leaves and dirt crunch under soles as my pursuer heads deeper into the church.

Crunch. Crunch. Crunch.

I was hoping I'd made it here fast enough that the guy would think I was long gone, but he must know these woods much better than I do—and the church is an obvious sanctuary.

Crunch.

He's heading away.

I draw a calming breath and slowly lift my head. It's so dark inside the church, all I can see are silhouettes. My heart just starts slowing down when my pursuer turns, and I catch sight of his profile.

A spike of fear washes me with panic, and my heart starts racing again.

Holy shit. He's fucking *huge.*

Something brushes the back of my hand, but I'm too transfixed on the monster who's standing less than a yard away, scanning the church interior as if he's trying to pick up my scent. Despite his size, he moves with the grace and casual ease of a hunter searching for his prey.

Which, in this case, is me.

My skin crawls, and it takes me a second to realize it's because there's something on the back of my hand, not just because I'm close to wetting myself.

It takes everything I have to look down.

A spider. And this isn't just a Daddy Long Legs. Nope. What's crawling on my hand is one nasty looking sonofabitch; all spidery fuzz and lethal-looking fangs. A scream bubbles in the back of my throat.

Without bothering to consider the repercussions, I flick it off me. The sleeve of my hoody snags on a bramble thorn. My urgent movements shake the whole bush.

The guy spins to face me and lunges forward.

I yell out, but the sound barely leaves my lips before he grabs my ankles and drags me out of my hiding place.

The knife. The fucking knife!

But he's too far away, and a moving target. If I have any chance of getting in a shot, I'll have to wait.

My chest closes, heart thumping like a wild stallion as I flip onto my stomach and furiously try to claw myself away from him.

One of my ankles is suddenly free. I glance back, and immediately try kicking the guy in the face.

He dodges effortlessly, and starts laughing.

The sound of that cold, heartless chuckle turns my marrow to ice. I scream, voice hoarse from fear, as I struggle and kick. He grabs the bottom of my hoody and drags me over cracked, dusty flagstones, until there's nothing left for me to try and grab for.

He straddles my lower back. I hurriedly close my fingers around the knife, trying to hide it until I'm ready to use it.

I buck my hips to try and throw him off but he's too fucking heavy.

"The fuck you doing in my town?" he growls.

In this position, I'll be slashing out behind me, probably just snagging on his clothes. I have to be facing him, or behind him, if I stand any chance of my knife doing enough damage for me to escape.

I throw out a scream of frustration as I wriggle like a fish on a hook.

He's going to kill me.

I'm going to end up just like Mom.

Is this karma?

Fear drains every last ounce of fight from me as I hear fabric rustle.

No, no, *no*! This is *not* happening.

Hot anger swirls through me. I reach behind me, trying to grab him or scratch him. A second later, he has my arms pinned at the small of my back. Fear pushes back my anger, and I'm filled with cold dread.

Can he see the knife?

More importantly, can I reach him with it?

My voice breaks as I yell out, "Let me go!" I wriggle so hard, my hoody falls back and my loose hair spills over my face.

"What the…?" The guy lifts his weight, but only long enough to grab my shoulders and flip me over.

My back hits the cobbles beneath me, and for a moment, both my hands are free.

The silhouette above me cocks his head, and bends close as he settles over my hips.

"You're a girl," he states in a flat voice.

BRIAR

Jesus—how could I ever have thought she was a guy? I can blame the dark, I guess. Or I could blame myself for not giving a fuck either way. She's trespassing. I don't give a fuck that she's a girl.

Even if she's a pretty little thing. Big, green eyes peer out at me from a delicate oval face. The plump mouth beneath her snub nose trembles. Now that she's between my thighs, I can truly appreciate how dainty she is.

I should have been paying attention to the rest of her.

When I make to grab the front of her hoody to haul her to her feet, the girl's fist comes out of nowhere. But instead of the punch I was expecting, a knife slices over my face.

I knock it out of her hand a second later, but I'm so shocked that I let her wriggle out from under me. She staggers and rushes to her feet. Then she glares at me for a second, as if weighing up her chances of recovering her knife before I can get up.

I guess she doesn't like her chances; a moment later, she's gone.

I stand, wincing as I touch the oozing cut on my cheek. It isn't a deep cut—thank fuck—but I think she knew it would be enough to distract me. I glance around until I see her weapon, and pick it up. I bounce it on my palm as my lips quirk into a smile. A compact switchblade.

"You're just making this worse for yourself," I holler after her.

She yells back "Fuck you!"

I let out a bemused huff, shaking my head. Got a bit of an attitude problem, my little stray. I'll have to teach her some manners.

A growl catches in my throat as I sprint after her.

INDI

I'm in the lead. I'm even sixty-percent sure I'm headed the right way. I can't hear the guy's footsteps anymore—just my own ragged breath. I discover a faint path and immediately follow it. A few minutes later, a definite track appears through the foliage.

My fear subsides; I'm headed toward civilization and away from that guy's massive hands and shadowy face.

I pause, glancing this way and that to make sure I'm well and truly alone.

Holy crap, that was a close call.

I run my hands through my hair and then drag my fingers down my face.

I guess it's time I started listening to people, right? I mean, yeah, my life sucks right now, but I just got a wakeup call like no other. Because anything—even *wonderful* Granny Marigold—is better than being gutted in an abandoned church in the middle of—

Hands grab me, jerk me off my feet.

I scream. Fingers cover my mouth, cutting off the sound.

He drags me backward before I can recover my balance. A gust of wind drives against him, bringing me his smell as he drags me off the path.

Crisp aftershave. Sweat. The mintiness of fresh mouthwash.

What the fuck? Killers aren't supposed to smell good!

I struggle, land an elbow in his washboard stomach, and completely fail to break free.

I guess he's not taking any chances this time. As soon as we're well and truly in the shadows, he pins the front of my body against a broad tree trunk and leans into me. He's powerful— even pushing against the trunk with everything I've got, I barely rock him.

He grabs my wrists and locks my hands against the bark above my head, leaving the other free to roam.

"Bad decision, angel," he murmurs into my ear.

Angel?

A sudden swell of anger leaves a bitter taste in my mouth. I struggle furiously, but all he does it press harder into me. Then he grabs the scruff of my neck. "You made me angry, having to chase after you."

"Yeah?" I snap. "Sounds more like you're out of breath."

It's the pent-up rage inside me talking, of course. He struck a nerve. Mom used to call me her little angel. What the fuck gives him the right to call me that?

When he laughs, his chest vibrates against my shoulders. His hand slides down my side as if he's trying to frisk me for more knives. And don't I fucking wish I had more?

"Chasing a little thing like you? Please."

"Fuck you," I mutter, wriggling furiously under him.

"Yeah, keep struggling," he murmurs into my ear, his warm breath tickling my skin. "It's getting me hard."

"You fucking sicko, get off!"

"Oh, I'm planning on it." His hand glides over my ass and dives between my legs.

I go stiff, my eyes squeezing shut as he brushes against my pussy. There's a lot of fabric in the way—I didn't bother trying on these jeans before I bought them, so they're super baggy—but still his fingers manage to make contact with my clit.

A dark thrill chases through me.

Then a whimper tumbles out of my mouth, timed perfectly with the ring of a mobile phone.

He ignores it, and it goes silent after a few rings.

"Not such a big shot now, are you, angel?" He presses into me at a different angle, and it takes me a second to realize why.

It's so I can feel his rock hard dick against the curve of my ass.

Fuck. Fuck!

My breath comes faster, my heart picking up speed.

I'm terrified—I know I am—but my body's doing its own thing. For some reason, some sick, fucked up reason, I'm getting wet from this monster touching me.

"Just let me go," I say, turning my head so I can look at him from the corner of my eye.

I've been avoiding eye contact. If I can't identify him, I don't pose a threat, right? But as soon as our eyes lock, I realize none of that matters. There isn't much light, but there's just enough to make out his features.

Eyes the color and warmth of a melting glacier fix on mine. Immediately, my willpower drains away because that wide, smiling mouth beneath his strong nose tells me everything I need to know.

I'm a rabbit, he's a wolf that enjoys playing with his supper.

CHAPTER THREE

BRIAR

All it takes is me pinning her to a tree and putting my dick up against her before she finally stops squirming. I won't lie, I kinda wish she'd keep at it. I love how it feels when her body writhes like that. Almost as much as I love watching her plump mouth spit out those dirty words.

"All out of fight?" I croon, grinding against her.

"I don't know who you are. If you let me go, I won't tell anyone—"

I stop rubbing her pussy through her baggy jeans and twist her around. My fingers go around her throat, my other hand keeping her wrists pinned above her head. "And just who you planning on telling, Angel?"

"The police," she says through gritted teeth as she scans my face.

I hope she's not looking for some sign of humanity. Anyone who knows me, knows I'm the furthest thing from a saint.

"Yeah?" I squeeze her throat, but all that does is make her eyes flare. Her eyelashes tremble, but I get the feeling it's anger, not fear. "Well, do me a favor and let the Sheriff know Briar says hi."

Her dark, unruly eyebrows draw together. "You're pathetic if you think that'll stop me," she says, voice dripping with disgust.

I laugh as I abandon her throat and instead run my hand down her chest, grasping first one breast, then the other.

In an instant, fear darkens her eyes.

Seems she couldn't care less if I strangle her, but using her body for my own depraved pleasure? Suddenly, I'm crossing a line.

My smile lifts as I rake my fingers down her belly and grab her pussy through her jeans again.

She lets out a hiss and stands on the tips of her toes. Even then, she doesn't reach my chin.

"I'm on my period," she says hurriedly, eyes filling with venom.

"Hmm…" I murmur, and lean close enough that my lips brush her ear when I speak. She turns her head away, but I just follow. "Guess I won't need to lube you up first."

When I straighten, her mouth is open in shock.

I run my thumb over her bottom lip, and she moves her face away from my touch. So I grip her jaw and force her head straight. Her eyes try to burn a hole through mine when I dip and rub myself against her so she can feel just how hard I am for her.

"Who the fuck do you think you are?" she whispers furiously.

I pause, my smile going crooked. "I told you, I'm—"

"Yeah, I'm sure you gave me your real name." She pulls her face free, red marks on her skin how I gripped her. "Well guess what, Whoever-the-fuck-you-are?"

I blink at her. How the fuck can she think talking back to me is going to make this any easier on her?

"You'll be pissing blood for a week."

Her knee lifts, but I twist away just in time. If she hadn't said anything, hadn't put me on my guard, I'd probably be writhing on the floor in agony right now.

My phone rings again. Just two rings, then it goes silent.

Time to go.

I release the girl, and drag my fingers down my jaw as I give her a long, slow once-over. "Run, Angel," I say quietly.

She slips away from the tree and backs up as if expecting me to rush her. Honest to God, I should…but I need to check my phone; I know it's important. So I just keep grinning at her until she turns tail and disappears into the night.

I lean against the tree and take my phone from my pocket. I toy with the girl's switchblade, turning it over in my hand as I wait for my call to connect.

"Hey…uh…" A voice breathes in my ear. I straighten, pressing the phone harder against my ear.

"Marcus?" I can barely recognize his voice.

"Yeah, 's me." He sounds short of breath, exhausted. "Can you…could you—?"

"Be there in five." I put down the phone without bothering to hear his response. Then I'm sprinting, my encounter with Angel already forgotten.

Marcus needs me.

INDI

I stop outside Marigold's house to hack up all the spit that's gone thick in my mouth. I stay bent over for a few panting breaths, and then straighten and haul icy air into my lungs.

Run, Angel.

And boy, did I obey.

On the plus side, I not only survived being murdered, but also the run back here. That must be some kind of miracle, right?

I push back my shoulders and stride toward the house. I have to give myself a mental shove before I can get myself to open the door.

Who'd have thought I'd be more reluctant to go inside this house than wait out here, in the dark, where a monster roams?

Marigold is nowhere to be seen when I let myself back inside her house. In fact, the house is so dark and quiet, I think she may have gone to bed already.

Crap, what time is it?

My legs quiver like jelly as I sneak upstairs, taking those unfamiliar steps one at a time because I have no idea which of them creak.

Turns out, all of them do. I give up on sneaking three-quarters of the way up, turn into the hall, and yell out when my gran materializes in front of me like the Mayflower looming from a fog bank.

"Holy crap, you scared me," I say, laying a hand over my thumping heart.

Marigold stares at me, nonplussed. "You do know you start school tomorrow?"

My throat tightens a little. "Of course."

"You should be in bed, not roaming around in the woods."

"But I wasn't—"

Marigold's hand lashes out. I instinctively close my eyes,

expecting a slap. But all she does is tug gently on my hair. I open one eye, and then the other. Then my shoulders drop.

She's holding a pine needle between her fingers. "While you live under my roof, you will do as I say, young lady." Her eyes bore into me, merciless.

My stomach twists. "I'm sorry, Gran—"

"Marigold," she snaps. "Now get to your room. We'll talk about your lack of respect in the morning."

She strides down the hallway, bristling.

Uh, gran, I was assaulted and damn near murdered in the woods? No? Not interested?

I slink into my room and press the door closed behind me. Eyes shut, I lean my forehead against the smooth wood. Hot tears press against my lids, but I will them back as I head for my bed.

All of this shit, I brought it on myself. I deserve nothing less. I should just have let that guy do whatever the fuck he wanted with me out there in the woods.

If I'd been at home last Saturday and not out partying, then Mom would still be alive. Or we'd both be dead. Either way, my life would have been so much better than the pig-shit swamp I'm wading through right now.

My backpack is beside the dresser, my two sets of *just* as ill-fitting clothes as the ones I'm wearing neatly stacked on top.

So I guess I don't have any privacy anymore, either? I have a feeling tomorrow's talk is going to involve a set of rules as long as my arm. And a nearly exhaustive list of the penalties I'll face for breaking any of them.

I head to my backpack, and spend a few seconds rummaging around inside. I'm far from the naive, idealistic innocent I was. My eyes have been opened these past few days. Opening up a hidden pocket inside my backpack for what I consider valuable seemed as good an idea at the time as buying that switchblade.

I've lost my knife, but thank God I haven't lost the flat, velvet-lined box I hid inside my bag.

After a quick glance over my shoulder, I hurry to my door to turn the lock.

Obviously, it doesn't have one.

So I grab the chair from the dresser and ram it under the handle. Not a sure-fire way to keep someone out if any of the hundred horror movies I've watched are anything to go by, but at least I'll have enough time to stash away my secrets before Marigold can come inside.

I perch on the foot of the bed and rub my thumb over the soft velvet case in my hands. It's a champagne gold color, and almost too heavy in my palms.

Bringing it up to my nose, I inhale deep.

Before long, it won't smell like her perfume anymore. But for now it still does, and I can't get enough of it.

Tears prick my eyes as the comforting smell of vanilla and sandalwood fills my nose. I lever open the lid and stare down at my Mom's favorite necklace. The heart-shaped sapphire seems to shift and dance as light falls on it. Through it.

I adjust the delicate chain so it hangs just right, a sad smile tugging at my lips. Then I snap the case closed and squeeze shut my eyes, refusing to let a single tear slip out.

It takes a great effort of will to stand and put the case back into my secret hiding place, but I make myself do it.

I was wearing this the night Mom died. I'd stolen it from her cupboard because I wanted to impress my friends.

Now it's all I have left of her. A constant reminder of her beauty. A never-ending testament to my betrayal.

You know what? Karma's a fucking bitch.

BRIAR

I'm driving too fast, but I can't make myself slow down. Fuck it, I don't *want* to slow down. Baker's house is five minutes from mine. Three if I floor it.

I slam down on my Mustang's brakes a few yards before I reach Marcus's gates. The Baker mansion is on a decent spit of land—several acres in each direction, their backyard disappearing into the tangled mess that goes up the side of the mountain. That's how we met, back in the day. We ran into each other in the woods, and been mates ever since.

Jumping out of my car, I leg it the rest of the way to Marcus's gates. I don't bother with the intercom—I assume his dad's home, and I definitely don't want to land myself on that guy's radar.

Instead, I climb the fence, and haul myself over using the thick branch of an oak tree. His dad's got cameras all over this place. After that stint of violent robberies last year, everyone in Lavish does, even after police charged a suspect. But Marcus knows where they are.

Which means *I* know where they are.

I make it to the side of their French Colonial a minute later, and climb up the trellises with ease. I've been doing this for years, so most of it's muscle memory. My actual muscles help, of course. Football's great for building bulk…and getting a practically absent father to pay attention once in a while when I make the Lavish Times cover story every now and then.

Marcus's bedroom window is open. I slip inside, whipping away the lace curtain that drapes my face, and stop to give my eyes time to adjust to the dark.

"Where you at?" My voice is deep and low. If his father's still around, the last thing I want is to let him know I've broken in again. If it wasn't for the fact that our fathers were friends, he'd have given me a beating too.

Still have to figure out why the fuck my father thinks Mr. Brandon Baker is the kind of person he wants to spend his time with. Honestly, I think he just feels sorry for the guy. Fuck knows it's got nothing to do with Baker's personality; Marcus's father has a mean streak the size of the Mississippi River. I think they may have been friends when they were younger, but Dad's never really spoken to me about it.

Especially after Mom's accident.

"Over here."

My heart sinks at the sound of Marcus's thick, rough voice. I hurry over to the bed, perching on the edge and reaching for the shape I can now make out.

When I touch his shoulder, he flinches away from my touch.

"Old man still here?" I whisper.

"No. Got picked up a few minutes ago."

I let out a long breath and work my shoulders while I wait for Marcus to gather himself.

Sometimes it takes minutes. Sometimes days. It all depends on how empty the whiskey bottle was before Marcus's father came to find him.

"You said you'd get out the next time he was here."

I know I shouldn't be blaming Marcus for any of this, but if he could have avoided another—

"I was asleep," Marcus croaks. "Smoked too much, knocked me out."

"Shit," I mutter, and rake my fingers through my hair. "Is it bad? Do you need ice or something?"

"I need a fucking drink." Marcus shifts, pauses, pushes up into a sit. His head is low, chin to his chest, as if it's too heavy to keep up. "Bring me a bottle."

"Marcus—"

"*Please.*" This time, he pushes the words through his teeth.

"All right, man. All right." I stand and leave his room, closing the door partway behind me. I move quickly, but I'm not fast enough. I hear Marcus let out a tortured sob, and my jaw clenches so tight, the scratch on my cheek starts to throb. I finger it gently as I make for the stairs, grimacing at myself.

Can't believe that little stray cut me.

I jog downstairs and head into the mansion's large den. This room always reeks of cigarettes and whiskey, but it's a stench I've gotten used to over the years.

There's a laptop on the desk, but it's closed. An empty crystal tumbler, an ashtray with a few cigarette butts inside. Evidence of Marcus's father being home.

But for how long?

Just like my dad, Marcus's father is away from home more often than not. You'd think he'd be happy to see his son, but all he does when he's in Lavish is drink, beat up Marcus, and then go out on 'business meetings' until the small hours of the morning.

There's a wet bar against one wall. I grab the bottle of vodka from it, not bothering with glasses.

I linger for a few seconds, mentally preparing myself to go upstairs, and giving Marcus enough time to pull himself together.

When I get back to him, he's standing by the window, staring out at his garden as he leans against the wall. I hand him the vodka and he takes it silently by the neck.

His Adam's apple slides up and down as he gulps vodka straight from the bottle. I can't see a single bruise on him, but that's one of his father's specialties—he never leaves a mark that his kid can't cover with his school clothes.

"Break anything this time?" I ask.

Marcus shakes his head. "Got a call. Had to leave." Then he glances at me, his dark eyes black in the low light. "Roof?"

I nod, and trail him out of his room. He walks with stiff legs and a straight back, as if his ribs are sore.

He should fight back next time.

He should tell the police, social services, something.

But we've been through all of this, time and time again. It's a never-ending cycle. Come morning, Marcus is always under the impression he somehow *deserved* the beating.

A low grade on a paper.

Fumbling a pass at the game.

Not hitting it off with the cheerleader he's been chasing.

It never matters what I tell him, so I've stopped trying.

But I'll never stop being here for him.

We've got each other's backs, Marcus and I. Have since we were kids. Every time he got into a scrape, I'd help him out. Just like he'd do for me, no matter how bad the shit was I got myself in.

I owe Marcus Baker my freedom, if not my fucking life.

He saved me, and I'll never stop trying to repay the favor.

It takes half the bottle of vodka before either of us speak again. We're sitting on the mansion's roof terrace, staring up at the stars that peek through a thin layer of cloud. Marcus brought his vape with, and he's been tugging at it between gulps from the bottle. Thankfully, the weed in his vape slowed down the drinking. Marcus can handle a lot of booze, weed, and drugs —as can I—but with finals coming up, we both need clear heads on us. I know Dad would be beyond disappointed if I didn't make my grades.

Marcus's father?

He'd likely put his son in the fucking hospital.

"Can I stay at your place tomorrow?" Marcus asks quietly. He shifts in his chair, wincing briefly before smoothing his face.

I lift my fingers from my knee where I've been toying with a fold in my jeans. "Sure, man. But what about tonight? Is he—"

"Doubt he'll be back so soon. I'll leave in the morning. Gives me time to pack a bag and shit." Marcus's voice fades away, his voice going thick. "Listen, Briar, thanks—"

I wave at him, and he cuts off. "You know what set him off?" It's none of my fucking business, but if I know Marcus, he'll be blaming himself for everything come morning.

I see him shrug from the corner of my eye. "He gave me a job to do, and I fucked it up."

"What, you didn't get the trash out in time?"

Marcus tips the vodka bottle to his lips in response. Fuck it, I shouldn't be prying anyway.

"You know what we need?" I sit forward, lacing my fingers together and letting them dangle between my legs. "Something to take our minds off this shit."

"Like what?" he asks, but with zero enthusiasm. Can't say I blame him—Lavish isn't renowned for its distractions.

I sit back again, stumped. "Dunno. But I'll come up with something."

Marcus nods a few times as he hands me the bottle. I take a small sip and hand it back.

One of us has to stay sober. It's a silent deal we've made ever since my party a few months ago.

"Wanna know something fucked up?" I ask quietly, tipping my head back to stare up at the stars.

"Sure."

"I don't feel weird coming back here."

Marcus rolls his head to the side, and I do the same. He

looks confused, and then barks out a laugh and looks back up at the stars. "'Cos of that shit with Jess?"

At the sound of her name, my chest constricts. He makes it sound so fucking nonconsequential.

That shit with Jess.

"Figures," he says, and then takes another sip of vodka. "You blacked out. Not like you actually remember anything, right?"

He rolls his head to glance at me, and I nod, my mouth tightening. "Right," I murmur, and gesture for the bottle.

For a while, I thought it was a mercy, me blacking out that night. But once the rumors began, I realized it was a very special kind of torture.

Ignorance is the furthest thing from bliss, especially if your entire life is on the line for something you can't even remember doing.

CHAPTER FOUR

INDI

I wake up with stiff muscles, looking like I was involved in some kind of zombie apocalypse.

Luckily, I won.

The shower stings my scratches and makes my bruises ache, but I ignore everything as I attempt to transform myself from a beast into a beauty.

When I'm done drying off, I feel a ton better than I did crawling into bed last night, but I still look like shit. Sleepless nights and a non-existent appetite does that to you.

I run my fingers through my dark, shoulder-length hair to muss it up, and then leave it to dry.

But before I leave the bathroom, my fix on the bruises on either side of my hips.

Slowly, I fold my fingers over those marks.

Holy crap. Briar—if that's even his real name—has got big motherfucking hands.

I'm whisked back to the past when I smell bacon and toast and coffee. Mom always made us breakfast on weekends. I'd wake up and smell this same delectable miasma of drool-worthy food and know it was gonna be a good day.

My heart aches with the memory, and I bite the inside of my lip when I imagine her spinning around wearing an apron, a spatula in one hand and a cup of coffee in the other.

Morning, Angel! Thought you'd never wake up.

I swallow hard at the knot in my throat. My swollen heart constricts painfully when I step into the dining room and see a single chafing dish set in the middle of the massive teak table. My grandmother is at the head, and my place is all the way on the other side of the long table again.

"Morning," I say, giving her a little wave.

Last night, I decided I was going to give this whole situation a good ole' college try. I mean, heck, my grandma doesn't deserve this any more than I do, right? Why the hell Mom made her my guardian is something I can't comprehend…but, then again, she never had anyone else after Dad died.

It's always just been Summer and Indi, the Virgo Troublemakers.

I take a careful seat, and stare at the dish. It's almost three feet away from me. For the first time in a week, I'm ravenous. Maybe it was my mad dash through the woods last night, or my brush with death, but I'm suddenly noticing a massive void in my stomach that needs urgent filling.

I open my mouth to ask if I can help myself to some food, but Marigold beats me to it.

"You've got another thing coming if you think I'll let you run around like a wild thing," Marigold states. She steeples her fingers in front of her, for all the world like a female version of Mr. Burns from the Simpsons. "You will obey my rules, or you will face the consequences."

"Yes, gra—Marigold."

"Rule number one." Marigold holds up a finger. "You will

maintain a B-average in all your classes while you're living with me."

I give her a thumbs-up. Academics was never an issue for me. Both my parents were smart, and I'm like them squared, so…

I point at the silver chafing dish. "Can I?" I stand, and drag my plate over the table. "You know, while you lay down the law."

Marigold's mouth tightens. "Rule two. You will be at school on time every morning. You will be home by latest five in the afternoon, unless you have extra-curricular activities."

"That all one rule, or are we doing like rule two point one, two point two…?"

When I lift the dish's lid, heavenly steam hits me in the face. I begin heaping greasy things onto my plate, listening to Marigold's droning with half an ear.

"Rule three. Your homework will always be completed in time. I don't own a television, so there will be no excuse."

I'm gonna make me a sandwich of epic proportions. Two slices of toast—nay, three!—and as many layers of fried egg, bacon, and onion as I can pile on top without it collapsing under its own weight.

"…will be in bed and asleep by nine o'clock—"

"So no one's told you about my insomnia?" I turn, piled plate held between me and Marigold like a shield.

Her eyes flicker to the plate and back to me as if I've somehow managed to offend her with my appetite.

"Insomnia?" Marigold says, voice hushed with disbelief.

"Yeah," I say, biting into a crispy piece of bacon. "It's this condition where you can't go to sleep—"

Marigold's fist connects with the table, rattling everything on it.

I pause mid-chew and widen my eyes at her.

Holy hell. I didn't think my grandma had a line, but I've obviously just gone and crossed it.

"Do not *ever* speak to me with your mouth full of food." She stands in a rush, spots of color touching her cheeks. "Did your mother not teach you any manners?"

Bacon turns into a nauseating ball of oily gunk inside my mouth. I bring the plate closer, spit out the half-chewed pork, and slowly set my plate down.

"If you'll excuse me, Marigold, I've inexplicably lost my appetite."

I turn on my heel, feeling her daggerlike eyes piercing the back of my head.

"You think I wanted this?" comes her yell.

I freeze on the spot, my body suddenly stiff with anger. "You?" I grate, turning on rusty legs. "*You* didn't want this?"

She crosses her arms over her chest, and for a moment—one brief moment—sympathy flashes over her face.

"You think I wanted to lose her, you fucking hag?" I scream. "You think I wanted to be stuck here with you in this stupid town? No friends, no family, *nothing*?" My voice bounces back to me, but I'm a wild horse that's got the bit in between its teeth; nothing's stopping me now.

"I hate being here. I hate this town. I hate you!" My chest rises and falls like when I got back from my run last night.

Marigold's face is the same color as her beige carpets.

I expect her to punish me for speaking to her like that. Maybe going straight to the phone and calling me a cab.

Instead, she comes around the table, eyes narrowing the closer she gets.

"Well," she murmurs, barely loud enough for me to hear. "Lucky for us, we only have to bear with each other until you graduate." She lays a hand on my shoulder and gives me a little squeeze. Her lips turn up into a fake smile. "Then you're on your own, young lady."

BRIAR

A dull headache forces me out of sleep. I stare at my bedroom's intricately molded ceiling, and shift my feet into the cool corners of my silk sheets as I try to ignore my morning wood.

I had a good dream last night. The girl in the woods starred in it. This time, she didn't get away.

I ignore my aching junk and go take a shower. I could jerk off in here, but I refuse to let my body dictate my actions anymore.

We're all animals. Some of us just hide it better than others.

I used to be able to hide it until my party a few months ago. Feels like a fucking eternity that I've been stuck with my new, shitty reality. What a brave new world; everywhere I go, the whispers follow. All based on rumors and gossip, not a single fact. And as much as they dig, they'll never find anything concrete.

Marcus made sure of that.

I shut off the angry stream of thoughts, squeezing my eyes shut as I turn off the heat and shove my head under the freezing cold jets.

Briar Manor is silent when I pad to the kitchen on bare feet. I eat a breakfast of dry cereal and coffee as I watch the sun rise over town. The family manor has one of the best views in Lavish, nestled along the side of the Devil's Spine mountains. Lavish stretches out far below, thousands of perfect little houses clinging to their winding country roads. The manor's surrounded by Blood Briar woods; our closest neighbor a property that once belonged to the Davis's. Might still, actually.

Maybe the girl in the woods last night is a Davis—some far-flung cousin that came to visit. Only their kin would be brave enough to venture into my woods without a second thought to their own safety.

Those first few months after my mother died, Dad was at home enough that we could have actual conversations. The loving husband and father I'd grown up with changed. He became bitter and spiteful. For months, he'd hold monologues at the dinner table, instructing me on how to protect my things.

My land.

My sense of self.

My heart.

Claim them as yours, son. Claim them and never let anyone else take them from you.

He blames himself for what happened to my mother, Natalie. Not the accident, of course. A patch of black ice and poor driving skills were at fault.

The fact that she was in her car is what he blames himself for. From all the little snippets he's told me over the years, I've pieced together the fact that Dad and Mom had an on-again, off-again relationship for about a decade before she settled down and became my full-time mother. That was several years after I was born, but my father never went into detail about why she wasn't around all the time. I don't ever expect him too—he's a private man by nature, and it's a miracle I know anything about the shit him and Mom went through.

I shake my head, draining the last of my coffee.

That girl shouldn't have been where she was last night. Everyone in Lavish knows about the wild animal that roams those woods.

Now she does too.

After breakfast, I try contacting my father again. I don't ever feel the need to ask his permission for Marcus to stay over, but it's a chance—an excuse—to speak to him. If he ever answered, of course.

His phone, unsurprisingly, goes to voice mail.

I don't bother leaving a message. He never listens to them anyway.

I stare out at the woods pressing up against Briar Manor's ornate fencing. Times like this, it feels like I'm the only person in the world.

A feeling I used to loathe. A feeling I now embrace.

INDI

The fuck is this?

I stare at the clothes hanging from the door handle of my closet.

"Gran—" I cut off with a grimace. "Marigold?"

My hands fist at my sides as Marigold opens my door.

"What is that?" I point at the clothes.

"That's your uniform, young lady."

Cold-hearted bitch—she's smiling, isn't she?

"No."

"What makes you think you have a choice?" The door closes behind me.

A school uniform? What the hell, am I five?

I glare at a black and gold school skirt while it taunts me with its perkiness. I strip down to my underwear and reluctantly step into the skirt. I sneer at my reflection. The thing barely reaches mid-thigh. Did Marigold get my measurements wrong or something?

Next is the white button-up shirt, then the tie. It's black with a fancy family-shield kind of emblem on the bottom in gold. There's a black, sleek-looking blazer hanging on the other door handle.

Blegh.

I rake fingers through my hair, consider then dismiss the possibility of trying to run a brush through the tangles, but even the thought feels like too much effort. Instead, I do my best to tame it into a bun.

My doctor said I could expect bouts of depression, anger… you know, all seven of those ugly fucking dwarves of mourning? Guess I'm back in the depression phase. Last night? Anger, of course.

Hang on, Indi—there's a long, bleak stretch coming up.

Marigold left a key fob and a printed map with directions to Lavish Prep on my dresser. The fact that she knows how to use Google Maps and a printer, but doesn't own a television confounds me. My grandmother is nowhere in sight when I thump downstairs, and I don't bother going into the kitchen to find food to take with to school. I've still got a little cash on me. It's all I've got until Mom's life insurance policy pays out. On Friday, when I'd phoned the insurance company to find out how far the process was, they told me the claim was with their investigation department. Because, apparently, being brutally murdered and raped gives them a reason to delay the payout to make sure there's no foul play.

I reverse out of the garage and start down the road. The key fob opens the old, creaking gates leading out of the property. Lavish is as pretty as it was last night. The sun's barely out, but everything gleams.

In fact, it's almost a little too shiny. Like how fake gold has to shine that much brighter to make up for the fact that it's as real as unicorn poop.

Yeah, I'm in a screwed up headspace this morning. I blame

Marigold, of course. And then I spend a few minutes blaming Mom. Then I pull over and thump my hands against the steering wheel until the urge to burst into tears subsides.

I have no one to blame but myself.

I reach Lavish Prep a few minutes later and park as far away from the front of the school as I can without looking like a weirdo. I check to see if anyone's in sight before I slip out of the car. A breeze slides over my bare legs, and I shiver a little. In my old school, we could wear whatever we wanted. I would sometimes wear a dress or a skirt, but nothing this revealing. Mom made sure I never looked like a whore when I left the house.

Her words, not mine.

I always wondered why she was so conservative, but after meeting Marigold, it all makes sense.

Right, now to get in without attracting attention. I guess, in that respect, the uniform helps a fuck load. I can just blend in with all the other kids.

I'm a ghost.

Just another shadow on the—

"You new here?"

I close my eyes, take a breath, and turn.

A girl with sleek blond hair fanning down her chest stands a yard or so away from me. Her backpack matches her neon-pink acrylic nails, and the tiny diamonds in her ears seem to have been chosen to accentuate the rhinestones glittering on her nail tips.

She sashays over and sticks out said glittering hand, jaw bunching as she chews on a piece of gum. "Addy."

I stare at her hand, and then back up at her. "Indi."

She turns with me and together we head for the school. It's all one big building with multiple floors. Despite the fluted pillars out front and the rigorously trimmed hedges, it looks more like a white-collar prison than a school.

I guess that's exactly what it is, and I'm just as guilty of being young and stupid as everyone else in this place.

"Where you from, Indi?"

"Not here," I mutter. Gees, what the hell do I have to do to get this girl to leave me alone? No way I'm walking into school unnoticed with her next to me. I bet the International Space Station can see her glittery nails from up there.

"Well, duh," she says through a laugh. "So where?"

"Look, Annie," I say, turning on my heel to face her.

She stops abruptly, her hair shifting like silk. "Addy." She shows me her teeth, and I feel like punching her because they're so damn perfect.

"Addy," I amend, starting to talk through my teeth in an attempt to remain civil. "I'm more of a loner kind of person, so if you could just—"

"Don't be such a fucking grouch," Addy says, rolling her eyes. She rummages in the pocket of her gold-trimmed blazer and pulls out a joint. "Not a lot of people around here smoke, and you kinda look like you might, so—"

I lift my hand, and she stops talking. "Addy? I think we got off on the wrong foot."

"**Y**ou're obviously not a morning person, are ya?" Addy says, her words punctuated with puffs of smoke.

We're in Addy's car—a cute little sportster that probably costs more than my mother's life insurance policy will pay out—with the windows wound up and our minds melting down.

I stare at her, and then burst out laughing. "It's that obvious?"

"Duh," Addy says with another exaggerated roll of her eyes. "You should come with a warning label."

"Yeah…sorry," I mumble around the joint. "It's been a short, yet *very* shitty morning. Week, actually."

I get ready to tell her to fuck off, knowing she's going to ask what happened, but instead she waves her hand in the air between us.

"So be glad it's over, and let's get our asses inside before they lock us out."

"They lock kids out?" I turn to stare ahead at the school building. "For real?"

Addy laughs as she kicks open her door. "You don't know the half of it. Come on, punk."

CHAPTER FIVE

BRIAR

Dylan, Zak, and Marcus are lounging in our regular spot by the front steps of the school when I arrive a few minutes before the first bell rings.

I pull my Mustang into my parking spot. It's always open; no one dares to park here anymore. Marcus steps closer, toking at his slim, silver vape as he sticks out his hand to shake mine.

Dylan yells out, "You cut yourself shaving or something?"

Shit. I'd been blasting metal on my car stereo, and it had taken my mind off everything—including my run-in with last night's little trespasser and the brazen memento she left me with. If Marcus had noticed it last night, he hadn't commented on it but now he's staring at it with a deep frown.

I grin at him, trying to ignore the aching cut on my cheek. "You know what happens when I look for trouble."

"You find it?" Marcus says, hitting his vape again.

Zak and Dylan stick out hands for me to fist bump. Dylan even goes as far as to tip his white baseball cap at me, and laughs when I cock an eyebrow at him. Then Zak and Dylan go back to talking about last night's game. We usually hang out on the weekends but with finals coming up, the three stooges's parents had grounded them for the weekend.

Bad things happen when parents start talking to each other.

Marcus doesn't join in on the conversation. He's staring at nothing, one hand draped over his knee, the other toying with his vape when he's not hitting it.

I click my fingers at Marcus, and he holds out his vape without looking. It could just be that he's hungover, but I know him too well. He's in a slump, and it's gonna take concerted effort to get him out of it.

I draw deep, grimacing around its sweet taste, and take a long, slow scan of the kids streaming into school.

A pair of girls come closer. I recognize Addison Green from my AP Literature class, but I don't know who the hell's with—

"Prince!"

I snap out of my trance, and throw Zak a scowl. The fucker knows better than to use my first name, but he doesn't even have the decency to look abashed.

"What?" I snap.

"You get any tail this weekend?"

I stare at him, and then shake my head. He's the only one in our crew idiotic enough to ask. They all know by now that I keep myself away from women.

It's too easy to lose control. If I'd had any doubts, last night proved I can't be alone with a girl.

When I turn back, Addison is only a few yards away.

"What the fuck, man?" I hear Dylan say, but I'm more interested in the girl walking beside Addison than in being interrogated by my posse.

It's the girl from the woods. This time, instead of some baggy jeans and an oversized hoody, she's wearing a school skirt that shows off a pair of slender legs. She's not wearing makeup, and her mess of hair's been drawn back into an untidy bun.

In daylight, she's even more petite than I witnessed last night, the shadows under her eyes more pronounced.

As she takes her first step up to the front of the school, Addy points a finger right at me. The girl looks up, spots me, and stops dead.

Behind me, Zak shouts, "Hey, who's the new chick?"

But those green eyes don't move. Her face contorts into a scowl. "You?" she yells, and I can't quite make out if it's anger or shock creasing her brow.

"Me," I say, grinning at her.

The girl surges forward. Addison tries to grab her, but she shakes her off without pausing. The little thing charges straight up to me and tries to slap me.

I catch her, of course, my fingers easily wrapping around her thin wrist.

"Easy there, Angel," I murmur.

She tries another slap, this time with her left hand. I was so busy gloating, I barely see it coming in time. I twist, and she falls forward, thrown off-balance when she doesn't connect.

Behind me, the guys burst out laughing. Addison's eyes are so wide, they look about to pop out of her head. But I don't think *any* of this is funny.

I grab the girl's wrists, pinning them together, and haul her against me. "What the fuck do you think you're doing?" I growl down to her.

"Me?" she barks out in disbelief. Her tits brush against my stomach as she draws one furious breath after the other. "You're the one that thinks you can just go around raping people!"

There's a scandalized gasp from everyone within earshot.

I shove her away from me so hard that she lands on her ass and I spot a flash of white underwear before she tugs her skirt straight. But even sitting on her ass in the grass, obviously overpowered and already surrounded by a decent crowd, fury blazes in her eyes.

"The fuck you on about?" I say, hardly recognizing my tight voice.

She scrambles up, fends off Addison when the girl tries to drag her away, and comes back for more. "Could you even stand looking at yourself in the mirror this morning?" she yells. Now there's an outright challenge in her eyes.

"The fuck?" I scoff, glancing over my shoulder at the guys. But they're all staring at me like they're just waiting for the other shoe to drop.

When I turn back to the girl, she's less than a foot away from me again.

"Let me cut you on the other side," she says through her teeth. "Then that face of yours will be all symmetrical again."

This time, when she goes to slap me, I duck under her arm, lunge against her, and force her to the ground. She lands on her back in the grass beside the school steps, and I immediately straddle her.

"Look, bitch," I spit, my cut aching how I'm clenching my teeth. "I don't know who you think you are, but you'd better get one thing straight."

"Briar!" Marcus calls out, but I ignore him.

She squirms furiously under me, but I catch her hands and pin them to her chest before she can try and scratch out my eyes or, judging from experience, try for an uppercut. Fuck, she's getting me hard, wriggling around like that between my legs.

"Get off me!" she yells.

I grind her wrist bones together so hard, her face goes white.

"Briar!" Dylan this time.

But she doesn't scream out in pain, or stop struggling.

"No one, *no one*, talks shit about me. Got it?"

"We both know what you tried to do," she whispers through a grimace, finally relaxing under me.

A whistle blows.

I'd been so fixated on her, I hadn't even seen Mr. Denard, the French teacher, walking up to us. As soon as I spot him, I let out a low growl and push up to a stand.

The girl scrambles up a second later, cheeks flushed and the whites of her eyes too bright in comparison. She points at me with a shaking hand. "Sir, this guy—"

"Are you the new one?" Denard asks, arching a single eyebrow at her. His lip twitches as if the mere sight of her disgusts him. He's dressed in black suit pants, a cream dress shirt, and a black suit vest.

"That she is," I say, stepping up to Denard and holding out my hand for him to shake.

Denard turns his attention to me, and his expression softens a little, but not enough. Thank fuck it was him who came out here to investigate.

I let out a low chuckle, grab his hand, and give it a good pump. "*Elle est tombée dans les pommes.* But don't worry, Sir, I have this under control."

"Wh-what?" the girl demands. She hasn't even bothered dusting herself off, or readjusting her clothes. Right now, it *does* look like I tried to get lucky with her.

Denard glances at her, and this time his lips pull into a full sneer. "Perhaps if you ate more, child, then you wouldn't be swooning all the time."

The girl blinks, and then glances over her shoulder at Addison as if for support. Addison drops her eyes, her mouth going into a line, but she says nothing.

Denard clicks his fingers at her. "What was your name again? Virgin? Virgile?"

Immediately, the crowd surrounding us begins murmuring, "Virgin," through a slowly building wave of giggles.

"Virgo!" The girl throws me a quick scowl, as if loathe to reveal any personal information in front of me. "Indi *Virgo*."

"Best get yourself to homeroom, Miss Virgo," Denard says. He's been teaching French at Lavish for over two years, but he still has traces of an accent.

I know it's on purpose.

"What?" Indi takes a step closer, her hands balling up as if she wants to attack the teacher next. "But, he just—"

"Now." Denard's face sets into an expressionless mask.

Around us, students start gathering, anticipating an even bigger showdown. Indi glances around, and as if realizing that her audience just doubled in size, she murmurs. "Sir, you don't understand. He tried to—"

Denard tilts his head. "Keep going, Miss Virgo. My detention class could always use more students."

Indi lets out a strangled sound. Her mouth opens and closes a few times, and then her shoulders slump.

"Is that all?" Denard asks, lowering his arm.

She nods, her mouth so tight it begins to tremble.

"Very well then." Denard sniffs. "Now get to class."

Indi manages a tiny nod, and her throat moves as she swallows.

Denard turns to walk away, and then pauses mid step to peer at Indi over his shoulder.

"Welcome to Lavish Prep, Miss Virgo."

INDI

Did that just happen? Did a teacher of this godforsaken school honestly crap me out after he saw that guy on top of me? I'm so pissed off, I can barely fucking breathe.

"Hey, virgin!"

I have no idea who the hell shouted that, but before I can find out, someone grabs the back of my shirt and tugs. In fact, they tug so hard that one of my buttons pop off. I'm hauled several feet away before I can free myself.

Addy glares at me when I turn to give her a piece of my flaming mind.

"Seriously don't know how to read a room, do you?" she mutters.

My eyes go wide. "You too?" I say, contempt dripping from every word.

Addison cocks her head. "Do you know who that was?"

"No," I say through an indignant laugh. "But if I did, I'd be at the police station, not—"

"That's Briar. Prince Briar, the Third."

I try to glance over my shoulder, a laugh rattling in my throat. "You're a fucking prince?" I yell out.

Briar cocks his head at me, a smile touching his lips. Then he spreads his hands to either side, as if to show off his mouth-watering physique.

Last night I barely got more than a glimpse of the guy; he was all shadows and square jawbone. Now in the daylight, I realize I was tousling with a six-foot-something teenage Adonis. Sandy, windswept hair, crystal blue eyes, and a face that captained those thousand ships launched for Helen of Troy.

Addy grabs my sleeve and rushes for the school, hauling me after her.

"Let go!"

"This is for your own good."

"What the hell's that supposed to mean?"

"Just shut up, Indi! Fuck!"

There's so much vehemence in Addison's voice, I stop fighting and let her drag me into the school proper. A few students flow in with us—obviously bored now that the morning's entertainment is over. Addison pulls me into a nearby corner and looks around as if this is a known mugging spot.

My chest is too tight to speak. The fists at my sides are aching how I'm holding myself back. But when Addison finally turns her gaze on me, all my anger—my indignation—melts away.

Her brown eyes are drenched with sadness, frustration, regret; her mouth an upside-down smile.

"What is it?" I whisper. "Addy, what's wrong?"

"Don't you ever, *ever* get close to that guy again. Hear me?"

I open my mouth, but she's not done.

"I mean it, Indi. If you see him coming down the hall, you go the other way. Got it?"

"Addy, I don't—"

"Say it." Addison's teeth flash white as she grits them at me. "Say it!"

I've had just about enough of being bullied by every second person in Lavish. But, at the same time, I'm utterly drained after everything that's just happened.

I can't handle this kind of shit. The last thing I want is people treating me different, but holy crap, what happened to just treating someone normally? I've never felt this out of place in my life. It's like I have this massive target painted on my back.

And why? Because I got pissed off that Prince—*Prince?*—Briar tried to get with me last night in the middle of the woods? That I don't feel he should be allowed to get away with behavior like that?

I want to fight. I so desperately *need* to fight, but I've got no energy left.

"Got it," I mutter. "Now tell me what the hell—"

"Later. I have to get to homeroom." Addison spins away from me, and I glimpse moisture glimmering on her lashes before she strides away.

My back thumps into the wall behind me. I stiffen my legs just in time before I can slide down and sit on the floor like an idiot.

I let out a soft laugh, and run my hands over my face.

What the hell have I gotten myself into?

BRIAR

"The fuck was that?" Marcus says.

I glance at him, and force my shoulders to relax. "The new girl, I guess."

"Yeah, but why was she saying all that shit?"

I can't look at Marcus. I already feel Dylan and Zak's eyes boring into me, demanding answers. I don't have their fucking answers. Not back then, not now.

"You saw who she was with," I snap, facing him in a rush. "Addison wasted no time."

"Fuck," Marcus mutters, hitting his vape. "Could be bad for you, mate."

"Yeah, no shit." I grind my teeth, staring back at the school building and wishing I could see through the walls.

Of course this is bad. Far from being afraid of me, it looks like this girl—Indi?—wants to rat me out for what happened last night. And it would be my fault, of course. Doesn't matter I was protecting my property against a trespasser.

I lost control, just like before, and now I'm stuck with the consequences…just like before.

Marcus moves in my peripheries, and I start nodding my head. If it weren't for him, I'd be in juvie, no doubt. Maybe even prison, charged as an adult instead of a minor, who the fuck knows?

I click my fingers for his vape. He hands it over, but even after what he just witnessed, I can see he's distracted. Probably wondering how long he has to stay at my house to avoid his father. Or rehashing whatever led to last night's beating.

"Thing is," I say slowly, before taking a tug. When I speak, my words escape with faint puffs of vapor. "She wouldn't be a problem if she's not going to school here anymore."

Marcus's eyes dart to me. He smiles, but the gesture lacks any real mirth. "Gonna take a lot for her to quit. Especially if her folks are hard set against her going to public school."

Lavish was so small, it only had two high schools—Lavish High and Lavish Preparatory School. The high school was probably just as good, education wise, but public schools in Fool's Gold have a hectic stigma attached to them.

"Far as I recall, we can be a tenacious fucking bunch," I say, sweeping my arm out to include Dylan and Zak. They chuckle to themselves, Zak elbowing Dylan in the side as if they're sharing a private joke. "And honestly, I think she's all bark and no bite."

Marcus nods, and focuses to the distant horizon. Hopefully to start planning the imminent demise of one Indi Virgo.

And thank fuck for that. Using Indi as a distraction would be the best way to get him out of his slump. And it'd make my life a fuck ton easier if she wasn't around as a constant reminder of just how little it takes for me to lose control.

"Think she's really a virgin?"

I snap out of my thoughts and frown at Marcus. He's wearing a strangely thoughtful expression, as if he's genuinely curious.

"Fucked if I know."

From what I saw last night? It's possible. But she's way too fucking beautiful to have not been a target of every single teenage boy in whatever high school she came from.

Except if she was homeschooled. She kinda looks like the type.

Hmmm.

"Love to pop me another cherry," Marcus murmurs, but as if to himself.

I let out a low chuckle, but then cut off and frown to myself. "When did you ever fuck a virgin?" I ask through a laugh.

Marcus glances at me as if surprised I'd heard me. "What? Oh." He laughs, and waves away the question. "Some fugly chick from MU."

I shake my head at him. We sometimes get students from Mallhaven University in Lavish. Karma Lounge plays the best hard house and trip hop on the weekends, and MU's students flock to it. Strange that I didn't know about him taking someone's v-card, but I guess Marcus isn't sworn to tell me every fucking ass he pounds.

"Virgo. Virgin." I pinch my bottom lip. "It's almost too fucking easy."

Marcus lets out a low chuckle. "Virgins usually are."

When I laugh, Dylan and Zak join me.

"Got any ideas?" Dylan asks, stepping up to me and Marcus.

"Plenty," I say through a grin. "Dylan, make sure that chick of yours knows something is going down in Homeroom today."

Dylan nods as he slides his phone from his blazer and types out a text to his fuck-buddy, Cindy.

For the first time since I climbed through his bedroom

window last night, Marcus's lips curl into a genuine smile. "This is gonna be fun."

I nod, having to force my own grin.

He doesn't know it yet, but if she doesn't back down then this shit's going to go way beyond anything considered 'fun.'

I'm sending Indi Virgo straight back to wherever she came from. She'll wish she never fucking set foot in my town.

CHAPTER SIX

INDI

Homeroom is on the second floor, and when I walk through the door, the first person I see is Briar. I'm not surprised he got here before me—I had to find my locker first, and then locate this classroom. Textbooks for each of my classes were already inside my locker, and I'd just stared at them. I know I can change the combination on my locker, but this doesn't bode well for my privacy at Lavish Prep.

Luckily, Briar hasn't noticed me yet. He's sitting in the far back of the class, busy on his phone.

Some of the other students are busy texting too, others doing last-minute homework or chatting with friends.

I'd hoped Addison was in my homeroom, but a quick glance establishes that's not the case.

Nope, just me and *Prince* Briar.

I'd chalk it up to coincidence, but after the morning I've had…I'm starting to think this is a conspiracy of global fucking proportions.

"You must be Indigo," a voice behind me announces.

I cringe at the use of my full name as I glance over my

shoulder. A lady stands just outside the class I'm blocking the entrance to, studying me.

This must be Ms. Parsons, my homeroom teacher. She's dressed in Bohemian-style clothes—a loose, flowing skirt, tasseled vest, and a blouse with full sleeves, all in neutral, earthy tones. Her tortoiseshell glasses are propped on a slim nose and her mousy hair—which there's a lot of—is gathered in a messy, loose braid.

"Why don't you go take a seat?" she says, her eyes curving as she smiles and points out the closest empty desk.

I nod and hurry to it, keeping my head down so I don't accidentally make eye contact with anyone.

Like Briar.

After what happened outside the school this morning, I'm doing my best not to attract unwanted attention. After all, it's been made pretty damn clear no one's on my side.

"Morning, class!" Ms. Parsons says as she makes her way to a desk overflowing with books, files, and wilted flowers. "Did we all have amazing weekends?"

A few "Yeah's," and "Sure's," are thrown back from just about everyone except Briar.

That's because the Prince of Lavish Prep has suddenly decided to train his attention on me. His gaze is so intent, I feel like I'm melting inside.

"Anyone have anything to share before I start with announcements?"

The general consensus is a mumbled, "No."

"All right." The teacher shoves aside a stack of papers and perches on the edge of her desk. "We have a new student to welcome this morning. Can you all give Indigo Virgo a nice—"

"*Indi*," I cut in with a grimace.

The teacher's mouth is still open, but it had to be said. If I don't nip this in the bud, every Tom, Dick and Jock Idiot will be calling me Indigo. And my new fun surname, Virgin.

"Oh?" Parsons nods her head. "Then let's all welcome *Indi* to Lavish Prep." She begins clapping, but only a handful of students bother to join her.

Every single student in homeroom decided to look at me, though, so there's that. I thin my lips and raise a hesitant hand, giving them a small wave.

Nobody waves back.

And then the murmurs begin.

That's the virgin?

Heard she fainted.

Got a thing for Briar.

Fuck.

Briar gives me another of his shark-like grins.

Holy crap. Tough crowd.

Maybe it's because I was brave enough to stand up to their deviant Briar. I guess that kind of stuff just doesn't fly around here, especially judging from that French teacher's response.

"Now, who would like to volunteer to buddy up with Indi for the first week?"

Wait…what?

Too late, I realize I'm gaping at Ms. Parsons, instead of declaring myself unfit for supervision. I mean, shit, I'm seventeen, not seven.

"I'll be happy to do her, Ms. Parsons."

The class roars with laughter.

Ms. Parsons—idiotic flower child she is—doesn't seem to notice Briar's Freudian slip.

I do.

My eyes go wide. My chest tightens.

Briar has his hand up real fucking high. He's wearing a grin that I can tell is both smug and weaselly, but one which Ms. Parsons seems to think is completely innocent.

"Why, Prince," Ms. Parsons enthuses as she stands, a hand to her chest. "That's marvelous." She turns to me, and points between me and Briar as if this is some kind of special school where your IQ has to be in the single digits before you can even apply.

"Indi? Prince will be your Lavish Buddy this week. He'll show you around and help you find all your classes."

Briar grimaces at that, and my panic flutters into pure ecstasy.

So I guess his first name's Prince and—just like me—he despises it to the nth degree.

But no one's staring at him. Everyone is staring at me. And the weight of all those expectant eyes compels me to let out a reluctant, "Thanks."

"Good." Ms. Parsons claps her hands. "Time for announcements."

I glare at the back of her head as she turns to get a clipboard from her desk. I bet bluebirds chirp around her head every morning when she wakes up, and she sings them a goddamn song about what a beautiful day it's going to be.

Mentally, I do my darndest—but her hair simply fails to catch on fire.

"The chess club has had to reschedule this week's tournament against Mallhaven High. A new date will be set…"

Briar stands up, and Ms. Parson's voice fades away as my ears begin to buzz in dread anticipation. He weaves through the desks until he gets to the empty one behind me, and lets his bag fall before dropping his ass in the chair with an audible thump.

"Morning, my little virgin."

I press my eyes closed. But, alas, along with the inability for me to set someone's hair on fire, I seem to have lost my talent for time travel and teleportation as well.

"Fuck off," I mutter, crossing my arms over my chest and slouching in my chair as Ms. Parsons starts rattling off the names of the students who were accepted into some or other club.

"Hey, I'm your *buddy*." The way Briar drawls the word makes my hair stand on end. "I got nothing but good intentions, Angel."

I glance at him over my shoulder, but somehow he fails to see my scowl.

The cut I gave him last night should have looked horrible, like all puffy and gross and oozing and shit.

Nope. All it does is give his face a roguish charm it doesn't need.

"Admiring your work?" His full lips curve up as he lifts a hand to finger the cut. He winces dramatically and inhales a hiss. "Buddies shouldn't cut each other."

I roll my eyes at him. "I don't need your help. I have a fucking map."

"A map?" Briar lets out a low chuckle. "You don't need a map. You need *me*."

He sits forward, lacing his fingers and sliding his elbows over his desk.

"Else how you gonna navigate the valleys and peaks of social class?"

Valleys and peaks? What a douchebag.

"Easy," I say through a grimace. "If they're friends with you, then they're losers and I stay away from them."

There's the tiniest tic of a facial muscle near his jaw. He sits back, shaking his head.

"This lack of respect won't do, my little virgin." He shows me his teeth, but it's far from a smile. "It just won't do at all."

I bolt out of homeroom as soon as the bell rings. Briar's still sitting in his chair, looking smug as the Cheshire Cat, by the time I hit the hall and risk a glance back.

Letting out a stale breath, I peek at my schedule.

AP Computer Science.

AP Psychology.

Calculus.

Guess whoever set the schedule must have thought it would be easier to tackle these classes when the brain's still fresh.

My first class is on the third floor, but first I make a stop at the restroom in a pathetic attempt to get a fucking grip.

As soon as I step inside, my legs lock in astonishment.

Holy *crap.*

Despite Lavish Prep looking like a prison, everything I've seen up to this point has been sheer luxury. Padded school seats, perfectly varnished wooden desks with electrical outlets for laptops or cellphones. I overheard one of my classmates asking for the school's wi-fi password.

The bathrooms? They look like something out of a five-star hotel. Orchids in planters decorate end tables. The fixtures are all black marble and gold, as if to match the school uniform. Spotlights line the outside of the vanity mirrors, as if to fool the girls standing there that they are in fact supermodels, not kids.

The face above those Hollywood starlet mirrors must belong to someone else though, because I've never looked this wretched in my life.

I splash water on my face, and blot it dry with a fluffy hand towel that smells of fabric softener. But even then, the face in the mirror still looks like shit.

So I slap it.

Hard.

The world goes white. I rock on my heels as I wait for my eyes to start focusing again. There's a big red handprint on my cheek, and as I wait for it to fade, I summon up every shred of dignity I still have and force my spine straight.

Fuck you, Lavish Prep.

Fuck *you*, Prince Briar.

I survived the death of my mother.

This?

This is a fucking cakewalk.

Bring it on, bitch.

CHAPTER SEVEN

My Computer Science class goes off without a hitch. Lavish is on the same timetable as my old school, so I'm only a week behind. But even so, after the teacher introduces me to the class, I barely register that I'm learning concepts a week into the future.

I *get* computers. I understand those basic programs everyone else swears at on a daily basis. Back before everything went to shit, I was the resident IT Girl on the block. Fellow students—even their damn parents—would send me sheepish text messages at all hours of the day asking for help with their issues.

Emails.

Internet browsers.

Blue screens.

I had no training beyond the basics that my school's computer programming classes gave, but it would never take me longer than a few minutes to figure out what the issue was.

Usually, it was the user.

At first, I was all nice about it. I'd suggest they tried things differently. Perhaps looked up new shit in Google before attempting anything.

But after a few years of being everyone's favorite IT Girl, that shit got me real jaded.

I went from being 'Indi the Genius' to 'That girl that fixes computers.'

The texts for me to help put a stop to email spam stopped. I was no longer the go-to person for clearing suspicious browser histories.

Instead, I only got called in on the level 3 shit: blue screens, failed updates, and porn pop-ups.

Now, for the first time in a week I'm finally starting to feel like myself again.

For the period of one class, I manage to forget Mom's dead.

I stride into AP Psychology with a smile on my face and a swagger in my step. There'd been a pop quiz for the last ten minutes of my computer programming class.

I aced it.

Afterward, the teacher called me aside to introduce himself formally. And then told me I had two days to catch up the last week of theory.

Well, damn. Guess I'd better cancel my plans for this evening.

I laugh to myself as I sink into my seat. Around me, the classroom's filled with a very familiar drone of friends chatting and the sound of chairs scraping back.

For a few, idyllic moments, I lose myself in that noise.

You know what? I *got* this. Whatever the world has to throw my way, I can handle it. This is a new chapter in my life. The fresh start I was looking for in syringes and rubber hoses. All I need is—

"What up, virgin?"

My thoughts collapse in on themselves like a poorly constructed house of cards.

Briar.

I don't turn, mostly because I'm frozen but also because I don't want to give him the satisfaction of seeing the shock on my face.

AP Psych.

Really?

The fuck does a jock like him need to know about Freud or Jung?

I ignore Briar, but he refuses to ignore me. The teacher starts taking us through the weekend's homework—of which I, obviously, did nothing.

Something brushes my hair. I jerk, and spin to glare at him over my shoulder. He sits back in his seat, a smug, crooked smile splayed over his mouth. "Jumpy," he comments.

"That's what happens when you almost get raped," I throw back, but in a whisper so as not to draw attention to myself.

Briar's smile inches up as he sits forward in his desk. He leans his chin on his palm, studying me intently. "I never heard you say no."

My eyes and mouth both go wide at the same time. I splutter a weak, "What?" before the teacher realizes I'm not paying attention.

"Ms. Virgo, is it?"

My body goes cold, but I spare a heated glare for Briar before I face the front of the class.

The Psych teacher, Mr. Veroza according to my timetable, is a balding eighty-something-year-old with liver spots.

He moves closer to my table and folds his hands at his waist, tipping his head to the side as if he's studying something pinned to a goddamn corkboard.

"Yes," I manage, trying to ignore the feel of Briar's eyes drilling a hole through the back of my skull.

"I'm not sure how things worked at your previous institution, but we don't talk during class, Ms. Virgo."

Institution? He makes it sound like I came straight from the fucking loony bin.

Veroza's gaze skates over my entire body, pausing for an uncomfortable length of time on my chest, before returning to my face.

"If you're uncomfortable sitting so close to Mr. Briar, I can arrange for a different seat."

Does he have every teacher in his pocket? How about moving Briar, who's obviously the one making me uncomfortable? But no, somehow even this is my fault.

I refuse to give him the satisfaction.

"I'm good, thanks," I manage, despite the fact that my heart's attempting to jackhammer through my chest.

Veroza nods as if this was far from the answer he expected. "No talking in my class, Ms. Virgo. Not unless I ask you a direct question."

"Hey, little virgin."

Squeezing my eyes shut, I start counting to ten.

But Briar interrupts me with a tap to my shoulder. "Can I let you in on a secret?"

"Shh!" I whisper furiously, without turning. The last thing I want is to draw Veroza's attention.

"You shouldn't have run last night," Briar murmurs.

I know I shouldn't turn around, but something about the tone in Briar's voice makes me so curious to see his face that I don't have a choice.

Briar's eyes light up when our gazes lock. His smile grows, and for some reason it makes me squirm in my chair.

"Why?" I mutter, casting a quick look to Veroza. But Teach is caught up in one of the student's questions on the far side of the class; we're safe for now, Briar and I.

"When you feed an animal, it isn't hungry anymore."

It takes me longer than it should have to process those words. I guess Addy's blunt has something to do with it. I'm not high anymore, but my brain isn't exactly sparking neutrons at its usual rate.

"Mr. Briar," Veroza snaps out with surprising harshness for such an old man.

Briar's smile fades as he faces the teacher. I sit back in my seat, crossing my arms over my chest and allowing myself a smug smile.

Guess you're not *this* teacher's pet after all, Briar.

Veroza adjusts his spectacles. "Since you're already an expert in this subject matter, tell me what kind of psychologist would describe depression as the result of an unconscious process where anger is turned inward as a result of repression?"

My eyes go wide. Holy crap. This must have been some of the stuff covered when I was inabsentia. My smile inches up. Yeah, Briar, what kind of—?

"Psychoanalytic," Briar replies woodenly.

Mr. Veroza seems at a loss for words, but when he opens his mouth, Briar cuts him off.

"Psychoanalytics consider depression a result of the unconscious activity of the mind."

"Yes, well, very good." Veroza shifts on his feet before lifting his chin in defiance of Briar's intellect. "Now, please pay attention."

As soon as Veroza turns his attention away, Briar lets out a low chuckle.

I don't know why, but despite how ominous that sound is, it kinda makes my insides go all gooey. Maybe it's just because he's proven he can actually read and regurgitate a textbook, I dunno.

And I don't care.

Briar isn't smart, he's cunning. Like a wolf. Which means he's set his eyes on me as prey.

For some insane reason I can't begin to fathom, the thought sends an illicit thrill through me.

I'm still scribbling down a few pithy notes from the blackboard when the bell rings to signal the end of the period.

Briar's been surprisingly quiet for the rest of the lesson, even when Veroza went into the hall for a few minutes to take a phone call. I haven't dared look around once—even when I saw movement behind me—because I don't want to catch feels again.

Briar walks past my table, but pauses right by the door.

"What? I snap, when Briar just keeps looking down at me.

"I was just imagining something."

When I look up and see the suggestive smile playing on his mouth, I grimace. "You're disgusting," I say, gathering my things so I can stand and get the hell out of here.

"Because I can't wait to see what you're wearing under that skirt?"

My eyes go wide. I snarl and stand in a rush, lunging around my desk. Briar's hands go up in mock surrender, a deep laugh bursting from him.

I don't get very far. Where I was picturing my hands around his throat, throttling him until he begged for mercy, I instead trip up and fall face-first to the ground.

I'd been moving so fast, my lungs are knocked clean out of

air. Gasping like a beached fish, I twist onto my side and stare down at my feet, which for some reason forgot how to move.

My shoelaces are knotted together.

Everyone still inside the class bursts into laughter. I push onto my knees, glaring up at Briar. He steps closer, grabs my chin, and tilts my head back so far my neck clicks.

"See? Everyone bows to the prince," he murmurs, those words meant for my ears alone. He rakes ice-blue eyes over me. Where he touches me, my skin tingles.

I tear my chin free and fall back. Moving awkwardly, I get my feet in front of me and start undoing my laces.

It had to be him of course. And someone must have seen him do it—we were sitting right in front—but no one said a word.

The laughter fades as students leave. Briar stays to watch me working furiously at the knots, as if proud that he did such a good job.

Mr. Veroza appears, brow wrinkled. "Ms. Virgo? Everything all right?"

"Yeah," I mutter, dropping my eyes. "Tripped on my shoelaces."

Briar reaches out a hand and grabs my arm, hauling me up. "You make sure they're real tight this time, Indigo."

My snarl transforms into a tight smile which I turn to Mr. Veroza.

Yeah, I can tell him. And suffer the wrath Briar will no doubt shovel on my head. Instead, I'll just turn the other cheek. Because, guess what?

If an animal goes long enough without eating, it fucking *starves*.

BRIAR

When I get into the hall, Indigo's nowhere in sight. She must have sprinted down the hall for me not to see her.

I smile to myself and head for my locker to put my books away before lunch. And here I thought my week was going to be same as usual. I'm kinda glad I stumbled into Indigo in the woods last night.

But I guess she isn't. I close my locker. Marcus is beside it, leaning with his back against the locker next to mine and tugging discreetly on his vape as he watches everyone move past us.

"Dylan said Cindy got it all on her phone," he says, before I can even open my mouth. "They're busy circulating it already."

"Good," I murmur, allowing myself a small smile.

"So I got my stuff in the car," Marcus says. "Still cool if I come over."

"Course." I wave at him, frowning slightly. "You know it is."

I take a second to scan my friend. His mood's improved a little with this whole Indi thing, but he's still standing stiff and proper.

"You see your dad this morning?" I ask casually, my eyes on my locker as I hunt around for one of my textbooks.

"Nah," he says through a sigh. "He's got some big project he's working on that'll keep him busy for a while."

"In Lavish?"

"Un-fucking-fortunately," Marcus says, shaking his head. "Should only be for a day or two though. That okay?"

I slam my locker closed, turn, and grab the side of Marcus's neck. "Dude, I said it's fine. For fuck's sake."

Marcus drops his eyes and gives me a small nod. "Thanks, man."

"No need to thank me. But you're buying the pizza tonight."

He laughs, and waves at me as he heads away. Then he turns, walking backward. "What's next for her?"

There are a few kids around us, but they all know by now not to pay attention to me or even attempt to eavesdrop. Then again, I couldn't give a shit if the whole school knew I have Indi in my crosshairs. Maybe then she'll realize she's better off being somewhere else, far away from me, and too far away to do any damage.

"I'll text you," I say, lifting my chin. Marcus gives me a thumbs-up and disappears up the stairs.

I let out a low chuckle as I run my hands through my hair and head for class. Around me, students part like water around a ship.

I'm used to the fear in their eyes by now. That uncertain look they get when they see me. They make me out to be a monster, larger than life, a deviant. But they have no proof, just gossip and rumors. Let them whisper. Let them play detective.

That shit didn't rattle me back then, it won't rattle me now.

Anyway, I have better things on my mind. Like the new toy I have to play with.

CHAPTER EIGHT

INDI

It starts when I hear the first giggle. I glance over my shoulder and stare at the pair of girls walking behind me. They make brief eye contact before staring down at their phones again.

Weirdos.

The giggles persist as I get to the ground floor. Here, several kids have stopped in their tracks—in the middle of the hall or beside their lockers—phones out and heads bent.

Guess something just went viral.

I'm suddenly glad I'm not on Lavish Prep's universal mailing list.

My phone vibrates with a new message.

I resist the urge to read it. Instead, I take my time shoving all my things back in my locker. I'm in two minds about whether I want to dare head into the cafeteria, or just hit up one of the vending machines in the hall and go have lunch somewhere quiet.

Like my car.

"Don't look."

I stop in my tracks, and turn my head a little to the side. "At what?" I ask.

"At your phone." Addison materializes in front of me with a scowl on her face. "It'll die down. It always does."

Now I'm burning to know. I reach into my pocket, but Addison snags my wrist and jerks my hand out again. "Don't do it."

"What's going on?"

"Someone took a video of you and Briar."

My heart stops beating. A cold, dreadful certainty fills me like cement.

"Of us in the woods?" I manage in a too-tight voice.

"The woods?" Addison waves away the suggestion with an annoyed flick of her hand. "You on your knees," she snaps. Then she lifts her chin, moves in beside me, and urges me forward with an arm around my waist. She snaps a large, pink bubble of gum and then throws a finger to the girls who were giggling behind me.

"Fuck them all," she states in a loud voice.

In the overwhelming relief flooding me, I let Addy sweep me down the hall. I even manage a sickly smile, purely because the horrifying thought that Briar's assault had been videotaped and aired to Gen Pop had almost given me a heart attack.

If Briar was pissed about me trying to tell a teacher this morning about what had happened…I can only imagine his fury if it was broadcast to the entire school.

I don't think I'd survive the fallout.

"Let's get something to eat," Addy says.

"Yeah. Let's."

We each grab a plate of roast turkey sandwiches and French fries and take a seat close to the windows. Chuckles and the word *virgin puppy* follow me, but Addison makes as if she doesn't notice.

I don't get it. What makes me so interesting to Briar? I mean, I'm a nobody. He's obviously a somebody—by the time we get to our seats and I hazard a glance around, I see his Majesty taking a seat in the middle of the goddamn cafeteria.

Two benches have been pushed together to accommodate his subjects, who are all currently transfixed by whatever tall tales he's lathering them with. Surprisingly, there aren't any girls at his tables, just a bunch of jocks and wannabes.

Leaning on my elbow, I point at Briar's table. "Him?"

Addy glances at Briar's table and then back at me so fast I'm surprised she doesn't get whiplash.

"Yeah?" she asks warily.

"You're going to tell me what his story is. Now."

Addy shifts as if the question makes her uncomfortable, and then gives a half-hearted shrug. "He's bad news, Indi. Just forget—"

"Bad news how?"

Addy purses her lips around her energy drink's straw.

"Like, he may look like a fucking god, but he's the spawn of Satan." Addy lifts a perfectly plucked eyebrow. "Prince Briar destroys everything he touches."

I lean away from her. "Personal experience?"

Addy sniffs, throws a glare in Briar's direction, and then turns her back to their bench. "He dated my friend, Jessica."

I point at her energy drink, and she hesitates before handing it over. I take a sip, grimacing at how sweet it is, as she carries on talking.

"They'd been going out a few months already. Jess said he

wanted to get serious, you know—sex?—but she wanted to take it slow."

My eyes go to Briar. He looks serious as anything, eyebrows drawn together and staring at his cellphone as his subjects make high fives and give each other fist bumps around him.

"Guys do that," I say dryly, thinking back to every single relationship I've ever had. It didn't matter how many times you said 'no', or how creative you got in telling them, they'd keep pushing and pushing and pushing.

I was tempted more than once to lose my virginity just to get it over with. I mean, sex has to be fucking amazing if guys are so hard up about getting laid all the time, right? Obviously I'm missing out. But it was never the right time, the right place, the right guy.

Story of my life.

Damn, but she wasn't kidding about Briar looking like a God. The day turned out warm, so he's only wearing his school shirt and a slightly loosened tie. He has his sleeves rolled up to the middle of his lower arms, setting off his dark tan. As I watch, he rakes the fingers of one hand irritably through his long, sandy-blond hair, mussing it up even further.

He should be gloating about the prank he pulled. The one currently circulating through the entire school's mobiles. Instead, he looks frustrated.

What could possibly piss off someone like Briar? I mean, does he not have enough rooms in his massive house? Because he's got to be super-wealthy to dare be so fucking arrogant. Maybe there aren't enough horses in his car's engine? Or is it because he's finally realized he's an asshole and no one will ever love him?

"We were at Briar's birthday party…"

I look away reluctantly from Briar, fixing my attention back to Addy. From the tone of her voice, she doesn't want to be having this conversation. She starts fidgeting with the straw wrapper, and I hand her back her can.

"What happened?"

"Everyone was drunk." Her eyes dart up to mine. "A lot of them were doped up too." Then she sighs and tugs at her straw. "I left at like one in the morning or something. Only Briar and his crew and a few of the cheerleaders were still around."

Addy gets a faraway look in her eyes and nods. "Dylan gave me a lift home."

"And Jess?"

"She stayed. I didn't want her to, tried to talk her out of it, but she was so drunk she wouldn't listen to me."

Addy grows quiet, and it takes everything I have not to press her to continue. After a few seconds and another sip from her can, she goes on in a low, barely audible voice.

"She called me in tears just before noon the next day."

My breath stalls as my gaze darts back to Briar. He's not looking at his phone anymore—he's looking straight at me. My skin flashes ice-cold, but as much as I know I have to look away, I can't.

"Said something had happened. That I had to come get her."

Even across the cafeteria, the weight of Briar's gaze pins me to the spot. I lick my suddenly dry lips, and he tilts his head just a little to the side, as if fascinated by this. He smiles at me, and those words he spoke in our Psych class come back to me like the whisper of a nightmare.

Everyone bows to the prince.

"When I got to the house, she was on the sidewalk. Barely coherent. She insisted I drive her home, and that's all I could get out of her."

"So you don't know what happened?" I ask, my ears starting to buzz the longer Briar stares at me. The guy to his left starts talking to him, but he doesn't bother breaking eye contact with me.

"There were rumors, of course." Addy reaches the end of her drink, and the rattle of her straw finally allows me to tear my eyes away from Briar.

"But I mean, you must have asked. Didn't she say?" I lean a little closer. Addy's eyes are too bright, as if she's holding back tears. "Addy?" I lay a hand on her arm, and she flinches before jerking away from my touch. "What is it?"

"All we have are rumors," she says woodenly, shaking her can as if wondering why it was empty.

When she looks at me, my stomach twists with dread. "Why?" I breathe. "Did she leave town or something?"

Addy shakes her head, her mouth a tight, trembling line. "Jess killed herself."

I zone out during Environmental Sciences as I try to piece together Addy's cryptic conversation.

There was a party.

Everyone got drunk.

Addy left.

The next day—but only at noon—her friend calls her to get her.

She's hysterical.

That night, she commits suicide.

Round and round my thoughts go. Where they'll stop, nobody knows.

When the bell rings signaling home time, I notice for the first time that the level of giggling and hushed whispers in the class has grown. I turn to look to the side, and feel something shift in my hair.

I sigh, reach up, and cringe inwardly when I touch a cold spitball lodged in my hair.

One of many, it turns out. I stay behind, picking the offending gobs from my hair, staring at everyone who walks past in an effort to narrow down my suspects.

And then one of Briar's friends, dark hair and dark eyes, the one who'd been sitting beside him at lunch, saunters past wearing a big, fake grin.

When I scowl at him, he begins tonguing his cheek in imitation of an obviously squint girl giving a sideways blowjob.

I throw him the finger, but that just makes him and everyone around him burst out laughing. By the time I get all the spitballs from my hair, all I want to do is go home and crash.

I drag myself to my junker and sit in the driver's seat, counting up all my fuck-ups for the day. A sharp rap to my window startles me out of the exhaustive list.

Addy's standing by my window, head cocked as if impatient for me to roll down the window.

"Hi," I say sheepishly, giving her a weak smile.

She leans her elbows on the window ledge. "Tomorrow will be better."

I squint up at her. "Why are you being so nice to me?"

Her smile is a touch nostalgic. "Because I was once the new girl. I know how much it sucks. It helps having someone on your side."

"Jessica?" I venture, my mouth pulling to the side.

Addy nods, and gives me a sad smile. Then she reaches into the car and squeezes my shoulder. "But I also know it gets better."

When I look up at her, her smile is warm and friendly. "Just take it one day at a time, and you'll do fine."

I have an overwhelming urge to tell her about the woods, but I can already feel she wants to change the subject away from Jess.

This is the worst time to mention anything about what happened between me and Briar.

Instead of making an ass of myself and getting Addy all worked up, I could try being her friend.

So I smile at her, and I let her think that her words are all the encouragement I need to make it through the day.

I guess she's right, in a way. I'll just take it one day at a time. When I close my eyes at night, I'll be cleaning the slate.

Tomorrow will be a new day, right, Mom?

I pull up to Briar Mansion, Marcus following close behind in his big-ass SUV. We had football practice until five in preparation for a game happening this weekend—the last before we hit finals. I'm physically drained, but mentally my brain feels like it's fizzing.

Sports always had a way to get me hyped up, especially football. No one cares how aggressive you get out there, long as you don't cross the line. Surprisingly, it's easier for me to do that on the field than in real life.

I guess that's mainly due to Coach Carter. Because fuck knows, that man's dressed me down until I was shaking with fury.

In real life, it's so much easier to get away with shit.

No witnesses? No crime.

Marcus jogs up to me, and then falls in line, his backpack over one shoulder, and two six-packs dangling from the fingertips of his other hand.

He's tall and thin and runs like a fucking Olympic athlete,

but he doesn't have the muscle to take down the bigger guys. We make a good team and coach knows it.

Marcus ruffles his short, dark hair and gives me a sheepish grin. "Gonna fucking feel this tomorrow," he says, shrugging his shoulders and wincing.

"You say that now, but wait till the only action you get is walking the stairs at Prep." Marcus loves letting off steam as much as I do, and I saw him on the field today—he was giving as good as he got.

I'm glad he has a healthy outlet for the shit he gets dealt on such a regular basis. My dad's never here, but that's a shit-ton better than if he was…and he was roughing me up every other night.

"So you decided if you're going to MU yet, or what?" I ask as I key in the security code on the mansion's front door keypad. I could have set up this place to work from my phone or smartwatch by now, but Dad's super old fashioned when it comes to this shit. I mean, we've got cameras and stuff inside, but they don't even get backed up to the fucking cloud.

Nope. DVD's all the way.

If Marcus's dad weren't such a fucking douche bag, I'd have asked Marcus a long time ago to get us a quote for a new security system.

When Marcus doesn't answer, I shove the mansion's massive front door open and block the entrance. "You okay, man?"

Marcus is staring at the ground, his mouth in an unhappy line. "Yeah, it's just…" He sighs, ruffles his hair again, and makes a face at me. "The old man seems to think I'm obligated to work at his company when I'm done with school."

"What? Fuck." I step aside, and Marcus trudges reluctantly inside. "But you told him you wanna be an attorney, right?"

"Man, he doesn't fucking listen." Marcus heads straight for

the kitchen. I follow him inside, watching as he sets our beers inside the double refrigerator.

Natalie designed this space. A few of the rooms, too. She was a fully qualified architect, and actually fucking good at it. But she seemed to think this house would be brimming with kids. Everything feels two sizes too big—the massive kitchen with its long island, the dining room table that seats twenty guests, the excess of guest bedrooms.

"Dude, you gotta level with him," I say, taking the can he hands me and cracking it open. "You can't go do something you don't—"

"I don't have a choice." He turns, staring out the window. "He's holding my trust fund hostage."

My eyebrows lift to my hairline. I'm speechless. I guess I shouldn't be surprised, but I thought at least in adulthood, Marcus's dad would cut him a fucking break.

"Wow…that's…"

"Cold," Marcus mutters. He swings back to me, lifts his can, and takes several long swallows. "Here's to the fuck-ups that call themselves dads."

I shake my head, but touch my can to his when he lowers it before taking a sip.

"Any idea when Indi moved to town?" Marcus asks quietly. My eyes snap to him, my heart suddenly beating harder than before.

"Recently, I guess. I think she's family of the Davis's," I say, coming around the island and leaning against it beside him. I've got about half an inch on him, but that's never seemed to bug him.

When Marcus doesn't say anything, I glance at him from the corner of my eye. He's gone all stiff, face leeched of color. "What's wrong?" I say through a chuckle.

"Nothing," Marcus says hurriedly, pushing away from the

island. He grins at me, and I wonder if I was imagining things. The light in this place can be a little too white sometimes. "Thinking of something else."

Fuck. What is it going to take to get his mind off his prick of a dad?

"Tell you what," I say, lifting my beer can and pointing at him with a finger. "Let's plan phase two."

Marcus's smile widens into something approaching manic. "Did you see the video today?"

I shake my head, gulping down more of my beer as Marcus rummages in his sweats for his phone. He beckons me with a finger, turning and resting his elbows on the marble counter of the island as a video starts playing on his phone's massive touchscreen.

The shot jiggles a little, and then steadies.

"What the fuck are those—"

"Lenses, dude. Or filters, or some shit, I dunno. Dylan's girl is fucking obsessed with the shit."

I crane closer, a slow smile spreading on my lips.

Cindy must have been quite close to get such a good shot of Indi on her knees. But whatever she did to the video, it introduced a pair of dog ears and a shiny nose to both me and Indi's faces.

It honestly looks like she's begging, and I'm standing over her smirking like a fucking king.

I bark out a laugh, and then snatch the phone from Marcus's hands, replaying the video.

"Fucking genius," I murmur.

"I'll send it to you," Marcus says, retrieving his phone when the video's done playing.

"Yeah, you do that." I'm still laughing as I make for the stairs. "Throw your shit in one of the rooms and let's bang out a few games of pool."

Marcus grabs his backpack and follows me up the stairs, detouring to his favorite guest bedroom—the one two doors down from my father's den. Apparently, he has a thing for balcony's, and that's the only guest room that has one. It doesn't have much of a view, but beggars can't be choosers.

While I'm changing into clean clothes, my phone vibrates on my bed. I go over to it, tugging a shirt over my head as the video comes through. I watch it again, but this time I don't smile.

This time, I'm trying to see past the ridiculous cutesy fucking dog ears and shit Cindy pasted on Indi.

I want to see her eyes. Those fierce fucking eyes of hers.

Yup, there it is.

She fucking hates me so much, it's bleeding through the phone.

"You coming, bro?"

My eyes snap up, and I toss my phone back on my bed. "Sure," I say gruffly, charging out of my room.

What the fuck's wrong with me? I should be elated that she hates me; it means my plan's fucking working.

Instead, I feel hollow inside. I chug the last of my beer before we hit the entertainment center on the ground floor, and immediately head for the bar.

"Shot?" I yell over my shoulder as I slide around the bar and grab a bottle of rum.

"Make it a double," Marcus says, taking a pool cue from the rack and weighing it in his hand. "Else you'll never fucking win."

I bark out a laugh, pour us a double rum and coke, and then add a shot of tequila on the side. I bring him the small shooter glass, and clink it.

"To fucking shit up," I say.

"Amen, brother."

INDI

I'm supposed to be catching up on a week's worth of school work, but instead I can't stop thinking about Briar. What he did to me in the woods last night. How it felt when he had me on my knees in front of him in homeroom.

I don't think I've ever met someone as enigmatic as him. There's danger in his eyes, but instead of running, I'm drawn closer.

My mother made a point of keeping me away from boys. She wasn't expecting me to lose my virginity on my wedding night or anything, but she impressed upon me how important it was to wait for 'Mr. Right', like she'd done with Dad.

But I haven't met my Mr. Right yet. Not even a Mr. Maybe. I'm starting to wonder why the hell I listened to her.

It's disrespectful. Downright rude. But as much as I loved her, as big a role as she played in my life…She's not here anymore.

I have to make my own decisions now. I have to decide who Mr. Right is, or if I even want to keep waiting around for him.

I slide that thin silver chain through my fingertips, a sad smile pasted on my mouth. I'm staring out my bedroom window while the smell of whatever Marigold's cooking downstairs wafts up to me.

Mom had lots of jewelry, but Dad commissioned this necklace from someone right here in Lavish for their 45th wedding anniversary…which he knew they'd never get to celebrate when he was diagnosed with stage four terminal cancer. Blue was Mom's favorite color, and he'd known the day he married her that he would get her a sapphire.

I would love to wear this necklace all the time, a way to carry her with me, but if all else fails…I might have to sell it to escape this place. It's worth seven hundred thousand, this stone.

I'm a hundred percent sure this is what they were looking for that night.

I got home at two in the morning. My phone had been ringing, but I didn't recognize the numbers. I'd had so much to drink, I didn't even think anything of it at the time. Multiple calls from random numbers? A mere glitch in the Matrix. Nothing for me to concern myself over. Especially when a hot guy from my school brought me three drinks, and seemed fascinated by everything I said. I thought we'd be making out by the end of the night, perhaps even screwing.

We never did.

By two, I could barely stand unaided. I'm convinced there was a guardian angel with me that night. A really trendy angel—one that knew I'd be better off getting pissed than staying at home with Mom. Because that guy could have done anything to me at the party, but instead he called me a cab.

I argued with the cab driver for a minute when he wanted to drop me off. I kept telling him he had the wrong house.

They'd extinguished the blaze about an hour before I got there. Smoke hung thick in the sky, and wreathed what was left of the upper levels of my home. My front lawn was littered with police, paramedics, and firefighters.

And then there was the crowd.

When I finally decided to get out the car and try to find a cab driver who actually knew Lakeview and could get me home, my next-door neighbor hurried over and threw her arms over me.

"My—God—Indi."

Then, finally, reality consumed me like molten lava.

I remember trying to run into the house. Men grabbing at

me, dragging me back. And then I don't remember much at all, because they fucking sedated me. My friend at the time, Sara, arrived a few minutes later. Her parents ushered me into their station wagon and drove me away.

The shit they gave me was so strong, I fell asleep in the back seat and only woke up later the next day.

Mom had been dead for almost a day before I heard the news.

I lift the chain and run the delicate links over my lips.

According to the police, it was a botched robbery. The thief —they could only find evidence of a single person on the scene —must have burned down the house to hide his tracks. He tried to make it look like a gas leak, but despite how badly burned my mother's corpse was when they recovered it, her autopsy revealed signs of a struggle and aggravated rape.

Mom was petite, like me. Father used to say she was his doll. He wasn't a large man, but she only reached his collarbones. It wouldn't have taken a strong man to subdue her, to force her—

A sob hitches in my throat. I squeeze my eyes shut and force away every last shred of emotion from my mind.

I'm just glad my father wasn't alive when it happened. It would have broken his heart. Just like he broke my heart and Mom's heart when he died from cancer. That was over five years ago. Sometimes I wonder which was better—Mom's abrupt, brutal murder, or my father's year-long struggle where we'd known weeks before that he would be leaving.

Guess it doesn't matter.

They're both gone.

But their deaths taught me the most important lesson of all.

Love is for masochistic fucks who enjoy the feeling of having their heart ripped out.

Right now, I'm free. I love no one, and I never will again. All that shit about it's better to have loved and lost?

I've done both. And in my mind, love's just not worth the fucking pain.

BRIAR

"So when you gonna grow a pair of balls and tell your Dad to fuck off?" I say. Well, slur is probably a better word. We've almost finished the bottle of rum; the tequila suffered severe collateral damage.

We gave up playing pool and went to go watch a rerun of the weekend's game. The plan was to figure out a strategy and suggest it to the coach for our game this weekend.

But as soon as our friendly debate began heading toward a screaming match, we decided to finally order a pizza and wait for it to be delivered on the front lawn.

That was ten minutes ago. Pizza takes a while to reach us out here in the rich part of town—sometimes up to thirty minutes. But we slump in a set of garden chairs and watch the moon rise while we wait, passing the last bit of rum from hand to hand.

Marcus snorts at my statement, and taps out a cigarette from a brushed steel case. We both stopped smoking a while ago, but on nights when liquor seemingly flows from the fountain of eternal fucking youth, nothing beats a cancer stick. He lights it, tugs at it, and passes it to me before replying.

"You make it sound so fucking easy."

"It is. You say, Dad…fuck off."

He laughs. "Yeah, and then he'll tell me to fuck off."

"And? Then you fuck off. Just make sure you got some money, and you're good to go."

"Yeah, money. You forget, my dad's a stingy fucking bastard."

I let out a massive sigh. "Jesus, then you save up. You get a fucking job. Or you could stay there and eat up his shit for the rest of your life." I wave a hand. "Your fucking choice."

"So I get enough money to make a move. Where would I go?" Marcus asks, but his voice softens as if he's actually really considering this shit. I'm fucking glad—it's only taken what, ten years to get my point across? I get that despite how flush his dad is, Marcus hardly has any walking around money on him. But if I were him, I'd have gotten a job a long time ago.

Where would he go?

"Here." I sweep a hand out behind me and take a drag of the smoke. "I got a couch in the living room that's got your name written all over it."

Marcus laughs again, trading rum for the cigarette. "Sure your dad will just love that," he mutters.

"He probably wouldn't even notice. I bet you could stay here for months, and he'd just think it was pure fucking coincidence that you're here every time he bothers to swing by and pick up fresh clothes."

"He still working so much?"

I press my lips closed. I don't whine about my personal life, because what kid my age wouldn't kill to be where I am? I'm one weekday-visit away from being an orphan. "I get the whole house to myself."

"He working on a new project or something?"

I shrug. "Probably. If I see him again this year, I'll let you know."

Marcus shakes his head as he laughs, and we trade again. "Might as well finish it, bro," he says.

There's about three fingers left, but I shrug and down it anyway. Not as if I'm driving home, and no girls around for me to assault.

My mood turns dark in an instant. I stand, aim, and throw

the bottle as far as I can. Marcus lets out a cackle when it hits the side of a hedge. "So close."

I slump back in my seat. "Give me a smoke," I say.

Marcus must have heard the tone of my voice, because he doesn't pass back the cigarette we've been sharing—he lights me a new one.

Kind of hate alcohol. The early stages are fine. But now, when I've just about reached my threshold, there are only two paths for me to follow.

Aggression or depression.

Guess Marcus and I have that in common. Except his highs and lows come regardless of how much rum he has pumping through his veins.

"Hey, so Zak's throwing a party after the game this weekend."

"Yeah?"

"Black-tie again."

"Swishy fuck."

Marcus laughs. "You gonna come?"

"What, alone?" I glance across at him. "Or are you offering to be my plus one? Forget it."

"You'd be lucky to have me, you fucking prick."

I wave away the comment. As if I could go to a fucking party like some normal kid. All those girls around, all that booze around. Even if I swore not to touch a fucking drop of liquor, not get close to a line of coke…I was perfectly fucking sober when I found Indi in the woods.

I can't risk that shit.

"You ever wish you could just go back to the way things used to be?" I ask quietly, sitting forward and resting my elbow on my knee as I drag at my cigarette.

Marcus is quiet for the longest time. "Man, you gotta get Jessica out of your fucking head."

"Easy for you to say."

"It is easy for me to say." Marcus sits forward in a rush, leaning forward until I look at him. "Get over her. Shit happened, we dealt with it, it's done."

I let out a soft huff. "So why the fuck does it keep coming up to bite me in the ass?"

Marcus laughs. "You honestly think it will just go away? It'll always be there, man, but you just gotta ignore it. If anyone had shit on you, it would have surfaced by now. It's been months, bro. Christ, almost a year, actually." He sits back in his seat, cigarette dangling from his mouth, and stares at me as if daring me to argue with his impeccable logic.

"When the fuck is the pizza getting here?" I mutter.

"I dunno. How long since you ordered?"

I twist to face him. "Me? You said you'd call."

We stare at each other for a second before bursting out laughing.

"Ah, fuck this shit," Marcus says. "Don't know about you, but I'm done."

"Yeah, fuck," I murmur, still smiling as I get to my feet. I wobble a bit, and Marcus slings his arm around my shoulder. We hold onto each other as we make our unsteady way back to the mansion, dodging rose bushes and concrete statues in the likeness of cherubs and shit.

"You ever think what it would be like to have a brother or a sister?" I ask idly.

The fuck was in that rum?

"Nope."

"Never? I'd have liked a brother."

"Younger or older?"

"Younger. Don't need anyone lording shit over me, you know?"

Marcus lets out a huff of a laugh.

"We'd have been good brothers," I say, flicking his ear.

"Doubt it. We'd probably have hated each other's guts." Marcus clears his throat. Maybe he's feeling all emotional and shit too. I'll have to make a note never to touch that brand of rum of again. "Plus, you can't choose your family. It's what makes life so much fun." With his flat tone, I know exactly where his mind has detoured.

By the time we make it upstairs, that last inch of rum I downed is blurring the world around me. I'm distantly aware of Marcus helping me stumble to my bed, murmuring something about no fucking way he was tucking me in, bros or no, and then he's gone.

Before sleep takes me, I swear I hear the sound of low, electronic beeps.

Beep, beep, beep, beep.

Did I lock the front door? Maybe Marcus is pinning in the key—I'm sure he knows it by now.

Fuck it—if someone breaks in, they'll have to deal with me and Marcus. Even drunk, we'd beat them to a fucking pulp.

CHAPTER TEN

INDI

Marigold looks up when I come thundering down the stairs and into the dining room the next morning. She called me down for breakfast fifteen minutes ago, but I lost my appetite when I remembered the hellhole I had to attend today.

"I need clothes," I say, shifting my hips to the side and crossing my arms over my chest. "And a longer skirt."

"I'm afraid my budget is already allocated for this week. You'll have to wait until the weekend."

"But I literally have like two pairs of underwear, and one's dirty."

"So best you wash them," Gran says, setting a delicate china cup down on its saucer. I scan the teak dining table and then shrug at her when I see there's no food on it. "I thought you said there was breakfast."

Marigold takes another tiny sip from her cup. "That was fifteen minutes ago."

"Isn't your job as my guardian to feed and clothe me?" I yell.

Marigold's shoulders melt at this. In response, my chest grows tight and I take a step back before I can stop myself.

"My job as your guardian is to make sure you don't fail school."

Shock slams into me like a wall of ice. I try to speak, but words utterly fail me.

Marigold gives me a cold little smile. "Aren't you running late for school? They take tardiness into account. I'm sure they won't hesitate to adjust your grades accordingly."

"I don't know how Mom could stand being around you," I say. My voice is so thick, I can barely understand myself, but Marigold doesn't seem to have the same problem.

"Leave," she says. "Before you say something you'll regret."

I laugh. "You know what I regret, *Granny?*"

My gran's already pale face goes translucent. She stands, her body quivering with righteous indignation, but I carry on before she can open her raspberry red lips.

"I regret not being in that house with Mom."

I'm surprised Marigold doesn't have something to say about this. In fact, to my utter astonishment, a tear flashes down her cheek.

"Get out," she whispers. "Get out of my house!" The last is a shrill yell. She charges for me, and I turn tail and run like the fucking coward that I am.

I slam the junker's door so hard, I'm shocked it doesn't fall off. I get to school in record time, everything en route just a blur of speed and tears.

I'm still sniffing back snot and blinking away my last tears when someone raps on my window.

Jerking, I spin to face the window. For a horrific moment, I'd thought it was Briar. The thought that he'd see me in hysterics makes me want to throw up.

But it's Addy out there, face wrinkled with concern. She whirls her finger in the air, demanding that I roll down the window. I comply, but with bad grace.

"What?"

"Have you—?" She ducks her head to get a better look at me, and even when I tip my head down she just follows. "Why are you crying?"

"None of your business," I snap.

"Yeah?" Her voice is as edgy as mine. "That's what you think." She shoves her hand through the window.

Pure instinct has me grabbing her wrist. She squeals, and tugs back at her hand, but I'm holding her tight.

Then I see the joint between her fingers.

It glitters.

It's gold.

I'm so very, very confused.

"Now you gonna let me in, or what?" Addy asks. When I look at her, she rolls her eyes. "It's edible gold," she mutters, before stalking around the front of the car.

I lean across and open the other door. Addy gets in with a sigh, smelling of weed and perfume, and immediately lights up the joint.

"Edible gold?" I ask, when she hands the joint over to me.

"Looks gorgeous. Tastes like shit." She glances across at me, and smiles as she blows out a plume of smoke.

Yeah, the paper tastes like shit, but the weed inside? Oh my fucking god.

"What is this?" I ask in a tight voice, keeping as much of that dank deliciousness inside my lungs as possible.

"Happiness," she says flippantly.

"I mean, what strain?"

She shrugs. "These guys don't grow strains. They just give you weed that will make you feel a certain way." She smiles around the gold joint, and then points to it with a long nail. "Happiness."

For a second—a brief, intangible moment—I wonder what it

would be like to be her. I mean, I wasn't always a slob—I used to wear makeup and brush my hair and wear pretty underwear. But that all seems so fucking pointless these days.

"Jesus, smoke more," Addy says, widening her eyes at me. "I swear you're oozing sad emojis from every pore."

I laugh, and then I cough. My dark thoughts disappear in a haze of artificial happiness.

BRIAR

"Dude, we're gonna be late. Briar. Briar!"

I groan, shoving the hand off my shoulder. When I open my eyes, it's no more than a slit. "Fuck," I groan up at Marcus.

"Yeah, today's gonna be fun," he says, squinting at me. "Want some coffee?"

"Please."

He's already dressed, but judging from how I feel, he's probably as hungover as I am. He leaves my room and I drag myself out of bed, scratching an itch on my side as I gaze around at the evidence of last night's rum intoxication. Sometime during the night, I stripped to my boxers. My clothes are scattered all over the floor, and the vase our maid normally keeps filled with fresh flowers on my nightstand is laying on the carpet, blooms already wilting.

Damn. Pity I missed all the fun.

After a shower and Marcus's cup of coffee, I can at least stand the thought of leaving my shelter.

"Driving with me?" I ask.

"Fuck yes." Marcus detours to his SUV and grabs out his sunglasses before going to my Mustang's passenger side. "I'm even considering skipping."

"Nah, come on," I say, opening my door and sliding in. "We got a newbie to torture, remember? Don't want her thinking we're backing off, do we?"

"Forgot about her," Marcus says. He puffs at his vape as soon as I put my car into gear, and doesn't let up until we reach Lavish Prep.

By then the coffee's kicked in, and if I keep my sunglasses on it doesn't feel like the sun's trying to scoop out my eyeballs with a spoon.

We're late, so the steps are empty.

"They'd have locked already," Marcus murmurs.

I'm real fucking tempted to turn back. But I meant what I said—I'm not letting up on Indi any time soon. The whole drive over here, she filled my mind. How she looked on her knees in front of me. I can't help picturing her naked, her mouth open real wide, waiting for my cock like the obedient toy she is.

After days and days of torture, I'm sure Indi will be more than happy to surrender herself to me.

I deserve nothing less.

She deserves nothing more.

"Earth to Briar?"

"What?"

"Christ, I don't know what you think you're gonna accomplish today, but I suggest you lower your expectations, bro. Like drastically."

I snort at him, and gesture around the building. "The gym door should be open. You know how coach likes his fresh air."

Marcus sniffs at himself. "Ain't gonna have much of that if he catches a whiff of either of us."

We're both still chuckling as we head for the side of Lavish Prep's massive building.

I'm coming, my toy. Hope you've had a good night's rest, because this is gonna be one taxing day for you.

CHAPTER ELEVEN

INDI

I lay awake for hours last night wondering what Briar had in store for me today. But I've been in homeroom for more than ten minutes and he hasn't even bothered looking up at me.

He's busy on his phone, and there's that same frustrated frown on his face.

I sit back in my seat and force myself to face Ms. Parsons as she starts off with some announcements. She hasn't mentioned the buddy thing again, but I have a feeling that she'll keep that for the end of class if she plans on bringing it up.

"Good morning, Indi."

I flinch, recognizing the voice, but unable to process those polite words. I turn in my chair, and scowl suspiciously at Briar. "What do you want?"

I discretely move my feet to make sure he hasn't somehow managed to tie my laces again, and then casually run my fingers through my hair in case I missed any early morning spitballs.

Briar's smiling. It looks genuine, and that's extremely concerning. Then again, he's wearing shades, so maybe that's why he has me fooled. That grin makes me think he knows something I don't.

I feel a nervous tic coming on.

"You rushed off so fast yesterday, I never got to find out how my Lavish Buddy enjoyed her first day."

"Which part?" I snap, cocking my head at him and not bothering to lower my voice. "The part where you had me on my knees, or where your friend decided to spit in my hair?"

I realize my mistake immediately. Phrasing, for one. Two, whose class we're in.

"Children?"

I catch Briar suppressing a smile behind a big hand as he sits back in his chair, but Ms. Parsons already has a hand on my shoulder, turning me to face her. "Is everything all right, Indigo?"

"Indi."

Parsons nods. "Indi?"

"Everything's fine, Ms. Parsons."

She tilts her head like I'm covered with spots and still trying to deny the fact that I have measles. "You can always talk to me, Indi. That's what guidance counselors are for."

There's a faint snigger from somewhere in the back of the class. I catch a few words, enough to make me blush. Something about asking her how one goes about losing my virginity. Someone else said Briar would sort me out, no problem.

"I'm fine," I say through gritted teeth. Ms. Parsons shakes her head, and then looks past me at Briar.

"You should take Indi to the stables during your free period today." Then she looks back at me. "Your transcript said you enjoyed horse riding. I'm sure Briar would love to take you for a ride."

The class bursts out laughing. Ms. Parsons hurriedly straightens, and then adjusts her tortoiseshell glasses as if the sudden movement knocked them awry. "Quieten down, class.

There's nothing funny about feeling out of your element at a new school."

"Really, I'm fine. I don't want to go—"

Ms. Parsons turns to me, her little rosebud mouth pursed with disapproval. "Horses are very therapeutic."

"I don't want—"

"Well, I insist." She crosses her arms over her chest. "Lavish expects its students to be fully involved in everything the school has to offer." She gestures toward Briar with a limp hand. "Briar's a wonderful rider, and I'm sure you'd love to see—"

The class erupts into fits of laughter. Ms. Parsons blushes furiously, but surprisingly, stands her ground. "To see the rest of the school."

Goddamnit Parsons. It would be a real dick move for me to refuse and embarrass her further. I mean, I'm even starting to blush just imagining Briar and willowy Ms. Parsons rutting like animals against the blackboard with their—

Woah, Indi! No.

Now my cheeks are on fire too.

"Okay," I say in a strangled voice. "I'll go."

"Good." Ms. Parsons nod firmly, makes a point of not looking in Briar's direction, and then goes back to her desk and starts eating an apple with such determination, I wonder if she's maybe a closet stress eater-cum-bulimic.

"I'm gonna enjoy riding you," Briar says, just loud enough for me to hear.

"You mean riding *with* me," I correct him, my focus still on Ms. Parson's squirrelly little bites.

"Not even a little."

I turn to him, but he's decided something on his phone is more important than being the subject of my wrath.

I glance at my class timetable. Two classes, a free period, then one class before lunch.

Oh wait. There's a typo on my schedule. I tilt my head to the side and shove the timetable into my blazer pocket. Free period is meant to say 'horse riding with Briar'.

Don't get me wrong—the thought of getting in a few minutes on horseback sounds like heaven. It wasn't just me being smarmy on my transcript—I do love horse riding. And, luckily, it was an elective at my last school. I refuse to do dressage or jumping or any of that craziness, but just riding was an awesome experience.

Maybe I can race away from Briar, lose him on the grounds, and get the rest of the period to myself.

I risk a quick glance behind me. Briar's got his arms crossed over his chest, muscles bulging against his blazer and a smirk all over his face. Is it just me, or his hair a little more tousled than normal? It would be nice if he had a sleepless night too.

A girl can dream, right?

BRIAR

I must admit, I'm kinda surprised when Indigo arrives at the stables. I thought she'd hide in the bathrooms until the period was over. I even messaged my crew, putting them on alert in case I needed them to go root her out. This couldn't have been a better way to get Indi's guard down than if I'd planned it myself. I think I'll send Ms. Parsons a gift when I get home. I do so love to make that teacher blush.

"Pick your poison," I say, sweeping my arm over the row of stabled horses. These aren't your teenage girl's ponies. Every horse in the stable is a thoroughbred with more certifications and paperwork than a surgeon.

Lavish Prep takes three things *very* seriously.

Football.

The chess club.

And their horses.

Bit of a mixed bag, agreed. But the faculty is pretty eclectic, so I guess it makes sense.

Indigo looks past me, crosses her arms, and gives me a smug little smile. "I forgot to mention…" She tugs at the hem of her skirt, showing off an extra inch of her thighs.

I swallow, and force myself to keep my gaze fixed on her eyes instead of letting them slide down her dainty little body. "That you're a girl?" I say, cocking an eyebrow at her. "I believe I've already confirmed that."

"I can't ride in a skirt." She turns around and gives me a little wave over her shoulder. "Suck it, loser."

She doesn't make it very far. When I grab her around the waist and spin her around, she lets out a squeal that does Neanderthal things to my body. I shove her away, but not hard enough for her to fall, and regret that I held back when she spins to face me wearing a scowl. "What the hell?"

"Don't you know you can't postpone a date with the devil?" I say, showing her my teeth.

I don't like the way my heart's knocking against my ribs or how I got a semi back there for the brief moment our bodies connected. This girl is trouble. I should just let her go already so I can get my head back in the game. Fuck it, I think the only reason I ended up drinking so much last night was because of her. To get her out of my fucking head. Didn't do me any good —the only thing I seemed capable of expending mental energy on was figuring out ways to harass Indi.

"I'll get a fucking rash if I—" she begins, but cuts off when I swarm past her.

Lavish thought of everything, of course, girls in skirts

included. I open one of the lockers inside the stable and pull out a pair of leggings.

Indigo snatches it when I toss it at her and glares at me.

She looks around, her glare slowly fading. "Where's the—?"

"Changing room?" I cut in with a smirk. "There isn't one. But I promise, I won't look." I turn around, crossing my arms over my chest, and wait.

Indi makes an angry sound, but sure as shit, there's the sound of rustling fabric a moment later.

When I look over my shoulder, I catch a glimpse of one ass cheek before she sees me looking.

"Briar!"

I chuckle and straighten again. "Hurry up, virgin. There's a fuck load of shit to see."

She grumbles something under her breath, and walks down the stalls, touching the noses of the horses who are looking over their doors. She takes her time, and I couldn't be gladder.

For some reason, my cock decided that glimpse of her ass was good enough to rouse it from sleep. I shift my weight, willing my dick to stop being so full of itself.

The only way I get that right is by forcing the thought of Indi's smooth skin out of my mind.

Christ. Soon, one of us is going to break. I was convinced it would be her…but I'm starting to think I overestimated my self-control.

INDI

I fidget on my saddle, trying to hook my underwear out of my ass crack.

Leggings *suck*. Not only does this pair cling like nobody's fucking business, but they're causing serious tension between the two halves of my ass. Peace talks broke down as soon as I hoisted myself onto my gelding's back, ignoring Briar's suspiciously gentleman-like stirrup he made with his hands.

Now? A minute into our ride and my ass crack is the fucking Gaza strip.

"Show jumping, right?"

I pluck away my hand out from under my skirt, fully aware that Briar caught me trying to adjust my panties, and tighten my grip on the reins. "Please," I mutter, too flustered to be snarky.

"Dressage?"

When I look across at him, I can't help but laugh at the disgusted look on his face. I pat the side of my horse's neck. "This," I say. "Just this."

"Leisure rides?"

I shrug a little and squint into the distance. "They said I was too big to be a jockey."

This time, Briar lets out a snorting laugh, and looks half-surprised at himself when I glance at him. "You? Really?"

"Turns out they only employ midgets and dwarves," I say.

I never applied to be a jockey, of course. I like galloping, but for me it's more about spending time with horses. I've always loved them—whipping them into a frenzy just to win a fucking trophy? Hard pass.

"I didn't think you'd come," Briar says quietly.

I frown a little, and peek at him from the corner of my eyes. He insisted I put on a helmet, which I'm glad I did because it's doing a good job of shielding my eyes.

He left his blazer back at the stable, as had I, but he still looks every inch a natural with his blond hair sticking out from under his helmet.

"Why'd you think that?"

"Because you hate everything and everyone," he says deadpan. He turns to me with an eyebrow cocked. "Am I wrong?"

"I don't hate everyone." I lift one side of my mouth. "I just hate jocks suffering from Short Dick Syndrome."

He lets out a rough laugh. "Yeah, that's not it, Angel" he says, but more to himself than me.

"So you're not an asshole because your pinkie's bigger than your penis?" I ask, blinking innocently at him.

Another laugh, but this time he deigns not to answer me. Instead, he glances behind us and then ahead, squinting like a cowboy in one of those spaghetti Westerns.

I must admit, I'm kinda glad I wussed out and came. Initially, it was just to tell Briar off—using my lack of pants as an excuse—but now that I'm here?

That same feeling of strange familiarity flows over me. I lose myself to my gelding's rhythm, letting my hips melt into the saddle.

The breathtaking scenery helps, of course. Lavish Prep is built on a rise, and as soon as we crest it, the suburbs of Lavish spread out in front of us. Everything is so neat, so tiny and tidy, that it feels like

I'm looking at a built-to-scale replica instead of the real thing. There's a mid-morning haze over the town, and the sun's warm light suffuses everything with amber.

"Beautiful, isn't it?"

I purse my lips, pissed that Briar dared to break me out of my blissful moment. But when I turn to him, he's staring at me, not the view.

Did he…was he talking about *me*?

"Come on," he says, before I have time to process the thought. "I'll race you to the tree line."

The tree line? I look ahead, narrowing my eyes a second before Briar lets out a loud, "Ha!"

His white mare—Princess Snow—lunges forward and breaks into an astonishingly smooth gallop. Sunlight washes him in a warm glow as he races down the incline. His shirt whips against his hard body, and he glances at me over his shoulder, a fat grin on his face.

My heart feels like it wants to explode from my chest. He's a *fucking* good rider. It's like he was born on horseback. He's standing in his stirrups, ass a few inches from the saddle as he urges his horse to pick up speed, his entire body moving in time to the creature's rocking gait.

My gelding tenses between my legs as if it wants to run after its friend.

"Ha!" I dig my heels into my gelding's ribs. It whinnies at me and, when I loosen up the reins and urge him forward with my knees, he leaps into action.

Hooves thunder over the grass. The wind runs cool fingers over my skin and tugs at my shirt, flattening it against my breasts and tummy as I lean forward.

"Come on!" I yell. I slap the horse's rump with my hand. "Ha!"

My gelding snorts, ducks its head, and speeds up. Briar made a good start, but since he obviously thought he was in the lead, he didn't bother to push his mare. But he must have heard my gelding's hooves eating up the distance between us because he glances behind him—still wearing that smug grin—and does a double take when he sees how close we are.

I grin to myself, and give my gelding another smack on the rump. "Ha!" Prince Charming flicks his head, and I give him even more rein. He rewards me by gaining another two noses on Briar's mare.

I can almost reach out and touch Briar's leg. But instead I give the two horses enough room so they don't feel crowded, while keeping them close enough that they'd have to be wearing blinkers not to see each other.

And boy does the sight of Prince Charming so close on her heels give Princess Snow a kick up the rear. She tosses her head until Briar gives her some slack and then the little bitch puts a yard between us.

But she's starting to lather, and I have a feeling Prince Charming's just about reached the end of his gallop too.

I lean down, my hips sinking and rising with every stretch of the gelding's legs, and yell out, "Come on, Prince! We can beat them! Faster! Ha!"

Briar glares at me, and I laugh as Prince Charming gains a little.

But then Briar looks ahead, and his face goes blank in shock.

"Indi, stop!" he yells, his reins tightening instantly.

I'm a little slower to react, because I think he's pulling my fucking leg. So when I do face forward and realize Prince Charming is galloping straight for the fence that surrounds the massive stretch of grassy knolls we've been riding around on, jerking back on my reins isn't good enough.

I dig my knees into his ribs, but even that only seems to encourage him. When I pull on the reins, but he pulls right back.

Fuck! He's got the bit in his teeth!

How the fuck did I manage to piss off this Prince too?

"Indi, stop!"

"Can't!" I yell back. "He's got the fucking bit."

And just like that, Briar's not in my line of sight anymore. It's just me racing for a very high, very intimidating fence.

Fuck, fuck, *fuck*!

I hunker down, throw my arms around Prince Charming's neck and cling to him with aching thighs as I wait for impact.

BRIAR

Slowing down is the hardest thing I've ever had to do. In a second, Indi is yards away, her chestnut gelding galloping straight for the fence.

I shouldn't have made such a pretend fuss when she'd chosen that horse. Then she wouldn't have been so stubborn and stuck with her choice.

All because of his name?

Prince Charming is a show horse. He's been teaching the kids at Lavish how to show jump for the past two years, if not longer.

And he's a competitive prick. You know all that shit about short dick syndrome? Well, they cut his dick off. Imagine how that shit messes with your personality?

But if I don't stop, if I keep pace, he'll keep accelerating. As it is, he seems to be slowing down a little, but I can sense he has no notion of missing that jump.

It's a fucking high jump. Not so much for Prince fucking Charming, but for a little thing like Indi, who's never jumped before…?

Fuck this. I can't just sit here.

"Ha!" I urge my mare into another gallop, despite her whinny of complaint. She's one of Lavish's best racers, but even she has her limits. She needs a cool down right now, not more galloping. But if Indi doesn't make that jump…if she does something to unbalance Prince Charming…

"Ha!"
Faster.
Faster!

CHAPTER TWELVE

INDI

I'm holding onto my gelding so tight I can barely breathe. I wish I could close my eyes but they just keep popping open, fixating on the hooves flashing under me.

I guess I fucked with the universe's plan for me; I should have been home that night Mom was killed. Karma's decided to right a wrong, and tax me for my stolen days on this earth. I get that. I understand. But it can't expect me to like it, for fuck's sake.

Everyone fights in their last moment of clarity. Even those that decide they've been dealt a shit hand and fold. Goes to show how much of the animal is still left in us.

Prince Charming's gait changes. His steps shorten.

Beneath me, the horse's muscles bunch and it's like I'm gripping a rock between my thighs.

No more thundering hooves.

No impact.

We're flying.

If I could breathe, I'd be screaming. But all I can do is stare wide-eyed as the fence flashes beneath us.

The air is knocked from my lungs by the impact of Prince Charming's landing. He takes a few lunging steps and then slows into a canter, a walk.

My face is wet. My arms and thighs are trembling so much I can't even think about pushing up into a sit. Prince tosses his mane and snorts as if he's getting pissed off with my fierce hug. I think I peed myself a little.

"Fuck y-you, Prince. You alm-most killed me," I say, my trembling jaw chopping up my words.

"I can't believe you expect me to shoulder the blame for this," a voice behind me announces.

I glance over my shoulder as Briar jumps down the last foot of the fence and lands with a spring in his step. He swaggers up to me, shaking his head and making tut-tut noises. His helmet is off, his sandy hair utterly mussed.

"You gonna get off him now?" he asks.

"I'm good."

"You'll have to get down sometime, Indi." Briar ducks his head a little, and squeezes my shoulder. "You did good though, kid. Though I think if you held on any tighter, Prince Charming would have choked to death before he took the jump."

I push the words, "Fuck you," through my teeth.

Briar's smile melts away. He trails a knuckle down my cheek. "Hey," he murmurs, frowning hard. "You're okay, Indi. You made it."

Fuck, fuck, *fuck*! In the comedown from that massive adrenaline spike, my body's gone all PMS on me. Tears leak from my eyes unbidden, and my lips start trembling.

No, please. I can't start sobbing in front of Briar.

"It's r-relief," I stutter. "Just relieved I didn't fucking die."

He grabs my waist and hoists me up off the saddle as if I was nothing more than a bag of potatoes.

But he sets me down carefully, almost gently, takes off my

helmet, and hangs it from Prince Charming's pommel. When he wipes at my cheek with his fingers, I flinch away, my heart hammering in expectation of some cruel joke.

Instead, Briar's eyes narrow, and a crease forms between his wild eyebrows. He studies me like he's never seen me before.

The uncertainty in his eyes holds me captive.

He slides a hand around the back of my neck and draws me closer. I move stiffly, my thighs still aching from their grip on Prince Charming, but he keeps urging me forward until there's no space left between our bodies.

"Where'd you learn to be so brave?" he murmurs down to me. "Any other girl would be bawling her fucking eyes out."

"Any other girl wouldn't have made the jump," I say, trying desperately to inject my melting brain with a little indifference.

It doesn't help, because my comment just puts a spark of a smile in Briar's eyes. He grabs my chin, tilts my head back, and brushes his lips over mine.

That gentle caress sends alarm bells clanging through my body.

No, Indi. No! This is the worst idea you've had since you decided to steal your mother's jewelry and go partying!

But instead of pushing him away, my body sags against his like my spine's turned into a piece of wet string.

His breath butterflies over my lips, sending a tingle rushing through every inch of me. It converges between my legs and burrows deep.

"I...can't..." I mumble, but while I'm still leaning into his feathery attempt at a kiss.

"Why do you *keep* fighting me?"

Fighting him? Him? It's not him I'm fighting. It's fucking temptation.

This man is a monster. I can't allow him to worm his way

through my defenses. This is some kind of prank. A trick. And it won't work on me. I'm not a fucking idiot.

In the distance, the school bell rings.

I summon every ounce of strength I have and shove against Briar's chest. He steps back, a tiny smile on his mouth as if he's expecting some more banter to pass between us. But as soon as he sees my determined expression, his face sets like marble.

Swallowing hard, I clear my throat. I have to get out of here, away from his hypnotic eyes, that incredible smell of fresh earth and pine that envelops me whenever he's close.

In a rush, I hoist myself onto Prince Charming's saddle. I glance around, my eyes traveling down the never-ending span of fence between me and Lavish Prep.

"How do I—?" I gesture at the fence. "Is there a gate, or—?"

Briar watches me without expression, but his eyes are as stormy as an approaching hurricane. The side of his mouth quirks up in a most familiar smirk. He takes a few steps back and flourishes an arm. "I dunno, Indigo." He shrugs theatrically and takes his phone from his pocket. "But you're gonna be late for next period if you don't find it soon."

Icy hatred washes over me, leaving my fingertips tingling and my throat too tight to answer him. I glare at him and nudge Prince Charming into a trot. My eyes are cast ahead, studying the fence for a gate or opening of some kind, but I can see Briar climbing over the fence to get back to his mare.

Briar's already heading back to the stables, sitting on his horse like his fucking namesake, when I finally spot the fence. I let out a dry laugh. It was so close to where we were standing, Briar must have known it was there all along.

I fume all the way back up the hill and into the stables. Briar's not there, but one of the stable hands is giving Princess Snow a cool down, a damp towel draped over her back as she walks in a nearby paddock.

I don't see another person until I slip into the main hallway where my locker is. It's the period before lunch, so almost everyone's in the hallway by their lockers or heading for the restrooms.

Addison's on the far side of the hall, and I wave to her. She spots me and waves back, smiling as she hurries over to meet up with me.

I head for my locker, but a hand catches hold of my arm and spins me around.

Briar.

His blue eyes could have been chips of ice, his face carved from stone. His grip is so tight, I'm certain I couldn't pull loose even if I wanted to.

I swallow down a cry of surprise, but I shouldn't have bothered. A second later, he plants his lips on mine and kisses me with such fierce determination that my knees buckle. He slaps a hand on my back, keeping me up, and then breaks our kiss with an animalistic growl.

Sliding a hand over his mouth, he shoves me out of the way and strides down the hallway, stopping beside his locker like nothing's happened.

The entire hallway comes to a stop. Everyone's either staring at me or at Briar. I hear footsteps and whirl around, expecting a teacher, but instead one of Briar's lackeys—the guy who always wears a white cap—is standing in front of me.

"Don't mind if I do," he says, grinning.

"What?" I manage, but in a voice that barely resembles my own.

The guy slides a hand around my waist and tugs me closer. I'm so shocked, I don't even struggle when he ducks his head and kisses me.

What. The. Fuck?

"Indi!" Addison yells from the other side of the hall.

Yeah, fuck, Addy, no time to chat, girl. Apparently I'm a little fucking busy.

I shove against the guy's chest, and he falls back with a laugh.

My heart's in my throat. My legs are still shaky from the intense horse ride, and they threaten to deposit me on the floor any minute. All around me, the hall erupts into laughter.

What the fuck is happening?

"Yeah, me too!"

I turn to the sound of a voice, and a girl who'd been standing nearby grabs my face and kisses me. I shove her away, but a second later someone else grabs me and plants a kiss on my mouth. I've barely shoved the stranger away before a hand slides around my throat and I'm drawn back against a warm, hard body.

I catch sight of Briar. He's standing by his locker, a few inches taller than most of the kids around him.

He looks like he's about to commit murder. Shoving a kid aside, he surges through the crowd toward me.

But that's all I see before the guy holding me spins me around, grabs my hair in a fist, and crushes his mouth against mine.

Another one of Briar's friends, his BFF. But just as he forces his tongue in my mouth and I'm about to knee him in the groin, we're torn apart.

Briar has his friend's blazer in a fist, and from the snarl on his face, looks about to punch him in the face.

Addison is at my side the next second. She reaches behind me and I hear something tear free from my clothing. She holds up a note.

Kiss Me.

"I'm telling the principal," she says, turning on Briar with such a look of fury, I wouldn't be surprised if she punched him.

Briar shoves his friend away and steps up to Addy, his lip lifting into a sneer.

"Go ahead, Addison," he rumbles. "Go tell the principal what I did."

Addison goes as white as her school shirt, and makes a soft sound in the back of her throat. I step in front of her, my entire body stiff with anger.

How fucking *dare* he threaten my friend?

"Back off, loser," I say through my teeth.

He glances down, dismisses me, and looks back at Addy.

Bad move, Briar. You should know better than to dismiss me, you smug prick.

But when I throw a punch, he catches it almost absently, without taking his eyes off Addison.

"You know what happens to snitches around here, Addy," Briar says.

I look up at him, and my body goes ice-cold; all that hatred consumed by fear in an instant.

"We all know what you did, Briar," Addy whispers. "We all know you—"

"Then fucking prove it," he growls, stepping closer to her. I'm sandwiched between them, and it's only then that Briar seems to remember about me. He glances down at me and then does a double take. A slow, serpentine smile spreads over his lips. "But until you can, you keep your fucking mouths shut."

"Or what?" I say, pushing back my shoulders.

Briar inches closer, but I put my hand on his chest and move Addy and myself back. My hand stays, and for some reason I can't make myself take it off him. If Briar notices, he doesn't seem to care. Instead, those blue eyes spear through me, eating into my soul.

"Or you might become Lavish's next fallen angel," he

murmurs. A dark light fills his eyes as he reaches up and grabs my wrist, pulling my hand away from his chest.

The bell rings, signaling the start of the next period. But nobody moves.

Fallen angel?

No…Angel *Falls*.

Behind me, Addison chokes. Her warmth disappears as she steps away. My mind scrambles. I thought Addison was accusing Briar of rape or something but now…? Could she honestly believe he had a hand in Jessica's death? Why? Because she'd rat him out? He'd probably be sentenced to a year or two in juvie, if anything, and that's if his parents didn't throw enough money on the situation to make it disappear.

But what if he didn't realize that at the time? Briar hasn't exactly proven himself to be a calm, rational human being. He's aggressive, impulsive, passionate.

What if…?

"You did it," I whisper, disbelief dripping from each word. "You killed her."

Briar's smile drops away. "If you're so convinced, then it's best you stop tangling with me."

He steps back, glaring at me as if to impress that last threat on my mind, and then heads for his locker.

Around me, students start moving again. A quiet hush fills the air as I make my way to my locker, by hand throbbing like I had it under too-hot water.

Briar might think he's invincible, but I felt his heart under my palm.

It was racing.

Not with anger…but with fear.

CHAPTER THIRTEEN

BRIAR

A P Psychology.

I stare at the textbook in my hands, and then toss it back into my locker. I slam the door, making the kid next to me jump nearly a foot off the ground, and then I'm striding to the exit.

No way I can deal with Mr. Veroza's old-man stink right now.

Or Indigo's reproachful gaze.

That little girl ruined my fucking day.

Again.

That soppy shit that happened out there by the fence shouldn't have happened at all. But I lost control for a moment. Forgot my purpose, my plans for Indi. The 'Kiss Me' prank was supposed to be a fucking hoot, but instead it made my fucking blood boil every time another kid helped themselves to Indi.

Her mouth? It's mine.

Her lips? Mine.

Indigo? I own every inch of her.

She just doesn't know it yet.

INDI

Addison pulls me into the restroom, and slams the door closed behind us. Everyone should be in class, so I doubt we'll be bothered, but she obviously needs to ensure we can't be overheard.

"You gonna tell me what's going on?" I ask quietly.

She drags a hand through her sleek blond hair, mouth twisting and squirming as if she wants to spit.

"He killed her," Addy murmurs.

My blood runs cold. "Jessica?"

Addy spins to me, eyes wide, and gives me a silent nod.

I shake my head, frowning hard at her. Despite my flurry of thoughts, I'm suddenly filled with doubt. I mean, how could anyone—even Prince Briar—get away with cold-blooded murder? "You said she committed suicide."

"That's how he made it look," she says. She tosses her hair over her shoulder and gives herself a hard hug. "But Jess would never...I know her. She would never do that." Addy's lips tremble and she shoves a knuckle into her mouth. "He pushed her. He must have." Addy turns around, still chewing at her finger.

"When did all of this happen?" It could explain the way the students acted around Briar. I'd have imagined the girls around here throwing themselves at him. Instead everyone gives him a wide berth.

I'd thought it was respect...But now I'm starting to think it's fear.

"Ten months ago."

"And the police?"

Addy rips her hand away from her mouth and lets out a bitter chuckle. "Yeah, Indi, the police did a real good job of locking him up."

"I mean," I say quietly, trying my best to keep my cool, "did they know about the party? Did you—?"

"Of course I told them," Addy says, frowning at me like she thinks I hit my head. "But they never found anything. There were no witnesses that night. The last people to leave saw Jess having a fucking blast with Briar and Marcus."

I sigh as I run my fingers through my hair. "I don't know what to say, Addy."

She starts pacing, her long legs barely taking three strides before she's done the length of the bathroom basins. "I don't want you to say anything." Her green eyes narrow, focusing her anger on me like a laser. "I want you to stay away from him. Stop antagonizing him."

"Antagon—" I splutter before cutting off with a wretched laugh. "Fuck, Addy, you don't think I want him to leave me alone?"

"What do you mean?" She stops pacing.

"He…"

Fuck. I should have told her yesterday, but I was a chicken shit little bitch.

I shift my weight from foot to foot, holding up a hand when Addy opens her mouth, mentally willing her just to give me a few seconds to get my mind sorted out.

What'll happen if I tell her about the woods? She'd say I have to file a report with the police.

In a case where a teenage girl 'killed herself', they did nothing.

Here, it's my word against Briar's. Plus, I didn't tell anyone, and they'd probably flag that as suspicious.

Why now, Indi? Why didn't you tell your grandmother, your new friend, your fucking guidance counselor?

Yeah, I tried telling a teacher, and a whole bunch of kids—Addison included—saw how well that shit went down.

Telling Addy will change nothing. She already suspects Briar of having killed Jessica—saying he mauled me in the woods before letting me run away isn't going to help.

But it might incense her to the point of random violence.

"You've seen how he is with me," I say weakly. "He's had it in for me since he saw me."

"Yeah…" Addy plants her hands on her hips, and studies me from the corner of her eye. "What was that about? You made it sound like he'd done something."

Her eyes widen, and it's like watching dawn rise over a fog-shrouded hill.

"We've met before," I say, hoping my brain will catch up in time and provide me with enough ammunition to lay down some covering fire.

"You and Briar?" Her knuckle goes back into her mouth. "When?" she asks, the word muffled around her finger.

Yes, when, Indi?

"Sunday night," I say slowly, my brain still scrambling.

She tilts her head expectantly. "What did he do?"

"He, uh…" I glance away and will myself to form a lie out of nothing. "It was my fault. I, I trespassed. I went onto his property."

"And?"

"He…chased me off."

Addy's eyebrow quirks up. "That's it?"

"What?" I snap. "It was fucking dark. I was terrified."

She lets out a little snort, and then shakes her head. "This is what I mean. He's fucking dangerous. Stay away from him, got it?"

I shrug. "Why wouldn't I?"

The corner of Addy's mouth crooks up. "Briar has a way of… getting under your skin. Trust me, it's best if you just pretend like he doesn't exist."

She leaves the restroom with a final glance back in my direction.

Easy for you to say, Addy. But, if anything, I've gotten under his skin. And all he seems to want is to destroy me. Kinda difficult to ignore the damn school bully.

CHAPTER FOURTEEN

INDI

Briar doesn't show up to our Psych class, and he's not in the cafeteria at lunch either. Addison and I sit in our usual seat by the window, and take turns keeping an eye on Briar's table. Addy toys with a French fry, dipping it repeatedly in her little plastic tub of ketchup as she idly glances over to Briar's table.

For someone who told me to avoid him like the plague, she can't seem to stop thinking about him.

"This is ridiculous," I mutter, shoving away my plate. "I can't just stick my head in the sand and wish this all goes away."

"What are you talking about?"

"Briar." I point in the direction of his table with my chin. "If he's guilty, then there must be something we can do to prove it."

Addy drops her eyes. "Like what? The police closed the case, Indi." She shrugs and drops her fry back onto her plate as if her appetite disappeared.

"We gotta dig up some dirt on him. Maybe someone saw something. Maybe one of his friends—"

"That's the point. They're his friends. They won't rat him out."

"Unless they don't realize they're doing it."

She frowns at me. "What?"

"All we need to do is catch one of them out in a lie."

Addy lets out an expressive sigh. "You have a plan?"

I drag my plate back and shrug as I pop a fry into my mouth and wash it down with some soda. "Who was there that night when you left?"

Addy starts counting on her fingers, the glitter on her nails catching the fluorescents.

"Briar, Marcus, Dylan, Zak, Jess. I think one of the cheerleaders too…" Addy squints, and scans the cafeteria. "Don't look now, but there's a girl with a blond bob a few benches away. Tiffany. She was there."

I chew on another fry before glancing around. I spot Tiffany a few seconds later. "You friends with her?"

Addison snorts. "I'm not friends with anyone after what happened."

"What do you mean?"

Addison's eyes darken a little. "They all think I'm full of shit. I tried to speak to everyone about that party, if they'd seen anything." She grins and tips her head. "Why do you think I hang out with you now?"

I laugh. "Because I'm the only one who's willing to spend time with a lunatic like you?"

She points at me with a ketchup-dipped fry. "Eg-fucking-xactly." The fry disappears into her mouth. "But see, you're new. You haven't besmirched your name for the sake of justice. You can speak to Tiffany."

I nod, discretely studying Tiffany's table. "They all cheerleaders?"

"Yup," Addison says glumly.

"Were you one?"

She lets out a most unladylike snort. "Please. I have better things to do with my time."

"Well," I say, grabbing my tray. "It's been nice knowing you, Addy."

She gives me a lopsided smile. "Good luck."

"Yeah…" I glance over to the bedazzled, glittering, fake-eyelashed crowd on that bench and my stomach tries to turn inside out. "I don't need luck. I think I need a fucking exorcist."

Addy chuckles as I leave our table. I could have made a scene, made it look like we were fighting, but honestly I couldn't give a shit.

My strength doesn't lie in fudging the truth—I get by on stubbornness alone.

Heavily mascaraed eyes turn to me when I slide my tray onto the side of the cheerleader's bench.

"Sorry to disturb you, ladies, but I heard a rumor one of you slept with Prince Briar."

The table immediately falls silent, until a girl I can only assume is the head cheerleader rushes to her feet. "Fuck off, virgin."

"So it was you then?" I ask, lifting my eyebrows as if this is all the confirmation I need. I lower my ass, and the girl closest to me scoots over to make room for me. I stick a fry in my mouth and chew, staring at the standing cheerleader with utter fixation.

"He got a big dick?"

The girl's cheeks turn pink. "I didn't fuck Briar," she says, and then glances at her friends. "I swear, I didn't!"

"Didn't…or didn't *want* to?" I inquire with a deep frown.

A chorus of gasps break out. Suddenly everyone except

Tiffany's looking at their plates. I glance across at her for the first time, and make sure she sees me looking at her.

Yeah, she saw me, if her glare's anything to go by.

"I gotta go," she mutters, standing.

"Yeah?" I get up too. "Mind if I walk with you? This new school is so confusing…"

Tiffany stares at me for a second, and then shrugs. "Whatev." She strides away, and I have to hustle to keep up with her.

I stop her outside in the hall.

"What?" she snaps, her bob swaying as she turns to face me.

"I just want to talk," I say, lifting my hands, palms up.

She narrows her eyes at me. "I didn't screw Briar."

I slip a hand in my pocket and draw out one of Addy's golden joints, but only far enough for Tiffany to see it glitter. "I just want to hang out," I say, putting as friendly a smile on my face as I can manage. "You in?"

Her eyes dart to the joint. Is she one of those teetotallers that doesn't smoke, drink, or fuck during school? She sets her mouth to the side and gives me a nod.

"Sure."

She shows me a cool little sesh spot by the bleachers, mostly blocked by a supporting wall and the mesh of steel framing. We light up and pass the joint silently between us. It's half done before I speak.

"Anyone else in that group know you smoke?"

Tiffany shrugs. "Some. Not the bitches, obviously." Her words escape with wisps of smoke. "Did Addison send you to talk to me?" Tiffany asks as she hands back the joint.

"What makes you—?"

"Cut the shit." She squints at me. "India, right?"

"Indi," I say.

She shrugs as if she'd gotten close enough for it not to matter.

"That chick's got a fucking bug up her ass about that whole thing with Jessica."

"So you don't think anything freaky happened at Briar's birthday party that night?"

I'm leaning with one foot up behind me on the wall, she's perched on one of the bleacher's struts. After another shrug, she squints into the distance, twisting her fingers around each other. "Freaky things always happen at parties. It's kinda the point."

"So tell me."

Tiffany sighs and drops her head between her arms. "I told her everything already." She looks up, frustration outlined by the unhappy curve of her mouth. "We were all fucking wasted. Then the guys started doing coke. That's when I left."

"And Jess was still fine when you left?"

Tiffany lets out a tiny snort. "Course she wasn't fine. She was drunk as fuck. Briar was higher than a kite. Marcus…" She shakes her head, her blond hair swaying. "I'm sure ten minutes after I left, every one of them passed out."

"Were you friends with Jessica?"

Tiffany shrugs. "She was on the squad, so yeah, kinda." Tiffany reaches for the joint, which I'd forgotten I was holding, and then clicks her fingers at me for the lighter. She cups her hands around the joint and lights it, hitting it hard before handing everything back to me. "But we never braided each other's hair or shit like that. Jess kept to herself a lot."

An antisocial cheerleader? Addy didn't mention that.

"Who was her closest friend besides Addison?"

Tiffany lifts her eyebrows in thought. She purses her lips and says, "Briar, I guess. It was always just the three of them."

"*Addy* was friends with *Briar?*"

"Yeah," Tiffany says through a short laugh. She sits back and gives me a faint smile. "Everyone said they were…" She squeezes shut her eyes, clicking her fingers, "—fuck, what's the word?"

"Polyamorous?"

"Yeah." Tiffany nods enthusiastically. "That's it. What you said. Everyone said they were like menaging and shit."

Another thing Addison didn't bother to mention, unless it was just a rumor.

"Did you see when Addison left?"

Tiffany nods. "Oh yeah," she says through a laugh. "*Everyone* saw when she left."

"What do you—?"

"She was cussing out Jess so fucking bad." Tiffany's eyes are wide as she swipes her hand back and forth. "I don't know what they were fighting about, but that shit was crazy. They looked like they wanted to claw each other's faces off."

My skin prickles and I bring the joint to my lips, pulling at it without even realizing what I'm doing. I shouldn't—I'm stoned enough—but I need something to help with all these unexpected revelations.

"You know what the fight was about?"

Tiffany shakes her head. "I was way too pissed. But it was probably about Briar. You now, 'cos they were both doing him?"

No, I *didn't* know, but thanks to Tiffany, my understanding of the situation is a whole lot clearer.

And with clarity, comes anger.

Who the fuck does Addison think she is, using me as a pawn in some twisted game? Maybe *she* killed Jessica, and she can't live with the guilt anymore.

Or...

Stay away from him.

Was she really *protecting* me...or was she just trying to protect herself?

"Thanks, Tiffany."

"Thanks for the weed," she says, grinning brightly at me. "This day was sucking donkey balls."

"Better now?" I ask with a laugh.

She gives me a double thumbs-up as she gets to her feet. Then she's off, headed back to the school building. I grind out the rest of the joint under my heel and take Tiffany's seat.

I can see a small section of the fence from my vantage point.

The fuck do I know about any of this? I'm a fucking outsider. Then again, as an outsider, I have no vested interest in any of the parties involved. I'm like some out-of-town detective called in to deal with a small-town murder where everyone's a fucking suspect.

Didn't know I'd be acting all Nancy Drew and shit, but I guess it's better than hanging around waiting for Briar to bully me.

The rest of the afternoon passes in a blur until Addy finds me outside my locker. I haven't been actively avoiding her —I just minimized trips to my locker and used my height—or lack thereof—to my advantage.

"You don't answer your phone anymore?" she asks, cocking an eyebrow as she leans her hip against the locker next to mine.

I close my locker door and give her a shrug. "In case you've forgotten, I have a week of school to catch up."

"Oh." Addison drops her eyes, and gives me a sympathetic smile. Yesterday morning in the car I told her that I'd lost my mother. Not *how*—no one needs that shit in their head—but again, instead of gushing, she changed the subject. Back then, I thought she was a real swell gal for being supportive without being nosy.

Now I'm wondering if she's just stacking up good karma points to use when I confront her with all the juicy tidbits I discovered today.

"Well, then maybe we can go to the mall and grab an early dinner tonight?"

I know all she wants is to find out what Tiffany said, but I'm still processing everything. After all, in my role as Detective Virgo, I need to ensure every interaction with the possible suspects can be used to the best of my advantage. If I'm going to feed Addison info, I have to make sure she's giving me something in return.

Yeah, I'm still baked as a fucking potato. I can't deal with this shit right now. All I want is to get home and wash this day off me.

I haven't gone girly since Mom died, but I really need some me-time tonight. I'm thinking rose-scented bubbles and possibly —*possibly*—some wine. A glass…maybe two.

"Tomorrow."

Addison pouts, but then smiles away the sulkiness. "Okay. Tomorrow." She holds up her phone. "But at least just reply to my texts? I worry."

I nod, patting the pocket of my blazer. The hard case of my mobile makes a comforting tapping sound against my fingers.

"Meet you tomorrow for our morning blunt?" she asks, lifting up the side of her lip with a shrug.

"Only way you're luring me back to this hellhole," I say through a laugh. Addy nods, looking satisfied, and waves as she disappears into the crowd.

Hopefully, by then, I've figured out what I'm going to tell her. And the questions I'm going to ask.

CHAPTER FIFTEEN

BRIAR

I get in my car and peel out of my parking spot. The growl of my Mustang's V8 engine rumbles through me as I tear down the road.

You killed her.

I rub a hand over my chest, and fist my fingers when I realize what I'm doing.

I need a fucking cigarette. Marcus and I both quit smoking last year so Coach would stop shitting on us for getting out of breath on long passes, but right now I couldn't give a shit if I never score another touchdown.

After picking up a packet of cigarettes at one of the filling stations, the cab of my Mustang fills with smoke. I turn up the radio till I can't hear anything anymore, even my own thoughts.

Because fuck it, I'm done having Indi in my head. Thinking about how soft her lips were against mine, how sweet her mouth tasted. The tiny sound she made when I—

I push my foot down on the gas, overtaking a slow-ass hybrid. It honks its horn at me, and I shove my hand out the window and flip it the finger.

Minutes later, when I realize where I'm headed, I slam my foot on the brakes. I'm on one of the roads leading out of town, and luckily I'm the only one in sight, because my Mustang fishtails. I grit my teeth, barely managing to keep her from spinning out of control.

I end up in a cloud of dust on the side of the road, my engine rumbling angrily before I turn off the ignition with a trembling hand.

What the fuck is wrong with me?

I run my fingers through my hair.

I need space.

I kick open the door and rush outside, hauling a deep, dust-tainted breath and coughing. When I turn to hack up and spit into the bushes alongside the road, a nearby road sign catches my eye.

Angel Falls

1 Mile

I glare at it, my jaw aching until I force myself to stop clenching my teeth. Killers are always drawn back to the scene of the crime, aren't they?

"Fuck!" I swing around and drive my fist into the hood of my Mustang. My yell echoes back to me, but the thump of flesh meeting metal doesn't.

When I lift my hand, there's a dent in the hood.

Because I destroy everything I touch, don't I, Addison fucking Green? I'm the Robert Oppenheimer of Lavish.

I force a grim smile onto my mouth as I get back in my car.

Guess what, Indi?

You're next on my hit list.

I 'm driving aimlessly, taking back roads I know don't have speeding cameras on so I can open up the Mustang. I almost forget how shitty my fucking life is for like five seconds.

Then Marcus texts me.

I pull onto the side of the road and stare at my phone. I'd forgotten he was bunking with me. That I'd given him a lift to school.

Stellar friend, aren't I?

I throw the Mustang into a turn and head back to Lavish Prep while I tug at another cigarette.

He's waiting for me on the school steps like I'm some kind of absentee father who was placing one last bet at the racecourse before coming to get his son.

"Where'd you disappear to?" Marcus asks as he tosses his bag into the back seat and collapses in his bucket seat.

"Had to clear my head."

"It work?"

I don't answer. Ahead, I spot Indi walking out of school, head down and totally oblivious to the world around her. I throw the car into reverse and squeal out of the parking, leaving tire tracks as I head for the exit.

"Wanna talk about it?" Marcus asks.

"No," I snap. I immediately regret the tone of my voice, but I refuse to apologize.

Marcus lifts his hands, steals one of my smokes, and lights it up without a word.

"I lost my shit today," I say, glaring through the windshield.

Around me, pines begin dotting the landscape as the road inclines. Lavish always looks so fucking perfect. Sometimes, its beauty is like nails on the chalkboard of my fucking soul. Especially on days when I recognize just how far from perfect I am.

"Yeah, I kinda noticed." Marcus hands me his smoke, and I let him hold it out for a second before I take it.

I exhale a plume of smoke, drumming my fingers on the steering wheel. "Let's just…let's drop everything."

"What, Indi?" Marcus chuckles. "A'right."

I glance at him, but he seems genuinely unconcerned.

I open my window to ash, and leave it rolled down despite how the air tears into the car.

"Why'd you kiss her?" I ask.

"What?" Marcus leans closer, eyebrows lifting.

It's loud in here, but it's not *that* fucking loud. He's a fucking dick sometimes, Marcus, but he's still my closest friend.

In fact, he's my only true friend.

He did what no one else would even have contemplated, and I didn't even have to ask.

"Why'd you fucking kiss her?" I bark, slamming my palm into the steering wheel.

Marcus snatches the smoke from between my knuckles. "'Cos she's got a sexy little mouth?"

I want to ask him why he felt he had to put his hand on her throat first. Pull her against him like that. But my chest's too tight.

"It wasn't part of the plan."

"Thought the plan was to make her look like an idiot. I think we succeeded."

I grit my teeth, but don't respond. I never openly told him Indi was off-limits. I'd never thought she was. But when he touched her, when he dared put his mouth on hers…I could have spontaneously combusted how pissed off I was.

Can't tell him any of that without revealing just how much Indi's clawed her way into my mind. And then he'd be just how he was when I was catching feels with Jessica; telling me to fuck her and get her out of my system already.

I don't know why, but Marcus seems to think love and all that shit is something reserved for old folks and bros that accidentally knock their chicks up. Anything else is just a one-night-stand. A fling if it happens with the same pair of tits more than once.

I thought I was in love with Jessica. Honest to God I did. But what I did to her wasn't love. It was pure lust.

"You're right. She's not worth the effort," Marcus says, sounding as if the thought's coming from fuck-far away.

I say nothing, glancing at him from the corner of my eye.

He shrugs, and turns to me, holding out the smoke. "We got finals and shit coming up, bro."

I let out a snort. Marcus has never cared about finals, so why the fuck is he using them as an excuse? I drag hard at the cigarette. The filter's grown hot and damp how we've fucking raped it between the two of us, and I grimace as I flick what's left out the window.

"Finals? Why don't you tell me what's really going on? You got the hots for her? You too chicken shit to admit it or something?"

"Course not." Marcus crosses his arms over his chest, staring out the passenger window. "You're the one who's fucking obsessed with her. And you know what happens when you get obsessed."

Despite how quiet his voice is, it feels like he shouts the accusation at me. We're about ten minutes from my house—more like five if I keep going at this speed—but I can't deal with his snide remarks anymore.

I slam on the brakes. Marcus grabs the dash, glaring at me as the car skids to the right before coming to a halt. "The fuck, man!"

"I'll see you at home," I mumble, staring at the distant line of trees while my jaw bunches to the point of aching.

"Briar, come on, I was just—"

"Get out."

He releases a heavy sigh, grabs his bag from the backseat, and climbs out. When he slams closed the door, my Mustang rocks on its shocks for a few seconds before settling.

Marcus doesn't look back, but I watch him until he turns off the road and into a side path that leads straight to Briar mansion.

Then I sit in my car and wonder why the fuck I just threw out my best friend.

I've been walking through Briar woods for what feels like most of the day but what couldn't be more than two or three hours. After throwing Marcus out of the car, I did a u-turn and grabbed a bottle of whiskey from the closest liquor store. The cashier's been selling me booze for the past three years—he knows I tip really well. The bottle's half done; closer to half-empty than half full. I could have grabbed a bottle from home, but Marcus might still be there. I guess, despite what an asshole I was to him, he'd still prefer to stay with me than head back home and see his dad.

Fall's almost done with Lavish; the nights creep in sooner every day. It's already twilight by the time I surface from my ocean of dark, dismal thoughts.

But I don't escape with clarity, or logic.

After hours of silent fuming, my brain's fizzing with anger, frustration, terror. The cocktail turns me into a speechless, knuckle-dragging Neanderthal with only one thing on my mind.

Indi fucking Virgo.

Twilight teases shadows out from under the trees. Under that darkness, the bramble's thorns grow longer and sharper than before.

Wicked.

That's what this place is.

That's what *I* am.

Wicked as a bramble thorn, and just as merciless.

I can't blame Marcus for taking advantage of the situation earlier today. I'd told the crew what I wanted, and they made it fucking happen.

That's how this shit worked.

But I couldn't stand seeing those sloppy lips all over *my* girl.

Yes, mine.

From the moment I saw her in the woods, she became my property. My toy.

My prize.

I stumble through the last of the tangled woods and hastily step back into the shadows, clutching the whiskey bottle to my chest like a sleepy kid with a teddy bear.

Ahead, the tacky Davis house sits on their small strip of land like the house in Wizard of Oz after it landed on the witch.

This must be where Indi's staying. It's the only way I could have encountered her in the woods.

There's only a single light on in the house, on the second story.

Too far away. A yellow blur.

I glance around, but there's nothing to see except more shadows and the deep purple of approaching night. Setting down the bottle, I push away from the cover of the trees and rush over the lawn. My back presses into the house's wooden slats, and I count a few hundred breaths before daring to peek out at an angle. I'm almost right under the light. The window is small, so it must be a bathroom or something.

Fuck knows why, but I want to be inside. I want to see her again, even if she doesn't want to see me. And the fact that I can't fight that feeling scares the living bejesus out of me.

You're losing control again.

You should be leaving, not breaking in.

But my hand's already on the doorknob of what I assume is this place's back door. My breath already stifled in an attempt to make as little noise as possible. I'm drunk, sure, but I've been sneaking around houses since I was a little boy. This stuff comes naturally to me. I take off my sneakers and leave them outside before inching my way into the quiet house.

Despite my precautions, I can't prevent the floorboards creaking under my weight. If it weren't for the roaring in my ears, I might have thought twice about proceeding. But I'm already in the middle of a dark kitchen, and my thumping heart practically propels me forward.

As does an intense urge to know what the fuck makes this girl so special, how the fuck she's capable of messing with my mind. I haven't fucked anyone since Jess because I didn't want to lose control again.

Honestly, I haven't even felt the urge, until I met Indi.

I'm facing stairs. It's nothing like the sweeping stairways and magnificent landing at Briar Manor with its massive fuck-off chandelier.

I'm halfway up before I realize I never had any intention of turning back. I knew I was going to be inside this house right after I kissed Indigo in the park. Which raises a fuck load of questions I am too drunk to answer.

A stair creaks loudly under my foot. I pause, my heart jumping into my fucking throat. But there's no 'aha!' No one demanding that I leave.

And when nothing happens, I push on.

Light shines under a closed door midway down the hall. The air here is scented with something girly—flowers, or candy, or something.

I stop outside the door, and stare for a second at the inch-wide gap.

It's not even closed all the way.

Which, to my beer-goggled mind is better than a golden, hand-lettered invitation.

CHAPTER SIXTEEN

INDI

"*Mmm, mm, mmmm, mm, mm.*" I tap my foot against the end of the bath, splashing water everywhere. My earbuds are on full blast, sending wave after wave of cathartic heavy metal deep into my ear canals.

Yeah, kill them all, you fucking motherfucker.

"*Mmm, mmmmmmm, mm.*"

I need more wine. I grab a metal goblet from the rim of the bath, and shiver a little as a light breeze caresses my arm. I glance over at the bathroom door, and frown hard.

The fuck? Did I leave it open?

Admittedly, I'd already had three glasses of wine—some really decent red—before remembering I wanted to submerge myself in a mountain range of bubbles.

I gulp at the wine and set it back on the rim. Breaking off another block of chocolate from the slab, I slip it into my mouth.

"*Mmmm, mmm, mmmmm.*"

Kill other motherfuckers, kill them fucking dead.

My foot resumes its splash-tapping.

When I take another sip of wine, another breeze slides over my damp arm.

I glance at the door and freeze.

The wind's pushed it open almost a foot.

"Fuck…" I groan. There's no way in hell I'm getting out of this deliciousness to close the door. Marigold texted me earlier to let me know she had a prior engagement tonight; I have the house to myself.

I squirm in the tub, and take out my earbuds. Heavy metal is awesome if you want to get rid of residual frustration, but porn is even better.

Marigold would probably never be caught dead with something as radical as wi-fi in her home, but I got a good data deal with my mobile back when Mom—

I gulp at my wine, and rest the goblet on my tummy as I flick through the thumbnails on the first porn site that came up when I googled 'nasty rough sex'.

Yup, I'm a freak like that. Then again, who isn't?

"There we go," I murmur.

At a creak behind me, I twist in the tub fast enough to send a wave of rose-scented suds over the side.

I'm tempted to say, "Hello?"

I burst out laughing at the thought and sink back into the bubbles.

The wind, Indi. It's the fucking wind, you paranoid freak.

I drain the rest of my wine glass and set it down on the rim. The last block of chocolate goes into my mouth, and my free hand slips under the bubbles.

My back arches as my fingers make contact with my clit. I circle that sensitive nub of flesh, goosebumps breaking over my skin.

"*Mmm.*" The chocolate's melting in my mouth, and that's elevating everything to the *nth* fucking degree.

I slide a finger inside myself, closing my eyes and resting my head back on the rim as warm water tickles its way deep inside me.

I juggle the phone, almost drop it in the water, and let it fall on the bathroom mat instead. Fuck it, I don't need porn to get off. I'm full of red wine, and chocolate, and all I need is…

Briar's blue eyes fill my mind.

The feel of his strong, soft lips against mine.

His big hands on my throat—no, wait, that was Marcus, wasn't it?— fuck it, his hands on my throat…

"*Mmmmmm.*" My back arches, and water splashes around me as I spread my legs as wide as they can go in the confines of the tub.

It's not wide enough.

I drag myself out of the water, shivering when cold air hits my wet skin, and perch on the rim of the tub.

Much better. I hold onto the rim with one hand, using the other to massage my clit. The door creaks, but I'm too far gone to be bothered with the chill factor right now. Although my nipples have pebbled into rock hard buds and I'm covered in goosebumps, this feels way too good to stop.

I climax a few seconds later, my entire body stiffening so much I almost end up on the bathroom mat.

I let out a long sigh, and giggle to myself as I realize what a fucking mess I've made. Well, luckily, I have this big bath of bubbles right—

I hear the sound of a car coming up the drive.

Fuck, Marigold's home already? What time is it?

I twist, and in that precise moment, Marigold must hit a bump in the road. Headlamps shine right through the bathroom window as I stand and turn to grab a towel.

There's someone standing in the doorway, watching me.

I scream, and immediately clap my hands over my mouth in surprise.

The headlamps move, and the hallway outside the bathroom door is once again in shadow.

I hear a key in the door, and my body freezes. I expect to hear Marigold demanding to know who's in her house, because no way was there enough time for the guy who'd been standing in the doorway watching me—*watching me*—to have gotten downstairs fast enough.

Unless he's still in the house.

"Granny!" I shriek, grabbing the towel and wrapping it around me as I rush for the hallway.

Yeah, I'll be the first to die in any horror movie ever made. But I saw that shape move—whoever it was, they didn't want to be seen. I doubt they'd be waiting right outside the door.

"Indigo?" comes Marigold's voice from downstairs. "Why on earth are you yelling at me?"

I run to the far end of the hall and begin throwing open doors. He could have gone in any direction, but it makes more sense that he'd head away from the stairs and try and get out through one of the windows.

But every room is empty, and feels slightly stale; no one's been in them for a while.

When I open my bedroom door, I immediately know he was in here. My space feels different. My sanctum defiled by a stranger's presence.

My window's open, and I know I should run to it and look outside to catch a glimpse of the invader, but I'm rooted to the spot, watching the lace curtain shifting in a breeze.

"Indigo?" Marigold calls from the stairs.

I only saw him for a second, and the light cast strange shadows on his face and leeched all the color from his skin. But I could have sworn it was Briar standing there in the hallway, lips parted, eyes wide.

He'd been pushing open the bathroom door, not the wind. Watching me.

Watching me.

BRIAR

I sprint for the tree line, not bothering to look over my shoulder. If she were to look out her window, she'll see me way before I reach the safety of wood's shadowy ground, and I don't need to give her a good look at my face too.

Why the fuck didn't I leave?

The fuck did I decide to stay and watch her bathing for?

As soon as darkness swallows me, I falter and stop running. My breath is coming fast, but I'm nowhere near winded. That's not the problem. The problem is I have a hard-on that's causing me immense fucking grief.

I slam my back into a tree and shove my hands into my hair.

Keep running, you fucking idiot. Don't let her get to you.

But for fuck's sake, how's that possible? I can't get the sight of her wet, naked body out of my damn mind.

I don't know what I'd expected to see under her clothes.

She's fucking perfect.

Nothing like the bulimic skeletons attending Lavish Prep.

She has curves and a pair of perky tits I was aching to grab.

Fuck, I *have* grabbed them before, but through all those clothes, I had no idea how magnificent they truly were.

And she shaves…everywhere.

My cock throbs, and I grimace as I try to fight off each new wave of lust crashing through me.

It was like I was in a trance, back there. I'd had one hand on my cock, throttling it through my jeans as if that would somehow control the dark, savage urges flooding my body.

It hadn't helped.

Fuck.

Fuck!

If someone hadn't arrived…

I was seconds away from stepping into that bathroom and claiming Indi for my own. No more of this fucking around. I wanted to pin her to the bathroom floor and fuck her until she begged me to stop—and then screamed my name when she came. I wanted to leave marks on her pale body, on those glorious curves of her.

My eyes flash open, and I stare reluctantly at my cock where I have it in a fist.

What the fuck is this girl doing to me?

I stroke myself once, with every intention of shoving my dick back into my pants.

But once is never enough, is it?

My arm trembles as I try to hold back, but then I remember how Indi threw back her head and moaned as she came, absolutely gorgeous as she fell apart.

I groan, and let the torrent of lust that's been building since I first saw her slender foot tapping on the side of the bath wash over me.

I stroke my cock slow and hard, urging precum from the crown so I can use it for lube.

How fucking long has it been?

I don't allow myself this pleasure, not after what happened with Jess. The more I feed this wretched beast, the hungrier it gets. The *stronger* it gets. And the less likely it becomes that I'll be able to keep it chained up.

The forest swallows my next groan as I speed up my rhythm.

Indi's mouth.

My fuck, what I wouldn't do to have it over my cock right now. Sucking. Her tongue sliding along my shaft. Those fierce green eyes glaring up at me.

She'd try to bite me.

But what if…

I'm getting close now, my back arching away from the tree.

What if she didn't have a choice?

She'd have to swallow every drop of my cum, and tell me that she loves how it tastes. That she wants more.

Fuck.

I come with a deep-throated growl.

In my mind, Indi's mouth opens wide, and I empty myself on her tongue while her eyes glitter with hateful tears.

I sprint home, dodging trees and brambles best I can. If the ground hadn't been this cold, it wouldn't have numbed my soles to the point where I could run.

I left my shoes behind. But I can't go back. Not now. They'd be on high alert. Hopefully, no one will look behind the shrub where I left them. If they do, then I'm pretty fucked.

I keep pushing, pushing, pushing.

The euphoria's long gone. And although I try to outrun the rest, it follows me as doggedly as my fucking shadow.

First comes the shame. It burns through me in an incandescent wave.

Next; guilt. Heavy, leaden, it drags down my feet and makes

my body ten times heavier than it should be. My sprint becomes
a slow jog.

Lastly, always…anger.

It eviscerates my reservations, logic.

Every fucking thing.

All I want—need—is to break her…even if I can't put her
back together again. Then that beautiful, broken girl will be all
mine.

I like broken things, but I love breaking them even more.

CHAPTER SEVENTEEN

INDI

I eventually do find remnants of an earlier, happier time in Marigold's house. For reasons I can't quite explain to myself yet, I don't tell her about the intruder. Instead, I claim I saw a spider terrifying enough to make me run wet and partially naked from the bathroom.

She went to bed still wearing a grimace. That had been for the almost empty bottle of wine she spotted in the kitchen though, not my tale of arachnophobic horror.

Briar's blue eyes kept me awake for an hour before I abandoned the concept of sleep altogether.

Intent on getting some warm milk, I head down to the kitchen. I walk past a hallway that heads to the back of the house, one Marigold never bothered to include in her initial tour. I always thought the room went to a study or a smaller sitting room, perhaps, so I never even bothered investigating.

The door's locked. But there's a hallway closet nearby I hadn't seen before. I open the closet and rummage through the shelves.

I find a few photo albums and some dilapidated sporting

equipment—a baseball bat and mitts, faded roller skates, a scratched bicycle helmet.

Weighing the bat in my hand, I purse my lips at its solidity. Then I grasp it tight and take a swing at an invisible enemy.

Not a bad self-defense weapon. Good to keep close at hand, should a certain Prince decide to sneak into my fucking house again. Fuck knows if I'd even use it. I should at least pretend that the fact that he's not just a rapist and a murderer, but a creeping tom to boot, scares the living shit out of me.

Because it really should.

Somehow though, it doesn't.

I guess after all the shit life's dealt me recently, a run-in with a young Ted Bundy seems tame in comparison.

BRIAR

Marcus's SUV is still out front when I finally get home. Inside, the mansion is quiet as the grave.

I find him in the pool house, immersing himself in weed and video games. He doesn't even hear me come in—with such a dank haze in the room it doesn't surprise me at all.

There's beer inside the fridge—I take out two cans and bring them over to the sofa.

Marcus twitches when I move into his peripheral view, and then pauses his game and settles back on the sofa as if getting ready for battle.

I hold out the can until he takes it, and then I lower myself onto the seat with a sigh.

Marcus scans me with black, unreadable eyes, pops open his can, and says, "The fuck happened to your shoes?"

I laugh and wave away the question. Taking a sip of beer, I sit forward and grab a joint roach from the ashtray. I'm still hunting for a lighter when Marcus holds out a hand and flicks on his Zippo.

"Look, man, about earlier…" I trail off, expecting him to stop me, but he just watches with dead eyes and a line for a mouth.

"Yeah?" he prompts after a few seconds.

"I'm sorry."

He shrugs. "Told you, that girl's got you fucking obsessed." He narrows his eyes. "Where've you been?"

"Sorry, love, I meant to call," I say dryly. "Time just got away from me."

He snorts and returns to his game. "You met up with her, didn't you?"

I turn to him, wide-mouthed with disbelief. "The fuck, Mar—?"

"Did you at least fuck her this time, get it out of your system?"

I don't know if it's because I still have way too much alcohol in my system, but déjà vu slams into me like a glass door.

Just fuck Jess and get her out of your system already.

Marcus had said that right after I told him that I had feelings for her.

When I don't reply, he glances at me and then does a double take. Throwing down the game controller without bothering to pause this time, he says, "Tell me I'm wrong," while cocking his head at me.

"I've known her for less than a week." It's a shitty defense, especially since he knows I liked Jessica from the moment I saw her, but it's all I got.

"Well she's obviously set off some kind of fucked-up chemical response in your brain." Marcus grabs his dime bag of weed and starts rolling another joint, his eyes flickering up to me every other second as if to make sure I don't launch myself at him while his attention is diverted. "That's the only rational explanation, isn't it?"

"That's not—"

"You want the same thing to happen to Indi?"

Now he's staring solid at me and I don't know what the fuck he means. Is he talking about the rape or the murder?

Cold fury bubbles inside me.

"I never asked you to do anything."

"Yeah?" Marcus runs his tongue along the joint and then slips it through his lips in one movement. "Guess I should just have let her go to the police. Testify against you in court. You'd have done hard time, you know that, right?"

I swallow, but it's as if all that guilt is stuck right there in my throat. "You didn't have to—"

"But I did, bro, because that's what friends do!" Marcus stands in a rush, toking hard at the joint before stabbing it in my direction. "We look out for each other. And I'm telling you, this chick's gonna get you in a world of fucking trouble. Think the fact she's buddies with Addison is a coincidence? Addy's been looking for a way back into your life for months now. She's got that chick wrapped around her finger."

"Addy doesn't have any proof."

"'Course she doesn't," Marcus says. I look up at him, and ignore the joint he's holding out to me. "'Cos I made it all disappear, remember?"

His head tilts to the side, eyes so dead they could have been chips of coal.

Is he seriously expecting me to thank him? I'd been in such a state after Jess left Marcus's house that afternoon, when he came and told me that she'd jumped off the bridge at Angel Falls, I'd broken down like a fucking baby.

For three months, I'd been hanging out with Marcus, going to school with him, letting him stay over at my house when his dad was in town.

Three months before I found out the truth about Jessica's death.

Just goes to show how deviant I am. When he did tell me, instead of beating him up and dragging him to the police station, I said nothing.

I've never said anything to anyone.

Because that's what friends do.

I won't thank him. What he did was wrong. Just like what I did was fucking inexcusable. But we keep each other's secrets like best friends should.

It doesn't explain why I keep thinking he wants to screw me over.

"You're right," I say, nodding slowly. Marcus takes a slow drag of the joint, watching me with unveiled suspicion.

I hold up my hand, palm facing him. "No, seriously, you are. This chick's gotten into my head."

The simple truth.

"If she stays in there much longer then no, I don't think I'll be able to control myself."

Marcus nods, hitting the joint again.

"So we stick to our plan," I say.

"We get rid of her."

I don't like the sound of that, so I add, "We'll turn Lavish Prep into her own personal hell. She'll be begging her parents to send her back."

Marcus smiles around the joint and sticks out his hand.

I grab it, squeeze it, shake it.

Then I take the joint from him and lift my eyebrows as my eyes slide to the game controller. "Duo?"

"Yeah, sure." He grabs the spare controller off the game console and brings it to me.

I watch him as he sits, and can't help but shake my head in reluctant admiration.

You'd never think, looking at him, that he murdered a girl in cold blood. I guess pushing someone off a bridge isn't as chilling as stabbing or gunning them down, but still.

"What?" Marcus asks, and I realize I'd been staring. I look away, grab my beer, and chug at it.

"Thinking how I'm gonna kick your ass."

"We're on the same team, Briar," Marcus says slowly. "Always will be."

Of course we are. I don't know why the fuck I ever doubted him.

CHAPTER EIGHTEEN

INDI

I slept much better last night with the baseball bat leaning up against my nightstand. Although, taking into account the nightmare I had, I wish I hadn't slept at all.

I shoot out of bed just before six, my heart pounding and holding Mom's necklace in a fist. I've taken to sleeping with it. That way, I can almost pretend she's beside me, her smell encompassing me as I drift off to sleep.

A hard rap to my bedroom door makes me yell out, and I barely manage to drag my sheets over my body before my gran is inside my room. "I heard noises," she says, her nose twitching.

I shift, and realize my thighs are coated with my own arousal. God, can she smell me? My cheeks glow but I shrug, and try to sound diffident. "Maybe it came from outside."

"No. It came from here." Her eyes narrow. "You don't have a radio in here, do you?"

I shake my head. I'm too fucking tired for snark, and that would just get me into hot water again. Instead, I stare down Marigold until she sniffs and leaves my room. I hold up Mom's necklace, watching light glimmer from it in rays of blue and white. I'm tempted to wear it under my school clothes, but then I'm sure the smell would wear off too soon. I take it off and put it back in its box, and then hide it in the back of my closet. Then I grab my uniform and dash to the bathroom for a quick shower.

Not wanting to run into my grandmother again, I sneak out the front door while she's busy in the kitchen, climb carefully into my car, and freewheel the first few yards before turning the ignition.

I glance in the rearview mirror, expecting to see her standing on the porch, arms crossed and lips pursed, and breathe a sigh of relief when she's not there.

Most of the trip to Lavish Prep I spend thinking about Addy. In all the fun and excitement lately, I'd forgotten I have a bone to pick with her.

I park and head over to her sports car. She gets a fright when I rap on the window, and I frown at her as she unlocks the door.

"Everything okay?"

Her hair isn't as smooth as it usually is. She's only wearing a touch of mascara, as if she was in a rush or couldn't have been bothered to do her usual morning makeover routine.

"Yeah, course." She smiles at me, and grabs a joint from the ashtray. Half of it's gone already.

So that accounts for the red eyes. I thought she'd been crying.

She unlocks the passenger door for me, and hands me what's left of the joint as I slide in. It's already lit, and I hit it hard as she starts to speak.

"So you ready to—?"

"Why didn't you tell me you argued with Jess that night?" I exhale a plume of smoke.

Addy looks away, grabs the steering wheel, and straightens her arms. "I didn't?"

"Tiffany said you two had a huge fight."

"Tiffany exaggerates about everything."

"So you didn't fight?"

Addy licks her lips. "I've never seen her that drunk before." She glances at me and then stares straight ahead again. "But she didn't want to leave."

"That's it?"

"Yeah."

"So your fight had nothing to do with the fact that you both had a thing for Briar?"

Addy's hands fall into her lap as she lets out a rough laugh. When she turns to me, her eyebrows are arched. "What did you say?"

"You. Briar." I use the joint to gesture from one side to the other, trailing smoke. "Nothing going on there?"

"*Pfft.* As if. He's a fucking prick."

Which isn't a no. Not even close.

But I'm also not getting any jelly vibes from her.

"Sure there's nothing else I need to know?" I lean to the side a little, trying to catch Addy's eye. "I mean, we are about to go after this guy for rape and murder. I need to know what I'm getting myself into."

Addy grabs the wheel again, and chews on her lip. Then she snatches the last bit of the joint from me and finishes it. When she grinds it out in her ashtray, her long manicured nails come back dusted with gray.

"I…after the cops dropped the case, I went…I kinda went a bit nuts."

"How nuts?"

Addy shrugs, and then clicks her fingers at the cubby hole. I open it and take out a packet of wet wipes. She plucks one out and cleans her fingers, eyes downcast. "Briar almost got a restraining order against me."

"Wh-what?" I say through a laugh. "You're shitting me!"

"I know he did it, Indi. I fucking know it." Addy's throat moves as she swallows. "Turns out I was the only one." When she looks at me, there's moisture welling on her bottom lids.

"Can you prove it?" I murmur.

Addy's silent for the longest time.

"Addy?"

"Proof," she says. "Everyone always wants fucking proof. We don't live in a perfect world. If we did, people wouldn't get away with shit like this."

She blinks fast, and then turns away to stare out the window.

"I hear you," I murmur.

My mom's murder case is still open, but before I left Lakeview, the police told me they had no suspects. Despite the mess the thief had made, he hadn't left much useful evidence behind besides a partial fingerprint, and it wasn't in the system.

Either it was his first crime, or it was the first time he was careless enough to leave a clue.

I don't know if Mom's murderer will ever be found, and even if he is, who knows if he'll get the justice he deserves? I hear about cases being thrown out on technicalities all the time.

Cases like Jessica's.

Because who's gonna investigate a suicide?

I reach over and squeeze Addy's shoulder. It makes me think back to when she did the same to me a few days ago.

"We'll get him, Addy. You hear me? He's gonna pay for what he did."

"How?" She throws up her hands. "I'm not even supposed to be talking to him. If the principal sees me anywhere near him, then—"

"Then it's a good thing we're friends, isn't it?"

Addy glances over at me. "Talking isn't going to help. I've tried that. No one saw anything."

"Briar did."

Her eyes narrow and she shakes her head. "I don't like where you're going with this."

"You know what they say about why boys pull your hair, right?"

Addy rolls her eyes. "He's done more than just pull your hair."

"We're not kids on a playground anymore."

"So what, you're gonna seduce him? Get him drunk? Hope he tells you everything while you record him?"

I purse my lips, sticking my fingers through a gap in my shirt and rubbing my collarbone. "Not a bad idea."

"It's a fucking *terrible* idea. Jess was his girlfriend, and you know how she ended up."

"I'll be careful."

"You'll be dead." Addy's brown eyes are round, her lips in a thin line. "Don't do this. We'll think of another—"

"You're right," I say, waving away the idea with a grimace. "I mean, he's probably forgotten all about his new bully victim."

Addy nods, and gives me a tremulous smile. "We'll figure something out."

I let out a long sigh and sink back into the seat. Is it weird that I kinda wish I could go ahead with everything Addy said? I've never tried seducing someone before—I've usually been the prey, not the predator. Could be fun, especially with an arrogant prick like Briar. Getting him to bend to me, instead—

"Shit, we have to go," Addy mutters. "School's starting."

I sigh again, reluctant to move. But she's right—we won't be solving any crimes sitting stoned in her car.

I have to get close to Briar. Maybe even through one of his friends. Addy said his whole crew was still there when she left. One of them must have seen something.

Especially that guy that sticks to him like a burr.

"Yeah, let's go," I say, levering my stoned ass out of the car. "Do you still speak to any of Briar's friends?"

Addy laughs. "As if."

Damn. Guess I'll have to work my way into their circle by myself. If I can figure out who the weakest link is… maybe, just maybe, I can get someone to talk.

CHAPTER NINETEEN

INDI

I'm lost in a fog of jumbled thoughts, moving on automatic as I head for my locker. I'm vaguely aware that Addy's chatting to me, but I honestly couldn't have remembered a word she said if she'd held a gun to my head.

There's a strange smell in the air when I reach my locker, but there are so many different smells inside a school that I don't think anything of it.

I should have.

My locker opens easily. Too easily.

I yell out in surprise. Red roses spill out and land on my shoes, thorns scratching my bare legs.

Music blares out of my locker, and everyone around me stops to stare as something blue tumbles out and lands on the floor.

Like a virgin, touched for the very first time.

Madonna screeches out to my massive audience.

Like a vi-ir-ir-ir-gin—

The entire school erupts into laughter. Addison pulls up short and throws me a wide-eyed stare before slowly coming closer. She reaches down to pick up the thing on the floor where it lays in a pile of long-stemmed red roses and petals.

"Don't," I say in a strangled voice.

But everything moves like a dream, and my warning comes too late. Addison picks it up, holds it out.

Lingerie.

Dark blue, ridiculously sexy, lingerie.

I snatch it from her. Then I fumble around inside my locker until I find the offending Bluetooth boombox, and pluck it out so hard that it goes silent it hits the floor.

But that doesn't stop the laughter. That does nothing to prevent red-hot shame flooding my face.

I see movement further down the hall.

Briar.

He's at his locker, the door partly open, but with zero interest for what's inside.

Instead, he's watching me.

Waiting for my reaction.

Hey, maybe it's because I'm still stoned. Or maybe it's because I have a fucking death wish.

Instead of running away to go sob in the bathroom like anyone else in my position most likely would, I push back my shoulders, take out the lingerie, and hold it up for him to see over the laughing crowd of students.

"How thoughtful," I yell out. "Guess it's a good thing I'm the same cup size as Jessica."

"What are you doing?" Addison murmurs, coming closer and making a grab for the underwear.

I move out of her way and hold the piece of erotic blue fabric even higher. "I mean, it's not as if she'll be needing it anymore, amiright?"

Briar's face turns to stone. He slams his locker so hard it

rattles, and storms off down the hall. His entourage breaks away from their lockers and follows him like sheep.

All except one.

I catch sight of Marcus. He's wearing an open leer on his face, as if he's picturing how I'll look in the lingerie. I hurriedly shove it back into my locker.

When I look up, Marcus is gone.

Addy steps closer and leans in. "What the fuck was that about?"

"Briar pulling my fucking hair again," I say, crossing my arms over my chest. I grab a bunch of the roses, sniff at the offending piece of underwear sitting in my locker, and slam closed the door. "Catch you later, Addy. Gotta trim my roses."

BRIAR

Fuck, I'm tired. Marcus and I stayed up until two in the morning playing video games, drinking, and smoking weed. And when I finally did get into bed, I spent another hour thinking up kick-ass pranks for my little virgin. I've already been in homeroom ten minutes, and I'm about to put my head down and take a nap when I hear someone nearby murmur, "There she is."

Indi storms inside the classroom, faltering when she sees me in the far corner. She purses her lips like she's bitten into sour candy and flings herself down in her usual seat close to the door.

I allow myself a grim smile, but it doesn't last long. I'd thought she'd been sobbing in the bathrooms, but she just looks angry. That prank was legit—she should be a blubbering mess—but that's not how Indi fucking Virgo rolls, is it?

My phone vibrates with a new message. I sigh and take it out of my pocket as Ms. Parsons starts going through the day's announcements.

Leave Indi alone.

I frown at the message, and then at the strange number. Who the hell sent this? When I look up, my eyes latch onto Indi. She's glaring at me.

Was it…?

I've known her less than a week, but she's not the type to threaten me with a message. She'd rather get up in my face and say something, like she did in the hall this morning.

She's either really brave, or very stupid. And I have a feeling she's more than just a pair of tits on legs.

I type out a quick reply, and immediately look up.

Who is this?

Indi doesn't move, but a second later I get another message.

I have proof.

My skin prickles.

Addison Green. It's the only thing that makes sense. But she doesn't have jack shit. Marcus took care of everything. And even if she did, she'd never have waited until now to use it. She'd have shown it to the police, and I'd be in jail right now.

What if she *did* show it to them? What if they found it inconclusive…or my father called in a favor?

Addy must have gotten herself a new number; I'd blocked her old one months ago after the hundredth message and threatening voice mail.

Crazy bitch.

Why the fuck is she dragging this all out into the open again? Is it because of Indi? Did she…?

I look up and lock eyes with Indi. She'd been staring at me with a soft frown on her face, no doubt trying to figure out why I look so fucking pissed off.

I draw a huge breath, and slowly let it out. Then I get up and walk over to her, ignoring how Ms. Parson's stops talking mid-sentence, and take the seat behind Indi's desk.

Ms. Parson's doesn't pause for long—she starts yammering on about something happening at assembly on Friday—but Indi's acting like I'm a viper that just slithered up to her and now she's too scared to run in case I lash out and bite her.

I lean in, my elbows on the desk and my fingers laced. "How much did you tell her?"

Indi's sitting in her seat at an angle, and turns her head just enough to catch me from the corner of her eye. "What?"

"Stop playing dumb. Did you tell Addy about us?" I'm gripping my hands so hard, my fingers are starting to tingle from lack of blood.

Indi shakes her head.

"Sure about that? Not a single thing?"

"No." Another shake of her head. "And even if I did, it's not like she'd believe me. Not after all this time."

I narrow my eyes at her, but I can't argue with her logic.

But if it wasn't that, then what? Something had to have spurred Addy into hounding me again.

I lift my chin. "What's she been telling you?"

Indi shrugs, and blinks innocently at me. "Lots of stuff."

Fuck, she's gloating about what happened earlier. I shouldn't have lost my cool and left like that. We could have teased each other until the bell rang. Instead I stormed off like a kid throwing a fucking tantrum.

I grind my teeth. "About me. What's she saying about me?"

"I think you know," Indi says, turning. She lays her arm on the back of the chair and tilts her head.

"I don't know what she thinks she has on me, and I don't give a fuck." I grab Indi's hand before she has time to move out of reach, digging my nails into her wrist. "So you tell

Addison I'll leave you alone as soon as she gets off my fucking back."

A crease forms between Indi's dark eyebrows. "What makes you think she's got something on you?" But a second later, her face clears. "And fuck you, she's not my baby sitter. I can take care of myself, asshole." She rips her arm free and moves her chair closer to her desk.

"Don't think for a moment that Addy's your friend," I say, my eyes turning to slits. "Jess made that mistake too."

Indi sneers at me. "And you sure showed her the error of her ways, didn't you?"

Anger wells hot and thick through me, strangling any words I could possibly have produced. I shake my head and push away from the desk, leaning as far away from Indi as I can.

Fuck Addy and her empty threats. She did this before, and for some reason she's gotten the balls to do it again. Maybe it's Indi's influence. If I weren't so pissed off right now, I'd have to admire this tiny chick with her fierce green eyes.

I curl up one side of my mouth. Indi turns her head, staring suspiciously at me from the corner of her eye.

"Wish we'd met under different circumstances," I say.

Indi lets out a single, bitter huff of a laugh, her lips barely parting. "Really?"

"We'd be hot as fuck together."

Her eyes widen in surprise, but a second later she's glaring at me. "Never! You're the biggest prick I've ever met."

My smirk becomes a suggestive grin. "I also have the biggest dick you'll ever see."

In a flash, red tinges her cheeks. She opens her mouth in shock, but if she was going to retort, nothing comes out.

"Not even close, my little virgin." I lean forward again, make a show of looking at her lips, and then shake my head. "You'll have to open *much* wider than that."

INDI

Oh man, there's some fucked-up shit going on in my head right now. Even as I'm snapping my jaw closed, my mind takes a mental screenshot of just how wide open my mouth was.

He's gotta be bluffing.

I turn in my seat, hoping to hell I don't spontaneously combust. As if the movement catches her eye, Ms. Parsons turns to Briar and me and grins wide.

Shit.

"Indi, Briar? Did you two enjoy your ride yesterday?"

I groan, squeezing my eyes shut with my fingers in dread anticipation.

Wolf whistles, choruses of, 'virgin', 'cherry popping', and God knows what else erupt from the class.

Ms. Parsons's attempts at hushing the kids are unsurprisingly ineffectual.

"Yeah, we did," Briar says, raising his voice over the noise.

I let out another groan. Of course he'll milk this as much as—

"In fact, we just decided to go out again today. Bare back, this time."

The crowd only just settled, but now they all burst out laughing again.

Ms. Parsons is probably as red as I am, but this all ends in about five minutes for her—I'm not that lucky. I'm going to be on the receiving end of every horse-related sex pun for the next week until Lavish Prep's gossip machine finds new fodder.

I'm terribly tempted to announce that I hate horses, Briar, and everything in between and just be done with this farce…

But despite what I told Addy this morning, I'm convinced that getting closer to Briar will give me—*us*—the answers we're so desperately looking for. After all, we had a moment out there, yesterday.

It could have been because we were alone, with none of his classmates or friends around to impress. If that's the case, then maybe it can happen again.

"I've always wanted to try that," I quip, doing my best to ignore how hot my cheeks are. I turn to Briar, giving him a frigid smile. "Oh, and I've still got that gift you gave me this morning. Should I wear that?"

Briar blinks, his smug expression freezing. Then his face melts into grudging admiration. He gives me a small nod. "Good one, angel," he says, his voice only loud enough for me to hear.

"I learn from the best."

When Briar shakes his head and a rueful smile touches his mouth, my chest feels like it wants to explode. I face forward, brimming with victorious glee. But I know this feeling won't last. Something rattled him earlier—that's why he came to sit behind me, why he started talking about Addy.

Fuck it—I know the war's far from over, but I won this battle and I'm gonna celebrate.

CHAPTER TWENTY

BRIAR

I meant to throw her off-balance, but Indi has her sea legs already. Despite all this shit with Addy and Jess, I'm looking forward to riding with her again. Just to get her alone, of course. If I can lure her far enough from school, somewhere secluded…

She'd never let me, of course. I'm the predator, she's the prey—and she's spotted me.

Now the dance begins.

We're riding different horses than last time. Indi chose Queen Sophia—a black mare with a white blaze on her nose and I'm sitting a seventeen-hand tall chestnut gelding named Duke of Hearts.

Yeah, Lavish brims with thoroughbreds and corny names.

"No fences," Indi says as soon as we exit the stable, a finger held up in warning.

"No fences," I agree with a rueful smile.

"And no galloping."

But despite the stern tone of her voice, I hear a certain something. Excitement? Pleasure? I can't be sure, but I have a feeling she's enjoying this as much as I am.

All that bullshit happening in school feels miles away. Out here, it's just us, our steeds, and Lavish's picture-perfect backdrop. Fuck, I wish this was how I'd met her.

Not Sunday night.

Not Monday morning.

Now. Here.

Just two kids out for a ride.

I wish she'd never met Addison either. That poisonous bitch salted the earth for me. After everything Addy's no doubt been ramming down her throat, it doesn't matter what I say to Indi, how I act from here on out—she'll never think I'm anything more than an animal.

"Why so glum, chum?" comes Indi's cheerful voice from a few feet away.

I snap to the present, and glance across at Indi. She's wearing a fat grin, melding with her horse on every step. The hand she has on the reigns seems a mere afterthought—her thigh muscles bunch as she guides Sophia with her knees. When my eyes reach Indi's again, she's blushing a little. She glances away, and then her hand does tighten as if she's just remembered exactly who she's with.

I can't change the past. I can't go back and meet Indi again in better circumstances.

I'll always just be an animal to her.

Fury eviscerates my good mood in an instant. What the fuck was I thinking? We'd go on a horse ride and tomorrow we'd be holding hands and doing our darndest to figure out just how alike—or dissimilar—we really are? That shit's for pussies and hopeless romantics.

I'm neither.

There's no point in beating around the fucking bush anymore.

I clear my throat, and Indi gives me a curious smile. She

opens her mouth, a smile forming around whatever she's going to say, but I cut in with a rough, "You should go back to wherever the fuck you came from."

Indi makes a soft, surprised sound as her eyes widen. "Excuse me?" She sounds more confused than offended, but I turn my voice to steel.

The time for pranks and teasing is over. Should have been over a long time ago.

"You heard me." I keep my eyes forward. "Tell your parents you don't like it here. Tell them the boys are mean to you. Tell them whatever the fuck you want."

"I…" But she doesn't finish her statement.

"I can keep doing this all year long, Indi. And it'll only get worse for you."

It's best for everyone, honestly. She's the one that stirred the pot—getting rid of her will reset the clock.

Plus, she can't like being here—new school, new town.

But she stays silent.

"You tell me you're leaving, this all goes away." When I look at her, she's staring forward again. Her jaw is set, her eyes blinking furiously.

Ah, shit. Is my little virgin gonna cry?

I let out a rough laugh. "Deal?"

"Fuck you," she whispers furiously.

"Come on, Angel, it's piss easy. You sit them down at the dinner table tonight. You say, 'Mommy, Daddy, I don't like it—'"

Indi kicks Princess Sophia in the ribs. In a second, she's tearing away from me.

I laugh. Fuck, guess that finally got the response I needed. Should have done this from the start. But I'm not done with her yet. If it takes me forcing her to jump another fence, I'll do it.

"Ha!"

I race after Indi, banking when she does, following her through the knolls. She glances over her shoulder, grimacing when she sees I'm on her heels. "Leave me alone!" she screams over her shoulder, flipping me off.

Really? She waves a fucking red flag in front of a bull and expects it to go quietly back into its stall?

"Ha!"

Duke speeds up. In seconds, I'm close enough to grab hold of Indi's arm. She tears herself free, but doesn't look at me. I urge Duke forward.

Light gleams off Indi's face.

Her cheeks are wet, her mouth a quivering line. Her chest is heaving as heavily as Sophia's, and her grip on the reigns is white-knuckled.

What the fuck?

Maybe she really *is* on the rag. There's no way what I said could possibly have made her cry.

"Hey!" I bellow. "Slow down."

In response, she spurs Sophia on.

Duke follows. I know Sophia could beat my gelding, but Indi's so busy wiping at her face that she's not controlling her animal. Sophia flags, and I take the opportunity to catch up, lean over, and grab Sophia's bridle.

Dumb ass move, but when I want someone to stop, they fucking stop.

Sophia's hooves churn up dirt and grass as she slows, and Indi swats at my hand as if she's somehow grown strong enough to fight me.

Our horses slow to a canter, a trot, a walk. But Sophia's barely even stopped before Indi hops off her and takes off running.

Fuck! What is it with her?

"Indi!"

I tie the horses's reigns together so they can keep each other company, and then I'm sprinting after Indi. She's fast, but she's not an athlete. She's still climbing the fence when I launch myself up behind her.

I grab her ankle.

She kicks me in the face.

So I let her climb over, and then I go after her.

The shadow of the small strip of woods hugging Lavish Prep's northern grounds cool my skin a second before I grab Indi's hair and haul her up short.

She yells out in pain and then starts thrashing around, digging her nails into my wrists and trying to untangle my fingers from her hair.

"What did I tell you about running?" I growl, dragging her against me.

She fights me for another second, and then she goes limp.

Jesus, finally.

Now, should I pin her to a tree again, or just shove her to the ground? Either has appeal—

Her body shakes as a sob wracks her.

Goddamn it.

"Hey, what the fuck's gotten into you?" I turn her around. Her eyes are squeezed shut, her mouth trembling. I swipe angrily at her cheeks to dry her tears, but more flash down her face an instant later. "Stop crying."

"F-fuck off."

I give her a shake, but she doesn't even seem to notice. "This could all be over, you know. Just say the word. Say you'll talk to them and I'll—"

"I f-fucking c-can't, you moth-therfucking *asshole*!" What starts out as a blubbering mess of words becomes an enraged yell.

Her veracity hits me like a club. I release her and step back, wondering if she's gonna attack me. The way her hands are fisted at her sides, her body stiff, I wouldn't be surprised.

I lift my hands, my mouth lifting up. "Just say the—"

"They're dead, you piece of shit," she says through her teeth. She advances on me and slams her fist into my chest.

I barely feel it. I'm staring into eyes bright and green as a water lily pond. "Dead?" I manage, but it feels like someone else is talking with my mouth.

Her fists start drumming against my chest. I gather her up, hold her tight. She fights me, but then another round of sobs takes control. She sags against me, and I let us both sink to the forest floor. I drag her with me as I lean back against a tree trunk. A second later she's in my lap, bundled up into an impossibly small ball.

She grabs my shirt, nuzzling harder and harder against me as if she wants to burrow inside my ribs so I can keep her safe.

And fuck me, I wish she could. Then I would always have her close, could feel her heart beating beside mine.

I wrap my arms around her, rocking her, willing her to pour out every last sliver of anger, pain, frustration, sadness. I don't care if all that negativity leeches into me.

I'd fatally poison myself for her and not regret a thing.

I stroke her hair and press my lips to the top of her head, but I doubt she registers a thing. If she did, she'd still be fighting.

Who the fuck wants to be comforted by a wild animal?

Indi

My legs twitch. I come to with my heart beating in my throat. I'm on my side, draped in shadow, but surprisingly I'm not cold. The green and brown enveloping me slowly comes into focus.

The woods?

I shift a little, a headache thumping in my skull.

There's an arm slung over my waist.

Panic scurries through me and converges in my chest, forcing out every last bit of air. I lie still as death.

Briar's behind me, body flush with mine.

What did he do to me? But an internal check produces nothing except the tight headache of a good sobbing session, and a dull ache where a rock's pressing into my hip.

A warm, steady breath washes over the back of my neck. Goosebumps scatter over my arms and legs, and I slowly turn to look at Briar.

We're under the boughs of a massive oak tree. The floor is mossy here, only the odd stone. My head is on his arm, and he's sleeping.

I remember crying. How he held me so tight.

I've never felt that…safe before.

None of it makes sense. If anything, I should have run away. Briar's not someone I want to be alone in the woods with. I grasp his wrist and lift up his arm. It's heavy, and long, and I already know I won't be able to move it much without waking him.

I barely lift him an inch before his massive hand grabs my belly and squeezes. I go stiff in shock.

"Briar." His name catches in my throat, mingling with a gasp when his lips touch the back of my neck.

"Jesus, you smell so fucking good," he says, those words chasing warm puffs of air over my skin.

Oh God, why did I wake him? Now I can't move away if I wanted to. It feels like the forest's claimed me and I've gone and taken root.

Briar's lips skate over my neck, my jaw, my cheekbone. He rains a flurry of light kisses over my face, hesitating when he reaches the edge of my mouth. He pauses, his warm, sweet breath fluttering over my lips as the hand on my belly moves down.

Get up. Run away. Don't let him pull you under!

Briar groans as if he can't hold back anymore, and his mouth crashes against mine. He takes without asking, dancing without letting me lead, all the while ignoring my mewls of protest.

A frantic ache bursts into my core, thumping in time with Briar's furious kiss.

How the fuck could I want someone so badly? I don't care if I never breathe, eat, sleep, or regain consciousness again. All I want is him. I want to give him everything. More and more and more, until there's nothing left for me to give.

Nothing left for him to take.

I shiver violently at the thought, and Briar pulls back with a reluctant exhale. "You cold, Angel?"

As if offering up the heat of his body, he pulls me hard against him.

I can feel every muscle on his body.

And his rock hard cock.

How easy it would be to just lie here and let this happen. To let him slip a hand up my skirt and tug down my leggings. For his cock to—

I shove at him and scramble up. He lifts his hands in mock surrender, a strange half-smile on his mouth as he stares up at me. Lowering his hands, he props himself up on one elbow.

Laying on his side, he should look defenseless, weak. He doesn't. He could be a leopard waking from a catnap.

His earlier words tumble back into my mind.

Just tell them you don't like it here.

Thankfully—*thankfully*—I don't have any tears left. He drained them out of me like the sun drains the deserts.

He doesn't deserve to know, doesn't even deserve an explanation, but I'm hoping it will be like a thorn in his paw. Something small, seemingly insignificant, but that will drive him mad over time. And the only mouse around to take it out would be me.

"My father—" I swallow hard, and fist my hands at my side. "Stage four Hodgkin Lymphoma. Know what that is? It's a cancer that attacks your lymph nodes. They thought they got it in time, that they could cut it out." My voice fails for a second, but I bite the inside of my bottom lip hard enough to taste blood, and then force out the rest. "They kept cutting and cutting, but that didn't stop it spreading. Eventually, there was nothing left for them to cut out. Not without killing him outright." I let out a soft laugh. "They dragged it out for a year. A fucking year. That was when he told me and my mom that he'd had enough. That he just wanted the pain to end." I hold up my hand, fingers spread. "He died five years ago."

Through my entire toneless monologue, Briar's expression doesn't shift an inch. But his eyes keep darting all over my face, like he's scanning me for the first hint of a lie.

Just thinking about Dad, repeating that story, brings a visceral image to mind; how pale and thin he looked on his bed, skin the same color as the sheets but more translucent. He'd insisted on coming home—said he didn't want to die in the hospital—and I hated him for that because I knew that, when he died, his spirit would haunt us forever.

And it did.

A black cloud hung over our house every second of every day after he passed away.

My legs go weak, and I hurriedly sink to the ground before I fall.

On my knees, ass on my heels, hands on my thighs—here I sit in supplication to Prince Briar. Am I begging him to stop tormenting me, or for him to go through with his threats?

He watches me with that same intrusive glare as before; silent, unreadable.

Probably waiting to call bullshit on my train wreck of a life.

I smile, but there's fuck all warmth in it, because my soul is frozen solid. I've been a fucking Ice Queen for half a decade. And my frozen heart? Some random, sadistic fuck shattered it a week ago.

I grip my hands together so they'll stop shaking.

"Eleven days ago, someone broke into my house and murdered my mother."

Briar's mouth twitches, but that's it.

One. Fucking. Twitch.

"Case is still open. No suspects."

I lean forward, pressing my palms onto the moss.

Briar slowly sits up and runs his hand through his hair with that same silent scowl on his face.

Guess you wish you could take back all that shit you said earlier, huh?

"One guy. That's what the cops said. Could have been more, but they only found traces of one—"

I cut off.

Fuck, I can't do this. What the fuck's wrong with me? This is private shit. I've made my point.

I push up, but Briar darts forward and stops me in my tracks. We're both on our knees, our bodies a few inches apart. I have to look up at him to see his eyes, and he's gazing down at me like I'm some kind of forest fairy that's about to grant him a wish.

My stomach coils uneasily as he slides a hand around the

back of my neck, the other on the small of my back.

"Don't stop," he murmurs, back to scowling.

"You sick fuck." I turn my head a little, bile-bitter saliva flooding my mouth. "You sick, *sick*—"

"Tell me."

I swallow hard. "What, so you can get off on—"

He squeezes the back of my neck, and I cut off, taking it as a warning. He dips his head a little lower. Suddenly, he doesn't look angry or frustrated or smug. There's an intensity to his gaze, some kind of urgency.

"Wh—?"

"You've never told anyone this, have you?"

My stomach flips over. I shake my head, not trusting my voice right then.

"Then tell *me*. I can take it, whatever it is. Tell me, and forget about it. I'll keep it for you."

I frown at him. *Keep* it? What the hell—?

He grabs my hand and puts it on his heart. Just like when I shoved him away from Addy the other day.

His heart pounds like a racehorse's.

"Feel that? It's going strong. And it can still take a fuck load more."

I tense my fingers, burrowing my nails into his flesh through his cotton shirt. His lips part, and his breath washes over me as he lets out a sigh.

"They—*he*—tied her up." My heart starts pounding harder, faster. Blood roars in my ears.

Briar's eyes light up, but not for the story. I'm confiding in him, and for some reason he's eating it up. I can't think about what this means, not right now.

I've reached the top of this fucking roller coaster, and there's nothing left to do but close my eyes, hold tight, and hope I don't fucking die.

CHAPTER TWENTY-ONE

BRIAR

Indi's story comes out slowly, reluctantly. But then it builds speed. I'm swept along like a leaf down a river running heavy with snowmelt.

I want her to stop.

I want her to keep going.

I want to hear everything.

And then I want to forget I heard anything at all.

Because I can do that for her. I can take away her pain, her suffering, her nightmares.

Christ, how can she *not* have fucking nightmares?

Her eyes glow, but this time her anger, her hate, it isn't directed at me. But it's just as fucking beautiful as if it was.

"I went out that night. The night he killed her." Her voice grows thick before she clears her throat. "Random house party, wasn't even anything special."

Indi blinks, but the movement is frozen in time. I can't look away from her eyes, but at the same time I feel drawn to watch her lips as she speaks. Could be because she's barely more than whispering.

I understand. A secret this dark, this depraved—no one should ever have to hear it.

I lean in until her face is a blur. Until every word touches my mouth in a flurry of her breath.

"Got drunk. Got easy. But then I had to go home. Always gotta go home, right?"

I tighten my grip around the back of her neck. I want to cut in, to tell her home isn't the end-all and the be-all of this fucking life. Take it from someone whose home is nothing but an empty shell. Or from a guy like Marcus, where home is a rusty bear trap just waiting to slam shut.

Not unless that home is with me.

"I thought the cab driver took me to the wrong address." A soft laugh puffs against my lips, and I lick them on instinct. I lean back a little, cradling her face in my hands. Not wanting her to stop, already feeling her sense of relief as these words spill out of the dank, dark hole she shoved them in.

"It was all black, my house. And still smoking. Hardly anything left of the place." She shakes her head, and I tighten my grip until she stops. Her eyes fix on me, draw at me until I want to kiss her. Instead, I smooth away a chunk of hair from her forehead.

"I got a bit mental when I figured out what had happened. When it all sunk in. They gave me a really strong sedative. It was better then. Everything wasn't so loud anymore, so bright, so fucking real. But I still knew what was going on. Guess the other people didn't know that. The cops and shit."

Her eyes drop, but I tilt her head back until she looks at me again.

"I overheard two of them talking. If I hadn't been so fucked up, I'd have covered my ears, walked away...*something*." She shakes her head. "But I just sat there. Listening to every fucking word.

"They said he'd…he'd had to have done this kind of thing before, because it didn't look amateurish. The ropes, the knots he used. How rough…how rough he'd been when he'd raped her."

My heart feels like it wants to fucking implode under the weight of Indi's words. But I swore to her I'd listen, that I'd take this burden from her. I have broad shoulders and a big heart. She's a tiny thing. No one like her can withstand this kind of shit. I can. I've done it before, I can do it again.

"He stabbed her with one of our kitchen knives. Not just once, but over and over and over again. And then he strangled her with his belt."

She should be sobbing again, but it's as if there's nothing left.

"He left her tied up. Wrists and ankles, face down on the bed. There was still…he'd used a soda bottle to, to—" Indi shakes her head hard, signaling the end of the morbid recitation.

I crush her against me, inhaling her scent. She's stiff at first, but then she relaxes. I can feel her heart pounding against my chest, just as I'm sure she can feel mine.

But slowly, ever so fucking slowly, her heartbeat grows softer, steadier. I like to think I tame it. That, as an animal, only I could know how. But if that were true, then I'd have learned to tame mine a long time ago. And I haven't. If anything, it just starts beating harder the longer I have her against me.

Because I *still* want her. Right here, right now, despite everything I've just heard. Perhaps *because* of everything I've just heard. I want to drown her sorrow with ecstasy.

But it's not right. It's not decent.

And it may never be. And I'd have to be okay with that.

I never knew she was this broken. But now all I want to do is force that darkness from her mind.

But how can I, when all I have to offer is more darkness? More depravity? More violence?

Dark doesn't consume dark. It festers and grows and expounds.

The last thing Indigo Virgo needs in her life right now is a sick fuck like me.

INDI

I finally understand what he meant by letting him 'keep it'. He's eaten out my pain like a bad cancer, leaving me disease free.

For now, anyway.

But what about him? How can he take on such brutality without succumbing to it in some way?

Then again, I know nothing about Briar. He said he can handle anything…and maybe he can. Maybe he's been eating his own pain for so long, it doesn't taste spoiled anymore. Maybe he even enjoys it. Like it's an acquired taste that makes normal people retch, but makes his mouth water.

I'm fully aware of how hard he is for me. And for some disgusting reason I can't fathom, I'm wet for him too. But instead of putting his hands on me, he moves back and pushes me away. Separating us.

We'd be hot as fuck together.

The same can be said of wood and a butane fucking torch.

I've stopped trying to out-think Briar—it's too exhausting. But I expected him to say something. Anything.

Not, 'sorry.'

Not, 'it's gonna be okay'.

Neither of us are that fucking naive.

But he's silent. Distant. Cold, even. He stands, watches me

until I do too, and then slips a hand in his pocket. He takes out my switchblade, hands it to me, and then leads us out of the woods.

As soon as I see where the sun's sitting, my stomach drops an inch.

It's past lunchtime already. How the hell could we have been gone for so long?

We walk back to the stables, silent and more than a yard apart. Briar's head is constantly turning—looking for our horses, I guess. But when we get to the stables and Mr. Denard and Ms. Parsons step out of the shadowy depths of that big barn…well, I kinda get a premonition about why we didn't find our valiant steeds.

"So where were you?" Addy whispers.

I'm toying with the corner of my notebook, flipping the pages over my thumb as our teacher drones on in the background.

"Horse riding."

"And what, you lost track of time?"

I sigh and look up at Addy. "That's what I said." She's sitting beside me, pretending to look at the board as she interrogates me from the side of her mouth.

There's a detention slip burning a fucking hole in my left breast pocket. Briar has one just like it.

Apparently, extending your free period to an over two-hour-long leisure ride in Lavish Prep's foothills is frowned upon. As are boys and girls disappearing off the grounds together.

Ms. Parson's got as much of a dressing down as we did for pairing us up. Denard had her pegged as some kind of pedophilic matchmaker, and I've never felt as sorry for her in that moment as I did right then while Denard's forehead grew pulsing veins.

Even Briar's rapport with the French teacher did nothing to reduce our sentence. We each got a week, and Denard's sincere vow that our parents would be notified about our lack of attendance before the day was out.

I almost laughed at that, and I caught a glimmer of something that might have been amusement in Briar's eyes. If anyone can communicate with the fucking dead, it's Mr. Denard.

"So…was he a good fuck?"

My eyes snap over to Addy. Her nose is up in the air, her jaw bunched like she's gritting her teeth.

"The fuck, Addy?" I whisper furiously. "Nothing happened."

"Mmm," she says.

"Addy."

But she ignores me, now and for the rest of the fucking class. Even my texts go unanswered, and I give up with a growl of irritation that makes our teacher glare at me.

As soon as class is over, Addy's out the door. I'm only a step behind her, but fuck she's got long legs.

"Addy. Addy, come on! Just—" I break off with a frustrated curse and put all my effort into catching up with her.

She's waiting for me around the corner, wearing a mask of such cool indifference it's like she transformed into a robot on the way over here.

"Thanks," I say, trying to talk and haul in a breath at the same time. I really gotta take a look at getting my fitness levels up. I mean, fuck, racing after Addy, running away from Briar? Then again, if shit keeps on like this, I think I'll be ready for the Olympics come Christmas.

"Thanks for what?" Addy prompts, crossing her arms over her chest.

"For listening."

She shifts, and glances away. "You haven't told me anything yet."

"Not for lack of trying."

Her brown eyes settle on me, but they flit away an instant later like nervous butterflies. I sling my arm through hers and start walking. I have one more period before home time. If I don't iron this out with Addy, who's to say she'll even listen to me tomorrow? She obviously thinks I broke her trust by sleeping with Briar. I can only hope she'll listen to reason.

"We didn't…there wasn't any sex."

She rolls her eyes at me.

"We just…spoke."

With that, Addy spins to face me. "About?" Her eyes are wide with expectation.

I look away before I can look at her again. "Not that. Not yet."

My skin starts crawling. As much as I thought this whole amateur sleuth thing would be a blast, I don't think I'm cut out for it. I keep feeling eyes on me, and it doesn't matter where I look, I can't spot who's watching me.

Paranoia. Just some standard high-school geek paranoia, Indi. It'll pass, most likely when you're twenty-five and high school is nothing more than a bunch of vague and slightly disturbing memories.

"I shared stuff with him," I say.

"Like herpes?"

I close my eyes as a laugh bubbles out of my mouth. When Addy glares at me, I shrug. "I know you don't like this, Addy, but it's working. I think he's opening up to me."

She shakes her head, but more like she can't believe how stubborn I am. Stand back, Addison Green—you ain't seen nothing yet. "Next you'll be telling me you're pranking him back, just for fun." Her words are heavy with sarcasm, but I let out a little squeal of joy and hug her arm.

"That's a fantastic idea!"

"No, it wasn't—" Addy cuts off with a sigh and another shake of her head. "You're fucking nuts, you know that, right?"

"Guess that's why we're friends." I stare at her until she gets what I'm saying and her imperious expression finally cracks into something resembling a smile.

"Fuck you, Indi."

"Thanks, but I don't swing that way."

Addy jerks her arm out of mine with an exasperated sigh and then brushes off her clothes. She stabs a manicured nail in my direction, frowning. "I'm not gonna keep reminding you how dangerous he is. You promise me you'll be careful."

I nod, and grin.

Well, I try to grin.

Of course I know how dangerous he is. He's a savage wolf, and I'm a baby lamb parading around him without any wool on, going on and on about how tender my flesh is.

I feel like a traitor thinking this, but out here in the glaring fluorescents of Lavish Prep's hallways, all that sentimental shit that happened back there feels more like the memory of an acid trip than real life.

Addy's right—I keep forgetting that Briar gets off on pain. But if I'm fast enough, nimble enough, I can get what I want out of him before his teeth can break skin.

CHAPTER TWENTY-TWO

BRIAR

I can't concentrate on a single word Kruger is saying, but I don't need to. I've read the whole textbook already, and memorized most of it. I only bother paying attention when Kruger goes into detail on something, and that happens rarely. I'm not a fan of Business Studies, but I prefer learning at my own pace. That is, a month or two, not twelve.

If this were psychology, of course, I'd be paying attention. As much as I loathe Veroza, he drops nuggets of his time as a practicing psychiatrist all the time. I think it's technically unethical, but he can never remember his patients's names, so I guess it's cool.

I can't wait until I get real world experience in that field. I'm keeping my options open, but I decided a long time ago that I want to work with people. I'll probably intern as a social worker for a while to build up my experience, and then move onto something else. I'm easily bored, so I can't imagine myself settling down long enough to open a practice or anything like that.

With my trust fund maturing on my twenty-first birthday, I

don't have to do anything. But that would be boring as fuck. What's the point of traveling around the world and merely existing for the sake of being alive, when there's no one to do it with you?

A yawn cracks my jaw. I stretch into it, rocking back on my chair until it creaks. The gesture makes the note in my pocket crumple.

I snort softly to myself.

Detention.

I don't think I've ever had detention. Why the fuck Denard thought my abscondence was bad enough to punish me, I can't begin to—

My chair legs thump back onto the carpet, jarring me.

Addison.

The bitch.

No one else would have bothered to report me. But she's got a fucking stick up her ass of late. Probably thought I was out there raping her friend. Explains why Denard was being such a asshole to Parsons. Ms. Parsons is a wallflower, but I've seen her standing her ground before. She obviously knew she was in the wrong, because she gobbled up Denard's bullshit with a spoon and asked for a goddamn second helping.

I thump my fist down on the desk before I can control myself.

Kruger stops talking, and stares at me for a long moment.

Don't come over. Don't come over. Don't—

My mental plea works—Kruger gives the class a haughty once over before carrying on with his lecture.

I haven't eaten yet. Should let Marcus know we're stopping for food somewhere before heading home.

I pull out my phone, but before I can open my messenger app, a new notification comes through.

Told you to stay away.

I'm torn between anger and disbelief. She rats me out to the teachers, and then she still has the audacity to fuck with me?

I can't even remember how many times I told Jess that Addy wasn't good for her. The jealous bitch always had something catty to say to me behind Jessica's back. I didn't mention it at first, but when Addy started getting personal—asking if I'd fucked her friend yet, or if I was stringing her along for another month—I lost my cool. I had a long talk with Jessica and laid it all out.

Jess chose Addy's side, of course. They'd been BFF fucking pinkie friends and shit since kindergarten.

I couldn't get it into Jessica's head that people change. Sometimes, for the worst. No one likes to think that. We're all real fucking precious about everyone that's been in our lives for longer than a year or two, but it's the goddamn truth.

People lie.

People change.

But when it's a friend, we're blindsided.

Think I'm bluffing? Let me show you…

I'd been so caught up in my thoughts, I hadn't even typed out a reply. I sit back, inhaling a heavy breath as I wait.

Yeah, show me what you got, Addy. This oughta be fucking good. Wish I'd got me some popcorn.

A download icon appears.

I glance up, making sure no one's paying me any attention.

What the fuck is it? Lavish Prep's wi-fi is fucking fast—if it weren't, the students would have rioted years ago—so I can't understand the delay.

But when the file finally loads, it all makes sense.

My screen goes black. I narrow my eyes. A video? My finger instinctively moves to the volume button, but I'm too slow. Before I can silence my phone, Marcus's voice rings out loud and true.

"She's so fucking trashed, bro."

My skin goes ice-cold. My phone's already back in my pocket before I lift my head, but that doesn't help.

Kruger tilts his head at me and beckons.

I swallow hard.

He beckons again.

Fuck!

I stand, take my phone out of my pocket, and glance down to make sure it's locked before I hand it over to him.

He takes it without a word, slips it into his top drawer, and points back to my seat.

I go reluctantly, my mind whirring like a spinning top.

She's so fucking trashed, bro.

I remember Marcus saying that. I remember that exact moment. It's a little vague—there'd been so much vodka, weed, and coke flowing through my blood, I'm shocked I managed to make it up Marcus's stairs.

To his bedroom.

That's where it happened.

Marcus's bedroom.

Nausea floods me, and I think I'm gonna puke right here in Kruger's class. But I fight it back with iron determination. Again. Again.

It dissipates, but reluctantly.

Think I'm bluffing?

The frame was too dark—I have no idea where the camera was that took that shot. But it was close enough to catch Marcus's voice.

Far from damning. Except...I never got to see the rest.

What if whoever took that footage followed the three of us— Marcus and Jess and me—up those stairs? What if they hung around on the landing and recorded whatever sounds could be heard through the door?

I remember sitting down on Marcus's bed.

Jessica, looking hot as shit in her little blue dress. Marcus by the door, looking high as fuck, silhouetted by the landing light.

That's it.

If it was a book, then all I'd read was the fucking prologue before skipping straight to the epilogue.

I woke up the next morning with the worst hangover I've ever had. I was on Marcus's bed, spooning Jessica. She was naked. I was naked.

I bask for a few seconds, counting my blessings and all that sentimental crap before the feeling went away. Because try as I might, not a single memory came up when I searched. So I thought we hadn't sealed the deal, maybe just fooled around a bit. We'd done that before. Some kinky shit.

But then I drew back the covers and I saw the dark streaks on my dick, and I knew I'd taken her virginity.

Unbelievably, I was more pissed off that I couldn't remember anything than I was about the fact that we'd both obviously been too drunk to remember.

My first virgin.

My *first virgin*, and I couldn't remember a thing.

And then Jessica woke up.

There was a moment, this brief, strange moment, where she smiled at me, and I could picture myself waking up beside her every morning for the rest of my fucking life. And then it suddenly didn't matter anymore if she'd been my first, because right then and there I'd decided she would be my last.

But then her expression changed. She frowned. Her lips thinned. Her arms darted under the covers, fumbling around down there. Shock widened her eyes, and parted her lips, and turned her face a whiter shade of pale. Words tumbled out of her mouth while I lay speechless beside her.

You…

How could you?

I didn't…
You raped *me.*

Kruger's lecture goes on for an eternity. I know it's just because I want to know what's on the rest of that clip. I have to know.

Because as much as I'd argued with Jessica—

I don't remember—

You never said no—

Prove it, Jess! Fucking prove it!

—I'd never know exactly what happened, because she had all the proof she needed. Her pussy was torn, and my dick was full of blood.

One and one make two.

I have to endure a lecture from Kruger about phones in class before I can snatch it from him and leave the classroom. I rush to the closest restroom and lock myself in the stall. Flipping closed the seat, I perch on the edge and plug my earphones into my phone.

The video plays.

A black screen.

Marcus: "She's fucking trashed, bro."

Me: "Tha' was the point, wa'nt it?" I'm slurring so much, I don't know how the fuck I was even able to stand.

The film's so dark, I don't even know if I am standing. Obviously, whoever took it used a very poor quality camera phone.

Marcus: "Almost there."

Me: "Jess? Still with us?"

My stomach clenches in anticipation, but Jess remains silent.

A few pixels appear on the screen. The vague outline of a

doorway appears. And then a silhouette. But it cuts off before I can make out anything useful like where the person taking the shot was standing, whose silhouette it was…anything.

That's it?

I replay the video, cranking up the sound and zooming in on every pixel I can see.

Nothing.

I'm a second away from hurling my phone at the wall before I can control myself. As soon as I manage to curb my hand's furious shaking, I type out a message.

That's it?

I wait, feet tapping on the tiles.

There's only one new message on my phone, and I read it before considering a reply to Addy.

Marcus: Thanks for the drinks.

So Marcus's father has left again. Good for Marcus. Although I wouldn't have minded having him at my house for a few days. At least the house doesn't echo as much.

I hesitate, and then type out a reply to Addy.

That's your proof? You haven't got shit.

I wait, but there's no response. She's probably in class already, not daring to take out her cellphone. I wait another minute, my hand in my hair, but no response.

Fuck this. I've probably scared her off. If it was just a voice recording, I hardly see how it could be evidence. Whatever her plan was, it didn't work.

I head for my next class, doing my best to keep Addy from my mind. Unfortunately, all that does is let Indi slip in.

Christ, her mother was *murdered?* There was no way I could have known, of course, but I still feel like shit for what I said to her. No wonder she went off the fucking rails.

I should apologize. But would she let me? She looked pretty pissed off when Denard handed her a detention slip.

Hmm. I get to have detention with my little virgin.

INDI

I have no idea if Marigold's been notified about my detention yet, and I have no wish to find out either. Addy and I meet for a late lunch at a bistro down one of Lavish's prettier roads. We smoke before going in, so I'm baked when we take our seat outside in the dappled shade of one of the many oak trees lining this street.

Addy orders a milkshake and some fries, but I need proper food. I missed lunch, after all, and tears are a poor source of sustenance. I upgrade my order to a burger, double thick strawberry milkshake and a massive plate of fries.

"Wanna know something weird?" I say, toying with my straw as I watch the play of light on the brick road. Sitting out here makes me think of what it must be like dining in Italy or something. "Briar seems so different when we're alone."

It's the weed talking, of course. I would never have brought up the subject if I hadn't been robbed of my inhibitions by a few solid hits of Kush.

"Serial killers are like that," Addy says dryly. "Handsome, charming psychos."

I laugh. "Serial killer? Damn, that escalated quickly."

Addy rolls her eyes. "He'll turn into one if he isn't stopped."

I shrug. "I just mean, if you hadn't told me about what had happened to Jess, I would never have suspected he was…capable of doing something like that."

I don't mention Sunday, obviously. In my mind, it turned out to be an anomaly. I can't explain Briar's behavior that night

—maybe he was high or something. I don't do drugs—to me, weed doesn't count—so I may have missed the clues.

"I need to get him alone again," I murmur, nodding my head as I take another sip of my milkshake.

"You wound up getting detention last time," Addy says, pursing her lips.

"You know, for someone who's determined to find out who killed her best friend, you're making this very difficult." I narrow my eyes at her.

She shrugs a little. "I don't want you to get hurt."

"I won't."

Our food arrives. I hurriedly sit back, swallowing drool as the server sets our plates down. I don't even bother with dousing my fries in ketchup—I go straight for the money shot. Grabbing my cheeseburger in both hands, I tear out a chunk with my teeth.

Fucking delicious.

I chase it down with a slurp of milkshake and then dab a napkin to my lips as if that will somehow make up for being a pig.

"But you're right," I say, wagging a finger at Addy without releasing my burger. "School's not the place."

"You planning on rocking up at his house and hoping he'll let you in? Because he will." Addy grabs a fry and stabs it in my direction. "But who knows if you'll ever leave?"

I laugh, and she glares at me. "Stop being so dramatic."

Her glare intensifies. "Stop being so stoned."

"Would if I could, but your shit's gooood."

We grin at each other over our food, and tuck in for real. She gets a message on her phone a few minutes later and types out a reply without looking up. Then she flips her phone over and gives me another grin.

"What?"

"Don't you have detention with him tomorrow?"

I pause with my third-last fry by my lips. "Fuck. I forgot about that."

"That's a whole hour with him."

"Yeah, but we won't be alone."

Addy drops her eyes. "True. But you could pass messages or shit."

"We're not five, Addy. And plus, you know he wouldn't dare put anything incriminating on a piece of paper. The last thing he wants is to give us proof."

Our eyes lock. Addy stops chewing. She nods a little, and then looks away to take a last sip of her milkshake. Her phone vibrates again, but this time she ignores it.

"Then I don't know," she says after a bit. "It's not like we move in the same circles anymore."

"Well, maybe we can change that."

Addy looks at me with narrowed eyes.

I push my plate aside and lean in. "Let's wave the white flag. Tell them we're done."

"He'll never—"

"After today, he just might."

Addy's eyes touch briefly on my mouth before darting away. "And all it took was a horse ride?"

I lick my lips, sigh, and sit back in my seat. Addy watches me from the corner of her eyes.

"We...kissed, okay? That's it. Then I told him about my mom and we left."

"Must have been a long kiss."

The last thing I want to do is admit to Addy everything that went on. I'm not a gossip, and my private life has always been just that—private.

"We rode around for a while. None of us wanted to go back to class. We decided to skip class and walk around in the woods."

Addy doesn't seem convinced, but I shrug at her and she eventually looks away.

"He won't trust us. Me, especially."

"We'll never know if we don't try."

Addy purses her lips and lifts a hand, signaling for the waiter to bring our bill.

I reach for my backpack, but she tuts me and lays a cool hand over mine. "It's on me."

"I have money."

"I have more." If there'd been even a shred of condescension, I'd have flipped over the table. Well, I'd have tried. But it's obvious that she's just stating a fact, and she doesn't even look even vaguely interested in noting my reaction.

"So…we'll do lunch with them tomorrow?"

Addy shrugs and smiles at the waiter when he hands her the bill folder. "If they let us, sure."

"Can you behave yourself for long enough?"

She snorts, tosses a bill in the folder, and snaps it closed. "I'll do my best," she says dryly as she hands the folder to the waiter without breaking eye contact. "But no promises."

I laugh at her, shaking my head. It's not the greatest plan, but if today was anything to go by, then it might just work. Briar hasn't pranked me again, so maybe he'll be receptive to us becoming friends.

I know he wants to fuck me. As much as Addy doesn't like thinking about it, maybe I can use the promise of sex to lure him into unburdening his darkest secrets.

It kinda worked for me, didn't it?

BRIAR

I head straight home after school, and spend the rest of the afternoon studying and shoving food into my mouth. It almost feels like a normal Wednesday. I have one more assignment to do, then I plan on vegging out in front of my X-Box. But I'm interrupted by another message from Addy.

Hey, handsome.

I frown at the message and do my best to ignore it as I carry on with the assignment Kruger gave us for homework today.

My phone vibrates a few minutes later. When I flip it over, the new message shows up on my lock screen. It's so short, I don't even have to open my app to read it.

Smile. You're on camera.

My stomach twists into a cold knot. I stare at the phone for a few seconds, waiting for more, but nothing comes.

Fuck this. All she's doing is trying to get into my fucking head.

I turn off my phone, sigh, and stretch.

I should go for a run, clear my head.

If I'm lucky, I might even run into Indi.

CHAPTER TWENTY-THREE

INDI

Denard came through on his promise. When I get home, I see Marigold's car parked out front, not in the garage, which means she came home specifically to crap me out.

Count on Marigold not to do this face-to-face.

Bitch.

I slam my car door shut and walk inside bristling, ready to handle whatever shit storm's blowing my way.

Cigarette smoke taints the air. I hesitate, then track it down the hallway. I stop outside the door that's always locked. The smell's definitely coming from here. I lick my lips and carefully knock on the door.

There's a thump, and then Marigold's wavery voice calls out, "Come."

I turn the knob and walk inside. After two steps, I stop.

This isn't a study. It's a bedroom. Paintings litter the walls—most done on letter-sized sheets of paper. Some pencil, some paint. Two large canvases dominate the wall opposite the bedroom's large windows. But there's no time to take in any details, because my eyes fix on Marigold.

She's sitting in the middle of the floor, an ashtray beside her and a cigarette in a long holder trailing smoke into the air.

Her back's to me, but I don't need to see her face to know she's been crying—the pile of tissues beside her legs is evidence enough.

I stand there, not knowing what to say, and instead finally take scope of the room.

I'd recognize my mother's art anywhere. She had such a unique style. Her art concentrated on mythical creatures that looked somewhere between elves and fairies. She called them pixies, but they were nothing like the Tinkerbell I grew up with. Her pixies have sharp teeth and long limbs. Jagged nails and evil eyes.

The backdrops were always breathtaking. Fantasy settings full of strange flowers and twisted trees. But in each piece of art, there would always be one of her creatures. You wouldn't see it at first—she liked to hide them away—but once you did you couldn't stop looking.

I'm still staring at the right-hand canvas, trying to spot Mom's creature, when Marigold speaks.

"The Lakeview police department called."

My heart flies into my throat. I hurry forward, turning so I can see Marigold's face. She's got a photo frame in front of her on the floor. It's a photo of my mother, probably no older than seventeen.

She looks just like me, but so, so much prettier.

"What…what did they say?"

Marigold takes a long pull at her cigarette. Then she gets up, moving stiffly but batting away my hands when I reach out to help her.

"They've closed the case."

I grab her wrists, holding on even when she tugs at me. "They found him! They found him!"

Marigold's red-rimmed eyes narrow. "Course they didn't, you stupid child." She tears herself free, her mouth twisting into a grimace. "The police these days are a joke. They said there wasn't enough evidence for them to continue their investigation."

"Can they do that so soon?" I throw my hand into the air. "It's barely been a week."

"I'm not a police officer, Indigo."

I snap my mouth closed. Tears prick at my lids, but I refuse to let them fall. Despite the fact that I know Marigold's been in here crying—possibly for more than an hour, judging from the ashtray—it would feel like surrendering.

I spin around, the paintings blurring as the first tear works its way past my defenses.

Moments later, I'm in the woods. It was the only place I could think of to go where I'd be alone with my thoughts. Where I could scream, and no one would hear me.

Except Briar, perhaps, if he happened to be out here. But what are the chances, right?

The straight lines of the church pull me out of the thoughtless fog I'd lost myself in. I stop walking, staring ahead at the blackened shell of a building.

Now I regret coming here. It reminds me too much of my house that night; black and gray and white with char, ash, and smoke.

Marigold must have heard wrong. No one can close a case that quickly. Maybe she's overreacting. I'll contact the Deputy and speak to him. That's what I should have done instead of coming here. The sun's already dipped behind the Devil's Spine mountains. It'll be dark soon.

But maybe I want to get lost in the woods again. At least, then, I'd have something else on my mind.

I push on, stepping into the church and taking my time to look around.

It must have been a stunning sight with its white walls and stained glass windows. Enough of the shell is still standing—I can see it was built in the shape of a Christian cross, with the pulpit up near the top and the pews down the longest branch of the cross.

Before the fire.

It's beautiful now, how the forest has reclaimed it. The brambles don't even look as sharp as they did that night—

I shove away the thought. I'm trying to stay positive; thoughts of Briar won't help.

I run my fingers over the back of a burned pew, rubbing the black char into my skin and lifting it to my nose. It hardly smells burned anymore. Guess this happened a long time ago.

Who builds a church in the middle of—?

Footsteps.

I freeze, too terrified to turn around.

See, this is what happens when you think about someone too much. You end up summoning them.

I turn to face him, because fuck, I wanted to be alone with him, didn't I?

But the figure headed for the church isn't Briar.

It's Marcus.

Something primal takes control. I drop into a crouch and glance around, scurrying to the back of the church, to the small area behind the pulpit.

It's dark here—most of the wall is still intact, and the spreading boughs of a tree act as a roof a few feet above my head. I carefully wedge myself behind a bramble bush and try to stop breathing.

Footsteps crunch closer.

What the hell am I doing? If Marcus sees me, he's gonna think I've lost my mind. I should just have greeted him and left.

But he won't see me here, and that's the fucking point. I won't have to speak to him, explain my presence.

Crunch.

Crunch.

He stops walking. My heart pounds harder as I wait for him to move again. Despite every atom in my body screaming at me not to, I lean to the side, craning around the bramble to try and see if I can spot him.

He's standing close to the main entrance of the church, head bowed. Even if he were to look up, I doubt he could make me out in these dark shadows.

Head still down, he starts walking toward me with utter precision, one foot in front of the other, heel touching toe.

Is he measuring the distance from the door to the pulpit or something? Sure looks that way.

Shit. I shift further back, huddling into a ball. If he comes much closer, he might spot me.

For some reason, the thought terrifies the living shit out of me.

Closer.

Closer.

Closer.

Then he stops. There's a soft sound, like he's scraping dirt off the floor with his shoe.

"Hey!"

I almost wet myself. I squeeze shut my eyes and try desperately not to have a heart attack.

"What are you doing here?" Briar's voice echoes through what's left of the church. Too loud, too cheery.

"What, now I can't come here anymore?" Marcus says grimly. "This place out of bounds or something?"

"Course not." Briar sounds either flustered or out of breath. "Just didn't know you still came here."

"Hardly ever."

Briar's footsteps stop. "What's up? Your dad come back again?"

"Was out for a run."

"What, in your school clothes?"

Marcus makes an angry sound. "Christ, I'm sorry I dared set foot in your fucking church, asshole."

I can't help myself—now I have to look. Moving as carefully as I can, I peek out behind the bush again. There's almost no daylight left, so both guys are just silhouettes. Marcus has his arms crossed, and Briar's are on his hips. "What the fuck's wrong with you?"

Marcus puts out his hands like Briar's about to storm him. "Nothing, man. Just…I was just thinking about stuff."

"Sorry to interrupt. But I'm kinda glad you're here."

"Yeah? Why?"

Briar moves back and leans against the pulpit. "Was there anyone with us that night, when we took Jessica upstairs?"

Every single hair on my body stands on end. I stop breathing in shock, leaning forward as I strain to hear Marcus's response.

"What the fuck are you on about?"

Briar runs a hand through his hair. "There, on the stairs. Did someone come up with us?"

"No. Course not."

"You sure?"

Marcus shrugs. "I don't remember seeing—"

"She sent me a video."

She? She *who*? Dammit people, use your words!

"You're shitting me," Marcus says, a light laugh in his voice. "What's on it?"

"Nothing much. Us talking. One of us opening your bedroom door."

"That it?" Marcus snorts. "What's that prove? Nothing."

"Yeah, but she says there's more."

Marcus shakes his head, but before he can say anything, Briar starts talking again. "How fucked were you that night?"

Marcus steps back, and his profile changes as if he's tilting his head. "The fuck you suggesting, bro?"

"Is it possible someone saw us? Came up with us? That you didn't notice?"

"I was fucked, but I wasn't *that* fucked." Marcus swipes his hand through the air. "You know what, I'm done cleaning up your messes, Briar. This one's on you."

"I thought you cleaned this up already," Briar growls.

My stomach sinks into my shoes.

Oh my fucking God.

He did it.

He raped Jessica.

Most likely killed her, too.

My body starts trembling, part rage, part terror.

It's still my word against theirs. Who the fuck would believe that I just happened to eavesdrop on this conversation out here in the middle of nowhere?

My phone! I can record this—

I pluck it out of my pocket without thinking and unlock it.

A glow envelops me. I shove my phone under my school blazer, but it's too late.

"You see that?" Briar says, his voice changing direction.

Because he's looking straight at you, you fucking idiot.

My eyes roll into the back of my head as I await my fate. Dry leaves and grit crunch under shoes as someone heads over to where I'm hiding.

Fuck. If they know I overheard them…

My skin goes ice-cold.

Closer.

Closer.

Fuck!

"What does she want?" Marcus calls out.

Briar stops walking, and his shoes scrape as if he's turning to face Marcus. "I dunno. Justice, I guess."

"If she wanted that, she'd have gone to the fucking cops."

"Then what?" Briar storms back to Marcus. He sounds so furious, I wouldn't be surprised if he lands a punch on his friend.

No, not his *friend*. His fucking accomplice.

They did this together, Briar and Marcus.

Bile floods my mouth.

No wonder no one could prove anything—Marcus helped Briar cover it up. Probably his other friends, too. So much for breaking into their little group and finding a weak link. No doubt they've all vowed to keep Briar's horrible secret.

"So why'd she do it, huh? Just to put me on a guilt trip?"

I've never heard such venom in Briar's words. I cringe back, hugging myself hard. Oh God, Addy wasn't kidding. This guy's a fucking psycho…and I was alone with him.

Willingly.

What the fuck does that say about me?

"Addy's a vindictive bitch," Briar continues, "but she's gotta have a better reason than that."

Addy? That's who they're talking about?

My mouth drops open.

"I bet you it's money." Marcus points at Briar, nodding. "I hear her folks's business is going belly up. Tax evasion or some shit."

Briar cocks his head. "You're shitting me."

Marcus shakes his head. "You'll see. She's gonna extort you for everything you've got."

"Fuck!" Briar whips around and punches the closest wall and that thump feels like it goes straight through me.

I don't think I've ever been this scared in my life.

Those two silhouettes don't look like high school boys. They look like full-grown men.

Dangerous.

Edgy.

Psychotic as fuck.

I press my lips into a line, and do my best to vanish into the bramble bush.

"But…she *can't* have anything, can she?"

They're blocked out by the brambles now, but when Marcus answers, I can tell from his voice that he's lost interest in the conversation.

"Whatever, bro. Pay her, don't pay her. Maybe she's bluffing, who the fuck knows. That bitch is crazy enough, she'd do anything to get you to confess."

"I'm not confessing," Briar grates out.

I bite my lip, giving my head a small shake.

At least Addy won't have to try convincing me anymore. After tonight, I know for a fact that Briar is every inch as guilty as Addy claimed he was. My jaw bunches as fury wells inside me. My hands fist, digging into my sides as I squeeze myself.

I let this monster touch me.

"Whatever man." Footsteps signal Marcus's exit.

For a terrifying moment, I think Briar's heading back in my direction. But I guess he has a lot on his mind, because a second later he calls out, "Hey, wait for me," and hurries after Marcus.

No wonder they're so close. Blood brothers usually are.

I have to speak to Addy. I have to know what she has on

Briar. And then we'll figure out a plan, once and for all, to take these fuckers down.

My quest for answers is met with failure. As soon as I'm back home, I try calling Addy.

Her phone is off.

Screw this. Have car, will drive.

But before I've gone more than a foot out of the front door, Marigold's imperious voice brings me up short.

"Where do you think you're going?"

I haven't even bothered to change out of my uniform yet. I adjust my blazer, facing down Marigold as best as I can. "Out."

Marigold lets out an unpleasant chuckle. "Not a chance, young lady. One of your teachers called a few minutes ago. Said you have something for me?"

She holds out her hand. The other's gripping the edge of her golden cigarette holder.

I never even knew she smoked, now she's a chain-smoker?

"I don't know what you're—"

She clicks her fingers at me like I'm a dog, and I bite off the rest of my pathetic excuse.

I storm up to her, rip my detention slip from my pocket, and hold it out for her to take.

She snatches it from me, drags at her cigarette as she scans it, and then hands it back.

"You should have gotten two weeks."

My shoulders slump. I shake my head and open my mouth, but she beats me to it.

"Go upstairs and get ready for bed."

"I'm going out," I say slowly, in case she's already going senile.

"You're grounded."

My mouth falls open. "You can't ground me."

Marigold tilts her head. "Really? Did I miss a few months and not realize you've turned eighteen already?"

I bite so hard at my bottom lip, a piece of skin comes off. I swallow it down, grimace at Marigold, and storm upstairs.

CHAPTER TWENTY-FOUR

BRIAR

I'm woken by a new message from Addy. I have to read it twice to get it through my sleep-fogged mind, and then I let out a dry laugh and collapse back on my bed.

I try calling the number, pissed off with this childish back-and-forth, but it goes straight to voice mail.

Her phone's off.

So I call Marcus instead.

"You were right," I say as I head downstairs to get a cup of coffee. "She wants money."

"How much?"

"Five hundred kay."

"Shit," Marcus breathes into the phone. "You even got that kind of green laying around?"

"Jesus, no. How rich do you think we are?"

"Pretty fucking rich," Marcus says, but it sounds as if he's about to laugh.

"You think this is funny?"

"Dude, relax. If she wants money, it means she can be bought. Which means she's probably willing to negotiate."

"Didn't sound like it. And anyway, what guarantee do I have she'll get rid of that video? She could keep it and then pull this gig a month down the line."

Marcus is quiet for so long, I glance at my phone's screen to make sure we're still connected.

"You there?"

"Yeah. Lemme think on it." Marcus hangs up and I toss my phone onto the kitchen's granite countertop.

I drum my fingers, waiting for Marcus to phone back, but by the time my cup's finished, he still hasn't.

Fuck this. I'm done having Addison Green fuck with my life. If her plan was to get a rise out of me, then it worked. But she seems to forget—keep poking at that tiger, and he might get pissed off enough to break open his cage.

And then you'd just better run like hell.

I stick around in the hall at Lavish Prep that morning, hoping to catch a glimpse of Addison, but I have a feeling she's not gonna show up today.

Why should she? She's got such a tight grip on my balls, she doesn't even have to be in range to squeeze hard enough to make me puke.

I'm just about to head to homeroom when I spot a dark head bobbing through the crowd. If I hadn't been so tall, I would probably have missed her—Indi being a few inches shorter than most of the seniors.

She spots me and instead of dropping her eyes or changing direction, heads straight over.

I lean my hip against my locker, a smug smile touching my mouth as she gets near. Strange how just the sight of her can change my mood.

"Morning, Angel," I say.

Astonishingly, instead of giving me one of her usual death glares, she smiles. It's a bit stiff, but it's a fucking smile.

What the fuck?

"Morning." She looks around, and then turns back to me and shrugs. "You seen Addy anywhere?"

I bark out a laugh. "Yeah, I keep real close tabs on her."

"So that's a no?"

I narrow my eyes at Indi. What fucking game is she playing? A comment like that would have deserved some snarky response, not a polite reply.

Then I remember about our talk in the woods yesterday. I guess, for this chick, every day's a roll of the dice. I rub the back of my neck, and turn up my smile a little.

"Think she's off sick," I say.

"Shit." Indi shakes her head and lets out a long sigh. Then she glances up at me through her lashes.

My body straightens on cue.

That look makes my nether regions start paying way more attention to this conversation than before.

"You busy?" she asks. "I don't know if you smoke, but I usually have a morning blunt with Addy, and now I can't find her, and I just thought...maybe..." And then she bites her bottom lip.

The fuck did I just get a semi for? I turn back to my locker and open it again as if I forgot to take something out, willing my dick to get its head out of the fucking gutter. I shove an extra textbook into my backpack and close the door again.

I pivot. She's holding one side of her blazer away from her small, curvy body. It takes me way too fucking long to see anything more than her cotton shirt clinging to her perky little tits. In fact, she has to wiggle the joint she's letting peek from her pocket before I spot it.

"Oh, yeah. Okay. Sure." I rip away my hand from the back of my neck and nod at her.

She smiles and lets out a rough laugh that makes my skin grow warm. "You okay?"

"Yeah, sure. Just…" I grab her elbow and hurriedly steer her through the crowd of students milling about the hallway. "We probably shouldn't be seen together."

"Right, detention and shit." She laughs again. "My first time, but probably not yours, right?"

I let out a strangled laugh and hesitate. We'll be in shit if we're spotted anywhere on the grounds.

"We could just drive around the block?" Indi says.

I glance down at her and do a double take, but in that instant her expression changes.

"Yeah, sure. Sounds good." I release her and head for my car.

Was I imagining it, or had there been trepidation in her eyes?

No, of course not. Only time I've ever seen anything resembling fright in those fierce eyes of hers was when I had her pinned against a tree.

And she wouldn't suggest we go someplace quiet if she was scared of that happening again.

I hesitate at my car door and glance back over my shoulder. She's standing a few yards away, a hand on the strap of her backpack, no expression on her face.

So why is she suggesting this?

But there's no time to give it more thought—as if she comes to some kind of decision, Indi heads for me again.

This time, she's wearing an expression I'm more familiar with.

Determination.

INDI

Briar's car smells just like him, but with hints of leather and car polish thrown in for extra manliness. I won't lie, the inside of his Mustang is as stunning at the exterior—white, red-trimmed bucket seats, a red console, and immaculate everything.

A gift? He sure looks after it as if it were one.

And it suits him like a well-worn glove.

I run my hands over the leather console, my fingertips thrilling at the feel of the supple leather. Briar climbs into the driver's seat and watches me before turning the ignition.

"Like it?" he asks.

He twists, sliding an arm behind my seat as he stares out through the rear windshield. I jerk at his unexpected closeness before I can stop myself, and the tiny twitch of his mouth tells me he noticed.

Shit, Indi, get a fucking grip. He's supposed to think you're crushing hard, not pissing yourself with fear.

Am I doing the right thing? Will this hare-brained plan of mine even work? I wish I could have spoken with Addy before making a decision but…Seems she's been lying to me again. Or, at least, withholding rather important fucking intel.

I mean, she must have something solid on Briar, right? Else he wouldn't have sounded so pissed off last night. But why did she hold onto it until now? Why didn't she give it over to the police? Why didn't she *tell me*?

Thoughts like these drove furrows through my mind as they raced back and forth last night.

It doesn't matter what Addy has—I can't trust her anymore. And this thing has gone further than rape and a dodgy suicide.

Marcus and Briar conspired. Who's to say they didn't have this planned out like cold-blooded murderers?

Boys like these…they become the type of men who torture and kill and then set houses on fire.

Even just for the sake of my own sanity, I have to find out what happened to Jessica.

"You try calling Addison?" Briar asks in a tight voice as he guides his Mustang out of the school gates.

"Phone's off." I toy with a button on my blazer, doing my best to avoid eye contact.

I shift a little, shrugging my shoulders. I left my hair down this morning—and I even fucking brushed it—but now it's just irritating me. My makeup went up in smoke, and Marigold was still in her room when I left this morning, so I couldn't sneak in and steal hers.

Mother's room was locked again.

So I put a brush through my hair, left off my tie, and undid the first three buttons of my shirt.

Which reminds me…

"Gosh, is it just me or is it getting warmer every day?" My voice cracks a little, no doubt because improv is far down on my list of polished skills, and I blush as I struggle out of my blazer. "That's better," I say through a sigh, and hastily turn to look out the window in case Briar catches sight of my red cheeks.

Holy shit, I didn't think this was going to be so difficult. Honestly, I thought I'd be more scared than flustered.

But again, just like it has before, Briar's no longer some monster straight out of a Grim Brother's story.

"Haven't really noticed," he says. "Should I turn on the—?"

"No, this is fine." I roll down the window and tug the joint from my blazer. It got a bit smushed from my struggle to undress, but I squeeze it back into shape and look around for a lighter. Briar pulls a gleaming zippo from his pocket and holds it out for me, already lit, without taking his eyes off the road.

So smooth, Briar. Did you pull these moves on Jessica too?

I light the joint and puff on it until it takes. Briar watches me from the corner of his eye, and then indicates and turns away from Lavish Prep.

My heart kicks up a notch, but I manage a semi-casual, "Where are we going?" I pass across the joint, but he waves it away.

My limbs start tingling. Fuck, he isn't going to smoke? Is that so he can make sure he has the upper hand?

I force a deep inhale, and smile at him as I shrug and take back the joint.

Fuck it. Might as well meet my maker while I'm high as a fucking kite.

"Thought we'd go pay Addison a visit. Make sure she's all right," Briar says.

Puffs of smoke escape my mouth as I splutter out, "What?"

Briar gives me a strange smile. "You don't want to check on your friend?"

"Of course. I mean, yeah. Obviously." I nod a few times, and then wonder if I should get more stoned. Before I can come to a decision, Briar turns down another road and starts slowing. Ahead, a golf estate's boom bars our way.

Oh, thank God. No way Addy would let us—

Briar leans across the car. I cringe away, thinking he's gonna grab my leg, but instead he just pops open the glove compartment. He rummages around inside and comes out with a remote control. When he presses it, the boom lifts.

Fuck.

"That's…convenient," I say quietly, repositioning myself on the seat so I don't look like I was trying to climb out the window.

"Dylan stays here."

Course he does, whoever the fuck he is.

Briar drives to one of the units and parks outside. There are no cars in the drive, not even Addy's little sports car.

"Guess she's not home," I quip, before stabbing a thumb over my shoulder. "At least we checked. Should probably get out of here before—"

Briar's hand closes over my thigh. My skirt's up to mid-thigh, and his hand easily fills the space between my knee and the hem of my skirt.

It's warm, firm, so fucking big. When he speaks, I realize I was staring at his long fingers. "We should at least knock, right?"

I don't turn to look at him, because I can see enough from the corner of my eyes. Plus, he's so close, if I *did* turn, he could kiss me.

And my stupid brain keeps telling me that's somehow a good fucking thing.

"Of course," I manage, fumbling for the door handle.

"Cool." His voice is so smooth, so calm and collected, I know he's up to something. But I don't know him well enough to even try and guess what the fuck his plan is here.

I follow him, glancing around to check if there's anyone in sight as he leads me to the front door. How does he know where Addy stays? Then again, he did date her best friend. He probably picked her up from Addy's house a few times.

The house is a modern, sprawling split level. Briar walks straight up to the front door and knocks, ignoring the buzzer beside the intricately carved paneling.

We wait for a while, and I'm feeling more stoned by the second.

Addy never comes to answer the door.

"Maybe she had errands to run or something," I say, taking a step back and hoping he will take it as our cue to leave.

"Yeah," Briar murmurs, glancing around. "Maybe."

When he turns, the morning sun catches on his hair, turning his sandy strands into sullen gold. He squints at me as he passes, and extends an arm.

I don't move, not sure what he wants, and he ends up draping his arm over my shoulders. "Where's that joint, Angel?"

That pet name sends an illicit tingle through me that I do my best to ignore. "Here?" I whisper back, glancing around. There's an old lady watering her garden a few houses away.

"You paranoid? Fine, we'll go check the back. Maybe they left the door open."

I almost stop walking, but manage to catch myself in time. Briar takes the joint from me, lights it, and hits it hard as he maneuvers me down a side path of cobblestones heading to the back of Addy's house.

"This shit's good," Briar says around the filter, looking down at me as he strokes his thumb down the side of my neck.

Unnecessary goosebumps break out all over my skin.

"It's from Addy's guy," I say, desperate to do anything but blush.

It doesn't work—my cheeks heat up anyway.

Why in the fuck did I think I would be in control in this situation? How? You'd swear I'd started smoking before I thought up this cockamamie plan.

Oh, right. I pictured this happening at school, not in Addy's backyard.

Which, by the way, is fucking gorgeous. The area's completely enclosed—Briar opens an ornate metal gate to let me in—and the walls seem to consist entirely of trailing ivy.

There's an intimate swimming pool, a hot tub, and a closed-off porch. It looks like something out of a home design magazine.

Briar heads straight for the glass sliding doors and tries the handle.

He turns to me and shrugs. "Locked."

"Darn," I say, snapping my fingers and then instantly wishing I hadn't. Note to self—don't ever quit your future day job to take up acting. You suck at it. "Well, best we get back to school. Don't wanna rack up more detention time, do we?"

"Relax," Briar says, hitting the joint as he walks back to me.

God, it should be illegal to look as hot as he does. With his swagger, and the way he's holding that joint, he looks like a young heartthrob actor taking a break between scenes of some gritty romance movie.

Focus, Indi. Or have you forgotten what the whole point of this excursion was?

I straighten, clear my throat, and make grabby hands for the joint. Briar cocks his head, a smirk playing on his mouth as he swaggers closer.

Good God, I think I'm going to combust if he keeps looking at me like that.

I squeeze my thighs together as he walks near and try to snatch the joint as soon as he's close enough. But he lifts his arm, putting it ridiculously out of reach. And then he just keeps walking until he's right up against me. Until I'm forced to take a step back.

Then another.

Another.

"Briar…"

He hits the joint, dips his head.

Before I can manage another protest, his mouth is against mine. His tongue teases my lips apart. Hot, dank smoke pours into me.

I inhale greedily, my hands sliding around the back of his head so I can kiss him back and create a seal around our mouths. For the weed smoke, of course. Not because I could devour this man alive right now.

"Mmm," he murmurs. That vibration flows through my entire fucking body. "Greedy little virgin, aren't you."

"So I like getting high," I say, my lips slipping over his with each word. "Sue me."

"I'd rather fuck you."

Air leaves me in a throaty groan at his words. There's a hand at the small of my back, another on my neck. He's pressing me tight against him, but still walking me backward.

I try to stiffen my legs, but then he kisses me for real, and my world explodes into pure bliss. I lose all motor function, relying on his strong arms to keep me upright as the pressure of his body against mine moves me like a piece in a chess game.

The back of my legs hit something soft but firm. I go, "uh," into his mouth in surprise, and for some reason that makes him growl.

"Jesus fucking Christ," he grumbles, tearing his lips away from mine and instead moving them to my ear. "How the fuck can you make me so horny with one little sound?"

I don't have time to reply—Briar scoops me up and plops me down.

I expect to hit the ground—bricks around here, if I'm not mistaken—but instead I land on something soft.

My eyes flutter open just long enough to take in my surroundings.

He has me on a day bed, the covers drawn back, the beige cushions supporting me.

Fuck.

It's happening.

But I can't let it.

This wasn't the plan, Indi!

I mean...this was *part* of the plan, but the timeline's accelerating waaaay too fast.

Get up.

Shove him away.

Do something, you dumb fucking slut.

So I do the stupidest thing I've ever done. I kiss him.

Briar shoves a hand up my skirt, and scrapes his knuckles over my pussy. My body responds on instinct, arching off the cushions as I let out a long groan.

"Fuck." Briar sounds so pissed off, a shiver of fear races through me. He grazes the side of my neck, my throat, my collarbone. All hard enough to sting.

Indi, get your fucking head straight! You can't give him what he wants. Not yet.

Quid pro quo, you dirty slut.

"Briar, no." I shove at him, wriggle furiously, and sway as I drag myself to my feet.

He lays there like the king of this fucking golf estate, propped on an elbow like yesterday in the woods, and watches me as I start gesticulating wildly.

"This is crazy. We have to get to school. I can't do this. Not now. Sometime, maybe, but not—" I clamp my lips shut, but it's too late.

"Sometime?" Briar drawls as he slowly rises.

God, has he always been this tall? This fucking hot?

"Yeah," I whisper. "Maybe."

He moves to touch me, but I step back in case my entire body revolts against me.

"So why'd you want me alone, huh?" Briar tilts his head. "Do you have any fucking idea what it does to me, to have you so close, and then you just fuck off?"

His voice drops so low, it's as if I'm feeling the vibrations of each word instead of hearing him speak.

I step back, lifting my hands. "I wanted to say sorry."

He stops, frowns. "What?"

"For yesterday." And then the words just pour out of me. The weed greased the wheels, but honestly, this shit was one of the reasons I couldn't fucking sleep last night.

"I didn't mean to tell you all that shit yesterday. You don't need to know that stuff. No one does."

The edges of Briar's mouth curve up, his lips parting. "Your mother?" he asks quietly, stepping closer.

I should move away, but his eyes narrow and focus on me like blue lasers. I'm pinned in place as effectively as if his hands were on my shoulders, keeping me in place.

"I went too far. I just wanted to…shock you."

He grabs my shoulders. If he pulled me close, I would have fought him, but instead he just dips his head so our eyes are level. "I told you to tell me. I *wanted* to know."

"Doesn't matter." Jesus, fuck, I feel tears coming. I blink furiously, willing them back. I thought I was done with this shit already.

Mom's dead.

Case closed—literally. There's no bringing her back. There will never be justice for the man who fucked and sodomized her with a soda bottle.

No justice for Mom.

No justice for Jess.

No.

Wait.

I *can* do something about Jess. But only if I keep my motherfucking head on straight.

And God, that seems easy as finding unicorn poop right now.

"Indi."

I must have zoned out—Briar's right against me again and I didn't even see him moving.

"I meant what I said," he murmurs. "Give your pain to me, and I'll take it. Every bit of it."

I stare up at him, transfixed by the play of light in his

cerulean eyes. Does he even know how beautiful he is, when he's not scowling or being a massive fucking prick?

"How?" I put my hands on his chest and lean in. "Why?"

"I have experience," he says. His eyes dart all over my face. This time, it doesn't feel like he's scanning me. Instead, it's as if he's searching for something.

"With what? Pain?" The words come out before I can stop them; hot and bitter to boot.

But he doesn't even flinch, he just nods his head. When his eyes lock with mine, something ephemeral flows through me.

Understanding.

Compassion.

Maybe even sympathy.

"My mother died in a car accident when I was thirteen."

My lips part. I want to say I'm sorry, but I know it would be hollow words. I shake my head. "That must have been…"

"Not even close to someone murdering her."

I'm dimly aware that there's no space between us. That his breath washes over my face every time he speaks. That his hip bones, his fading erection, are digging into my belly.

But I can't move.

I'm frozen.

He's right. A car accident—random chance.

Murder? Brutal torture and rape? Nothing random about it.

"Now…Is there something you want to ask me?"

My eyes fly back to Briar. My stomach twists, shooting sour bile up my throat.

Of course I do. More than anything. I swallow. It takes everything I have, but I eventually gather enough courage to ask.

"Did you…" I haul in a breath, but Briar waits, patient as the motherfucking grave.

"Did you rape Jessica?"

The world undulates around me as I wait for him to answer.

My body responds, pulsing and throbbing as if I'm connected on some cosmic level.

Holy shit, that weed was strong.

No, it's not that. It can't be.

It's Briar.

It's this unfathomable connection we have.

I don't understand it one bit—and I don't consider myself a stupid person—but somehow, we're the same.

I should have asked him if he killed her. That's the greater sin here, right? But it doesn't seem important right now. I can't explain it any more than I can explain the fact that I'm still here, allowing him to touch me, allowing him to be part of my world when I should be miles away.

"I…" Briar's throat moves. He looks away, but I grab his jaw and force him to look at me. My heart pounds, and I feel his jaw bunch under my fingertips, but I don't release my grip.

And he doesn't pull away, although it would be the easiest thing in the fucking world for him.

"Did. You. Rape. Her?"

His eyelids droop. His shoulders sag. A soft sigh washes over my face as he briefly squeezes closed his eyes before flaring them wide open.

"I don't know, Indi." When he looks up, his eyes are the softest I've ever seen him. Inside those blue irises, a maelstrom of confusion and frustration swirls.

"I can't remember a fucking thing."

CHAPTER TWENTY-FIVE

BRIAR

We drive back to school in silence while my heart pounds along to some sullen beat. I don't know what happened back there, and I don't like it one bit.

It felt like someone—something—else was steering me. Even when Indi pushed me away, the urge to claw her back, tear off her clothes, and claim her was so strong I almost couldn't fight it.

But I did.

It took more than I thought I ever had in me, but I *fought* it.

And then I told her the truth.

Something I never thought could feel that good. But it should, right? Why the fuck haven't I been doing it since day one?

Did you have sexual intercourse with Jessica Hamilton?

I don't know, officer. I don't fucking know.

But it's not the truth, is it? It's a thinly veiled attempt at a lie.

I know what I saw that morning when I woke up beside Jess. There's no denying that I took her virginity. And if she didn't consent then it's rape.

But is it still a crime if I don't remember doing anything?

What if I slipped into some kind of a fugue state or something? Veroza would back me up on this—that shit's real. When your brain chemistry gets unbalanced enough, shit goes down. Shit you wouldn't remember, even under hypnosis.

But it doesn't add up. I wasn't mentally unbalanced. I was happy as fuck.

Fuck it, I was in love with Jessica. I used to wake feeling like the sun had risen solely to bake me in its beatific rays.

So why would I have fucked out like that? Could it have been the drugs? I'd only done coke once before, and I was on my sixth line when Marcus and I took Jess upstairs to go lie down.

My intentions had been pure, too. I wasn't even thinking about sex. All I wanted was to get Jess somewhere quiet.

Because I was worried about her.

Why was I worried about her? She'd gotten trashed before. We both had. But something was wrong that night. Something—

"You don't want your face to get stuck like that."

I glance at Indi, no idea what to say because my thoughts scatter away like marbles on a mirrored floor.

Her eyebrows draw together. "You okay?"

I hurriedly look back at the road. I had too many tokes on that joint—I feel woozy and lazy and fucking crazy.

And I'm rhyming. That can't be a good sign.

I eventually get out a far from reassuring, "Sure."

Don't look at her. Those hypnotic eyes. That expressive mouth. Keep your eyes on the goddamn road.

"You really don't remember anything?"

Just like Addy, with the constant questions, the nagging, non-fucking-stop. I've told her more than I've told anyone except Marcus, and she still wants more?

"Drop it," I snap.

I catch her flinching from the corner of my eye, but I bite

back the apology brimming on my lips. I've done months's worth of thinking and theorizing on this shit. I'm not gonna keep giving myself grief over it.

It's over.

Whatever happened, happened.

If there's still some karmic debt for me to pay, then I'll pay when the universe is good and ready for me.

Indi licks her lips, and I narrow my eyes as if that will somehow diminish my peripheral vision. It doesn't. If anything, it intensifies it. She sits back in her seat, and I can clearly see her breasts pushing against her shirt.

God, I can so vividly recall every curve of her body gleaming with water. How her back arched and the sound she made when she rubbed herself out on the rim of the bath.

I shift, tugging at my slacks as my dick starts hardening.

I should just have fucked her back there in Addy's yard. Would have been done with all these thoughts, done with her filling every inch of my mind, *done* with losing control.

My hands tighten on the steering wheel.

Thoughts blur through my mind.

There's a camping spot a few miles ahead, if I take the next turn off. I can strip Indi naked, shove her in the backseat of my car, and fuck her till I'm done and finished with her.

Till she's begging me to stop.

Did Jessica beg for me to stop? Did she scream?

I should remember something like that, right? How could I not remember that?

My hand dips down to the indicator, but before I can signal to turn, my phone vibrates in my console. One glance is enough to see the short message on my lock screen.

$250,000.

My heart stops for a second, and then slams against my ribs like a wild animal trying to get out.

Marcus was right.

She's desperate for money.

"That's a lot of dough," Indi says, her voice light. "You buying a new car or something?"

My jaw bunches. I put both hands back on the steering wheel and keep heading for Lavish Prep.

"When did you last speak to her?"

"Addy?" Indi shrugs. "Yesterday afternoon."

"She say anything about me?"

Indi pauses for the longest time. "She always says stuff about you."

I grind my teeth. "Anything specific?"

Indi shakes her head. "No."

She's lying, but I'm not surprised. She's always been on Addison's side. Maybe she even knows about the messages.

Was that what this was? Was she trying to find out if I was going to bend over so Addison can fuck me up the ass? She was reluctant to go to Addy's house, but it could have been part of the act. She probably already knew Addison wasn't there, or wouldn't answer.

Are they *both* setting me up?

I should pull over and kick her out of my fucking car. She can walk back to Lavish, and get extra detention days tacked onto her sentence.

Or…

I reach across and lay my hand on her leg. She twitches, but doesn't move her leg away.

No girl in their right mind would let me touch them. Not unless they had some kind of ulterior motive. My mind scrambles, the weed helping fuck all. But by the time we pull into Lavish Prep's parking lot, something akin to a plan is swilling around in my head.

"This was fun," I say as I pull into my parking spot.

"Yeah," Indi says, not skipping a beat. She turns to me, her face blank before she smiles at me. She moves forward a quarter of an inch, and her lips part.

I could call her out on this ruse of hers, let her know I have her all figured out. Or I can play along, and toy with her until I'm done.

Leaning in, I stop just close enough that my breath whispers over her mouth. "Addison's gonna be pissed off if she sees us together."

"I don't give a fuck."

She's a good actress, my little virgin. I almost want to believe her. I touch my lips to hers.

One tender kiss, so soft my lips are left tingling sulkily when I draw back.

Indi's eyes flutter open, her pupils narrowing like she's coming down from E. She licks her lips and hurriedly sits back in her seat.

"But—" Indi pauses, clears her throat, "we should probably not let her find out. You know. Manners and shit."

Yeah, manners and shit.

I smirk at her and tip an invisible hat. "See you around, my little virgin."

Indi's already pink cheeks darken, and she drops her gaze. Her mouth opens, but she slides out of my car without saying another word.

My eyes drop to my phone. I unlock it and stare at Addison's message.

$250,000.

I let out a low laugh, pressing my eyes closed with my fingertips. I didn't even have to negotiate with her. Maybe if I let her stew longer, she'll end up settling for a few bucks and a goddamn confession.

INDI

My head feels like the teacup ride at an amusement park.

I don't fucking know.

Yeah, right, you fucking psychopath.

It's so easy for them to turn off emotion—because they're only pretending at it. I got to see the real Briar today. It was a spectacular revelation, and he played his part to perfection.

I don't fucking know.

I let out a bitter laugh as I push open the school door. First bell must have just rung, because there are only a handful of students hurrying down the hall.

Except one.

He's not hurrying.

Marcus ambles over to me like he has all the time in the world.

Instead of speeding up, my body slows like I'm trudging through a snowdrift.

He stops walking.

And so do I.

We're only a few feet away from each other, still his hatred washes over me like an icy wave.

He *knows* I know.

He saw me last night.

He's going to—

Marcus stares straight at me until I hear the door whoosh open again behind me, then his eyes dart past me. "There you are," he says, before his eyes are on me again.

"Here I am," Briar says. He walks right past me, even

knocking my arm with his as if he's suddenly gone blind in one eye.

Marcus's gaze dashes back to me, but then Briar has his arm around his shoulder, swiveling him around.

"You're stoned," Marcus says, frowning at Briar.

They could have been brothers with their long legs and narrow waists.

Blood brothers.

Goosebumps break out on my arms, I turn and hurry the other way. If I'm fast enough, I can make it to homeroom before Briar and avoid seeing Marcus again. Avoid his aura of penetrating evil from touching me.

I'm still reeling when I arrive at Ms. Parson's class. I slip into my seat by the door and draw out a notebook, flipping it to a random page. I put my head down and start doodling like my life depends on it, desperate to untangle the spaghetti-mess of thoughts clumped in my head.

I don't get very far.

My phone starts vibrating with an incoming call. When I see the name on the screen, my fingertips start tingling.

Addy.

I could take it in the hallway—there are still a few minutes before the second bell—but that might mean bumping into Briar on his way in. Possibly seeing Marcus again too, depending on where his homeroom is.

Instead, I take a quick look around, turn in my chair, and put my phone to my ear.

"Hey, you okay?" I say.

"I guess," Addy replies in a thick voice, like she's been crying.

"What's wrong?"

"Just…family stuff." Fabric rustles against the speaker. "Listen, I'm not coming to school today, but Maxine told me Dylan's throwing a party."

A party? The fuck do I care?

"Addy, do you have something on Briar?"

But she ignores the question and keeps on talking right over me.

"You should try to get in. I know I said I didn't like your plan but…I think it's the only one that'll work. I'll see if I can work something out but—"

"Addy. Addy, listen—"

"—I might be gone for a few days, so I don't know if—"

"Indi?" At the sound of Ms. Parson's attempt at a stern voice, my stomach drops.

Dammit.

I end the call and slip my phone into my pocket. When I turn around, Ms. Parsons is a few feet from my desk, arms crossed and her rosebud mouth puckered tight.

"No phones in my class," she says, enunciating every word with utter precision. "Understand me?"

Holy crap, I'm obviously not in her good books anymore, am I?

"Sorry, Ms. Parsons."

She lifts her chin, shakes her head, and mutters, "I'm so disappointed in you," as she walks away.

I glare at her. She was the one who suggested the fucking horse rides. What the fuck did she think would happen? Naive little—

"Don't want your face getting stuck that way, Angel."

My eyes snap up and track Briar as he saunters past my table. For a heart-stopping moment, I think he's going to sit behind me. But he winds his way through the aisles and takes his seat in the far back of the class without making eye contact with me again.

I sink back in my seat and run Addy's conversation through my head. When the second bell rings, I almost jump out of my fucking skin. As soon as Ms. Parsons starts reading out the announcements, I smuggle my phone out of my pocket and send her a text.

Do you have evidence against Briar?

I wait, glancing up every millisecond to make sure Ms. Parson's doesn't catch me on my phone and decide to confiscate it.

My message sends but, by the end of homeroom, it still hasn't been delivered to Addy's phone. It's not even half an hour's wait, but those minutes could have been an eternity. A very special kind of hell that I barely survive.

As soon as I'm out the door, the bell for the next period still clanging in my ears, I'm on the phone to Addy.

My call goes straight to voice mail.

What the fuck?

I might be gone for a while…

My mind races back to everything I heard Briar and Marcus discussing last night at the church. Is her family's business really in jeopardy? She never said she was having problems—

What, in the handful of days you've known her? Shocking how private people can be about money.

I laugh quietly at myself as I head for Psychology. I'm so lost in my own thoughts, it takes me a full minute to realize someone's following me like a second shadow.

When I glance over my shoulder, Briar gives me one of his smirky grins. "What up, Angel?"

I face forward and speed up, but I'm a cat trying to outrun a cheetah. Briar skips ahead and stops in front of me. When I try to detour around him, he slides an arm out to stop me. When I try to go the other way, he does the same with his other arm.

Boxing me in with my back to the wall.

Students stream past, and none of them seem the least bit interested in my predicament.

"What do you want?" I ask, and realize my voice isn't anything approaching sexy or seductive, which is a problem. I don't have enough information to change tactics, not yet. Until I can get hold of Addy again, I have to keep up pretenses. I try fluttering my lashes, but I'm not sure if it works.

Briar leans in a little. "You're joining me for lunch."

I tamp down an automatic protest, and give him a coquettish smile. "Oh, sure. Wonderful."

His smile cracks a bit, but then he hitches it up even higher. He grabs my chin, tilts my head back, and plants a chaste kiss on my mouth.

Even that brief contact ignites my body like a fourth of July firework special.

I'm still blinking at his retreating form when I realize I must look like a complete moron, and push away from the wall.

Lunch. Perfect. I can study Briar in his natural environment, perhaps figure out who else in his crooked brood may have had a part in Jessica's murder.

I hardly feel stoned anymore, but as I'm about to step into Psych, I feel eyes on me again.

I want to dismiss it as paranoia, but it's too strong. I pause outside the class, take a step back to study the number above the door as if checking if I'm at the right class. Then I slowly pan my gaze left and right, taking another step back.

I don't think my theatrics fool Marcus though. For one, he doesn't seem to care that I know he's watching me.

Secondly, when our eyes lock, he gives me a smile that makes my skin crawl. He purses his lips and pantomimes a kiss before turning on his heel and walking away.

I'm so shocked I can't move.

What the hell was that? Why would he—?

A hand closes on my shoulder. I gasp and whirl around in fright.

Mr. Veroza studies me. When he opens his mouth, I'm sure it's to ask how my relationship with my father was.

"Class has begun, Ms. Virgo."

I nod and hurry inside. As I turn to take my seat, my eyes just happen to lock with Briar's.

No, it wasn't an accident. He was glaring at the door, waiting for me to come in.

And when I sit, I can still feel his eyes on me.

Why do I suddenly regret poking the tiger?

I smile to myself as Indi takes her seat in Psych, looking flustered as fuck. Would never have thought a simple invitation to have lunch would have put such uncertainty in those green eyes of hers, but I guess there's a lot I don't know and can't fathom about her. Like how on earth she thinks her attempts at playing dumb are going unnoticed.

It's hilarious that she thinks fluttering her eyelashes at me will make me forget who she's friends with, or how much I've told her. How much she *knows*.

I don't get the point of this elaborate cat and mouse game, but I'm willing to play along until I grow bored enough to end it. And since I can't get hold of Addison, Indi might be the only way I can figure out how damning the evidence is against me.

I watch her through the rest of the lesson, and from the way she keeps squirming and doing her best not to look around, I know I'm getting under her skin.

I don't want to chat with her in class, not unless I know a teacher won't interrupt us, but it's taking everything I have to keep my cool until lunch.

By the time that bell rings, I feel ready to run a goddamn marathon. I throw my stuff in my locker, watching for Indi to come down the hall, but I don't see her. I linger for a minute or two, and then head for the cafeteria.

Fuck it, I'll wait for her there.

Ten minutes into lunch, it's obvious she's not coming.

Chicken shit little bitch. Honest to God, I didn't peg her for such a coward.

"…haven't R.S.V.P.'d, Briar?"

My attention swarms back to the present as I turn blank eyes to Dylan. "What?"

"My party, man. You gotta like—" Dylan waves a hand "—RSVP and shit."

I almost roll my eyes, but manage to stop myself. He always takes these things too damn seriously. "Yeah, don't think I'll make it."

"What? Why?"

I shrug, and start scanning the cafeteria again.

"Looking for someone?" Marcus asks. I glance over at him, and then down at his food. He hasn't touched it and, judging from the way he's toying with his fork, there are no immediate plans in his future involving the consumption of that congealing Al Fredo.

I shrug. "Wondering if Addison was gonna show."

I'd texted him earlier about Addy's new message, but he'd never even responded. Maybe he meant what he'd said about letting me sort my own shit out. I'd hate to have to remind him that what he did, he did on his volition. He's been in a pissy mood again lately. Could be more shit at home—wouldn't surprise me in the least. I have a feeling if I ask after his dad he'll just fly off the handle. I don't want to straight-up invite him for a sleepover—we're fucking dudes, we don't do that shit—but he needs to know he's welcome to crash, even if we're spitting mad at each other.

"Wanna get a drink this afternoon?"

Marcus shrugs, and eventually gives up on his food. He pushes away his tray and leans back, stretching as he surveys the cafeteria. "Sure, why not."

I slap him on his shoulder, and he gives me a vague smile.

Well, since my little virgin decided to abscond, I might as well dig in to my sandwich. There's one bite gone when everyone around me suddenly goes quiet.

I finish chewing, swallow, and turn in my seat.

Indi's standing a few feet behind my side of the bench, her eyes flittering across all the guys seated around me.

Chicks are trouble, so I don't make a habit of keeping company with them anymore.

Until now.

Until *Indi*.

I'm breaking all my fucking rules for her, and I still have no idea why. She's a liar, friend of the enemy…and the most interesting person I've ever met.

Even now, inches shorter than every guy at this table, completely out of her element, there's nothing approaching uncertainty in her eyes. Instead, she's looking at my crew like she's trying to pinpoint who will crack the first joke at her expense, and take him to task before he opens his mouth.

But no one does. Because I stand up, climb over the bench, and walk up to her.

This wasn't part of anything I'd planned. I'd invited her over here to get her guard down, to see if I could ferret out any juicy morsels Addison might have mentioned in passing.

Now all I want to do is taste her again.

Indi's my new coke. One kiss was all it took to get me

hooked, and now I can't go a few hours without experiencing withdrawal.

Fuck that.

INDI

That's a shit load of eyes on me all of a sudden. I shift my feet a little, and do my best to stare down every guy at the table. I can't wither up like a wallflower now—if I don't show them some backbone, they'll walk all over me.

Briar stands and comes over to me. There's a soft light in his eyes like he's thinking back on some fond memory, and I don't like it. It's not what I've come to expect from him. Then again, he's about as predictable as a goddamn tornado.

Before he can reach me, I take a step back. "I have to study," I blurt out, lifting a hand as if I would stand any chance at stopping him.

But surprisingly, he does. A frown touches his face, but in an instant his smug smile slips back on. "So why the fuck did you come all the way over here to tell me that?"

The condescending tone of his voice brings heat to my cheeks.

Motherfucking prick.

I turn on my heel, but his voice halts me a second later. "You know what, forget it. You weren't that good a fuck anyway, virgin."

I whirl to face him, eyes almost popping from my fucking skull. "What?"

All around me, students start laughing. Most of the guys at

Briar's table are openly smirking at me, and he turns back to them to accept a round of high-fives.

I stumble over my feet in my rush to back up and get the fuck out of this place. Why the hell would he say that? We never—

But he probably told all his friends we did. That's what dickheads like him do, isn't it? They lie and they exaggerate…

And they rape and they murder.

I stop in my tracks. My cheeks are on fire, blood pumping so hard through my veins I barely hear the laughs and the catcalls. I haul in a huge breath, fist my hands, and turn back to Briar.

He's about to sit again, but when he happens to glance over his shoulder and spot me, he pauses and then slowly straightens again.

All that smugness melts from his face, leaving only wary anticipation behind.

Congratulations, you fucking psycho. You landed yourself a wild card.

I cross my arms over my chest, and cock my head. My cheeks are still warm, but I ignore them just as hard as I ignore the murmurs around me.

They grow quiet, and it seems like the entire cafeteria is straining to hear what I'm about to say.

Better make it good.

"Really? You didn't enjoy it?"

Briar's head dips. Now there's open challenge in his eyes, a tiny smile teasing his lush mouth.

He's waiting to see where I'm going with this.

I'm filled with an overwhelming sense of pride in myself. Fuck you, Prince Briar. You don't scare me.

I shrug expressively, even lifting my hands a little. "Maybe next time you should be on top. Might last longer than a minute."

I drop my eyes to his junk long enough that everyone can see where I'm looking. My heart's pounding like a fucking drum, but I feel more alive than I have in a week.

Briar smirks at me and opens his mouth, but I pivot and head for the cafeteria door before he can get a word in.

The hushed silence lasts all of one second before the entire cafeteria erupts into gales of laughter. That sound puts a swagger in my step, and I'm even tempted to whistle a little as I step into the hallway.

But my excellent mood dissolves in a second when I see Mr. Denard heading in my direction. I turn around, but I'm not fast enough—he's already spotted me.

"Ms. Virgo."

Dammit.

I turn and give him a measly little smile. "Sir."

"Don't forget about detention this afternoon." His smile is wide and full of joy. I bet he jerks off to the thought of handing out detention slips.

I hitch up my frosty smile until it feels like my face is gonna crack. "Wouldn't miss it for the world."

His eyes narrow at my open sarcasm but he doesn't call me out for it. Lifting his nose into the air, he strides past me without another word.

Two in one day? Damn, Indi, you're on fire.

BRIAR

This is fucking bull shit. I don't know how she's doing it, but it has to stop. I take the jab as best I can, but she got a solid fucking hit in. I tear out a bite of my sandwich, barely chewing before I force it down my throat.

Fucking bitch.

"Hey, can I invite her to my party?" Dylan asks.

Conversation had barely picked up again, but at his question, it stalls like a car badly in need of new spark plugs.

"You wanna what?" I manage through a growl.

Dylan's grinning at me. I'll be the first to admit, he's not the sharpest tool in the workshop, but he gets by just fine on his charm. "My party."

I put down the rest of my sandwich, dust my hands, and put my palms down flat on the table. Then I'm about to tell Dylan to go fuck himself with a rusty pitchfork, but Marcus cuts in.

"Round two," he says quietly, for my ears alone.

Round...?

I don't turn to him—I'm too busy glaring at Dylan.

Marcus must know I didn't fuck Indi. Is he seriously suggesting I get with her at Dylan's party as revenge for her humiliating me?

I can't deny—it won't take much convincing on my part. I've been wanting to fuck her since day one. But she made it clear in Addy's backyard that she's not interested in sex. Apparently, the extent of Indi's interest in me is to lead me on for fuck knows whatever nefarious purposes.

Still...Booze and Indi?

"Bad idea," I murmur.

"You've had worse."

I let out a soft laugh, and Dylan nods his head, his smile inching up as if he thinks I'm agreeing with him.

Fuck it, maybe I am. I'd like to see Indi at one of Dylan's parties, if only to watch her squirm the entire night. She doesn't strike me as the kind of chick that likes to play dress up.

"Sure, Dylan."

My friend takes his phone from his pocket, but I hold up my hand to stop him. "I'll do the honors."

"Awesome!"

Indi's going to smell this trap a mile away. And after the shit I pulled here, she's no doubt gone cold on me. Lucky for me, I have until tomorrow night to warm her up.

"So you're coming too?" Dylan shoves a few fries into his mouth, his eyes fixed on me.

"Wouldn't miss it for the world."

CHAPTER TWENTY-SEVEN

INDI

As luck would have it, I don't have any classes with Briar for the rest of the day. And it drives me crazy, because I don't even bump into him in the hall, and I'm on tenterhooks to see how he'll respond to me after the shit I said at lunch. But no luck. By the end of the day, my ego's deflated like a birthday balloon a day after the party.

I trudge up the stairs to detention, feeling more than a little apprehensive at seeing Briar again. By now, he'd have recovered and thought up something nasty for me in exchange for embarrassing him in front of the entire school. And I have no choice but to be here in this classroom while he sets his plan in motion.

Room 301 couldn't have made a more perfect prison. For one, it's fucking tiny. The curtains on the windows block out all but the most stubborn chinks of light. I spend a few seconds thinking crazy thoughts about Denard and sunlight before I spot an old-school projector in the middle of the classroom.

Yeah, that makes more sense. But only barely.

Briar's all the way in the back, but the rest of the kids are all in front. There are seven of us in total, and one very righteous looking Denard leaning against a small desk near a projector screen.

As I enter, Denard pushes away from the desk and saunters over to me. He sticks out an arm, and for a terrifying moment I think he's going to touch me.

Cold, dry fingers and long nails—the stuff of nightmares.

Instead, he flicks off the lights.

"You're late, Ms. Virgo," Denard says as he walks back to his desk.

I barely manage not to roll my eyes. "Sorry, Sir."

He pulls his mouth to the side, but then flicks his fingers at the middle of the row of seats. "You can make up the time tomorrow. I have somewhere to be this afternoon."

Coffin shopping, perhaps?

There are enough chinks in the curtains to allow a little ambiance to filter through, but I still bump my knee on one of the seats as I weave my way past the filled seats. The closest open one is only two seats away from Briar, but it will have to do. As I turn around to sit, I happen to catch his eye.

His expression doesn't change in the slightest.

I sit hurriedly and pile my books on the tiny desk. Dammit, I thought I could use this time to study. I need to complete last weekend's assignment and hand it in to Mr. Veroza tomorrow. Then I have five chapters of Computer Science to catch up on. But it looks like we're about to be subjected to an educational video made in the eighties and narrated by a chain-smoking pedophile.

"So I've been wondering…you really a virgin, or what?"

My spine stiffens, more from the touch of warm breath on my neck than from Briar's question. In the gloom, I hadn't noticed him moving closer. Now he's right behind me, and the tiny fold-away desk between us is obviously not a big enough buffer to keep him away. His presence shouldn't have put me on edge—we're in a classroom full of students, after all, but it does, and that pisses me off.

"Fuck off, you deviant," I whisper, doing my best not to move my lips.

Denard fiddles with the projector until it clicks and whirs to life.

True enough, the gritty title, '*Getting High in High School*' blooms onto the screen. I grimace, and then shiver as Briar blows against the back of my neck.

"You trying to get yourself more detention?" I ask, glancing over my shoulder to glare at him.

He shrugs. "Got nothing better to do."

"Then why the hell not just go to prison, huh?"

Even in the low light, I can see darkness flooding Briar's eyes. He looks away, eyes now trained on the screen. Faded colors paint his face as the projector spews out its ancient lecture.

I face forward and do my best to zone out while the rest of the video plays, but less than a minute later, another breath warms the back of my neck. I stem the temptation of turning around and scowling at Briar. It won't do any good, anyway.

Hands slide over my shoulder. They're so big, his thumbs touch my neck and his pinkies almost don't have enough space.

"Why so tense, Angel?"

I grit my teeth, but I force myself not to say anything.

Why am I tense Briar? Because I'm getting a fucking shoulder rub from a rapist, that's why.

His thumbs stroke the side of my neck.

I immediately look up at Mr. Denard, but the teacher's head is down and he's busy on his cellphone. Everyone else in detention is either catching forty winks or busy on their phones too. Meanwhile, the video is playing so loud, I doubt anyone would hear us having a full-on conversation.

They definitely don't hear him dragging away his desk, or bringing his chair closer to mine.

I feel him shift—there's weight on my shoulders one second, gone the next—and then his knees wrap around my seat.

"You know what I think?" Briar murmurs as he settles down behind me. His breath stirs the fine hairs by my ear, and that makes me squirm in my seat. "I think you're too serious."

Serious about making you pay for what you did, yeah.

God, I wish I could just yell at him. Maybe I should go to the police. It would be my word against theirs but, fuck, it has to do something, right?

This is probably exactly what Addy had to go through all those months ago. Why she went off the rails and had to be told to leave Briar alone.

"You know what'll loosen you up, Angel?"

His hand slides down the front of my chest. He squeezes my breast hard enough to make me bite my lip, and then his hand sinks lower, and lower, and lower.

"Losing your v-card," he whispers, his lips touching my ear.

Fuck.

Fuck!

I should go sit somewhere else. Raise my hand and hope Mr. Denard will take my side for a change.

But if I lead him on, there's a chance we can pick up right where we left off.

I don't fucking know.

No, no more lies. The truth. I will squeeze it out of him one way or the other.

Briar slides his hand around my throat. I'm flung back to my episode in the tub, where the thought of him doing just this tipped me over the edge.

"Was it you?" I murmur, shifting despite myself as his other hand smooths my skirt over my thigh. "Were you in my house?"

Briar's soft chuckle warms the back of my neck and sends another flurry of goosebumps over my skin. "What the hell are you on about?"

It *must* have been him. I *want* it to be him. And how fucked up is that? Beyond-thought fucked up, that's what.

Briar grabs the edge of my skirt and draws it up my leg. Higher. Higher. Where his fingertips brush my skin, electric tingles crackle like branches of lightning through a stormy sky.

"You're tensing up again."

"Because you have your hand up my fucking skirt."

"Relax, Angel. I can't finger you out of being a virgin."

I let out a soft huff, and then clamp my lips shut when his fingertips reach the seam of my underwear.

If Denard was to look up... If any of the five students in front of us happened to look back…

I shift in my seat, and grab Briar's wrist. "Stop."

"Why?"

"Because—"

'Because I said so,' suddenly doesn't seem a good enough reason when Briar runs a knuckle over my underwear… right above my clit.

My head falls back before I can catch it, and our cheeks brush. I sit up straight immediately, blinking to force myself to focus. I squeeze his wrist hard, but he just strokes me again.

"You really don't understand the meaning of the word, no, do you?" I say it through a soft laugh, trying to be glib, failing miserably.

He grabs my pussy and squeezes so hard I almost gasp out loud. Luckily, I seal my lips just in time and sit up real straight.

My entire body responds to that merciless grip. Where I was getting all tingly and nice, I'm suddenly aching, the feeling so close to pain I can't decide if it's good or bad.

"And you don't know when to shut up," he whispers. "I'm doing you a fucking favor."

Heat blooms on my cheeks. I dig my fingers into his wrist until I feel wetness pooling in my nails. "Stop touching me, or I'll scream."

Something brushes the side of my neck, and I shiver when I realize it's his mouth. I squeeze his wrist again, but he doesn't notice. Instead, he eases up on my pussy and strokes me again.

The contrast between that fierce grip and his gentle caress makes my core clench like a fist.

What the fuck is wrong with me?

But it doesn't matter how many times I yell that mantra in my head, it doesn't change my body's response.

He's making me wet.

I don't want him to stop.

And I know that makes me some kind of twisted enabler but for the life of me…I don't want him to stop.

BRIAR

This isn't what I'd planned. I was going to tie her shoelaces together again. Maybe push her into the wall on the way out. Whisper obscenities in her ear that I would immediately deny when she ratted me out to Denard.

But that's the problem, see?

She's not fighting me. Sure, she's drawn blood from my wrist, but she could have stopped this a second after I grabbed her tit.

She *wants* me, and that blows my fucking mind.

Maybe she *is* a virgin. That's the only explanation I can come up with. Else why the fuck would she let me grope her like this?

I move my hand away. I stop kissing the side of her neck.

She's done it again. Somehow, this little slip of a girl's gone and made me lose control.

I have to get out of here. Out of this classroom, away from her intoxicating aura. I have to—

Her arm trembles, and that brings me back to the here and now.

Warmth spills from her pussy. Her legs were a little open, and there's still an inch of space between her thighs.

I could leave, but then she'd have won. Because Indi fucking Virgo doesn't seem to understand that I have all the power here. If I want to finger-fuck her in detention, then that's exactly what I'm gonna do.

"Open your legs," I whisper into her ear.

When she doesn't move, doesn't obey, I nip her earlobe.

She squirms frantically before opening her thighs.

"More." When she obeys instantly, I lick the side of her neck in reward and feel her shiver against my tongue. "More."

This time, when I run my knuckle over her clit, my skin comes back damp. My cock hardens at the thought that she's wet for me, that she opened her legs for me, that she still hasn't brought an end to her ordeal.

Fuck, how I wish we weren't in class right now.

The things I could do to her…

INDI

When Briar licks the side of my neck, every rational thought scatters. My body tightens and then relaxes, and my legs go as wide as they can.

I don't give a shit if anyone turns around anymore. In fact, I'm not even here anymore. I'm on planet Don't-Give-A-Fuck, and the weather's bea-u-tiful.

Briar slips a finger behind my underwear, and I barely keep back a groan as he traces my entrance with his fingertips.

I can't believe how wet I am, and that's just turning me on even more. As fucked-up wrong as this is, I don't think I've ever felt this good.

Then again, I've never gotten to third base with a guy before. Somehow, my own fingers have never elicited this kind of a response from my body before.

I'm heating up, but my flesh feels cold and prickly.

And then Briar slides his fingers inside me.

Deep inside me.

I arch, grabbing his wrist and forcing those fingers in all the way up to his knuckles.

He lets out a muted growl right by my fucking ear. "Jesus, you're so goddamn wet."

I've got my bottom lip in a death nip. I'm so scared I'll make a sound and get someone's attention. No one's paying us any mind, but fuck, all it takes is one backward glance—

"Take off your underwear."

"What?" The word slips out in a rush of breath. "No!"

For that, he sinks his teeth into the flesh on the side of my neck. I go rigid, panicking as pain flicks through me. Did he break the skin? But when he pulls away, he leaves only a dull throb in his wake.

"Take. It. Off. Or I will."

I slam my legs closed, trapping his hand. He pulls it out and lets out another soft, animalistic sound which I try to ignore. I lift my hips and tug my undies down my legs as fast as I can without making a sound.

"Give them to me."

I wad the damp fabric into a ball, hesitate, and pass it to him over my shoulder.

He's still taking it from me when his fingers wedge between my legs again. I hear him draw breath with another command, but I anticipate him and spread my legs again.

This time, he lets out a pleased murmur against the side of my neck as he slips a finger inside me.

"I like obedient little virgin," he whispers to me. "You should let her out to play more often."

I shudder when his thumb begins massaging my clit. His finger dips in and out, setting a breath taking pace that has my back arching from the seat. Lips touch the side of my neck. My jawline. I turn to him and give him my mouth as he begins strumming my clit.

His smooth, warm lips seize my mouth, drawing a mewl from me as his tongue forces its way between my teeth.

My entire body's vibrating from his touch. Skin stretched tight, breath coming hot and fast. He tastes so sweet, so good, but I can barely stand my attention being divided between his fingers and his mouth.

He abandons my mouth for a second, our air mingling.

"Come for me, my little virgin."

And god, his wish is my command.

He slaps a hand over my mouth a second before an explosive climax crashes into me. My back arches off the chair, and he moves with me, thrusting his fingers hard and fast into my pussy as he ekes out a final shudder with his thumb on my clit.

Then his mouth is on mine, urging a soft mewl as he tastes

me hard and deep. He strokes my pussy, first soft, and then harder.

"Again," he whispers.

The fuck? There's no way—

But then he's inside me again, beckoning me with a finger. I burn and I ache, my core constricting in anticipation.

"Briar, please," I mumble.

I can't. Not again. Not like this. Because I know I'll make a noise, something to attract attention. And then I'll get suspended, never mind fucking detention, and Marigold will be gloating at me as she watches me pack up my shit—

There's a loud *clack-clack-clack* from the projector less than a yard away from us.

I slam my thighs closed and yank away Briar's hand, smoothing down my skirt all in one go.

I face forward with burning cheeks and flustered breath, blinking furiously to try and focus my gaze.

Denard glances over at us, but I guess in the dark it doesn't look like anything suspicious was going on.

"See you tomorrow," he says, addressing the class as a whole, before heading for the exit.

He flicks on the light as he leaves.

The students in front of us stand in a rush, chairs scraping back over the hardwood floor. One or two of them glance back at me, and I hastily drop my chin to my chest.

"Stay behind," Briar murmurs in my ear.

Another command, but this one I refuse. I shoot to my feet, grab up my books, and rush for the exit. I knock into a few students on my way out, but I don't bother looking back.

Halfway down to the second floor of Lavish Prep, I remember I'm not wearing any underwear.

Grabbing the hem of my skirt, I keep it flattened against my leg as I do my best to run down the stairs.

I barely make it to my car in time before tears flash, hot and torrid, down my face.

Clapping both hands over my eyes, I cry myself out, fervently hoping that no one's bothered enough to look my way.

When I'm all petered out, I push hair out of my face, drag a hand over my nose, and let out a harsh breath.

Fuck this.

I grab the steering wheel with both hands, inhale steadily, and let out a long, slow breath through pursed lips.

Briar's just digging himself deeper in this grave of his. All of this is anecdotal—the woods, the fence, the forest, Addy's backyard, detention.

But it doesn't have to be just my word against his. In this day and age, proof is but a cellphone camera away.

I climb into my Mustang wearing a shit-eating grin and hum a nonsense tune to myself as I head home. I have to start getting Indi in trouble more often—especially if I can spend every detention with her.

My fuck, those sounds she made. The way she clamped around my fingers when she came…

I shift in my seat, but I don't will my erection to fade. This time, I relish it. I don't care how wrong it is letting myself get this close to her. I'm on a high I haven't been since Jess—

Squeezing my eyes shut, I shake my head. When my eyes pop open, it's to glare at the station wagon in front of me.

Now I get it.

When I'm with Indi, I forget that I'm a monster. That's why I can't get enough of her. If it hadn't been for Addy, we could have been perfect together. But the past will always creep in and contaminate what we could have had.

My phone rings, and I answer it through my car's Bluetooth audio system.

"Yeah?"

"Hey, bro."

I blink. Why the hell does Marcus sound so fucked off? "Hey, man, what's up?"

The brief silence that follows weighs a ton. "You still coming through or what?"

Coming through…?

Fuck.

Fuck!

"Shit, man, I forgot I had detention."

"Detention," Marcus repeats.

"Yeah, I told you yesterday. 'Cos of that shit with—" I cut off before I say her name, but that doesn't make it any better.

"That's cool man."

I blink, mouth still open to protest. "Oh. Okay."

What the fuck? I expected a meltdown of epic proportions.

"So you still coming through?" Marcus asks.

"Yeah. Sure." I glance in the rearview mirror and put on my indicator. "Be there in five."

We're two beers in when things start getting weird.

"Dunno what I'm going to do," Marcus says.

We'd been talking about coach's obsession with the 46 defense.

"About what?" I don't look at him, instead inspecting the rows of bottles stretched in front of us.

"Brandon's being a fucking prick."

"He's back already?"

Marcus shakes his head. "Called me. Wants me working this weekend."

"This close to finals?"

Marcus runs the rim of his beer glass against the bar's scarred surface. "Doesn't give a shit about that."

"He should. Your grades—"

"Mean nothing." Marcus drags at his cigarette before crushing out the filter in our ashtray. "He told me attorneys won't make close to what I will, working for him."

I bark out a laugh, but my face falls when Marcus turns blackly somber eyes on me.

"Dude, what does that even mean? There's no way you can make—"

"Not the security company," Marcus says, his eyes and voice dropping simultaneously. He leans in. "Brandon…his money never came from the company."

I sit back, my eyebrows lifting to my hairline. "Then where?"

Marcus shrugs a little, and then takes out his vape. He offers it to me, but I wave it away—I'm much more interested in what he's got to say than in getting high.

"My dad's into some dodgy shit, okay?" Marcus hits his vape again, considers it, and then slips it back into his pocket. He shakes loose a cigarette, and this time when he offers I accept. I cup my hands around it to light it, and hitch up one foot so it's on the highest rung of the bar stool. "Dodgy how?"

"Probably best if you don't know," Marcus says, his eyes going everywhere except to mine. He seems nervous, but it doesn't look as if this is news to him.

"You've known about this?"

"Yeah," he says, rolling the tip of his cigarette around in the ashtray until the ash forms a peak. "Helped him before. But…" He swipes at the air with his hand.

What the fuck is he trying to spit out? I do my best to be patient, but I realize I'm drumming my fingers on the table the same time Marcus does.

His spine snaps straight, and he downs the rest of his drink. "Forget it."

"No, man, don't—" I grab his shoulder and squeeze. "Just say what you gotta say."

Marcus shrugs off my hand, but after another pull at his cigarette, his dark eyes dart over to me and fix.

"The first time he asked…" He licks his lips. "He caught me on a good day. Or a bad one, I guess. Made it sound easy. So I did it, but it all went to shit. And then…" He shrugs, and lifts the hand holding his cigarette to stroke his jaw. Smoke obscures his face before he sits back as if to get out of that toxic cloud.

"I keep going back and forth—hating it, loving it, hating it. What if I stop hating it?"

"What did he ask you to do?"

Marcus's jaw bunches, and his throat moves as he swallows. But before he can answer, his phone rings.

I hold out my hand, telling him to ignore it, but when he looks at me, I already know he wouldn't dare to.

He pulls out his phone, and his shoulders sag as soon as he sees who it is.

"Marcus."

He lifts his gaze, and a rueful smile raises one side of his mouth. "What you gonna do, right? It's family."

My skin crawls at the bitterness in his words, but he pulls away when I grab him to keep him from leaving. He weaves his way out of the pub, lifting his phone to his ear as soon as he pushes on the door to go out.

Drumming out a relentless staccato on the wood, I finish the rest of my beer and order us another round. Hopefully, Marcus will feel more talkative after another.

What kind of dodgy shit could his father possibly be into? Money laundering? Drugs? Arms?

Christ, the list is endless, now that I think about it. And it's starting to make sense; why his father is always out, the random violence when he comes back. I don't doubt for a minute that you need to have a mean streak to make it big in the criminal underworld.

A hand falls on my shoulder, and I twitch as I'm hauled out of idle speculation.

Marcus sits, and taps his phone against his thigh for a few seconds before putting it away. He opens his mouth, but I don't let him speak.

"I'll call my dad tonight," I say. "If I can get hold of him, then—"

The bartender brings us our beers, and I wait for him to be out of earshot before I continue. "We've got like six months before the end of term. You can stay with me."

Marcus swings his head to look at me, frowning hard. "I can't do that."

"Of course you can," I say through a laugh. "I told you, my dad probably wouldn't even notice. But I'd rather ask, then he doesn't think I'm suddenly drinking twice the amount of beer as usual."

Marcus's lips lift into a phantom smile. "He won't mind?"

"Fuck no!" I lift my beer bottle and tap it against his. "And long as you don't hog the X-Box, then I don't give a fuck either."

Marcus lets out a laugh, but it sounds stiff and uncomfortable.

I clap a hand on his back, and lean in. "Now, wanna hear what I got up to in detention?"

INDI

You could have used my brain as the marshmallow bit for a Smore. I have a book open in front of me, but apparently it's all in pig Latin. No surprise here—I keep daydreaming about what Briar did to me in detention. Every time that happens, it's like I'm right back there. And trying to study while this fucking horny?

Impossible.

I'd been considering taking a long bath for almost fifteen minutes already when the house phone rings.

I turn a page in my textbook and do my best to read the words instead of replaying the sensation of Briar's thumb on my clit.

There's a knock on my bedroom door.

I twist on my bed and scowl at the wooden paneling, but that doesn't stop Marigold from coming inside.

Her mouth is pursed, and her eyes sweep across the room as if she's purposefully trying to find something wrong with this scenario so she can ground me for another month.

"There's a phone call for you," she says when her inspection is complete.

"Who?"

Her eyes narrow a little. "The insurance company."

I frown and scramble off the bed, trailing her to the phone in the hallway. She stands so close to me when I take the call that I can smell stale cigarette smoke mingling with lavender perfume wafting from her. I turn my back and cringe around the phone, feeling like I'm in a prison trying to have phone sex with my beau.

"Hello?"

"May I please speak with Indigo Virgo?"

"Her speaking." I take a quick peek over my shoulder and give my grandmother a glare that she ignores.

"Ms. Virgo, this is Mr. Fallow from the claims department. It regards your insurance claim on the property on 12 Northenden Drive, Lakeview?"

"Yes?" A thick wave of uneasiness washes over me. This is the first time since I called them about my rental car that I've heard back from the insurance company.

"Our claims investigator has submitted his report on the household contents section of your claim. Am I correct in believing that you were denied entry to the premises after the fire?"

"Yes."

Denied entry is putting it mildly. The whole place had been taped up as a crime scene, and it didn't matter how much I yelled, howled, or sobbed at them, they wouldn't let me go inside. After I'd come down off the tranquilizers enough to give my statement to the police, I had to stay with my friend until social services handed me over to Marigold, my closest surviving kin and guardian.

"Our investigator inventoried the remaining undamaged items. Fortunately, several of the high-value items specified on your policy were retrieved undamaged."

"Oh. Good."

I guess this guy does this every day, because you'd think he'd sound happier about the fact that he didn't have to pay out so much money.

God, why couldn't Marigold have handled this shit? My mind's already slipping away to much, *much* more pleasant things.

Detention, for example.

"…item we can confirm missing."

"Sorry?" I say, reluctantly dragging myself back to the present.

"There is one high-value item we can confirm as missing."

Instantly, my mind flashes to the necklace safe in its hiding spot upstairs.

I open my mouth to tell them I have it, but the claims guy doesn't give me a chance to speak.

"Since the value of this item is over five-hundred-thousand, we are now changing the type of claim from fire damage to theft."

Theft? Shit.

"Oh, no, you don't—"

"Our investigator contacted the Lakeview police department today. They have confirmed that they will reopen the case as a murder investigation. You may need to come through to the station to answer some questions, but they will be in contact with you directly to confirm the date and time."

Holy fuck.

If I tell him I have the necklace, they'll close the case again. But the insurance company obviously doesn't want to pay out half-a-mill if they can get the police to actually do their jobs and track down the thief.

The thief is *me*, but that's no one's business but mine.

"Do you think, I mean, the police said there wasn't enough evidence…"

Mr. Fallow lets out a low laugh. "Ms. Virgo, our investigator is one of the best in the country."

Obviously—insurance companies have a monetary obligation to unearth as many fraudulent claims as possible.

"So, what are you saying?"

"His report details several key pieces of evidence the police missed on their first sweep. Including, but not limited to the fact that the upstairs safe had been broken into."

My skin goes ice-cold.

Cigarette smoke envelops me an instant later, and I spin to face Marigold, gesturing her back with a grimace and a flick of my hand. But then I see the dread anticipation in her eyes, and I remember how she'd been sitting on the floor of my mom's old room, chain-smoking and emptying out a tissue box.

She's a hag of a bitch, but it's obvious she loved her daughter as much as I loved my mom.

My face melts, and I hold up my hand, mouthing, "hang on," before leaning against the wall.

"The motive behind this was most definitely theft, Ms. Virgo. Taking into account the fact that it was the only item missing, we must assume that the suspect knew exactly what they were looking for, and already had plans to sell the item."

I shift, nibbling the inside of my lip.

On a scale of one-year community service to a life sentence, how much shit will I get into for lying to an insurance company?

But if no one ever finds out… and if this little fib means the insurance company will keep pushing the police to find the person responsible for murdering my mother…

"Just tell me what you need from me," I say, forcing my voice out steady and strong.

"This will delay the claim payout, unfortunately."

"I don't care. I want to know who did this. I'm sure you do too."

Mr. Fallow's voice drops a little, but it doesn't soften a hair. "Of course, Ms. Virgo. I will be in touch. And again, condolences for your loss."

"Thanks."

I put the phone down, let out a long breath, and turn to Marigold.

The hand holding her golden cigarette holder is trembling. "Tell me," she rasps.

"They're reopening the case." For some reason, telling Marigold is putting tears in my fucking eyes. I blink hard and fast, and try to sound glib. "One of Mom's necklaces is gone, so they think this was a theft, not just…"

Marigold starts nodding, her mouth pursing tight. Then her face crumples up and she lets out a loud sob.

I don't even know I'm moving, but then I'm in her arms, and we're gripping each other so tight I can barely breathe. She's all skin and trembling bones—so frail I can't believe she's still standing.

I don't doubt for a second that I'm doing the right thing. We both need closure, and this is the only way.

After all, the investigator didn't exactly say *what* was missing. Who says I even know what my mother had in that safe? I'm a fucking kid.

I smile into Marigold's shoulder as I sniff and drag a hand over my nose.

Finally something in this fucked-up world is going my way.

My footsteps echo as I enter Lavish Prep's gymnasium. According to my timetable, this is where we have assembly on Fridays. It must be Friday already, or there's a special assembly, because the benches are packed.

But something's not right. The principal's podium is missing and it's too quiet.

With no teachers in sight, the kids should have been chatting and laughing and fidgeting, filling the gymnasium with a hushed cacophony that would only end once the principal called the assembly to order.

But no teachers.

No noise.

Just thousands of blank, expectant faces.

I'm nervous enough to be sweating, but at the same time I'm detached from my body. Like I'm floating, tethered to myself by a very short string as I lumber over the empty floor.

Everyone's looking at me, and it's no wonder. The only thing making any noise right now are my shoes.

Clomp. Squeak. Clomp. Squeak. Clomp.

Someone's behind me. I can feel their presence. But I can't turn; I'm too scared it's Briar.

As if the crowd read my mind, they begin to chant.

Briar.

Briar.

Briar.

Shoes thump on wood. Hands clap.

Briar!

Briar!

Briar!

Why *wouldn't* they cheer for him? They let him walk loose among them as if he's nothing close to the wild predator Addy suspects him of being. An animal I *know* him to be.

My skin feels a size too small.

I try walking faster, but my disengaged body just keeps plodding along at the same pace.

When I try to look behind me, my eyes remain fixed forward.

Briar! Briar! Briar!

Addy's standing at the foot of the benches wearing a pink, glittering cheerleader's outfit that doesn't look anything like Lavish Prep's gold and black uniform.

A pair of pink pom-poms dangles at her side as if she's lost every bit of enthusiasm.

I stop in the center of the gym.

Breath stirs fine hairs against my neck.

Shit, he's so fucking close.

Briar! Briar! Briar!

I want to close my eyes, but they stay wide open. I have no choice but to stare at Addy as she stares back at me.

No, not me.

She's looking past me.

Briar! Briar! Briar!

Why am I stuck? Why can't I move? I don't want to stand here in the middle, not with Briar this close. What if he pulls up my skirt or shoves me to the floor?

My insides grow tighter and tighter.

Briar! Briar! Briar!

Hands slide around my stomach, draw me back. A hand closes around my throat, firm but not too tight.

My core clenches as tingles start spreading through me.

Addy starts to dance. Her pom-poms dazzle, despite how reluctantly she thrusts them into the air. Her lips move, but her chanting comes from everywhere at once, like she's wired to a mic.

Who's number one? He only wants some fun.

Lips touch the side of my neck. My body aches in response, and I melt against the hard body behind me.

Who's perfect too? He's right behind you.

Addy twirls around and does a perfect backflip. When she straightens, there's a pained smile stretching her glossy lips.

The hand around my throat squeezes, while the other trails down my belly, heading for my navel. I shudder, my core clenching tight in pained anticipation as those fingers creep closer and closer.

Who's wild and free? Not you. Not me.

Addy spins around, shoves her pom-poms in my face, and then flips away from me again. Her brown eyes are slitted now, her teeth bared in rage.

Air rattles in my throat as the hand squeezes even tighter. But before I can protest, fingers scrape over my pussy.

I'm stark fucking naked but I remember the sound my shoes made just moments ago. What happened to them?

Shame battles lust which battles utter, desperate confusion. Addy's grin turns ferocious, and she bites at her bottom lip as if trying to be coquettish without really wanting to be.

Blood pools and trickles down her chin.

Give me a B!

Her pom-poms flash up, and she jiggles them until the glittery strands infuse the air with scattered reflections.

Fingers delve inside me. There's a hard cock pressing against my ass, sliding up and down. Inching closer to my pussy.

Give me an R!

I groan as I try to move. I have no idea if it's to get away, or to get closer. The tip of his cock presses against my entrance.

This is the furthest I've ever gone with anyone. The guy who was going to take my virginity at that party last week was too drunk to get more than a semi. But this doesn't feel anything like that. This feels raw, and wrong, and horrible and I don't know why because I know I *want* to fuck Briar. I know it like I know my own name. Like I know my mother's death was my fault.

Give me an I!

The entire crowd screams out the vowel. My knees go soft, but the hand around my throat tightens and drags me up again.

Give me an A!

Something's wrong. It's not just the blood dripping down Addy's chin, splashing onto her trippy cheerleading outfit. It's not just the fact that I'm about to get fucked in front of the entire school without a say in the matter.

Give me an R!

R!

My ears are ringing. I feel wet and tight and so fucking horny

I could die. But there are tears running down my face. The hand around my throat tightens. Tightens.

I gasp, struggle, but I'm pinned too tight.

What does that spell? Addy demands.

A double backflip has her right in front of me, teeth shining dark with blood, eyes lit with anger, frustration, betrayal.

I groan at her, caught on the cusp of an inexplicable climax that feels like it will never reach me.

Then her eyes flicker past me, over my shoulder.

Hands grip me, turn me. They must be Addy's, because that other hand—impossibly—is still around my throat. The other gripping my pussy.

My heart stops beating when I see who was standing behind me. Eyes the color of a basement at midnight consume me.

Marcus smiles, slides a finger deep inside me, and whispers, "Marcus Baker, bitch."

CHAPTER TWENTY-NINE

BRIAR

"**E**vening, Son."

I choke on my own spit as I'm walking into Briar Manor. When I look up, my father's standing in the middle of the kitchen, a wine glass in one hand and a cigarette in the other.

Suddenly, I'm very glad I didn't join Marcus for that last round of shots. It's only nine, but I'm a bit unsteady on my feet.

"Dad," is all I can manage.

"Been keeping well?" he asks, although his gaze is on the dark woods outside the kitchen windows. He's wearing a business suit, hair immaculately combed, freshly shaved.

"Yeah." I nod. "Yeah."

"That's good." He finally turns, and does a double take. "I suppose you didn't receive my message?"

I shake my head. I was distantly aware that my phone vibrated earlier in the evening, but I was deep in discussion with Marcus and hadn't bothered to check.

Dad shrugs. "I won't be here long. Just came to pick up one of my pieces to show a prospective client."

I can't even imagine how much my father makes his

insurance company sweat. That's one of the main reasons he comes home these days—to select a piece of jewelry usually well over the million range, and fly it with him to some far-flung part of the country to brag.

His success rate at scoring new clients is easily close to ninety percent.

"Where to this time?"

"Los Angeles. Actress." He smiles at me then, and for a very brief moment, I'm sickened.

His wife, Natalie hasn't even been dead five years and he's already scouting around for fresh pussy.

But then I realize his smile isn't roguish, it's almost apologetic, and the bitterness inside me subsides. I drop my gaze.

He's not cheating on my mother—he loved her as much as I did. We walked around like ghosts for close to a year after the accident. Not speaking to each other. Barely eating. If it weren't for our staff back then, we'd probably both have died in a dusty old house, leaving nothing but skeletons and grief behind.

In the past, I used to wonder if he was one of those guys that lead multiple lives. The ones that have like two or three families. Different wives, different kids, different jobs. All would include heavy traveling, of course. Sales, consulting, that kind of thing.

Here, at the Briar's, he's a gemologist. Earns a pretty penny designing lux jewelry. His specialty is designs utilizing precious and semi-precious stones as their centerpieces instead of diamonds. Says they're boring as heck, especially since they're hardly as rare as the people buying them think they are. He even designed a necklace for one of the state senators last year.

Wouldn't think someone like my father would have any influence over this town, but gold and jewels are revered like gods in this place. My father's many, many connections make him a big enough deal that sending a few pretty stones someone's way is enough to get them to look the *other* way.

His phone rings, and he answers it with a sedate, "Edward Briar."

His full name is Prince Edward Briar, but my father hates the family name of Prince as much as I do.

As much as grandfather did.

And yet, every generation, the firstborn gets those unwelcome letters thrust upon him, without a say in the matter.

I can change it, of course.

But then I wouldn't see a cent of any of my trust fund, or my inheritance.

"The meeting is at eleven," Eddie says. "I will let you know as soon as I do." Then the call is over, and his phone is back in his pocket.

Another prospective client, or one of his other kids?

"How long you in town for?" I head over to the fridge to grab myself a bottle of water.

"Until Sunday."

"Wow." I give him an appraising stare. "Almost long enough for us to have a conversation."

I immediately regret the comment, but I refuse to apologize. Dad lets out a world-weary sigh, and then all I hear are his dress shoes taking the stairs.

Well done on keeping your temper, Briar. What does it matter anyway? Not like there's anything he would actually enjoy talking to me about.

I snort at myself and chug down half the bottle of water.

I don't have the mental reserve to speak to my father that night. When I wake up, the promise I made Marcus keeps repeating through my head.

I make myself a cup of coffee, hesitate, and then pour a

second cup, adding cream and one sugar. Upstairs, I walk to the end of the hall and rap my knuckles on the bedroom door.

"Come."

Soon as I'm inside his bedroom, I do a quick scan for my father. I find him on the balcony, sitting in an ornate fretwork chair reading the morning newspaper.

"Morning," I say, putting down our coffee cups on the round table that goes with the outdoor set. His balcony is the second largest—the second-level entertainment area takes first spot—and there's more than enough space for both of us to stretch out our legs.

The sun's still coming up in the east, outlining the distant pines in yellow and gold.

"Sorry about last night," I say, doing my best to make my voice sound as sincere as possible. "Was in a mood."

"Perfectly understandable, boy your age. Hormones must be raging."

Instead of replying, I take a sip of my coffee and glance at my dad from the corner of my eye while he reads his newspaper.

Mom used to say we look like twins born two decades apart. I guess she's kinda right—I take mostly after him.

"I, uh, I have a favor to ask."

After I'd decided I'd speak to Dad about Marcus, Indi slipped into my mind like she'd been impatiently waiting her turn since last night.

I need to convince her about Dylan's party. And I know no better way of buying someone's affection than with jewelry.

"What is it?"

"Can I borrow something from your collection? On loan, of course."

My father snaps closed his newspaper and peers at me with narrowed eyes. Then a sparkle touches his eyes. "Of course. Do you have anything specific in mind?"

I twitch my mouth into a lopsided smile. "I was kinda hoping you could help with that."

"That's why I get paid the big bucks."

He brings his coffee cup with, so I bring mine too. He stores his collection inside a vault in his study. I know the combination of his study, but don't have a fucking clue about the vault. Plus, I know he needs a key to open it too, one he wears on a chain around his neck, one I've never seen him without.

I don't bother trying to watch him open the vault—there's no way I can see anything interesting—so I run my eyes over his study instead.

A place for everything, and not a hair out of fucking place. This place is so tidy, it makes my teeth ache.

"Come on," Edward calls out, and I trail him into the vault. It's slightly smaller than a walk-in closet, but it sparkles like the inside of a lit-up diamond. I narrow my eyes a little and squint around, but everything looks as glittery as the last. Stones in every conceivable shape and color vie for my attention.

There should be an epileptic warning on the vault door.

"What complexion does the young lady have?"

My eyes fly to Edward and I frown warily at him.

He lets out a low chuckle. "I'm sorry, was it wrong of me to assume it's for a lady?"

I roll my eyes at him. "Dark hair. Light skin. Green eyes."

My dad grimaces at me. "What is she, a mannequin?"

I cock my head. "What?"

"This 'fair' skin of hers…" Edward looks away. "Is it pale like cream, or a milky tea?"

"I don't…" But then I realize I know the answer. "Cream."

Father turns immediately and heads for a different section of the vault. "Hair black, brown?"

"Dark brown. Messy."

Edward quirks an eyebrow in my direction, but doesn't

comment. It looks like he's narrowing in on a certain area, but heavens knows how.

"And her eyes. Please elaborate."

"Greenish…"

His hand pauses, and he glances at me over his shoulder. "Do try harder, Son."

"Uh…there's a yellow color in the middle."

"Hazel or gold?"

"Gold…" I nod. "Yeah. Gold."

His lips curl into a smile. "And how does she make you feel?"

I blink, and slide my hands under my armpits. "I'm sorry, what now?"

My father narrows his eyes at me. "She makes you feel uncertain?"

"What? No. You're the one doing that."

My father laughs, and turns back. It looks like he's narrowed in on a few pieces with blue and yellow stones.

"When you were last with her, what feeling stayed with you the longest after she left?"

"Regret." I don't know where the word comes from. I don't know how I let it get past my lips. But if my father heard it, he doesn't seem to find it a strange thing for me to say.

"Yes…This is the one."

He swings open a glass door and takes out a bracelet with a trio of blue stones dangling from it.

I take it gingerly, fumble, and then hold it out.

"Wow," I murmur.

"Three ten millimeter round-cut blue sapphires on a platinum chain. And the diamonds are all one carat, of course."

The diamonds he refers to so glibly are embedded along the platinum chain in clusters like a crystalized form of Baby's Breath.

"Wow," I say again, and mean it just as much as I did the first time around.

"I designed it for a client, but he never took it."

My eyes dart up to my father's face. He looks lost in the past. "What? Why? It's fucking beautiful."

"He commissioned a full set, but when it came time to pay, he could only afford the necklace."

"Oh. Isn't that like…breach of contract?"

Edward shakes his head, inhales, and lets out a soft sigh. "He was dying of cancer, Son. Didn't feel right to hold him to it. And he did give me one of his wife's painting in partial payment. The one over the safe."

"Fuck, okay." I close my hand over the bracelet, and then hurriedly open it again. "Can I have a box or something?"

"Sure. Second cupboard on the right." As if he's coming out of a trance, my father waves his hand at me and leaves the vault.

As soon as I'm out, he pushes the door closed. "Leave everything as you found it," he says, heading for the study door. "And make sure to lock up."

"Dad, wait."

"What is it?" He turns back, and it's as if I'm talking to a different person. He looks rushed and almost irritated, as if I'm wasting his time.

But I promised.

"Uh, I'm sure it's okay, but I just wanted to let you know that Marcus is gonna be staying here for a little while."

My dad remains motionless.

"You know, so we can study and stuff," I add lamely.

Still nothing. If anything, it looks like my father's thinking about his upcoming meeting, not what I'm telling him.

"We've got enough room, so—"

"Marcus?" Dad snaps. "Marcus *Baker*?"

"Uh…yeah." I shake my head, and let out a soft laugh. "My friend Marcus."

"You're still friends with that delinquent? I told you to stop seeing him years ago."

My head moves back an inch. "Delinquent?"

"Have you let him into my house?" Father hurries forward, head moving to the side so he can study me from the corner of his eye.

"He's my fucking friend. Why wouldn't I—?"

"No." Dad shakes his head. "No. That boy will *not* set foot in my house. Not now, not ever!"

"What the—?"

But my father flicks his wrist and grimaces at his watch. "I have to leave." When he looks up, his blue eyes are ice. "This isn't up for discussion. That boy doesn't come anywhere near this house, understand?"

My mouth is still open. I want to yell at him, to demand to know what the fuck he's on about, but all I do is nod mutely.

He must take it as acceptance, because then he's gone and I'm left with one of his precious trinkets in hand and a mind whirling like a spinning top.

CHAPTER THIRTY

INDI

I'm late getting to school, and for the first time since arriving at Lavish Prep, it's because of Marigold.

We had breakfast together. It was weird, and awkward, and I don't think I've ever been that aware of the sound of my own chewing before in my life, but it felt like a step. I'm not saying we're BFF's, but something happened in that hallway last night that made us realize that there's a possibility that maybe—*just maybe*—we're not enemies. I guess that's what happens when you find something in common with another human being. In this case, it was Marigold Davis.

Denard looks pointedly at his watch as I slip through the main entrance at one-minute to first bell, and then closes the door soon as I'm through. It locks behind me with such finality that I can't help but glance over my shoulder. Denard follows me, and I decide not to risk stopping at my locker—I can always get my shit out after homeroom.

But as soon as I turn to head up the stairs, Denard's voice calls after me.

"Where do you think you're going, Miss Virgo?"

I pause, my hand on the railing, and frown back at him. "Homeroom?"

"It's Friday." Denard slows a little, turning his head to the side as if waiting for me to realize what that means.

Uh… Fri-yay?

"Assembly, Miss Virgo." He rolls his eyes as he walks past me. "Assembly."

It's my turn to follow Denard, and I do so with a hollow pit for a stomach. This is nothing like the dream I had the other night, but that doesn't stop my fingers from tingling, and my legs threatening to buckle under me.

Denard opens the gymnasium door for me, which catches me off guard. I do this weird little spin to frown at him, and then turn to the interior of the gym when I feel eyes on me.

All the eyes in the entire fucking school.

In an instant, my cheeks are burning. My feet try to tangle under me before I can sort them out, but luckily I spot an empty seat almost right by the door.

Which happens to be the exact same time I see Briar. Because he's the reason there's an empty seat.

He pats the space beside him, giving me a smile that does perverted things to my insides.

"Take a seat," Denard instructs behind me, and I swallow hard and force myself to go sit beside Briar.

"Morning, Angel."

I shift on the seat, grabbing both straps of my backpack and wishing I could worm my way inside it and disappear.

"Morning," I murmur back, keeping my eyes fixed on Denard as he heads over to the middle of the gym floor.

Nothing like my dream. There's a podium here, and a guy that has to be the principal standing nearby, talking with a teacher I'm not familiar with.

I flinch when a hand lands on my thigh.

"What are you doing?"

"I'd consider it pretty obvious," Briar says.

"Stop touching me."

"You weren't complaining yesterday." He inches his hand up, and I shift close enough to the edge of the bench to risk falling off. But Briar's got long arms and the stubbornness of a mule, so he doesn't seem to notice.

Wanna know what *does* notice? My fucking vagina. As if expecting action right here and now—in the middle of an assembly—I start tingling.

I consider standing, but that would mean drawing attention to myself, and that's the last thing I want.

Briar leans closer. "I have something for you."

I glance at him before I can stop myself. "Let me guess. An assembly I'll never forget?" I say dryly.

I wish I had the words back—it makes me think of my dream.

"You'll see."

Around us the benches are quietening down. The principal has taken his podium, but he's busy conferring with Ms. Parsons now.

"But first, I want you to promise me something."

I let out a soft snort. "Nope."

"You haven't even heard—"

"Don't have to. Not promising you anything." I cross my arms over my chest, and my body language screams for an end to the discussion.

"Morning, Lavish Preparatory," comes the principal's voice over the audio system.

The school sends back an unenthusiastic, "Morning Mr. West," but Mr. West nods as if he's been received by a standing ovation.

Briar squeezes my leg, and I glance reluctantly at him,

shrugging.

He smiles as he takes a rectangular, dark velvet box from his blazer. My eyes fix on it suspiciously as he puts it down on my knee.

"What's this?" I whisper.

"Look."

My mouth twitches to the side. I glance up, making sure no one in authority is looking in our direction, then I lever open the lid.

Light catches the blue sapphires inside and makes them sparkle. I snap the box shut again, my eyes boring into Briar's. "What the fuck?"

"Not as self-explanatory as I thought," Briar says, barely moving his lips, "But if you need me to elaborate—"

"I don't want it." I ram the box into the side of his leg.

"Sure?"

"Positive."

"Not even if you get to wear it to Dylan's party tonight?"

I glare at Briar, but he's staring at the principal, a faint smile on his face.

I'd forgotten about the party. About my promise to Addy. Does it matter that she's pulled a disappearing act if I swore that I would uncover Briar for the savage we both know him to be?

But something's not right. This is too convenient, the timing too perfect.

"Why?"

Briar's smile hitches up, but he doesn't look at me. "I think it would look good on you."

"I mean, *the party*. Why do you want to go with me?"

Briar lets out a low chuckle. I fumble with the box as Briar pushes it back onto my lap. "I haven't said—"

"But you will." When he finally looks at me, a thrill chases through my body that converges at my core. "Because we both know what's going to happen tonight."

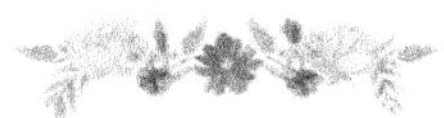

A *Simple Affair*
Hosted by Dylan Steward
15 Serenity Lane, Devil's Creek Golf Estate
22h00 till Late
Strictly black-tie

I stare at the image messaged to me by an unknown number a few minutes after assembly this morning. Fuck knows how the person who sent it *got* my number, but that's not really top of my mind right now.

A Simple Affair? This party doesn't sound simple at all. And what high school kid arranges a black-tie party? Or is that code for something else…?

I would have asked Addy, but she isn't at school today, and her phone is still off. I went to the office to ask after her, but they refused to hand out any details.

Guess I'll have to figure out the logistics by myself. It sucks, because my plan involved her as my accomplice. I have no idea how I'm supposed to pull this off without her.

I should be paying attention to Mrs. Winslow's lecture on sanitation policy in developing countries, but I swear she's speaking Ancient Sumerian or something equally as cryptic. All I can think about is the jewelry box in my pocket. When Mrs. Winslow starts writing out our homework on the board, I slip the box from my pocket and take out the delicate bracelet with its mesmerizing stones.

I let the bracelet slip through my fingers, twisting and turning the sapphires so they catch the light.

God, it's beautiful.

Which brings up so many questions, least of all—

We both know what's going to happen tonight.

I squeeze shut my eyes and inhale deep. No, Briar. You *think* you know what's going to happen, but you've got no fucking clue.

As I slip the bracelet back inside its box, I feel eyes on me. I put the box in my pocket and take a quick peek around the classroom.

Marcus is openly staring at me, his dark eyes as unreadable as his blank face.

I hurriedly face forward again, and start copying our homework into my notebook. As much as I try to ignore it, I can feel those black eyes on me for the rest of the lesson.

Will he be there tonight?

Fuck, why wouldn't he? He and Briar seem inseparable.

Does he have a date?

Why the fuck do I care? I have more important things to think about.

Like what the hell I'm going to wear.

BRIAR

When I spot Indi leaning against the wall of classroom 301, a smile twitches at my mouth. She's staring at something in her hand, and as soon as I come close enough to see it sparkle, my suspicion as to what it is is confirmed.

"Guess I'm not the only one who likes pretty things."

Indi starts, her hand closing guiltily over the sapphires. She slips the chain back into the box and shoves it into her blazer.

Her glare slides right off when I slip my hand behind her neck, draw her close, and bring her close enough to kiss.

Stiffening against me, her eyes dart over mine, anger swiftly replaced with confusion.

"I'll have to take it back if you say no," I murmur.

Her neck muscles tense under my fingers. "I don't have anything to wear."

"Dylan won't be amused if you arrive naked."

Color touches her cheeks, and she drops her eyes. "I mean… I don't really have—"

"Now that can't be true. You've gotta have something in your closet."

Indi's eyes narrow. "Yeah, I used to. Then some fucker burned down my house, remember?"

She steps back, tugs my hand off her neck, and walks away, turning her back to me.

Shit. How the fuck could I have forgotten about that?

My hand curls into a fist, and I thump it against the wall a few times as I stare at the back of Indi's head.

I step up behind her, and grab her stomach when she tries to step away. Gentle though, just enough pressure to keep her in place.

"There's a boutique in downtown Lavish. When we're done here—"

"No."

"You don't want a—?"

"I'll be at the party, and I'll be dressed, but it won't be in something you bought me." She tugs my hand off her belly and steps forward, turning and watching me warily as if convinced I would try and grab her again.

What Indi doesn't know is that I can be patient if I want. So I'll wait until we're inside before trying to change her mind.

Because now I can't get the thought of me and Indi alone in a changing room out of my head.

There are a handful of kids ahead of us, some leaning against the wall, others immersed in their phones, waiting for detention to start. One of them murmurs something about Denard being late, and I glance down at my watch. Weird—detention was supposed to start five minutes ago. I've never known Denard to—

"Afternoon, everyone," a voice calls out from behind us.

I turn, frowning at Ms. Parsons as she sweeps past us. "I'm afraid Mr. Denard has taken ill, so if you could all please follow me?"

"Where we going?" one of the kids up front asks.

Ms. Parsons turns, adjusting her glasses with a finger and giving him a wide smile. "I have a heap of fun activities planned for us this afternoon," she says, her eyes running over the small herd of students trailing her. "We'll be starting with some visualization exercises on the lawn. Come on, no time to waste!"

I'd been walking at Indi's side. At Parson's enthusiastic statement, we both break out in a groan. I glance at her, smiling, and she looks up at me and smiles back. But then her face solidifies again, and she surges forward, putting several feet between us.

Patience is my middle name, Indi, and I'm stubborn as fuck too. I meant what I said—tonight I'm making you mine.

You don't get a say in the matter.

CHAPTER THIRTY-ONE

INDI

I thought I had it all figured out, but I'd forgotten one very important element: Marigold Davis. When I arrive home after detention, she's already home and busy with something in the kitchen. I try to sneak past to my room, but she must have the hearing of an arctic fox, because I haven't gone two steps before she calls out to me.

"Indi? Join me, please."

I roll my eyes and drop my backpack on the stairs. Sweet cinnamon hangs thick in the air, and I can't help but inhale a greedy lungful as I step into the kitchen.

"What you making?"

"*We're* making snickerdoodles. And then shortbread, and some pound cake." Marigold peers at me over her shoulder. "Hurry and go wash your hands. We have a busy afternoon ahead of us."

"I…I have homework."

"And the whole weekend to finish it," Marigold says smoothly.

Fuck.

I hurry down the hall to the guest bathroom and wash my hands. When I come out, my eyes track down the hall to my mom's old bedroom. I glance toward the kitchen. An electric mixer turns on, and I use the noise as cover to race down the hall and try the door.

Locked.

Because why on earth should anything ever be easy?

I roll my eyes and head back to the kitchen. Marigold turns off the mixer, spots me standing idle, and frowns. "Don't just stand there. Make yourself useful."

I walk over to the eye-level oven and peer inside. "Are these ready?"

"What does the timer say?"

Back to good old Marigold, eh? I knew our truce was too good to last. "One-minute twenty-five."

"Then they'll be ready in one-minute twenty-five," Marigold says.

I roll my eyes again, and start clearing up some of the mess on the countertop. "What's all of this for?"

"The church has a fundraiser tomorrow." Marigold looks around and points at a lined baking tray. I bring it over to her, and her eyes dart up to mine before she starts spooning batter on the tray. "We'll be selling these."

We?

No, good God, say it ain't so.

"You know I have finals coming up, right?"

Marigold snorts. "You can't offer up a few hours of your time for God?"

I blink at her, caught off guard. I never knew Mom to be religious, and she'd never mentioned anything about Marigold's affiliations either. Then again, she'd only ever mentioned grandmother in passing.

"I didn't know you…went to church," I finish weakly.

"There's a lot you don't know about me, young lady." Behind us, the timer goes off. "Now get those out of the oven before they burn."

Shortbread, pound cake, *and* snickerdoodles?

So much for the damn party—I'll be lucky if I get out of this kitchen before midnight.

BRIAR

I stare at my reflection, frowning critically at the fit of my black tuxedo. It's a bit tighter in the arms than I'd like—I last wore this a year ago, and I've been bulking up my biceps since then—but I doubt I'll be keeping my jacket on for long. One thing about Dylan's parties? They might all start out as black-tie events, but by the end of the night they usually devolve into wet t-shirt competitions.

I've combed my hair back, but I'm not sure I like the city-slicker look it gives me. I tilt up my chin and adjust my bow tie.

My phone rings, and I answer it with a terse, "Hello?" without checking who's calling.

"Hey, man, you wanna take one car to Dylan's?"

I open my mouth to accept, but then I hesitate. I plan on bringing Indi home with me, and it's gonna be hella awkward if Marcus is hitching a ride.

"Actually, go on ahead. I have a few things to do before I pull through."

"Sure? I don't mind making some stops."

"Yeah, I'll just meet you there."

Marcus is quiet for a second. "Okay, sure."

I bite the inside of my cheek. He doesn't sound happy. He

also sounds as if he started the party early. It's an unspoken agreement—at these types of parties, only one of us drinks. Since the thing with Jess, it's almost always been him doing the drinking. I'd have thought common sense…

"Hey, you'll be keeping an eye on me, right?" I say through a laugh. "Make sure I don't get too wasted?"

Marcus laughs too, and I realize I was imagining things when he says, "Dude, of course. This is my last drink for the night."

I end the call with a smile, and turn back to the mirror. I guess it's good for Indi to see me all cleaned up and shit. Maybe she'll start to realize she's not dealing with some high school kid anymore, but a man.

Because fuck, I definitely don't look like a kid tonight.

There's a parking spot open beside Marcus's SUV—my usual spot. I guide my Mustang into the bay and turn off the ignition, taking a few seconds to soak everything in. Dylan's glass and limestone mansion is almost a mile away from Addy's house. It sits on a small rise looking out on most of the eighteen-hole golf course in the middle of the estate.

There are a ton of cars parked out here. I know Dylan has to jump through hoops every time he has one these shindigs just to get the golf course to accept this amount of strangers inside its boomed-off premises, but he gets it right every time.

I adjust my tie, run my hands through my combed-back hair, and head for the front door. One of the guys from our football team stands nearby, a clipboard in his hand. There's a line of kids waiting to get in, but I ignore them as I head straight for the door,

"Hey, man," I say, walking right up to Jeremiah. "Indi Virgo check in yet?"

Jeremiah consults his clipboard, and then shakes his head. I pat his shoulder. "Let me know when she gets here."

He nods and steps aside, unhitching the red rope so I can pass. I hear murmured complaints from the queue behind me, but none loud enough for me to make out actual words.

The bottom level of the house has a few separate lounge areas, mostly intimate, all crammed with girls in whorish cocktail dresses and uncomfortable guys in suits. There are already some loose ties and rolled-up sleeves—and the party hasn't even begun yet.

I find Dylan in the game room, playing pool with Zak and a few other guys from our team. The music thumping from the dance floor beneath makes it almost impossible to hear anything over the bass track.

I check my watch. Ten minutes to eleven. Did Indi honestly chicken out?

A hand lands on my shoulder, and I'm grinning before I even turn around. "My man," I say, chest-bumping Marcus. He's also wearing a tuxedo, but where mine is a little tight, his seems to be hanging looser than it did last year.

All the drinking, I guess. That, and I barely see him eat anymore.

"Let's get a drink," he mouths, cocking his head back the way I just came in. I slip my phone out, checking the screen to make sure I haven't received any notifications. Jeremiah has my number, so he's bound to call or text when Indi shows up.

"She not here yet?" Marcus says, raising his voice above the music as we head into one of the hallways leading to the smaller kitchen where Dylan keeps his alcohol.

"Not yet." I grin at him. "But she'll come."

Marcus doesn't look convinced, but I ignore him. She *will* be my date tonight. Even if I have to go to her house, throw her over my shoulder, and bring her back here myself.

CHAPTER THIRTY-TWO

INDI

I slide the last tray of shortbread into the oven. Marigold is snoring quietly, head in her arms on the countertop. I set the oven timer, push a strand of hair from my face, and bite back a sigh of relief.

Quarter to midnight.

Hey, it's not a party if it's over before midnight, right? If anything, I'll just be fashionably late.

Wearing what, exactly? My school clothes? A pair of baggy jeans and my hoody?

I creep down the hall and consider the stairs before grabbing the rail. Then my eyes track down the hallway again.

The brief thought that my mother may have left behind something suitable for the party tonight has been pestering me since I tried that locked door hours ago.

Locked, Indi.

But every locked door has a key, right? I just need to find it…

I creep up the stairs and hurry down the hall to Marigold's room. The door creaks a little as I push it open, then I'm inside.

Yup, just as I thought—it's as lifeless and dull as the rest of the house. It seems like the only room in this place that ever had any spirit was my mother's—and that's been a tomb longer than she's been dead.

I scout around for a few minutes, but I come up empty. Marigold doesn't have a drawer of trinkets, or a jewelry box, or any reasonable, logical place to hide a key.

Which means it's probably on her person.

I let out a sigh, and start opening her closets. But after tugging out the fifth shapeless, beige dress, I give up.

On her person…

I stand at the entrance to the kitchen, pushing my bottom lip against my teeth with a thumb so I can nibble it real good.

Worst case scenario? Marigold wakes up and thinks I was about to molest her. Honestly, she probably considers me a no-good deviant to some extent already.

But what if she *doesn't* wake up?

I go up to her and slide my hand in the pocket of her housecoat, but there's nothing in there except some lint and a damp tissue. I grimace and move to the other pocket.

My searching fingertips are met with the cold, jagged edge of a key.

Yes!

As I draw the key from her pocket, it catches on something and tugs at her coat.

Marigold wakes with a snort.

I drop to my knees behind her chair, not daring to breathe.

"Indi?"

The chair scrapes back, and I'm barely nimble enough to scamper back before it can slam into my face.

Marigold walks around the kitchen island, and I wait until she's standing in front of the oven before dashing out of the kitchen. I stand beside the hallway phone for a second to catch my breath, and then wait till the count of ten before easing up the stairs. They all squeak, of course, but I'm hoping the sound won't carry far enough for Marigold to hear. Especially since she's started mumbling about shortbread and the oven door and I don't know what other nonsense.

I slip into my room, close the door, and take a deep breath.

That's when I see my phone's light flickering. I hurry over and unlock it.

Addy.

She tried calling, and sent two messages while I was in the kitchen helping Marigold.

I listen to her voice mail first.

"Hey, where are you?" Her words are almost illegible over the bass thump-thump-thumping in the background. "Call me!"

The first message came in a few minutes after her voice mail, and reads:

Where are you?

The second, about thirty minutes later.

?

Shit. Well, I'm kinda glad she decided to turn on her phone again, but the timing couldn't have been worse. When I try and phone her... her phone's off again.

I hesitate for a second, and then send a message back to whoever sent me the image for the invitation to Dylan's party.

I'm running late - Indi.

I send it before I can second guess myself and squeeze my hand around the key buried in my palm.

That's when the stairs start creaking. My eyes go wide.

Marigold's coming to check on me.

I rush over to my bed and jump under the covers. I manage to tug them up to my neck just as my bedroom door opens.

"Indi?" Marigold whispers. "You still awake?"

I remain motionless, and force my chest to rise and fall like a sleeping person's would.

Marigold stays at the doorway for a few seconds before she closes the door and leaves. From the sound of her footsteps, she's headed for her room.

Holy hell, that was close.

I sit up, and jerk in surprise when my phone starts ringing. Addy.

"Hey," I whisper, hunkering down beside my bed as if Marigold's suddenly developed super-human hearing.

"Indi?" Addison yells in my ear. "Can you hear me?"

I cringe, and hurriedly end the call. I'm still busy typing out a message when Addy tries to call again, but I end her call without pausing.

Can't talk. Just text.

I send the message and wait, my lip getting another round of nibbles as time stretches out like taffy.

Addy: You still coming?

Indi: Have to sneak out. No dress, no makeup, no shoes.

Addy: What size?

But I already know Addy's twice my size, bust wise, height wise—practically everything wise. I send her my measurements anyway—for all I know, she has a baby sister that likes glitzy ball gowns.

Addy: Makeup, yes. Shoes, yes. Dress - no.

Indi: Can you pick me up?

Addy: Send me your deets.

I text her my address, and devour more of my inner lip while I wait for her to reply. I twitch at a distant door closing, but it has to be Marigold's en-suite bathroom or something.

Here's hoping, anyway.

Addy: see you in 15.

Shit. That's not a lot of time to get ready. I shove to my feet and grab my backpack from the dresser. It has everything I own inside, so there's no way I'm leaving it behind. Especially since I have this sneaking suspicion that Marigold might be throwing me out of the house tomorrow when she realizes I snuck out in the middle of the night.

My mother's bedroom door opens and I step inside the dark room. The white walls glow everywhere except where the dark shapes of her artwork cover them.

Should I dare to turn on her light?

God, no. If Marigold happens to come downstairs, the light will be a veritable beacon and I don't want to know what happens when Marigold realizes I'm disobeying her. I really, really don't.

My heart pounds in my throat as I open first one closet door and then another. Books, art supplies, rotting cardboard boxes.

This place feels like a museum, but the inside of the closets look more like a rubbish dump. It's as if Marigold took everything that wasn't nailed down in Mom's room and threw it in the closets.

Have these doors ever been opened?

The second to last door has what I want. As it swings open, something deep inside shimmers, despite the lack of light inside this mausoleum.

I reach in and grab a handful of slinky fabric.

Too many precious minutes have already ticked away inside my head, so I grab the fabric and tug it off its hanger. I shove it in my backpack as I'm easing my way out of my grandmother's house.

I spend a second at the backdoor, my hand clasped on the handle, listening.

That's when I see the shoes behind the shrub.

I stare at them for long seconds, minutes even, my brain scrambling to make sense of such an incongruous object. What the fuck is a men's sized pair of sneakers doing tucked behind Marigold's shrubs? My phone vibrates in my pocket, and I abandon idle speculation in favor of creeping around the side of the house.

I doubt Marigold's the type of woman to stare dreamily out of her window at night, but I keep to the shadows as much as I can, anyway, only breaking into a run when I'm obscured by some of the pine trees lining the long drive down to her gates.

Addy left her headlamps on. They illuminate me when I'm a few yards away from the gate. When I press the key fob, I'm entirely convinced that the gates won't open, that Marigold realized I've snuck out, and somehow locked them from inside her house.

But they do open for me.

Addy's passenger door unlocks with a quiet *snick* when I get close. I fall into her seat with a sigh, my backpack bundled against my stomach.

I glance over at her with a smile, and then do a double-take.

"Holy crap, you look fucking stunning," I blurt out.

Addison gives me a faint smile. "Thanks, lesbo." Then she's reversing, her attention on the rearview mirror.

I feel dirty and ruffled and all kinds of unsophisticated sitting beside her in this cute little sports car while she smells of strawberries and cream and I reek of snickerdoodles and despair.

Addy's dashboard clock mocks me with its massive digits.

"It's midnight," I say quietly. "Should we even—"

"What does your hair do when it's wet?" Addy cuts in.

I stare at her. "Uh…?"

"Does it curl, frizz, what?"

"It curls. Like…a lot."

"Good, because there won't be time to straighten it."

"I don't think there's any time for—"

"Shut up so I can drive."

I sink back in my seat, grinning like an idiot.

I'm going to a party. It almost feels like it's too soon, but fuck it…

I'm going to a party, and I'll be fucked if I don't try and enjoy it even a little.

The inside of Addy's house is as neat and contemporary as the exterior. Since I wouldn't dare tell her that I was sucking face with Briar in her backyard, I do my best to 'ooh' and 'ah' most convincingly when we pull up outside her duplex.

"Come on," Addy says, hopping out of her car. "Lots to do, not nearly enough time to do it in."

I follow her inside, but I stall in the living room.

There are boxes everywhere. The furniture's been wrapped in plastic. The walls have faint outlines where framed photos or portraits used to hang, the bare nails jutting out like a child's desiccated fingers.

"Addy?"

But she waves at me and trots up a pair of carpeted stairs without answering.

The house feels empty—where are her parents? But as soon as I step inside her room, the question doesn't seem that important anymore. Most of the room is taken up by a bare mattress, the rest by furniture that looks ready to be loaded into the back of a loading van.

She's busy packing out her makeup right over the sheet of plastic covering her dressing table, almost as if she doesn't see it.

"Addy."

She points to a door leading off her bedroom. "Shower, shave, shampoo. Then get your ass back here. I'm giving you five minutes."

My head's the human equivalent of a hard drive that's in serious need of defragging. And since I can't argue, I obey.

When I emerge from Addy's shower, squeaky clean and smelling like strawberries, she gives me a once over like she can see right through the towel wrapped around my body, and sniffs.

"I don't know if this is gonna work," she says, holding up the dress I shoved into my backpack earlier. "It's…like…really old fashioned."

I couldn't give a fuck if it's more suitable to Neanderthal man —the instant my eyes land on the shimmering silver dress, I'm incapable of looking at anything else.

"It's fucking beautiful," I murmur, walking closer like I'm in some kind of trance.

"Whatev," Addy mutters, and tosses the dress at me. "Don't you even try wearing underwear with that. It'll show." Then she struts over to me with a joint in one hand, and a mascara wand in the other. "Now sit, and let me work my magic."

I hold up a finger, but I don't waste any time grabbing the joint. She lights it for me, her green eyes twinkling as I hit it hard.

"Don't make me look like a whore," I say, wiggling my finger in her face. I extend another finger. "And don't tell me what I can and can't wear with this dress."

Addy cocks her head, but doesn't argue. I sink onto her dressing table's stool and tip my head back so she can apply makeup on my face. Meanwhile, I'm puffing away at her joint and hoping like fuck Marigold went straight to bed without checking my room again.

I'll be the first to admit, I'm probably a bit too sparkly, even for a black-tie event. But fuck it, I haven't felt this pretty in years, and I used to make a point of dressing up whenever I went out back in the day. Mom's cocktail dress drapes me like spun platinum. It hugs my body in all the right places, emphasizing tits and ass as if it was designed by the only heterosexual designer in high fashion.

Maybe it's the makeup. Addy's got a real fine touch—my eyes are big and green but not whorish at all. My lips dark, and full, but nothing resembling those of a prostitute's. My cheekbones glimmer, and this is the first time ever that I've noticed my décolletage.

Addy's shoes seal the deal. Black, understated, two inches high. I manage to walk in them, but only just.

But it's worth all the moments between steps when I'm not sure if I'll ever find the ground again. Because, fuck it, shit looks fantastic two inches up from my usual eye level.

"So you're moving?" I ask, twisting in front of Addy's mirror. I'm perversely fixated on how good this dress makes me look. And also slightly distressed how much I look like my mother, but I'm doing my good darn best to ignore that.

Maybe it's the hair. I don't know what the hell Addy has in her shampoo, but my hair has a life of its own. It tumbles down my back in a raven cascade of bouncy curls I've never seen before.

"Yeah," Addy says quietly. She's behind me, toying with my hair as she sticks a few glittering pins in it and hoists it up into a messy bun. "There's been some shit at my parent's company. We're moving south for a while until it blows over."

"Shit, Addy, that sucks."

She shrugs at me in the mirror and bends down until our heads are level. "Doesn't matter. You know what does matter?" She grips my shoulders and grins at my reflection.

I nod. "Getting even."

"Getting even," she repeats softly. She steps back and claps her hand. "You're ready."

I stand and take one last twirl in front of the mirror.

Fuck, I didn't think it would be possible, but I look amazing.

I hold up a hand. "Shit, hang on. I almost forgot something." I rummage around in my backpack until I find my mother's necklace.

"What's…?" But Addy's voice trails away as she comes to my side. "Fuck, Indi, that's…"

"It was my mother's." I hold it up and try to clasp it at the back of my neck, but Addy bats away my hands.

She secures the clasp and stares at my reflection with wide eyes. "You look gorgeous," she murmurs.

I drop my gaze and grab hold of the sapphire around my neck. The light catches on Briar's bracelet, and I stare at them with wide eyes.

It's as if they were made for each other.

"Let's get going," Addy says, snapping me out of the thought. "Else everyone's gonna be too trashed to notice when we arrive."

BRIAR

After the fifth pool game, I'm ready to leave. It's fucking obvious Indi isn't coming, so there's no point in me hanging around here. Not unless my only motive tonight is getting fucked up.

I head for the main kitchen in search of water and a clear head, and find Marcus cutting up lines of coke on Dylan's granite countertop. A few girls stand nearby, waiting patiently for their turn with the rolled-up dollar bill he's holding. I grab a water and chug down half of it before he realizes I'm nearby.

"Better get some before it's all gone," he says, swiping the back of his hand over his nose as he sniffs.

I shake my head. "Not in the mood for that shit tonight."

"Sure?" Marcus straightens, and one of the girls waiting for her turn at the lines of coke steps up. He grabs her around the waist, spins her around, and starts nuzzling her neck.

I roll my eyes, and I'm about to leave when he calls out, "Dude, she's not coming. No reason you shouldn't enjoy yourself."

I wave at him, shaking my head as I make my way to the front door. Fuck this—I've got a shit-ton of studying to do anyway. If I get a good night's sleep, then I can crack open my textbooks nice and early tomorrow, and get done by latest Sunday afternoon.

I'm trotting downstairs to the main floor when something catches my eye.

A glimmer of silver.

No, platinum.

A slight, yet curvy figure. A mess of dark hair.

Indi.

I stop walking, my hand gripping the railing tight as my phone starts vibrating in my pocket. She has her back to me, and from the expressive hand gestures she's flailing around, she looks mightily pissed off at the doorman.

My legs feel rusted in place, but I force them to take me downstairs.

Jeremiah flinches when I grab his shoulder. I hear something like, "I tried calling, but…" before I steer him out of the way.

"You came," I say like a moron.

Indi spins to face me. Her eyes are impossibly wide, gorgeously luster, unsurprisingly fierce.

"He said it's too late," she says, tilting her head to the side.

"She's with me," I say, my voice dropping several octaves below normal.

I won't lie—I've been spending the past hour and a half drinking in the hopes that I would eventually forget that Indi might show up. I'm more than a little tipsy, and ridiculously glad she's here.

"Me too, right?"

My eyes skip reluctantly past Indi. Addison's standing behind her, a head taller and seventy thousand times as arrogant.

If Indi hadn't grabbed my hand right then, I would have told Addison to fuck off. But when I look down into Indi's imploring gaze, I'm so off-balance, all I can do is nod.

Indi releases my hand, and the pair of them sweep past me without a second glance. I'm left staring at Jeremiah with a frown and an inexplicable urge to take Marcus up on his offer for a line of coke.

Instead, I follow Indi and Addison inside, feeling for all the world like a sheep who's only just realized who the fucking sheepdog in this situation was.

CHAPTER THIRTY-THREE

INDI

This house is a masterpiece of architectural genius. There's nothing cozy or open-plan about it—it's a sprawling collection of intimate lounges and hidey holes that seem custom-made for making out. No wonder Dylan throws these parties on the regular. If this were a club, he'd be making a killing.

Addison has hold of my hand, and I'll be honest, it's the only thing keeping me grounded right now. We had two glasses of wine and a fat blunt while I was getting ready at her house, and since my last meal was a sandwich at lunch, I'm flying pretty fucking high.

The temptation to turn around and see if Briar is still following is powerful, but I know I'll trip and fall if I try. I didn't want to let go of Briar's hand, but Addy's right—tonight, *I'm* in charge. If anything, it will piss him off so much, he's bound to take back control in the worst way.

And we'll be there, ready and waiting to capture every deviant moment.

Addy seems to know this place well. She tugs me after her without hesitation as she weaves around the kids littered throughout Dylan's house. Music thumps in the background, weed and cigarette smoke hang thick in the air, and almost everyone I pass stinks of booze. I haven't seen this many dilated pupils since I last partied at Queenies just outside Lakeview.

Addy sashays us through a kitchen, grabbing a pair of pink drinks from an ice bucket without pausing. The music gets louder. The congestion in the passages thickens.

Heads turn to follow us as we pass. Some envious, some considering, others openly leering.

I glimpse a big open-plan room with two pool tables, a dartboard, and a swarm of kids. Instead of heading inside, Addy leads me down a staircase.

It's dark down here—the only light comes from a projector screen that's playing some freaky fractals and a mirror ball that doesn't seem to be doing much good. Here, the music is a physical entity. It pounds into my body with relentless force, making me hesitate before Addy tugs me after her.

She spins around, hands me one of the pink bottles she swiped from the kitchen, and raises it for a cheer.

"To getting fucked up!" she yells.

"To getting fucked up!" I yell back, and clink our bottles.

Damn, the music is intoxicating. Even as Addy starts shifting to the rhythm, my eyes slide closed. I slip away from the here and now, and lose myself to the track.

I'm rudely drawn back to the present when hands grip around my waist, and I wonder what on earth Addy's doing. But when my eyes fly open, her eyes are locked on someone behind me.

A jumble of strange sensations flood me. That exact look had been in her eyes in that dream—hatred.

Marcus or Briar?

But as soon as I'm drawn back into the hard body behind me, I know it's Briar who's holding me. His smell envelops me, comforts me, arouses me all at the same time. I breathe him in, arching my ass against his groin.

In these shoes, I'm actually the right height for him.

I can't help the coy smile that touches my mouth when I feel him harden against me.

"Let's talk," he says in my ear, his hands sliding over my belly.

"Let's dance," I yell back, not caring if he can hear or not. Addy's turned her back on us as if she can't stand the sight of us dancing together, and it takes sincere effort for me not to giggle at her theatrics.

I spin in Briar's arms, drape my wrists over his shoulders, and start twisting in time with the beat. I'm far from an accomplished dancer, but what I lack in technical training I make up for in enthusiasm.

I can see the battle in his eyes—he wants to maintain eye contact, but his eyelids flutter how badly he wants to look at my curves.

And as soon as he crumbles and his eyes drag over my body, I snap my fingers in front of his face. "Up here!"

His eyes narrow, and his lip lifts up in a snarl. He grabs me and crushes our bodies together. His hands grab hard onto my ass, squeezing me through the dress. With those long fingers of his, he's almost touching my pussy.

I go on tiptoes, trying to move away from his touch, but he just gives me a bemused smile and grabs the back of my neck.

When he kisses me, everything vanishes.

The crowd.

The music.

Everything.

All that's left is the feel of his lips against mine. The urgency of his tongue; how he forces it deep, deep inside my mouth. The hardness of his cock; irrefutable evidence of how much he wants me.

Fuck, it's too much. I honestly hope Addy's paying attention, because I'm about to skip stage two-through-seven of our plan and go straight for the money shot.

BRIAR

It worked. Indi doesn't want to dance anymore. She breaks off our kiss, looking shell shocked and more than a little breathless.

"Come," I tell her, grabbing her hand.

She nods.

I turn and lead her out of the crowded downstairs room Dylan converted into his own private club a year or so back.

There are too many stairs between us and our destination. I start taking them two at a time, then three, until Indi pulls back on my hand.

She swoons away from me, grabbing on the railing and shaking her head.

Too fast?

Fuck it.

Too slow.

I jump down the two stairs between us, scoop her up, and ignore her distressed squeal as I race up the stairs.

"Briar, stop!" But she's laughing so much, she's barely coherent.

I reach the top floor of Dylan's house, and try the first door.

Locked.

The second door's open, but as soon as it swings open there's a yell from inside.

Occupied.

I back out, slamming the door behind me with a growl stemming in the back of my throat. That's why doors have locks, idiots!

Somewhere in the course of arriving here tonight and now, Dylan's house has transformed into a fucking opium den. Every room upstairs is either locked or occupied—the master bedroom by the fucker himself and three girls.

Jesus Christ.

"Briar, slow down. We can—"

"Shut it," I snap.

Sure enough, when I glance down, Indi's mouth is open, and her eyes are twinkling with anger. She squirms and twists hard enough to slip out of my grip. But she only gets two paces before I grab her arm and haul her back to me.

"Too late," I growl. "Should have run when you had the chance, my little virgin."

"Briar!" She yanks at her arm, but I just tighten my grip. "What are you—?"

Instead of letting her finish, I haul her toward me, push her against the wall, and cage her in with my arms. "I told you, we both know what's gonna happen tonight."

She opens her mouth, but words fail her.

Which suits me fucking perfectly.

I grab her ass, relishing the feel of her curves as I hoist her up against the wall. She's still fighting me but, fuck, we both know it doesn't matter.

My hands slide under her glorious dress, and I grab the side of her underwear. Tug. Draw it down her thighs. It gets stuck of course—her legs are wrapped around mine, so there's not much leeway—but I have access to her pussy and that's all I care about right now.

I kiss her. Ferociously, savagely, until she moans against my mouth. I can't make out if those sounds are laden with fear or passion, but I'm way past the point of caring. My need for Indi has surpassed anything remotely humane. I'm ready to burst, like an overripe fruit, if I don't fuck her, right here, right fucking now.

I zip down my fly, wrestle out my cock, and push it against her entrance.

Her wetness coats my crown, my fingers. I break off our kiss and haul much-needed oxygen into my lungs.

"Please, Briar," Indi chokes out.

I have to force my eyes open, and when they do, I see hers are brimming with tears. I swallow down a growl of impatience and rub the tip of my dick over her wet as fuck pussy. "What?" I manage, my voice so thick and low, I'm surprised she can even understand me.

"Not like this," she whispers in a shaking voice. "Please…not like this."

Maybe it's the way she says it. Maybe it's the look in her eyes. No longer fierce as a falcon, but desperate, hopeful, pleading.

I press my cock against her, my body trembling with its need to force my way inside her hot, wet pussy. But when she mewls into my ear, her fingers digging into the back of my neck as if she's bracing herself…

"Fuck," I murmur into her ear. "You're really…?"

I move away, shoving my complaining cock back inside my pants. Indi lets out a tattered sob, but as soon as her shoes touch the ground, the sound cuts off. When I step back, her damp eyes could have belonged to someone else. She glares at me, her mouth in a line and her hands fisted at her sides.

I'd just been kidding with the whole virgin thing.

I don't know why, but this changes everything. Our games, this back and forth. Right now, I feel like a filthy deviant for even attempting to be inside her.

I let my eyes fall down her body, but before I get far, they're drawn back up to her collarbones. I'm not a jewelry guru or any such thing, but I need all the distraction I can right now.

I grab the necklace hanging around her neck. The one that so perfectly matches her bracelet. "This is—"

"Briar! There you are."

My body moves on some subconscious level. I step back and let go of Indi's necklace without thought. From the corner of my eye, I see her shifting from side to side as she tugs up her panties.

Marcus strides up to us wearing a cocky smile, a girl from the cheerleading squad trailing him like a lost lamb.

"You know Jennika, right?"

I blink hard, shake my head. "Yeah, sure…"

Marcus cocks his head to the closest doorway. "She's got something to show you."

"Uh…Marcus…" I tug at my dress shirt, and glance back at Indi. She's glaring at Marcus, but as soon as I look at her, she must feel my eyes on her because she suddenly wraps her arms around herself.

"This isn't the right time…" I say, gesturing weakly at the girl as she comes to a stop beside Marcus.

But he's not looking at me anymore—his gaze is locked on Indi.

No, not her.

Her *necklace*.

"Where did you—?" he starts, pointing at her like she's grown a third arm. But before any of us can react, his face breaks into a warm smile. "Don't you look fucking gorgeous?" he says, cocking his head to the side. "Now I'm getting your vibe, bro."

I step forward warily, but Marcus doesn't move even though his eyes take on the gleam of a voracious predator.

"Makes Jennika here look like a ten-dollar whore," Marcus says.

Jennika squeaks out a protest, scowls at Marcus, and storms away down the hall.

"Dude, that's not—" I start, but I cut off when Marcus steps right up to Indi.

I stick out my arm, blocking him, and he does come up short, but without acknowledging me or the arm in his way.

"Don't you clean up nice?" Marcus says.

From the corner of my eye, I spot Indi grab her necklace in a fist. It makes the bracelet I borrowed for her gleam in the hall's subtle downlights, but Marcus seems less interested in that trinket than the stone around her neck.

I'm not surprised. That sapphire must have set her back half a bar. Or her parents, at least—there's no way she bought something like for herself. A family heirloom, then? Something that wasn't lost in the fire?

Or was that all a fucking lie?

I take a step back, raking my gaze over Indi.

She's dressed to the fucking nines, when just today she told me she didn't even have a dress. It can't be Addy's—Indi would be swimming in even the shortest, tightest thing Addy owns.

Suddenly, I'd rather stick my cock in a fucking vacuum cleaner than put it anywhere near Indigo Virgo.

I push past Marcus, dimly aware that Indi's trying to talk to me, but the super-heated blood rushing through my ears drowns it out.

Fuck her.

Fuck this.

Fuck *everything.*

CHAPTER THIRTY-FOUR

INDI

It's as if Briar was some kind of shield. The moment he turns the corner, I'm no longer protected by his presence. Cue Marcus—who's so fucked, I can't imagine how many drugs he's on. I push against him, my mind still whirling with how close Briar was to fucking me.

Marcus's jaw works feverishly as he steps closer. I keep backing up, but I'm only too aware that I'm running out of hallway with every step.

"I need the bathroom," I say.

"We all need shit, princess." Marcus grabs my necklace, and I freeze. I want to move away, but I'm too scared he'll yank and the chain will break. I can't risk losing the only thing I have left of my mother.

Then why the fuck did you wear it tonight, you egotistical moron?

Marcus's eyes dart up to mine. He smooths a curl away from my forehead, shaking his head. But his eyes aren't on me, not really. They're unfocused, his mouth moving as if he's talking to himself.

And when I catch him saying, "…she looked so peaceful…" I can't bear him being close to me anymore.

So I knee him in the groin.

At least, I *attempt* to knee him in the groin. But just like self-defense courses have become pretty much compulsory for women these days, it seems every dick head in Lavish knows how to sidestep feisty chicks trying to knee them in the cherry popper.

But it doesn't matter that I don't hit my target, because I'm free anyway. That's the thing with men—you drop a bomb next to them and the first thing they do is cup their ball sacks.

I race away from Marcus before I remember that I'm still wearing Addy's suicidal heels.

Which means I *start* running away, trip, fall, skin my knees, and almost twist my motherfucking ankle.

I spin around, plop down on my ass, and start crawling away, already feeling Marcus's hands on my ankles, my legs, my thighs.

But he's just standing there, watching me.

I stop and slowly slide off my shoes while my heart thump-thump-thumps so fucking hard, I swear he can hear it.

When my shoes are off, I stand.

Marcus's eyes track me, but that's it. His shoulders have sagged, and there's no expression on his face.

It's the most terrifying thing I've ever seen.

I back away, swallowing hard and wishing more than anything that I had enough guts to turn and run.

But I just keep backing away until I have to turn the corner to go down the stairs, and *that's* when I start running.

Addy meets me halfway down the stairs. She's so out of it, I'm almost past her before she recognizes me.

"There you are."

I cringe, hearing Marcus's exact words played through Addy's mouth. She tries to grab me, but I sidestep her easily. "Not now. I have to find Briar. I…I fucked up."

She starts smiling, but then schools her face with obvious effort. "Is it over already?" One side of her mouth twists up. "Fuck, I didn't think he was a quick draw."

I shake my head, waving at her. "It's not—just—" I break off with a frustrated growl and rush down the rest of the stairs.

I *did* fuck up, because I was scared.

I got sentimental about my fucking hymen.

Fuck knows why. Girl my age? Should have lost my v-card like three, four years ago.

But it's never seemed right.

Briar feels right. But that hallway didn't.

Because Addy wasn't there with her cellphone camera, duh.

I shake away the thought.

That's not it. I don't want my first time—consenting or otherwise—to be up against a hall in someone's house.

Admittedly, I wasn't expecting roses and fucking champagne, but…

Fuck that—I wasn't expecting *any* of this. Not Briar's passion. Not his animalistic urgency. Not the stutter of fear in my chest.

I know it will hurt. That's not it.

The fact that Briar will break me…*that's* it.

I don't know if I want someone like him to be my first. Yes, he ticks all my boxes. Yes, he's gorgeous as fuck and knows my own body almost—but not quite—as well as I do…

Am I a stupid romantic for thinking there'd be more? That

there'd be love and devotion and some kind of commitment; the most kids our age can ever promise each other?

My hand folds around Mom's necklace.

You *are* an idiot, Indi. You're weak, and sentimental, and you don't deserve to lose your v-card on a rose petal scattered bed at some hotel. You had what you wanted. The perfect camera angle, a brightly lit space. Addy was moments away—

No. *Marcus* was moments away.

I stagger to a halt, and lean against the closest wall. I'm in the kitchen, and a few people are lingering here already. Some look up at my arrival, most don't. That's because they're making out, zoning out, or purging, but I can't hold any of those things against them.

After all, we're just kids. This is the kind of shit we get up to when our parents are away. In this case, it's the kind of shit Dylan lets other kids get up to in his house when his parents are away.

And then I see Briar.

He's staring at me, smoking a cigarette like his life depends on it.

I've barely had more than two seconds to process anything since I've stepped past that red rope at the front door. And now, caught in this moment, I take my time to drink him in.

Screw that—he looks good enough to eat in his slim-fit tuxedo, biceps bulging against his shirt, bow tie at a roguish angle. I think his hair was meant to be slicked back tonight, but he's obviously been pawing at it like he does, because it's all over the fucking place.

Without realizing it, I move closer to him. At first, it's as if I'm trying to find a quiet space in the busy kitchen. Circulating around the other kids like a leaf on the surface of a rippling river.

Briar was in the small lounge area a few steps down from the kitchen. But the closer I move to him, the closer he moves to me.

We meet on the steps, and in a second I'm against the wall again.

But this time, he doesn't lift me up. His head is down, his mouth by my ear, and his hands are on my hips, holding me in place.

"I *will* be your first," he says to me.

A shudder races through me. He touches my chin, levers my head up. "And if that's not tonight, then I'll wait."

My stomach bottoms out. How the fuck could I ever have thought he was capable of anything Addy said he was? He might be rough around the edges, but Prince Briar's only ever been—

Rough?

Cruel?

Brutal?

More importantly, how on earth am I supposed to entrap him into committing a crime when he's just told me he'll wait until I'm ready? I can't do this. Any of this. My mind is in tatters.

I squeeze closed my eyes and turn my head away. "I have to go," I murmur.

He wraps his hands over my shoulders, but I shove them off.

"Wait," he says.

The command goes straight to my legs without involving my brain.

"I need you, Indi."

I hear his words, but they're gibberish. He *needs* me? For what? So he can get off?

I shake my head, but he catches hold of my chin and stops me. "If I can't have you tonight, then at least let me taste you."

Kissing? I glance away.

This, apparently, counts as consent in Briar's world. I barely have time for a yell before he's pulling me after him.

For a frantic, panicked moment I think he's dragging me back upstairs, and I almost dig in my heels.

But then he detours down a side hallway, opens a door, pulls me inside, and slams it shut behind me.

A bathroom.

Pristine, sparkling and shit…but it's still a fucking bathroom.

"Briar, I'm not—"

He shoves a finger against my mouth. And then his hand is up the skirt of my dress, grabbing my pussy.

Fingers raking over my skin, he gathers my dress and hikes it up to my waist.

Shit. None of this is going to plan anymore. Addy doesn't know where I am, I don't know where she is—

Briar yanks down my underwear so hard, the fabric leaves burning tracks down my thighs. He holds up the sliver of blue lace and considers it before turning his icy eyes onto me.

"Is this supposed to be a joke?" he says, dangling the underwear he'd shoved into my locker the other day from his finger.

"Ha ha?" I say weakly.

He shakes his head, tosses the pretty panties to the far corner of the bathroom, and sinks down onto his knees in front of me.

A second later, my ass slams into the marble basin behind me.

"Up."

He hoists me as much as I clamber up, my limbs moving like I'm stuck in a wet dream I have no intention of waking from.

Briar spreads my legs.

My cheeks burn as he studies my pussy with his head cocked to one side, like it's a piece of abstract art.

A second later, his lips are on the inside of my thigh and trailing closer to my pussy. I grab his hair—more in self-defense than anything else—but he hardly seems to notice.

Shit.

Shit!

His breath stirs against my slit, and I cringe away from him, both deeply embarrassed and impossibly turned on.

Fingertips dimpling my thighs, he grabs my legs and shoves them even further apart.

Briar closes his mouth over my pussy, moaning against my lips as if he's biting into the sweetest, juiciest fruit he's ever had the privilege of defiling with his mouth.

I let out a low groan and arch against that heat, his wetness, those strong lips. My feet lift and settle beside me on the countertop, spreading me impossibly open for his ravenous mouth.

If this is nirvana, then I'd better start behaving myself so I can die happy.

"Fuck!" I growl out, grabbing a fistful of Briar's hair. I force him harder against my clit. His tongue swirls against my clit before diving deep inside me.

Then he slides a pair of his fingers inside my pussy.

I jerk, moaning breathlessly before I start bucking against his knuckles.

Holy fucking hell, I can't even. Moments ago, I was ready for him to fuck me. But if this is what it's like when he goes down on me? The hallway wall isn't going to cut it. I demand rose petals and champagne. Maybe even a satin blindfold.

Oh God, even the thought of him blindfolding me sends a shudder through me.

What am I doing?

Fuck it, I don't care. The plan's already ruined. I'll try and pick up the pieces later, after…goddamnit I'm melting.

Briar's tongue is a live wire, sending wave after wave of electric pleasure through me. I fuck his mouth without a second thought, urging his tongue deeper and deeper inside me.

His hands bruise my thighs as he grips me, pulling me into

him as he licks me from ass to clit with the hunger of a starving man.

"Briar!" I yell, and it's barely a second before I come. I buck against his mouth, a rush of heat and pleasure capsizing me.

I hear a murmured, "fuck" from below, but I'm too busy having my mind blown to pay attention.

I force his mouth as hard against my pussy as I can, groaning as I ride out my climax. His tongue sweeps over my folds and flicks against my clit, and I shudder as a last tentacle of pleasure releases me.

My shoulders brush the mirror behind me. It's too cold, too hard, but there's nothing left for me to fight with.

Briar grabs hold of the edge of the basin and hauls himself to his feet. If he took out his dick now, I wouldn't have been able to stop him from fucking me.

Not because he's just given me the most spectacular orgasm I've ever had…but because I wouldn't have *dared*.

There's something primal in his eyes. Something dangerous, toxic even.

He drags the back of his hand over his mouth, drops his eyes to my spread-open pussy, and slaps me almost absently. I yelp, my legs trying to close but blocked by the slab of his body.

"Go home, little virgin," he says, his voice thick and rugged. "Go home before I change my fucking mind."

CHAPTER THIRTY-FIVE

BRIAR

Indi slips past me, heading for the corner of the bathroom where I tossed her underwear. "Leave it," I snap. She flinches, turning wide eyes to me, and then comes past on her way to the door. I grab a handful of her hair and haul her back. She protests when I kiss her, but I couldn't give a fuck if she's ever tasted herself or not.

I did.

I almost came undone how sweet she was. How wet. How her body shuddered when she came in my mouth.

My dick's already painfully hard—kissing her like this is only making matters worse. I catch a glimpse of tears caught in her lashes before I shove her out the door and slam it behind her. Then I lock it, just in case.

Jesus Christ, what the fuck just happened? One minute I'm furious enough to break everything in this house. The next I'm eating Indi out in a goddamn bathroom. There's a tentative knock on the bathroom door, but I ignore it.

I will my cock to soften, but it refuses. It doesn't help that I keep hearing Indi saying my name, hoarse and desperate, echoing in my mind.

Slamming my hand into the mirror, I yank out my cock and stroke it hard enough to make myself grimace in pain.

Punishment for losing control again.

But like so many things in life, that pain only makes the pleasure that much sweeter. That much more taboo.

"Fuck." I stroke my cock again, then again. Harder, until my face twists in pain.

But when I close my eyes, all I can see is Indi's rapturous face. Light gleaming from her lush mouth as it forms a perfect 'o'.

She's mine. I will *be her first.*

I speed up, grunting in the urgency to relieve myself of this deviant train of thought.

But I lied when I said I'd wait.

If life's taught me anything, it's that nothing is forever. People come and go like dandelion seeds. Drifting aimlessly for the longest time until a wind sweeps them away forever. I replay every second of what just happened, from Indi's glare when I yanked off her panties, to the way she fisted her hand in my hair. How she rode my face, and how deep my tongue sank inside her.

As she comes, so do I.

Marcus is waiting for me in the foyer, Dylan and Zak nearby like sharks who've smelled blood in the water. The party's still in full force, but the number of kids passed out on couches - or the floor—has increased since I last noticed.

"Where is she?" I ask, scanning the crowd in case she's still nearby.

"Left with Addison," Dylan says. "Dude, what happened?"

"She was crying," Zak adds, giving me a frowning once over from beside Dylan.

They were at the party that night with Jess, but both of them were trashed out of their minds. I doubt they remember much more than I do. But now? There's uncertainty in their eyes, faint disgust touching their mouths as they look first at each other and then at me.

"Nothing," I snap. "Did they leave in the same car?"

Everyone but Marcus shrugs at me. When I glare at him, he nods. "Addy drove."

"Fuck." She was way too trashed to be driving, even if it was just the mile back to her house. "I have to make sure they're okay."

I head for the door, but Dylan puts out his hand to stop me. "I think you've done enough."

Letting out a disbelieving, "What did you just say?" I step back and scan him with utter contempt.

"Just…go home, Briar." Dylan drops his gaze, but he doesn't step aside. His shoulders don't sag.

"I didn't do anything!" I yell, shoving him aside so hard he stumbles.

"But you wanted to, didn't you?" Zak says as he steadies Dylan.

"What are you saying?" I storm forward, and suddenly both of them are upright, standing shoulder to shoulder, eyes narrowed and hands fisted. If the two of them decided to gang up on me then yeah, I don't think I could take them both.

"Cool it, guys," Marcus says. "We're leaving, okay?" He steps in front of me, for all the world like he's gonna protect me.

I glare at Dylan and Zak over his shoulder. "Chicken shit pussies," I hiss.

"Come on, man, let's get out of here." Marcus turns,

scanning me as if he's checking for some last vestige of calm in my face.

I doubt he'll find it. I'm about ready to rip through skin and claw apart flesh.

How fucking dare they—?

—think I was gonna rape her?

I sneer at them, take a slow step back, and then another. That's when I notice everyone in the immediate vicinity is watching, wide-eyed and open-mouthed.

There are phones out, too.

People have been recording this shit.

I storm out of Dylan's house with blood singing in my fucking ears like a Valkyrie's Aria. Obviously, Addy's long gone by now—I just hope to all hell they made it back to her place without hitting anything on the way. She never seems to realize how much she's had to drink, Addy. And Jess was always too pissed to care how she got home—or if she even got home at all.

"Wanna go check on them?" Marcus asks.

I turn to him. I don't have a fucking clue if he's talking about Jess or Indi, but then I come back to the present with bitter finality.

"Yeah." I climb in behind my Mustang's steering wheel, and Marcus hesitates before getting into the passenger seat.

As I turn the ignition, my phone vibrates in my pocket. I take it out and hurriedly unlock the screen.

She's safe.

It came from the same number Addy's been using to blackmail me with. There's another message—one from my dad —but I'm too furious to read it.

"Fucking asshole," I mutter. I throw my Mustang into reverse, grabbing Marcus's headrest as I check behind me to make sure I'm not about to drive over some drunk kids.

"Who?"

"Addy. Bitch thinks she can get away with this shit, she's got another thing coming."

"What are you—?"

I make eye contact with Marcus as I turn forward, and he cuts off. "This bitch is done ruining my fucking life. You hear me?"

When Marcus leans away from me, I realize I'm yelling. I blink a few times and desperately try to compose myself before I slam my foot down on the gas.

It doesn't work.

If anything, it pisses me off even more.

She's safe.

Yeah, just like how Jess was safe all those times they went out to party without me. Those times my girlfriend called me from a strange bar to come get her because Addy was 'on something' and acting weird.

And she had the fucking *nerve* to demand Jess go home with her the night of Marcus's party. That between me and Addy, *I* was one who'd let Jess come to harm?

"Dude, slow down," Marcus says quietly.

I glance at him, and then do a double take. He has one hand on the dash, the other on the chicken bar above the car door. His face is a shade paler than usual, his lips a barely visible line.

I take my foot off the gas, inhale deep, and grip the steering wheel hard enough for my knuckles to go white.

"What happened?" Marcus asks.

"Thanks to you, nothing." I shake my head, taking turns glancing at the road and back at Marcus. "The fuck was wrong with you tonight? I thought you had my back?"

"She's trouble."

"Christ, you say that about every fucking chick, bro."

At this, Marcus shuts up. But now that he's got me riled up, I don't want to back down.

"What's with you and Indi, anyway?" He was like this with Jess, too, but it's worse with Indi. It's like he's taken her presence personally, as if every second I'm with her is an insult to our friendship.

"Nothing, man. Just drop it."

"You coming unhinged or something because of all that shit with your dad? Now you have to make my life worse than what it already is? It's not *my* fucking fault your life sucks."

Marcus twists in his seat, mouth wide as he lets out a disbelieving huff. "You think that's what I'm doing? You think I'm trying to ruin your fucking life?"

"Well, you haven't exactly been cheering for me to be happy anytime in the last two years."

Marcus gives a bitter laugh and thumps his hand on the dashboard. "I've been protecting you, bro. These whores all just wanna use you."

"And you know this because you're some kind of an expert? When last did you even try dating someone, not just fucking them?"

Marcus lets out a low growl. "Stop the car."

"Not a fucking chance. You're coming in there with me, and you're sorting this shit out. *With me.*"

"Fuck you, Prince." Marcus grabs the door handle as if he's ready to leap out of the car.

I slam my foot down on the gas.

Addy's house streams past—I barely catch sight of her racer before it's dwindling away to nothing in my rearview mirror.

"You know her from somewhere?"

Marcus grabs hold of the chicken bar again, gritting his teeth as if he's ready for me to crash us into a brick wall. "What?"

"Indi. Do you know her?"

"No! I've never seen her before in my fucking life."

"So what is it, Marcus? What is it about her that makes you fucking pissed off every time we're together?"

"She's not good enough for you! No one is!" Marcus throws me such a fierce glare, my foot slips off the gas. The Mustang slows, slows, almost stops.

I jerk up the emergency brake, and we stare at each other over the center console. Marcus's chest is heaving as if he's run a marathon, and my heart's pounding like I was beside him every step of the way.

"What…?" I manage.

Marcus waves his hand as if to dismiss what he just yelled at me. Instead of explaining himself, he fucks off on a different tangent. "You think you have it so bad, Briar?" He runs his hands down his face. "You don't. You've got everything you could ever want, you just can't see it."

"If this is about your dad—"

"Shut up about my fucking dad!" Marcus thumps the dash again. Veins protrude from his neck, and the way he's staring through the windshield—as if at something only he can see—is freaking me the fuck out.

I turn off the Mustang's ignition before the tick-tick-tick of its cooling engine can drive me mental.

"Marcus—"

"You snap your fingers, and girls fall at your feet. Always have, always will."

I let out a bitter chuckle. "You know that's not—"

"Yeah? Not anymore?" Marcus turns in his seat, one hand on the dash, the other on his knee. It might just be this confined space, but I've never realized how lanky he was. I definitely have more bulk than him, but where I knew Dylan and Zak could take me if they teamed up, I have no idea who would win in a fistfight between me and Marcus.

And I've never thought that. Not once.

Until now. Until I see some dark glimmer in his eyes that I can't identify.

Frustration? Regret? Anger?

"You get all A's. A mansion of a fucking house. The best family—"

"Woah, yeah, really?" I cut in with a laugh. "A dad who's never home, a dead mother? How the hell can that be—?"

"It beats a criminal for a father and a whore of a mother." Marcus scowls at me, and then rips his packet of cigarettes from his pocket and lights one. He expels a fierce stream of smoke, raking his eyes over me as if daring me to argue. "Fuck knows how many men she was screwing before she met my Dad. Then six years after I arrive—" He puts his fingers to his lips, blowing air over them. "Poof. Gone."

I have no fucking clue what I'm supposed to say to that. I keep quiet, watching Marcus's face to gauge where he's going with all of this. He takes a hit of his cigarette, and smoke fills the Mustang's cabin.

"Why didn't you say anything?" I lean a little closer, dropping my head. "I mean, I knew about your dad, some about your mom, but—"

"You ask your dad about me staying for a while?" Marcus asks quietly. He's staring through the windshield again, oblivious to my attempts at making eye contact.

"Wh—yes." I nod. "I did."

"What did he say?" Marcus's voice is cool and smooth as silk now as if we weren't just yelling at each other.

I'm tempted to tell him I didn't get around to it, but I'd just be delaying the inevitable. Best to get everything out in the open.

I shake my head. "I don't get it. He made it sound like you were..."

"What?" Marcus cocks his head and slowly turns to face me. "I was what?"

"A delinquent."

Marcus shrugs. "Aren't I?" He flicks his fingers in the space between us. "Aren't *we*?"

And then he laughs, and I swear to fucking God—I'll die a happy man if I never hear that sound again.

CHAPTER THIRTY-SIX

BRIAR

It's perversely sunny outside this morning, as if the world's mocking the darkness of my inner world with its godawful brightness.

Thought you were king of the hill, did'ya?

No one's gonna forget what I did. Not now, not ever. Might as well have served my time—maybe then people would have considered my debt to society paid in full.

We never did end up going to Addy's house. It seemed so much easier to keep driving until I came to Marcus's house. And then all I wanted was to go home and crash. I regret it now. I could have ended this last night. Settled the score.

But when I woke up this morning with a new text from Addy, and that unread text from my father, the culmination of the two messages broke the last restraint inside my mind.

I glare at the safe in my father's study. It was hidden behind the painting that's now leaning against the wall by my feet. This one's just as bright and colorful as the other abstracts in the room, but it depicts a fantasy forest of some kind instead of the seemingly random Rocher inkblot shapes of the others.

Not the greatest hiding place for a safe, but I have a feeling my father didn't really care much for the location of his safe compared to the security of his vault. Maybe he saw it as a second prize to anyone stupid enough to come in here and try to break into his vault.

This pin code I know. There's a handgun, our passports, and a few stacks of notes inside the safe. I remember the first time Dad showed gave me the code and showed me how to open it. I went around thinking we were part of an international crime syndicate for weeks before my imagination found something new to latch onto.

I know how to load and shoot the gun, but I've never had to use it. To the best of my knowledge, neither has my father.

I ignore it now—it's not what I came for.

I'm here for one thing only—Addison Green's motherfucking blood money.

I close the safe and hoist up the painting. As I'm adjusting it to make sure it's hanging straight, something catches my eye. I turn my head a little and stare at the demonic face of some kind of goblin hiding behind a tree just a few inches away from my nose. It's looking straight at me, it's eyes so realistic, there's no mistaking the gleam of evil flickering inside.

I brush my hands on my ass as I step back, grimacing. I glance at the right-hand corner, at the name scrawled in the corner, but I'll be fucked if I can make it out.

Christ, what a fucked-up painting. Once you've seen that evil little shit, it's ruined.

Indi

I force my eyes open, cringing at the pain. God, it feels like someone's gone and poured a whole bag of sand in them. Rolling onto my side, I focus on the shape beside me. It eventually resolves into Addy.

Which means…

I push up to my elbows, and scour the room I'm in.

Yup—cardboard boxes, plastic wrapping. And, if I'm not mistaken, I've been sleeping on a bare mattress.

My aching bladder—the reason I woke up in the first place —drives me to my feet. The world takes a slow spin as I head for the hallway, hoping against all hope that the first doorway will be a bathroom.

It is.

I let out a long sigh as I sit down and pee. And then groan when I see the bathroom is as bare as the rest of the house— toilet paper included.

Damn it.

There's a crash from downstairs. I drag up the sweatpants Addy loaned me last night as I stand, almost tripping in the process.

"The fuck?" Addy mutters as she stalks past the bathroom door.

"Addy, wait!" I run after her, just in time to see Briar bursting through the door. Addy and I both stop walking, Addy letting out a strangled gasp.

"What the fuck are you doing?" she shrieks.

And then she does the stupidest thing I've ever seen. She runs down the stairs and heads straight for Briar.

"Addy!" I hesitate for barely a second, and then I spin around and race back to her room. My backpack's on the floor. I snatch it up, my hand shaking and my skin ice-cold as I hunt through the pockets.

Where the fuck did I put it?

"Get out of my house!" Addy's voice sends a lash of panic through me. I'm just about to abandon my futile search when my fingers brush cool metal.

When I make it back to the landing, Briar's standing by the busted-open door, hand fisted on the straps of a backpack, the other opening and closing at his side. Addy was at the foot of the stairs, but when he remains silent, she storms up to him.

As soon as she's close, he throws the bag at her.

It hits her in the chest. She staggers to the side, clutching it to her as she bumps into the wall.

"Briar!" I'm convinced he's going to lunge at her, and I don't wanna know even a little where that will lead. He looks ready to kick, punch and bite the fuck out of anything that moves.

Despite the death grip on my switchblade, my legs lock, trapping me on the last step. For the life of me I can't force myself closer.

Addy pushes away from the wall, her teeth flashing. "What the fuck is this?" she yells, hoisting the bag up.

"It's what you wanted, you fucking bitch." Briar scans the now empty living room, and for a second I feel like I've stepped into some kind of alternate reality.

Where the hell has all the furniture gone? Is it truly possible I slept through moving guys dragging out a three-piece living room set, dining room table, and the leftover boxes I saw peeking out from the kitchen last night?

If I did, then why the fuck is Addy still here? Shouldn't she be headed wherever her stuff's going?

"I want to feel sorry for you, Addy. I do." Briar's voice is dangerously low, but calm. He sweeps a hand out to the empty living room as Addy drops the bag to her side and watches him warily through slitted eyes.

"Briar," I say quietly, finally getting my legs to unlock so I can move closer to them. Fuck knows how I can remotely help in this situation, but I don't want my gravestone reading 'Indi *The Yellow-Bellied Coward* Virgo.' For now, I tuck the switchblade into the sweat's elastic at the small of my back. Briar can easily overpower me, even with the knife—he's done it once before. All I have is the element of surprise, which will be a moot point if he realizes I'm armed.

"I mean, it's gotta suck, right?" Briar tilts his head, taking a slow step closer to Addy. She retreats, and draws the bag up to her chest again as if it can offer some kind of protection against Briar's fury. "Losing your best friend. Losing your mind. Losing every last bit of credibility you've ever had."

Addy's eyes go round, her mouth tight. "You don't know anything, you fucking criminal."

His eyes dart down to the bag, back up to her face. "Takes one to know one," Briar says, lips lifting in a sneer. "Now where the fuck is the video?"

I step closer still, but they're so fixated on each other, I doubt either of them knows I exist right now.

Should I call the cops? Marigold? Who?

Addy shakes her head. "What video?"

Briar throws back his head and laughs. The sound makes every hair on my body stand on end.

"You gotta be shitting me." He surges forward, hands raised as if he's about to grab Addy.

Before I even realize I'm moving, I'm between them. Briar grabs me instead of Addy, and there's the briefest look of confusion on his face before he tosses me aside like a trash bag.

There's nothing for me to hit, so I just stagger for a few feet before I find my balance, but by then he's gotten hold of Addy.

"You have your money, you fucking bitch! Now give me the phone!"

Addy screams as Briar backs her up against the wall. She lifts the bag, but he bats it aside with barely a pause.

"Briar!" I launch myself at them, grab his arm, and sink my nails into his skin.

He shakes me off with a growl. "Don't think for a second I'm leaving without that video, Addy."

I've never seen her green eyes that wide, that terrified. "I don't know what you're—"

Briar slams a fist into the wall beside her head, plaster pattering onto the tiles below.

"Where. Is. The. *Video*?"

Addy bursts into tears, shaking her head. Her hands are up now, pressing into Briar's chest. Not digging in, not fighting. Just keeping him back.

"Where is it?" he bellows.

Addy's eyes squeeze shut, and she lifts her arms over her head as if Briar's about to start pummeling her.

I surge forward, but my foot catches on the backpack. I go to the floor, grunting as the wind knocks out of me. I kick, trying to free my foot. When it remains tangled in the bag, I roll onto my ass and give it a furious yank.

The zipper was only partially closed. As I tug at the bag, it opens wider and spills out a neat stack of bills.

I stare at it. Gape up at Briar. Realize both of them are still totally fixated on each other.

"What's the… what's all this money for?" I ask, clearing my throat halfway through so I can get everything out.

"Don't think for a second I'll believe you're not part of this," Briar snaps, glaring at me over his shoulder.

"Part of what?" Addy says, and his attention goes back to her.

A video. A cellphone.

Evidence?

Is that what Briar and Marcus were talking about that night at the church? Does Addy have a video of Jessica's rape?

No, that makes absolutely no sense. Something that damning would have put them both behind bars. She'd have used it a long time ago.

Except if she only just found it. But when? How?

"Addy, what video is he talking about?" I ask.

Briar is the furthest thing from innocent here, but I knew that going in. Addy's been lying to me from the start. Maybe even now. Fuck knows why she'd want to assume innocence, but I don't pretend to know a thing about her or her motives.

"I don't know!" Addy shrieks.

"Who the fuck else could it have been?" Briar grabs her around the neck and pushes her against the wall. Addy breaks down into hysterical wails while I watch, feeling so detached from this moment I could be in a cinema.

"There was someone else there," I say. My feet take me forward even though I never gave them permission to move. "You said it yourself: you were fucked. Marcus was fucked. Someone else could have been following you up those stairs."

Briar releases Addy in a rush and pivots to face me. I expected shock on his features, but there's nothing.

Nothing.

"Suddenly you know everything," he says. Addy slides to the ground and collapses on her side. When she starts sobbing, she sounds so absolutely riven I want to fall down and start crying too. But I hold back everything—my fear, my sadness, my confusion.

I shove it far out of reach and match Briar for each of his steps until we're right up against each other and he could grab me by the throat and strangle me if he wanted.

"She says she doesn't have anything."

"She's a lying bitch."

"And you're not?"

Briar's mouth thins.

"You told me you didn't remember anything about that night, but that's a lie, isn't it?"

Still nothing. His face could have been carved from frozen cream. "How long have you been following me?"

He doesn't have to know *how* I know—the facts speak for themselves. Let him think I'm stalking him—they say crazy sometimes works at keeping other crazies at bay.

"And you know what?" I go on as if I didn't even hear him, palming my switchblade as casually as I can. "I hope whoever does have that video, that they send it to the police." I step closer still, until our bodies touch. The metal in my hand is warm now, hot almost. "Because evidence like that? That should be enough to reopen the case, don't you think?"

"I meant what I said—"

I flick open the switchblade and press it against Briar's throat. He doesn't move.

Not a flinch, not a twitch, nothing. It's as if he hasn't even noticed the metal against his skin. I drop my voice low, and force every word out steady. "Especially when I show them the shoes you left outside my house."

Addy's sobs are simmering down, but I doubt she's coherent enough to hear what I'm saying. But I go up on my tiptoes anyway and lay a hand on Briar's shoulders, nearly meeting him eye for eye as I press the flat of the blade against his throat in warning.

Okay, *hardly* meeting him eye for eye. But I'm trying really fucking hard.

"How you broke into my house. How you *watched* me."

"That won't—" His thick voice cuts off, and he glances away from me. "You know that's not—"

"The same as raping someone?" I whisper furiously, leaning in even closer so he's forced to look at me. "I dunno, Briar. I kinda feel it's one of the first rungs on the motherfucking ladder."

His eyes touch me then, and for the briefest, craziest moment, I *know* he's not a bad person. But see, that thought has nothing to do with common sense, logic, or facts. That's my fucking vagina talking again.

Briar is a criminal. He dodged the law once, but I've vowed to myself and Addison that it will never happen again. If that means he spends a few months cleaning trash on the side of the road instead of hard time in jail, so be it.

At least his record won't reflect the perfect imitation high schooler he shows the world. There will be a black mark on his name.

Until his father washes it off, of course.

Briar ducks, grabs the backpack off the floor, and backs up toward the door.

"This isn't over," he growls. He stabs a finger in Addison's direction, but doesn't take his eyes off me. He gives my switchblade a contemptuous smirk, and then he's gone.

My legs give out, but I don't feel anything when I hit the floor. Moments later, Addy's by my side. She throws her arms over me and starts crying again.

I would have joined her, but I have no tears.

My fury boiled them all away.

As soon as I'm in my Mustang, I take out my phone. My hands are trembling so bad, it takes three attempts before I can call Marcus. I put the car into gear and peel out of Addy's driveaway, one hand on the wheel and the other holding my phone to my ear.

"Pick up, pick up." I push the words through gritted teeth.

He answers on the next ring. "Yeah?"

"You at home?"

"The fuck else would I be?"

He's pissed off, but I can't blame him. "Listen, I need you to do something for me."

There's silence on the other end of the line. It could have gone so many ways—he could have laughed in my ear and put down the phone. He could have cursed me to the nth generation.

But Marcus was, and always will be, my closest friend.

"Tell me what you need, bro."

As I'm waiting for the golf estate's boom to rise, I re-read the message my father sent last night. Judging from the time stamp, and if I remember correctly, I was probably on my third game of pool and my sixth beer. No wonder I didn't hear it come through.

We need to talk.
11:45am
Angel Falls Cemetery
Don't be late.

I lock my phone and toss it on the passenger seat. My eyes slide to the clock on my dash. I thought I would have more time, but I woke up late, and it took me a while to get my head straight.

I push down harder on the gas, opening up the Mustang's engine. It tears down the freeway as my heart starts a slow th-thump in my chest.

We need to talk? Well that suits me just fine, because I have some questions for him.

Angel Falls Cemetery, poetically, is set in the small valley of Devil's Creek. At the entrance to the cemetery, you can see a few yards of the wispy waterfall that gives this area its name. However, the craggy creek it plummets into is hidden—accessible only by hiking down a steep ravine lined in pitch black rock.

Massive oak trees litter the cemetery, throwing dappled shade over the paved road my Mustang skims over as I head deeper inside.

I only come here once a year with Dad, and nothing much has changed since the last time. The leaves have only just started changing color, and it's a mess of green and orange out here.

And gray, of course.

Row upon row of concrete slabs and sad, pouting angels.

I park behind my father's pearl-white Mercedes and take a second to drag myself together before climbing out.

"You're late," he says, as soon as I'm in earshot, but with his back still facing me.

"Was busy."

I expect a reprimand, but he says nothing. He's wearing a black-on-black suit, his hair slicked back, hands clasped behind his back. This could have been a replay from last year's visit, until he turns to face me.

His blue eyes pierce through me like a spear, rooting me to the spot.

"What?" I ask, my voice too soft, too unsteady.

"Do I not give you enough, son?" There's open contempt on his words when his sneer could have sufficed to convey his disgust.

"I…what are you talking about?" I'd been gearing up for some of his usual sentimental drivel about my mother, not a full-on confrontation.

"Is it drugs?" He steps closer. I wish I could move back, because I've never felt such venomous anger flowing from him before.

"Dad, I don't know what you're—"

"Did you think I wouldn't notice? That I'm that fucking obtuse?" He doesn't raise his voice, not even a little, because he doesn't have to. I'm fucking terrified, and I still don't know why he's angry with me.

I lift my hands, palms facing him. That, at least, stops his slow advance. But it does nothing to the set of his mouth or the righteous indignation glaring in his eyes.

"Couldn't figure it out, even when I did it right in front of you, could you?"

Finally, my scrambling brain finds purchase. "The safe?" I blurt out. I wave my hands. "Dad, no, I have the money. All of it." I stab a thumb over my shoulder. "It's in my—"

"Did he promise you a cut?" My father lifts his chin, hands still clasped behind his back for all the world like he's having an idle chat with his son.

If you didn't take into account his eyes, of course.

"Who?"

"That Baker boy. And don't tell me he didn't have anything to do with this. I know it's him. It's always been him!"

Now my head's fucking spinning again. "Dad, please. I have the money from the safe. I can give it to you right now."

My father cocks his head. "And the files? All my clients's information? Do you also happen to have that in your car?" Sarcasm drips from every word. His face contorts into mock concern. "I'm assuming you haven't made any copies, of course?"

I gape openly at him.

His clients's…?

Beep. Beep. Beep. Beep.

Four digits.

I thought it was the front door, that night.

It wasn't.

It was the entry code for my father's study.

Beep. Beep. Beep. Beep.

How many times had he tried a different combination over the years? I know he never asked me about it, and I've never once been inside with him there. Dumb luck, or years and years of patient determination?

I stagger back shaking my head, doing my best to reign in a

thousand abrupt thoughts tumbling over themselves in their rush to be acknowledged.

That's why Marcus chose that room. It's closest to the study.

Was that why he was okay living with me? Why he was so pissed off when I said my Dad had said no?

He must have accessed my father's computer. Copied his files.

But when? Why? What use—?

"Dad, do you keep their addresses on file?" I bark out, my eyes wide and my hands already curling into fists.

Dad lets out a rough bark of a laugh, shaking his head. "Just admit you've fucked up, Son. Admit it, and we—"

"No, you don't—" I cut off, grabbing my lips and twisting them in an effort to work through my thoughts before my father thinks I've lost my fucking mind.

But then something else trips me up.

"How did you know it was him?" I step closer to my dad, lifting my hands when his eyes narrow to wary slits. "Marcus. And you called him a deviant. Why?" I spit out the words as fast as I can, and my father's suspicious glare slowly changes into a confused frown.

"The cat," he says. "He killed the cat."

I shake my head, laugh. "What fucking cat?"

"When you were six," Dad says, staring at me like I've just told him the sky is green and we're standing on air. "He killed your mother's cat."

I can't even. Blood sings through my ears, and my heart's pounding along to a 155 BPM track as I try to understand what the fuck my father's telling me.

Then I remember.

It's just a fragment of a faded memory, but it's there.

Natalie's white Persian, the one I always thought looked like it had run headfirst into a wall. Ugly as sin, but she loved that thing to death.

"You told me it ran away."

Father shakes his head. "Because that's what I thought. But when Baker tendered for one of my client's security upgrades, I went to his house for a meeting." Father waves his hand. "Brandon Baker, Marcus's dad."

I nod, but it's not with understanding. I'm not getting any of this shit.

"I saw its collar. That—" he snaps his fingers. "Diana? Deena? Can't remember what your mother called the thing. I designed it a collar." My father brings a hand to his throat as if he's about to strangle himself. "Beautiful thing. Put me on the map for pet couture."

"Where did you see it?"

"In Baker's house. That kid was looking at it. I only saw a glimpse, but I know my own work when I see it."

"How do you know *he* stole—"

"That whole family's rotten as a barrel of week-old fish." Father shakes his head, teeth flashing. "I told you back then I didn't want you seeing that boy."

We were so young. I thought we played in the woods because what fucking kid wouldn't if they had the chance?

But now I remember.

We played there because else I would get into trouble. And I only brought Marcus over when I knew my father would be out of town.

Over the years, I must have forgotten the real reason. So much has happened since then, I mean, fuck. Junior high, high school, Jessica.

Indi.

"I…forgot."

My father shakes his head, but I can see there's a touch of

doubt in his eyes now. "What were you going to use it for?"

I shrug. My father's mouth twists.

"The money! What was it for?"

"A loan, that's it."

"Like the bracelet?" Dad's eyebrow quirks up. "Is that in your car too?"

I shake my head. "No. I have to… I still have to get it back."

"Then get it back." Dad tugs at the hem of his suit jacket, twisting his neck. "The police are busy fingerprinting my computer and study. I already know what they'll find."

Because of course my fingerprints will be all over that shit.

But not his computer. I've never touched it. I knew it was off-limits.

"You're wrong about Marcus," I say. "He's never done anything—" I cut off, aware of the bald-faced lie I'm about to lay on my father. "He's a good guy."

Father lets out a soft laugh. "No, son. *You're* a good guy. Marcus? He takes advantage of good guys like you."

Dad's words play on end in my mind as I head home. I zone out so badly that the car behind me at the traffic light honks before I realize the light is green.

I coast down the freeway.

It doesn't matter which way I twist things, I can't fit the pieces together.

Of course, it doesn't help that my mind keeps going back to Indi. How vengeful she looked. How hard she pretended that she'd actually be able to hurt me with that little blade if she tried.

Liar.

When could she possibly have overheard me and Marcus

speaking about Jess? We know better than to run our mouths where anyone can hear us.

The church.

Was she there? Was that what I saw before I got so caught up in Marcus that I forgot?

What the fuck was she even doing there?

My hands tighten on the steering wheel. I lick dry lips and take a deep lungful of air.

No…what was *Marcus* doing there?

CHAPTER THIRTY-EIGHT

I stand at the threshold to the Davis house and my shoulders sag as if there's a ton of weights strapped to my back, not just a backpack.

There wasn't much to say to Addy after we'd both calmed down. She swears she doesn't know what Briar was talking about, and I so badly want to believe her.

When I asked, she said she was supposed to leave with the moving men, but she wanted to spend a few minutes saying goodbye to her childhood home.

I still don't know what shit her parents were involved in that made them a target for the IRS. She didn't elaborate, and I didn't ask her to. Right now, I just want to climb into bed and forget the past two weeks of my life ever happened.

Which is what I would have done if I hadn't run into Marigold.

She's waiting for me in the entrance hall, skinny arms crossed over her chest. The lecture begins before I've even let out my first long-suffering sigh.

"How far do you think you'll get in this world, young lady?"

"Quite far," I snap back. "Starting with moving fuck far away from this hell hole."

"And then what?" Marigold says, following me relentlessly up the stairs. "You get a job, your boss gives you an order, you throw it back in their face?"

Well, at least she's not expecting my boss to be male. That's gotta count for something, right?

"I dunno, granny," I say. "But let me think it over while I remain grounded for the rest of my life, yeah?"

I turn to close my bedroom door in her face, but she sticks out a hand before I get there. I scowl at her, and she glares back at me.

"This isn't the life your mother wanted for you," she says quietly.

"Don't you dare," I say, lifting a finger at her and wishing it was my knife instead. "Don't you dare!"

"She put me in charge of you, Indigo. Me." Marigold presses her fingers to her chest. "I'm responsible for her daughter. This —" she flicks her hand at me "This excuse of a child."

My mouth drops open. "What?"

"I never wanted kids," she goes on with barely a pause. "Did your mother ever tell you that? Not one. Until I had your mother, of course."

She shakes her head.

"That's when it all changes, you know. That one moment, when you're holding your baby in your arms. The burden you've carried for nine long months. The thing that made you throw up every morning, that made you spoil your bedsheets more times than you'd care to remember. That thing…"

Marigold blinks a few times, and I realize she's keeping back tears. "That thing consumed my life. She was everything to me. Everything!"

I start misting up. That's how I felt about Mom too, especially after Dad died. She was my world.

I like to think I was hers.

"But then I lost her." Marigold holds up a hand and extends two fingers. "Not once. Twice."

"I don't—"

"Your father took her away from me." Marigold flicks her hand, shakes her head. "Dragged her thousands of miles to that nowhere town. He kept us apart."

I open my mouth, but she doesn't let a word get out.

"And then someone killed her."

Those two fingers lift, trembling ever so slightly. "Twice, I've lost her. I'm not losing you too, even if it means you hate me. Because at least you're *here* to hate me. At least you're here."

She drops her arms to her sides, swallows visibly, and takes a step back. "Now think about what you've done." She nods, and a single tear breaks free to race down her wrinkled cheek. "You think about your life, Indi. And you don't come out of this room until you're ready to tell me how you plan to spend it."

Marigold grabs the door handle and shuts the door in my face. I stare at the wood for the longest time, and then slowly turn around and collapse on my bed.

I wish there were a way I could dump everything that's happened to me in the past two weeks onto Marigold. Maybe she can handle that shit better than I can. After all, she's still standing, and barely looks worse for wear.

Me? I feel like two-day-old roadkill left to bake in the sun. I'm a withered husk of who I used to be, and it feels like the only thing keeping me alive is my anger and my hate and my desperation.

Anger at Briar for lying to me.

Hate for the man who destroyed my life so wantonly.

And oh, how *desperate* I am to make them all pay for their crimes.

BRIAR

It's just after one when I get to the burned-out church. Empty, blackened, cast in deep shadow.

I haven't seen Marcus here in years. So why? Why did he track all the way over here from his house? It's further than mine —an extra fifteen, twenty minutes. Doesn't make sense, not if it was just to reminisce.

So why then?

I scan the building, trying to find anything that might be out of place. Some glaring sign that will point me in the right direction.

But it looks the same as it always does.

I head to the back where I thought I saw a flicker of light the night Marcus and I were here. There's a tangled nest of brambles back here. I crouch, take out my phone, and shine the torch on the ground.

There are a few scrapes through the dirt, some indistinct marks. A thorn ripped from the bramble. Was this where Indi was hiding?

I turn, crouch, and scan the church from my new perspective. The entrance is straight ahead, the pulpit a little to the left. She would have had a clear line of sight to both of us coming and going.

She must have seen what Marcus was doing. My finger hovers over my phone, but who the fuck do I call?

I try Dylan first. He's the one that sent Indi the video his girlfriend had taken of her on her knees in front of me in Veroza's class.

No answer.

I try Zak next, but his phone's off.

I know Marcus doesn't have her number, and the last thing I want is to potentially tip him off to my amateur investigation.

Instead, I wander around the church. Spot the difference, Briar.

My eyes are drawn to the mess of footprints coming and going. I follow them a few times, trying to decipher which ones are mine, which are Indi's, which could possibly be his. On the fourth circuit, I notice a pair of tracks detouring. It could be mine from the night I first followed Indi into this place…but it doesn't feel right.

For one, they're too perfect. Each precisely placed in front of the other.

I follow them down a row of pews, and stare at a scuff mark on the dusty tiles.

Crouching, I brush my fingers over the tile. It's not flush with the others. No surprise—almost nothing in this church is straight or narrow anymore. I heard that the church burned down in the early sixties, cause unknown. Apparently, no one was injured in the fire, but it was never reconstructed.

I wedge my fingernail under the lip of the tile. Reluctantly, it starts lifting. I put it down to one side and frown down at the dark rectangle of empty space it was obscuring.

I reach inside. The air in that small space is arctic. I grab the bundle of fabric inside and draw it out as goosebumps break out over my arms.

Did you get rid of everything?

Of course.

As soon as that blue fabric catches the light, I recognize it.

Jessica's hoody. The one she was wearing when she left Marcus's house the next day.

Why the fuck would he keep this?

I stand, gripping the sweater tighter. Inside one of the pockets, something crumples. I unfold the hoody, dangling it from my finger as I head out of the church. I rummage through the pockets, forcing a swallow when I pull out Jessica's lip balm.

It takes everything I have not to smell it. My hand slips into the other pocket.

A piece of paper, and something small, rectangular, hard, slick, cool.

Flash drive. I stare at it for a second before slipping it into my jeans. As I step into the small clearing right outside the church and the sun washes over me, I unfold the piece of paper.

I stop walking.

I straighten the paper, blinking hard.

I turn my head.

Am I fucking seeing things?

I rub a thumb over the penciled lines. They smudge a little, but that only convinces me that I haven't lost my fucking mind. My head darts up as a cold thrill scours my bones.

Indi.

I break into a sprint.

Jesus fucking Christ.

How long, Marcus Baker?

How long have you been playing me, you sick fucking psycho?

INDI

I t's too bright out to sleep. I'm too miserable to study. I
decide on a hot shower, and daydream about French toast
and hot coffee for after.

Marigold's gone. I heard her slam the front door a few
minutes ago. It's the only reason I dared to sneak out of my room
for the shower. With clean, wet hair and a body reeking of
lavender, I feel a little less wrecked than when I walked in here.

A little, but not a lot.

I pull on my baggy jeans and hoody, and drag my hair into a
messy bun, glaring at my reflection.

I look as bad—if not worse—than when I arrived here six
days ago.

Six. Days.

Feels like a fucking lifetime.

I slip my mother's necklace around my neck, lay back on the
bed, and close my eyes as I wait for the stone to go warm in my
fist.

Marigold said I should figure out what I want out of my life,
but you know what? I don't have a fucking clue despite having all
the traditional expectations thrust upon me while I was still part
of a full, functional family.

Doctor.

Lawyer.

The opposite of a starving artist.

My parents told me I could be anything I wanted, and I lived
life expecting that to be true. So I studied whatever took my
interest. History, the sciences, art. Briefly, accounting. Because it
didn't matter—I could be whatever the fuck I wanted.

When my father got sick, I didn't want to be anything
anymore. Didn't seem to be a point. He was young—not even

forty-five yet—and his life was over. All my hopes and dreams were pinned on his recovery. I prayed, I begged, I sacrificed.

It was never enough.

If there was a God, then he refused to listen. No one accepted my offerings.

After Dad died, the only thing I wanted to be was fucked. I drank, I smoked, I snorted.

There was nothing for me to rebel against, but I still found cause to yell at my mother and call her names.

And she just kept on doing what she'd been doing. She was my only constant in those years, and I was too much of a loose cannon to notice. She kept painting and drawing. Her work kept appearing in galleries and art shows.

If I'd bothered for even a second to pay attention, I might have noticed the sterling fucking example she was setting.

But I was too broken, and unashamed of flaunting my grief to the world. I didn't want to feel anything except pleasure, and I pushed away every bit of pain that came my way.

The police asked me if I knew my mother was on anti-depressants. That she was scheduled to appear at an art gallery for her latest collection the night she was murdered. That, instead, she left and then came home, heavily intoxicated with booze and pills.

I didn't. How could I? That would have required talking to her. Doing something other than yelling and disobeying her.

It was a blessing, they told me.

Meant she must hardly have felt a thing.

As if they were there when she was bound, gagged, and tortured. Like they had ringside seats to her brutal rape.

But they weren't.

No one was there that night except her, and the man who took everything from her.

The man who stole my life from me.

I come to with a start, and stare fuzzily around my room as I lick dry lips and push onto my elbows. Must have dozed off, but I don't remember even—

Someone's coming up the stairs.

I'm on my feet in an instant. It's not Marigold—those footfalls are too heavy, too slow.

Determined.

My eyes dart to the baseball bat beside my bedroom door. I left it there in case Briar ever came back, not sure if I could ever use it against him but wanting to keep my options open, just in case.

But this isn't Briar. I know it like I know there's some heavy shit coming my way.

I creep over the carpet, my breath coming in fits and starts as I take hold of the bat and wrap my fingers around the smooth handle.

My heart's slamming in my chest. My pulse is a soft roar in my ears.

He's on the landing now. I hear a door creak—the spare bedroom next to mine.

My door is next.

I hoist up the bat, flexing my fingers before wrapping them even tighter. It feels too heavy. My body too light. I want to tip over. I want to drop it.

But I clutch it for dear life instead.

Somehow knowing…this is life or death.

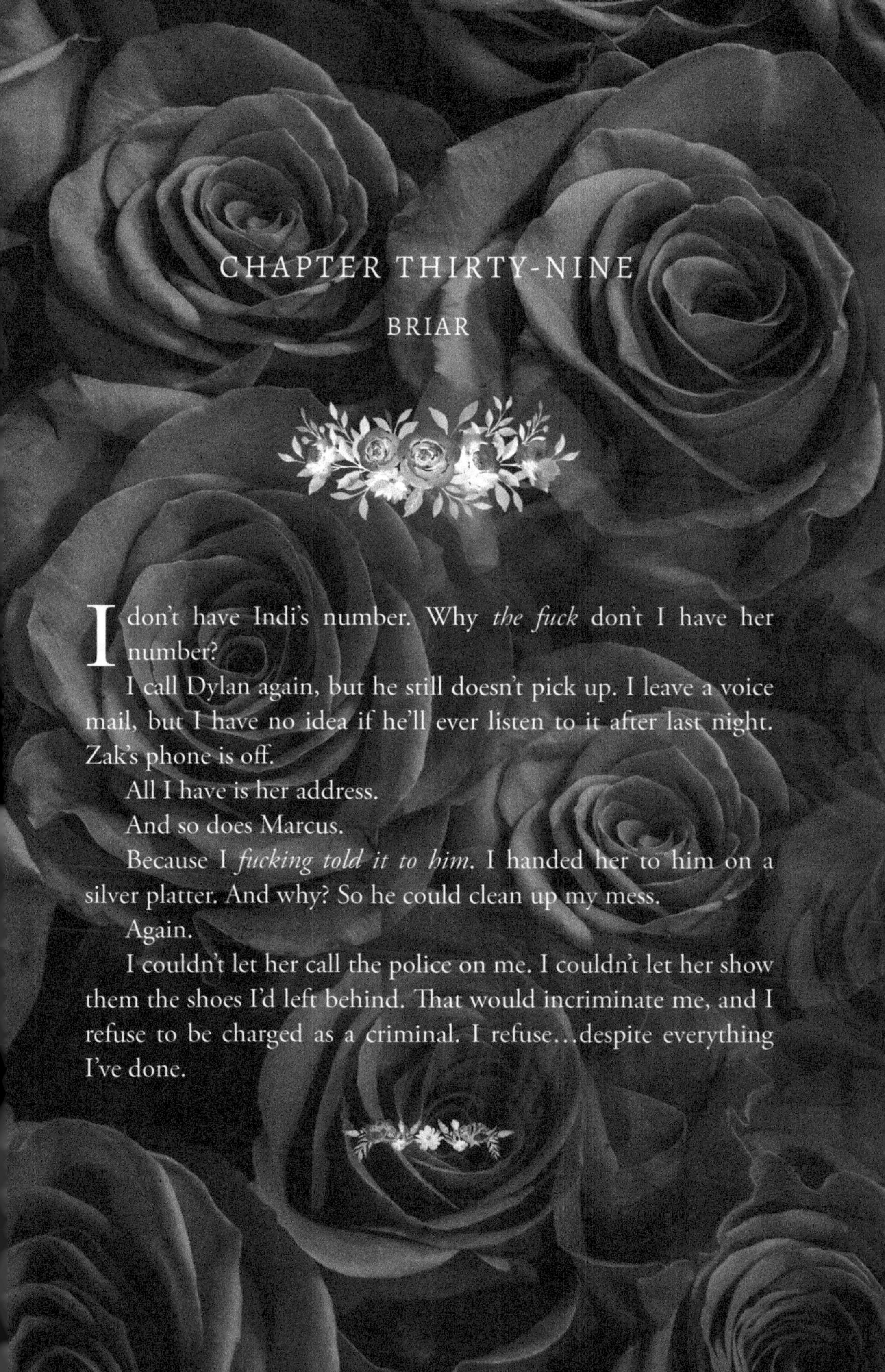

CHAPTER THIRTY-NINE

BRIAR

I don't have Indi's number. Why *the fuck* don't I have her number?

I call Dylan again, but he still doesn't pick up. I leave a voice mail, but I have no idea if he'll ever listen to it after last night. Zak's phone is off.

All I have is her address.

And so does Marcus.

Because I *fucking told it to him*. I handed her to him on a silver platter. And why? So he could clean up my mess.

Again.

I couldn't let her call the police on me. I couldn't let her show them the shoes I'd left behind. That would incriminate me, and I refuse to be charged as a criminal. I refuse…despite everything I've done.

I emerge from the shadows of Briar Woods breathing too hard, my vision swimming with stars. I ran as fast as I could, but I already know it's too late. *I'm* too late. The monster's been loosed. Wolf has already devoured Red Riding Hood.

But I still have time to cut him open, right? Isn't that how the story goes? The hunter cuts open the wolf, and Indi and her grandmother come out unharmed?

I sprint over the lawn, scanning Indi's house for signs of life.

It's just gone one in the afternoon. There are no lights to indicate whether or not someone's at home. Oh, how I fucking wish she wasn't here, but life has never been that cute, that perfect, that wonderful.

The back door is ajar, and that almost makes me stop in my tracks. Luckily—*luckily*—I have enough momentum to keep me going when my mind flags.

I dart into the kitchen. A white-haired woman spins to face me. I see her resemblance to Indi in the way she scowls at me, as if daring me to take another step.

"Where is she?" I barely manage through a wheeze.

"In her room, studying." The old woman lifts an imperious eyebrow at me. "And you are?"

I growl in response, and run for the stairs. My mind's begging me to slow down, to take stock. To stop being such a fucking fool.

But I can't.

I can sense him.

He was here.

Marcus was *here*!

"Excuse me!" Indi's grandmother calls from downstairs. "Indi is grounded. She will *not* be receiving guests."

All the doors on the landing are closed. I throw open the second one, the one I escaped through the other night. I instinctively knew back then that it was Indi's room, even though it could have belonged in a hotel's guest room, because she'd somehow left her mark on it.

Even now, standing at the threshold, I know this is her space.

And I know it was violated.

A second later, once my eyes have swept the room, they fix on a spot on the floor.

A splash of blood. Incongruous against the beige carpet. Unmistakable.

"Young man, just what the hell do you think—?"

"She's gone," I say, turning to the old woman working her way up the stairs. "He's taken her."

The woman glares at me, her lips working. Then she storms closer. "Nonsense. She was in her room when I left…"

The old woman steps into the room. It takes her a moment to spot the blood, and when she does she puts a hand on her chest and steps deliberately back as if it was a snake rearing to bite.

"No," she murmurs, shaking her head. "No."

"Call the police," I say. "Tell them it's Marcus Baker. He's got her."

I don't wait for her response—I'm already rushing down the stairs three at a time.

But where to?

My first thought would have been the woods, but I was just there. We would have passed each other. I would have seen him. So *where*?

Burning lungs force me to a halt a few yards outside the house. I fall to my knees, dragging air through a tattered windpipe as my fingers dig into the grass.

Back to where it all started, of course.

Back to the Baker house.

INDI

As my door opens, I swing the bat. There's a bark of pain from outside, the hand holding the door handle darting back into the hall.

Shit, too soon!

I rush around the corner, lifting the bat for another blow, but Marcus is too fast for me. He steps forward, grabs the base of the bat, and twists it out of my hands.

It happens so fast, my scream of rage twists into a shriek of pain as my wrists bend the wrong way.

I sag, desperately trying to pull my hands free, but then Marcus is inside my room, and the door's already slamming shut behind him.

He grabs the front of my shirt, draws back his hand, and slams his fist into my nose.

Heat, pain, blood explodes from my face. I yell, gurgle, fall to the floor. In a second my shirt is soaked.

Marcus grabs me again, hauls me to my feet. I splutter, coating his face in a fine spray of bloody mist.

He doesn't even notice.

"I have Addy." His voice is barely legible, not even a little human. Black eyes dig into my head like a migraine.

"Wh-?"

"I'll kill her."

I shake my head. "Pl-please—"

"Then walk." He shoves me so hard, I tumble over my own feet and land on the floor. I grunt, and a splatter of blood lands on the carpet by my hand.

That's it. One splatter.

That's the only evidence of this struggle.

And the struggle *is* over, I know it. I've already lost. Already surrendered.

I lift shaking hands. "I'll come. Just…I'm coming."

I don't know what's more terrifying—his expressionless face, or the way his dark eyes burrow into my skull.

He beckons me with a flick of his fingers, and I take a careful step toward him, hands raised.

Marcus grabs a fistful of my hair and uses that ferocious grip to steer me down the stairs. I bite back curses and tears, clinging desperately to the only thing I have left.

And it's Briar.

I'm too fucked in the head to understand why, or how, but he's all I've got right now.

BRIAR

Marcus's car isn't in his driveway, but he could have fetched it from Dylan's house earlier today, drove it through to Indi's house. More than enough time, what with me disappearing to the cemetery.

I've always been one step behind you, haven't I, *bro*?

I don't know why I believe I'll find answers at his house, but honest to God, I don't have anywhere else to go. I mean, where the hell do you take someone you've just fucking kidnapped?

I climb through Marcus's window and take a second to scan the room.

Has he always been this messy, or does his cleaning lady not work weekends? The bed's unmade, sheets twisted like he hosted a wrestling match on them. There are empty bottles of beer, coke and rum everywhere. Cigarettes and joint roaches clog up the air with stale fumes.

Was his father in here? Did he rough up Marcus enough to have caused this mess? Or did Marcus bring Indi back here—?

I cut off that last thought with ruthlessness and squeeze my eyes shut as I gather myself.

Must have been Marcus's father. Shit's been moved around, tossed to the floor, but nothing's broken.

My gaze lands on the laptop sticking out of Marcus's backpack. Was he going to study and decided against it, or was he in too much of a hurry to push it down all the way?

I'm all too aware of how much time is slipping past while I stand here motionless.

If Marcus used his car, then his GPS might be logged to an online app like my father's Merc. Fuck knows how that shit works—Dad mentioned it in passing during one of his visits a few months ago, and it sounded like pretty cool technology. Said he would know exactly where they were if anyone ever stole his car.

I grab the laptop and flip it open. Setting it down on the desk, I stare at the empty password field under a photo of Marcus smirking into the camera wearing sunglasses, a joint sticking out of his mouth.

Fuck.

I try a few random phrases, each more desperate than the last.

password
Pasword123
Marcus
Marcus123
I hesitate, then type:
Briar
Jessica

Nothing. My eyes slide to the default avatar of the guest profile next to Marcus's. I'm not exactly a computer boffin, but I know you can't access stuff on one profile from another, not unless you're the admin. Browser history, all that shit is profile dependent. It would be absolutely useless—

My fingers go hunting for a packet of smokes, an absent gesture as my mind grinds its gears.

But I don't touch a box of cigarettes. My fingers brush against the flash drive in my pocket.

Maybe not entirely useless.

I take out the drive, and swallow hard when it brings back a too-vivid memory of what Marcus had drawn on that piece of paper. He's no artist, but it was blatant how much time he'd spent on the sketch. The faint lines where he'd erased his pencil marks again and again to make sure every curve was just right.

I drum my fingers on the table as I wait for the computer to log me in and pick up the flash drive plugged into its USB port.

Squeezing my thumb and forefinger against my eyes, I do my best to rid myself of that image, but it's impossible.

Obviously, he lied to me. But I could never have imagined the extent of his depravity.

He killed the cat.

I let out a soft, bitter laugh, and open the flash drive's folder. Videos. Fourteen videos, all different file sizes. Porn, from the titles.

kayceegang.mp4

Castingcouch_HD.mp4

Bendingbecky.mp4

I scan the list, and my eyes immediately fix on the seventh, eighth, and ninth one.

Jess.mov

Jess (1).mov

Jess (5).mp4

Jess (6).mp4

I open the first one, chewing on a fingernail as I wait for it to load. It's the shortest one, so it doesn't take long.

A blur of yellow.

The camera focuses reluctantly.

"What are you doing?"

My heart clenches at the sound of Jessica's voice. Marcus laughs and suddenly the camera's on him. "What's up?" he says, giving a peace sign.

I remember this video. I inhale deep as Marcus focuses the camera back on Jessica. He was using his phone—a new one he'd just bought with a something ridiculous megapixel camera he couldn't stop talking about.

Jessica's wearing a bikini. I see myself in the background playing volleyball with a few guys in our team. This video is more than a year old, but the time stamp was from a few months ago.

And then I see why.

It's been edited.

The original video—the one Marcus had posted all over social media to show off his video skills—had been of him panning the beach, giving Jessica a fake interview about UV indexes and where she bought her designer bikini from, and then some macro shots of sand crystals and a lone starfish.

Only the interview was left.

When I'd watched the video on my phone's Facebook app, I hadn't realized just how close Marcus had been sitting to Jessica.

How uncomfortable she looked.

How tiny her fucking bikini was.

But I guess Marcus did, because he kept the video.

Sickened, I close the window and open the second video.

Sickened, but still curious as fuck.

Curious, but hoping against all hope this will reveal something I can use to find Indi.

I don't recognize the second video, but it's another faux interview with Jessica. She wanted to become an actress, so she was never shy of the camera. She's absolutely trashed in this video. She's in a bar, but it's one I don't recognize. Above the drone of conversation, music, and laughter, I hear another familiar voice.

Addy sounds as if she's having a conversation with someone else off-camera.

Jessica, however, is pouting and batting her eyes to the camera, explaining how easy it was for her to get cast for the latest Spielberg movie.

But it was obvious Marcus was less interested in what she had to say than in her mouth, her tits, and her legs judging from the close-ups and where he was pointing the camera.

Was this one of those nights I had to drive to the middle of nowhere to pick her up when Addy disappeared on her or took too many drugs to remember she was there with a friend?

I end that video prematurely, considering if I even want to watch the next. I don't know if I can bear watching another leering pseudo-interview.

Instead, I spend a few minutes hunting around in the computer's file system, trying to gain access to anything that might have some hidden meaning.

I find nothing.

So I light myself a cigarette and sit back in Marcus's desk chair, staring out the window as I smoke.

I shift, and the folded paper in my pocket rustles.

It's with morbid fascination that I take it out, unfold it, and smooth it open on Marcus's metal study desk.

I carry on smoking my cigarette as I do my best to look past the actual image and find any clues it might hold. A landmark, maybe, or a significant object. But there are precious few significant objects. Two, in fact. My eyes keep going back the necklace. That tear-drop cut stone. I know it to be encircled in diamonds, but Marcus's skill with a pencil doesn't do it justice. He almost tore through the paper how he colored that stone near-black.

Indi's necklace.

But Indi's not the one wearing it. The woman is about two decades older. A bit plumper.

Indi's mother.

And Marcus drew her exactly how Indi described her in her final moments.

Bound.

Gagged.

Naked.

There's an object between her legs. It's as darkly filled in as the stone around her neck.

I close my eyes and try to will away the image, but I can't.

I'll never be able to unsee that soda bottle.

CHAPTER FORTY

INDI

I wake with a throbbing headache, a stiff, cotton-dry mouth, and utter darkness. There's a hand on my upper arm, and it squeezes me tight enough to pinch. But when I cry out in pain, the sound is stifled.

Because I'm gagged.

Icy snakes of fear worm through my bones as I'm hauled up and out of a car.

Marcus's SUV. I remember a little now, although much of it's still groggy. He led me out of my gran's house to his car. Fuck knows how he got past the gates, but that doesn't matter now, does it? He shoved me in the back, and was beside me an instant later. Like lovers getting ready for a quickie in the back seat.

I tried fighting him.

Don't let them take you away.

Never change locations.

Rather die than let that happen.

Which is all sterling advice…if you have a fucking choice.

I didn't.

Marcus the goddamn football player is twice my size. I didn't stand a chance at resisting him. After the first kick, he had his ropes out and lashed around my ankles. And the first time I tried to scream, he gagged me. Once my hands were bound, there was literally nothing more I could do.

But he wasn't satisfied. He brought out a syringe, and jabbed it into the side of my neck. Whatever was in it took effect in seconds. I don't remember anything else—not how long I've been out, or if he did anything to me while I was unconscious. A mental scan of my body only tells me that my ankles and wrists are aching, and that I really need to pee.

My legs sag under me, and Marcus leaves bruises in my flesh as he props me up beside him and starts walking. The hood over my head is a new addition. When did he put it on? How long ago was that?

More importantly, where the fuck are we?

CHAPTER FORTY-ONE

BRIAR

Ifinish my cigarette before I can force myself to watch the last video. As it is, I almost decide against it. Marcus's actual depiction of a crime scene didn't give me any fucking clues— what would another fake interview with my dead ex-girlfriend help? But it's not as if I have anywhere to go. Any other leads to follow. I could scour the entire town of Lavish and not find him in time before he—

Thumping my hand on the table hard enough to rattle the ashtray, I let out a long breath and stab the spacebar.

A shaky camera focuses on Jessica's sleek hair. She turns her head, and grins wide at whoever's holding the camera.

"What's up, princess?" Marcus asks.

Jessica's eyes go wide in surprise, and then she slaps playfully at him. "Don't call me that."

"Why not?"

She tilts her head, lips pursing. "'Cos you know Briar will catch a fit if he hears you."

"Why? I'm just protecting you from scavengers," Marcus says. The

camera phone zooms in on Jessica's face. "Shouldn't have left such a fine specimen by herself."

Her eyes narrow. "You're the scavenger, Marcus." She's jostled to the side as a pair of arms encircle her, each hand holding a red Solo cup. My face comes into view, eyes glassy and unfocused, hair a mess.

Christ, I'm drunk as fuck.

I give Marcus a lopsided smile and lift a cup for Jessica to take. Her eyes narrow at Marcus as if in warning, and then she spins in my arms and kisses me. Beer sloshes out the cups, but I don't even seem to notice.

The longer the kiss goes on, the emptier both cups get, but then a bottle of vodka appears in the camera's view. Marcus pours a few solid glugs into one of the cups—the one I'd been about to hand to Jess before she kissed me.

The bottle disappears. "Drink up, guys!"

I come out of my kiss wearing a wide, sloppy smile.

I was so happy. I can see it in my own face watching this now, and my heart squeezes before I can push away that unexpected swell of emotion.

Jessica peeks at Marcus over her shoulder. "He's had enough," she says, and then snatches the red cup from my hand as I'm bringing it to my mouth.

"It's his birthday, Jess," Dylan says as he appears in the shot wearing his white baseball cap and slings an arm over my shoulder.

"Yeah, Jess," Marcus parrots. "It's his fucking birthday."

Jess scowls at Dylan, and then her gaze returns to Marcus as she drains what's left of my cup. She staggers a little and then takes a few gulps from her own.

She's just as drunk as I am—perhaps even more—but how couldn't she have tasted the vodka in her cup? It must have been strong as fuck. Jess never liked hard liquor. Beer was always her first choice, then wine. But she's throwing back her drink like it's watered-down beer.

"I hope you're gonna put out for my buddy tonight," Marcus says, handing a lit cigarette to me. Smoke briefly obscures the video. "Seeing it's his birthday and all."

Jessica's mouth drops open as she turns to me. "You told him?"

My grin widens.

Christ. I'm so far gone, I don't even realize how much shit I'm getting into.

Marcus lets out a low chuckle and reaches for Jessica's shoulder. She shrugs him off immediately, throwing him another heated glare.

"Ssstop it," Jessica slurs.

"Think your girl's a bit fucked," Marcus says. The shot focuses on Jessica's face, and she swats him away as she twists her mouth in disgust.

The camera jolts and noise stutters through the laptop's speakers. I hurriedly lower the volume, glancing over my shoulder at the closed door behind me. It's ridiculous to feel paranoid in an empty house, but I can't help it.

This is the video Addy sent me. It's much higher quality, but there's no mistaking where this was taken.

Really still think Addy sent you this?

My hands curl into fists on either side of the laptop and I close my eyes in utter disbelief. I never suspected Marcus, because evidence against me would be evidence against him covering up for me. But if it was Addy blackmailing me…?

His plan fell through. Or maybe he hadn't thought it out well enough.

"Tell you what, bro. I'll help you get the princess to bed, yeah?"

"Bed sounds good," I say. "Don't it, Jess?"

She giggles at me.

The video ends.

I stare at the square of black on the laptop screen, my heart thundering in my chest.

But then, a new video begins playing.

Jess (6)

The last video.

A black screen. The sound of breathing, shoes sloughing over carpet, fabric rustling.

"She's so fucking trashed, bro," Marcus says.

"Tha' was the point, wa'nt it?" I slur back.

"Almost there," Marcus says.

"Jess? Still with us?" I ask.

There's the faint outline of a doorway. A silhouette approaches it. Opens the door. A low light from inside splashes over the guy's face.

It's me. I'm standing in the doorway to Marcus's bedroom, swaying as I hold open the door for him.

I turn in the chair and stare at the closed door. My stomach tightens, and for a second I'm convinced I'm going to puke. When I face the laptop again, it's with a grimace and slitted eyes.

I don't want to watch this any more than I wanted to look at that picture Marcus drew. Because I know what happens next, and I don't want to have to face it like this.

But if I don't, then I'll never know if she said yes or not. It's always been her word against mine, but now—

Judging from how drunk she is, I already know she couldn't possibly have consented to anything.

I tap the spacebar anyway. And I force myself to watch.

"But it's your birthday, bro," Marcus says. "She's supposed to be giving you head right about now, not passing out in my bed."

"You're th' one that got her this drunk in the first place," I say.

Got *both* of us drunk it seems. On the contrary, Marcus's hand is steady, and his words come out just fine.

Marcus brings Jess over to the bed, but instead of gently putting her down, he collapses on the mattress with her, letting out a theatrical groan.

She tries pushing his arm off of her, and then starts giggling.

My chest grows tight again.

Nothing could ever get Jessica down for long. She was always so happy, so fucking optimistic. My little Hollywood starlet.

Until I ruined her. Until I broke her so badly that no one could put her back together again.

I squeeze my eyes shut, and move to close the laptop lid. I can't watch anymore. Just thinking about what comes next sickens me—

From the laptop comes the unmistakable sound of a door closing. And then Marcus speaks. What he says makes my eyes shoot open and sends a flood of bitter bile into my mouth.

"Give the birthday boy a goodnight kiss."

"What?" Jessica says, laughing. "Get out, Marcus."

"Come on. One for the camera, princess."

"Fine," she says through a sigh, but sounds only too happy to comply. The camera jolts. Light blooms and then Marcus's arm retreats behind the lens again. The lamp on the nightstand throws a golden aura over the bed. I perch unsteadily on the edge of Marcus's mattress, my bare feet on the floor and my knees wide apart, and drag Jessica onto my lap.

She straddles me clumsily, her back to Marcus as he moves away from the bed. Her skirt rides up her thighs when she leans in to kiss me, both of us swaying like reeds in a high wind. She seems to have forgotten all about Marcus as our kiss deepens. I grab her ass, dragging her hard against me. When she mewls into my mouth, Marcus steps to the side to get a better shot.

"Yeah, that's it," he murmurs.

Cold sludge slides down my back as my lips slowly part.

On the video, my hands move clumsily as I try to take off Jessica's shirt. I end up tangling it in her arms, and she starts giggling uncontrollably as I struggle to undress her.

The video blurs and then settles. Marcus's face obscures the shot, a pale smudge until he steps back.

My hands clench into fists. Marcus's pupils are crowding out his irises. It can't just be the low light in the room causing that—that must have been the coke and shit he was on that night.

"Marcus to the rescue," he whispers to the camera, his mouth inching into a coy smile. He points at the camera. "Who's the greatest wingman ever?" He points at himself with his thumb. "I am, and don't you ever forget that, bro."

He grins, smooths down his hair with his hands, and spins around to face me and Jessica on the bed. Creeping up behind her, he slides his hands under her shirt and pulls it over her head.

She doesn't even seem to notice it wasn't me undressing her. With her eyes shut and her body arching against mine, she looks lost in the moment.

And so am I. My hands move to her bra, but Marcus brushes them away and unhooks it for me. I claw the straps from her shoulders, baring her tits, and Marcus draws the lacy bra out between us and tosses it on the floor.

He should have left then. I could have stomached all of this, up to this point. He was high, so he thought he would help me. It was all innocent.

But what comes next makes my skin grow cold.

He moves up against Jessica's back and starts kissing the side of her neck. Her moan reaches the camera, but then cuts off abruptly when she snaps out of her trance and leans to the side to get away from Marcus's mouth.

"Wha' ya doin'?" she demands sulkily.

My eyes open, but it seems all I care about is making out with Jessica. If I see Marcus past her shoulder, I don't seem to notice, seem to care.

I slide my hands up Jessica's neck and draw her back for a kiss. She struggles and breaks free. "Get out, Marcus!"

"Yeah, Marcus," comes my slurred voice as I kiss Jessica's throat. "Get out."

"Is that any way to treat your wingman?" Marcus slides his

hands down Jessica's waist, and she arches away from his touch and deeper into mine.

"Marcus," she says, her voice dropping in pitch.

"Shh, princess." Marcus swipes her hair off her shoulder and plants another kiss on her skin.

"Briar, tell him to get out," she whines.

Instead, I grab her ass and throw her onto her back on the bed.

Because I never was a gentleman, was I? Whenever I got hard back then, I couldn't think about anything except what I wanted to stick my dick into. It had been Jessica for months already, and I'd been more than fucking patient.

My jaw's aching how I'm gritting my teeth, but I'm past the point of ending the video.

What happened to Jessica was all my fault. I will watch every second Marcus recorded and live with the torturous consequences of having that night forever etched in my mind.

It's the least I deserve.

I expect Marcus to leave, now that it's been made apparent I don't want him there. I guess that's what I thought back then too, in my drunken haze.

Marcus takes a step back, turning a little as if considering. It's impossible not to notice the erection tenting the front of his jeans. And as if he just became aware of it himself, he runs a hand over his groin, flattening his dick against himself as if suddenly embarrassed that we made him horny.

On the bed, Jessica starts moaning as I stick a hand under her skirt. But I'm slowing down, my movements becoming clumsy and heavy-handed. She hisses as I begin fingering her, and then squirms out from under me.

"You're hurtin' me." Her tits bounce as she sits up and runs her hands through her hair. Her face is slack from alcohol, her mouth a sloppy, unhappy crescent.

Marcus is still in the shot, but he's still as a statue—perhaps not wanting to draw our attention to the fact that he's still in the room.

"Sorry, babe," I mutter, pushing up so I'm on my knees. "Lemme make it up to you, yeah?"

I grab her hips and drag her closer, and then I flip her around. She arches and lets out a low moan as I squeeze her tits, kissing her neck until she's writhing against me.

My voice comes through on the camera, but it's unintelligible. Marcus looks at the camera, his mouth opening like a naughty kid who's just heard his first swear word, and then he does the unthinkable. He takes his fucking dick out of his jeans and begins jerking off.

I thumb my eyes closed and sit back in the chair, forcing back nausea. I've known Marcus since we were kids, but I never thought he'd be capable of doing something like this.

But I can't stop watching now. Because, up to this point, Jessica gave me full consent.

What if I *didn't* rape her? What if she let me take her virginity, and then had a change of heart in the morning?

It won't bring her back, but it might make those fucking nightmares stop, knowing I'm not guilty.

The bedsprings start shifting, and I make myself open my eyes.

I hold my hand out to block Marcus from the video so I don't have to witness him getting off from a few feet away while I screw Jessica.

Except…I've still got my jeans on.

Jessica's skirt is off, her panties tangled around her knees, but all I'm doing is finger fucking her.

I lean forward in my seat and go to skip the video ahead.

I fold over Jessica's back.

My hand freezes an inch from the laptop's touchpad.

Here it is.

This is where she yells at me to stop, and I don't.

I slide my hands down Jessica's ass, and ease her open. Marcus chose a perfect spot on the mantel—if the light in the room hadn't been so dim, this would have made a pretty decent porn flick.

But instead of taking out my dick and shoving it into her, I slide off her and onto the mattress.

Passed out?

I press both hands to the desk's cool metal surface, biting the inside of my cheek as Marcus stops jerking off.

On the bed, Jessica arches her back and makes a crooning sound. When she seems to realize I'm not trying to mount her like a wild animal, she glances to the side and sees me laying on my back, one hand on my chest the other flung out, chest already rising and falling in steady sleep.

She straightens on her knees, giggling, and tries to tug her underwear up her thighs.

But she can't, because Marcus catches hold of them with a finger. She struggles for a second before throwing a glassy look over her shoulder. It takes her too long to focus on Marcus, and when she does, she first smiles, and then frowns.

"Whad'ya doin'?" Her frown deepens as Marcus slides onto the bed behind her.

"Hush, princess," he murmurs.

"He's passed out," she declares, still trying to pull up her panties as if she doesn't realize Marcus is the one keeping them down.

"And the bastard left you high and dry," Marcus says. He slides a hand up the inside of her thigh, and strokes her. Her eyes stutter closed, and she lets out a low moan. "What kind of gentlemen would let his best friend's girl go to sleep all horny and shit?"

"Wait, no. Don't," Jessica grates, but she's doing fuck-all to stop him rubbing her clit.

My stomach's so tight, I'm surprised I haven't puked yet. I narrow my eyes, not wanting to watch what comes next, but at the same time unable to look away. It's a car crash. Body parts strewn on the road as haphazard as broken auto parts. And I'm craning my head to see, because I'm horrified and fascinated at the same time.

"No," Jessica moans, as Marcus shoves his fingers into her. *"Please, stop."*

Marcus puts his hand between her shoulder blades, and urges her down onto the bed, doggy style.

His dick is already out, and he positions himself at her entrance, fixed so entirely on his task that he seems to have forgotten about me, the camera, every-fucking-thing except wet, drunk Jessica.

"No. No!"

He thrusts so hard into her that she lets out a hoarse shriek.

It must have hurt like hell—Jessica's body goes stiff a second before she begins thrashing under Marcus's hand. He just bends over her, his other hand going to the back of her neck to keep her down as he begins fucking her even harder than before.

When she starts screaming, he grabs a fistful of sheet and shoves it into her mouth.

And, all the while, I'm laying right next to them, passed the fuck out.

I'm frozen where I sit as I watch it all play out. Bitterness floods my mouth, but I keep swallowing it down, forcing it back.

He keeps talking throughout. Princess this, whore that. Slapping and grabbing her ass as he watches his dick sinking into her.

Marcus comes quickly—maybe a minute or two in—while Jessica's still sobbing around the sheet he used to gag her with. When he pulls out, there's no mistaking the streaks of blood on his dick.

I sit forward in a rush, blinking hard.

That doesn't make any sense. *I* was the one with blood on my dick. That was how I knew I was guilty when Jessica confronted me the next—

Marcus sits back with a long sigh, stroking a last few drops of cum from his dick, and then slaps Jessica's ass so hard that even her muffled squeal reaches the camera.

Then he looks down, and slowly lifts his hand to study his palm.

His body tightens, and he scrambles off the bed, gaping at his hand.

He didn't know she was a virgin, and why would he? I never told him that's why she wasn't sleeping with me—just that she hadn't put out yet.

"Fuck," Marcus's voice comes through the speaker. "Jesus, fuck."

Jessica slumps to the side, and yanks the sheet from her mouth with trembling hands. "You fuck!" she says through a sob. But she's staring at me where I've passed out beside her. She thumps my chest with a fist and breaks into a string of sobs.

Marcus moves around to my side of the bed, waiting until Jessica burrows her head in her arm before climbing up beside me.

What. The. Fuck?

He unbuttons my fly with shaking hands.

No.

I begin shaking my head, my breath coming too fast, too hot, scorching my throat with every exhalation.

He pulls my dick out of my pants, and then stares at it, face devoid of emotion.

Then he begins jerking me off.

"Fuck!" I push away, closing my eyes as I slap the laptop closed.

That's why I had cum and blood all over my fucking dick that morning. That's why I never doubted Jessica when she said I'd raped her. How the fuck could I, with that much evidence stacked against me?

INDI

Marcus grunts as he hoists me up and cradles me to his chest. I buck, moaning into my gag as I struggle to get out of his arms. He grabs my hair and tugs so hard I see spots. I go rigid, and then relax into his embrace as he starts walking.

It's impossible to tell where he's taking me. It feels like late afternoon, but it could just as easily be a shady area we're in. For some reason, I keep thinking of the church where I first met Briar, where he and Marcus were conspiring. It would be kinda poetic, him taking me there for whatever nefarious purpose he has laid out for me in his deranged head.

As I feverishly attempt to place myself, both in time and space, memories come to me. Fragments, like raindrops splashing on my face, each one jolting clarity through me.

He had a pair of sneakers in his hand when he came to my bedroom door. The same ones that were outside.

Was it him that night, watching me?

I bite the inside of my lip, willing away the feel of his hands on my thigh and shoulder. His footsteps crunch over something.

Twigs? Dry leaves?

The church then.

It'll end where it all began.

What did he say to me in the hallway at the party last night? How peaceful someone looked. Her. She looked so peaceful.

Had he been talking about Jess?

"I didn't hurt her," Marcus says.

I flinch at the unexpected sound of his voice, and get goosebumps when my mind latches to his words.

Get out of my fucking head!

I make a sound through my gag, and Marcus laughs. "You don't believe me? You'll see. She's just fine."

Who the fuck is he talking about?

But then he's setting me on my feet. Pushing on my shoulders until I sit on something hard and smooth.

A light breeze touches my cheek, bringing me the scent of burned wood. I squirm, blinking back tears when Marcus steps back.

He doesn't even bother lashing me to anything. What would be the point? Where would I run, bound and blind?

There's a soft sound a few feet away, and I freeze.

Someone else is here, but who? And why are they so quiet?

Briar.

It's an irrational, panicked thought, but that doesn't make it any less terrifying.

It's been the both of them all along, hasn't it? Was this all just some sick game for them, keeping me guessing? The one luring me in, while the other stalks me from the shadows?

"*Please,*" I push through the gag. "Don't hurt me."

There's a sharp intake of breath, and then I hear a muffled whimper.

Not Briar. Addy.

I should have been relieved, but I'm not. At least if Briar was here, I might have stood some chance at getting him to let me go. I know I didn't imagine the chemistry between us. That inexplicable connection we've had from day one.

But he's not here.

Maybe he'll never be. Maybe he doesn't even know I'm gone.

In which case it's just me and Addy…

And Marcus.

CHAPTER FORTY-TWO

BRIAR

I stand in a rush, pressing a fist against my mouth until the urge to puke dissipates some. All this time, I was convinced I was a rapist.

The worst part is, I was kinda okay with that. Thinking about it brought the occasional fit of guilt and rage, but at the same time I felt numb to everything. Like it was all happening to someone else.

Because it *did*.

Because I never raped anyone. I never told Marcus to get rid of Jessica. He did it by himself. To protect himself, in case Jessica's memory came back.

And the idiot kept proof. Fine, he didn't exactly keep it laying around the house, but it didn't take that long for me to find it. Did he honest to God think this video would never be discovered? And the drawing? He sure loves his trophies.

Fucking psycho.

I glance to the side, and avert my eyes when they touch on that perverted drawing. But then I do a double take. At the angle

I'm sitting, the person depicted in the picture looks even more like Indi than before.

Thought she was lying about the murder. About the fire. Just like she thought I was lying, I guess. Meanwhile, I was bumping fists and buying drinks and playing X-Box with the person who raped and tortured her fucking mother.

I bow my head and rub my fingers over my lids.

Is that what he's doing right now? Does he have Indi at his mercy, while I sit here with my fucking thumb up my ass? I alerted the police, but what the fuck else can I do?

I thump the desk hard. Then again. Again. Welcoming the pain, drawing it deep inside to douse the guilt and shame drowning me.

I can show the cops everything—the video, the drawing, the hoody—but what would that help? It might as well just be Indi in that drawing, because I know deep down that's exactly what he'd do with her if he got the chance.

Bound.

Gagged.

Nak—

Marcus's bedroom door bursts open. I jerk and twist around in the chair.

Brandon Baker is standing in the doorway.

"The fuck you doing in my house?" the man belts out in a hoarse voice.

Christ, he's drunk. I move to the window, but slowly like I'm backing away from a wild animal.

I guess Marcus got his build from his mother, not his father. Brandon Baker is wide and tall as an ox with a thick neck and a broad nose. Marcus's features are more delicate, almost fox-like in comparison.

This is only the second time I've met Brandon. The first was more than five years ago, when Marcus and I were still teens.

He'd been in better shape back then, but still a hulk of a man. Alcohol abuse has webbed red veins over his nose and cheeks, and turned his eyes a shade too yellow for a healthy person's.

"Thought Marcus was home," I say, trying to inject casualness into my tone. "But I see he's not, so I'll leave."

Brandon's bloodshot eyes fix on the laptop before coming back to me. "You looking at his stuff?"

"No, course not." It's probably an idiotic thing for me to do, but there's still a bit of space between us—and Marcus's bed—so I do it anyway. "You maybe know where he is?"

Brandon's laugh turns into a phlegmy cough before he's done. "Prolly sticking it in some cunt or other." His eyes narrow. "Or an asshole, all I know." He gives me another long look, as if trying to determine if that might have been my asshole before.

I lift my hands. "Fair enough. I'll just be on my way." Those stilted words are barely out of my mouth before Brandon takes a few lumbering steps closer to me.

From what I remember Marcus telling me, he started out working as a bouncer at a night club. That was before he started his own security company, of course. Which is how he met my dad. A security company that obviously does well for itself, if this house and its location in Lavish is anything to go by.

But Marcus also said his father was into some dodgy shit. That would better explain their finances than a security company in a town where there isn't an electric fence in sight. Not unless installing a safe at some rich guy's house made him enough…

Client lists.

Addresses.

I tilt my head, and advance a step before I can stop myself. "You made him do it, didn't you?"

Brandon ignores the question. "Pissed tha' m'boy isn't actually your fucking bestie, you queer prick?"

I scowl at him. "The hell you on about?"

Fuck knows I can't take him down, but I'd love to try. Even if it meant being bludgeoned into a coma, I'd love nothing more right now than to crack my knuckles into this ogre's jaw.

My mind feels like scrambled eggs. I shake my head, frowning hard. "What are you—?"

Brandon's face hikes up in a grimace, then he turns and spits into the corner of Marcus's room. "Beat the fag out of him one of these day." He laughs, rough and loud, and makes to grab me.

I sidle away, and reach behind me. My fingers touch the windowsill, and the relief that escape is so near almost drives me to manic laughter. *That's* why Marcus's father kept beating him? Did he honestly think his son was gay?

Brandon's obviously close to a psychotic break or something. Perhaps he's schizo. Would explain the alcohol abuse, the domestic violence, the paranoid delusions.

"You're crazy," I say, moving back until my thighs brush the window sill.

In an instant, Brandon is in my face. His fist is a blur as it heads for my jaw. I half-fall, half-push myself out the window. I barely manage to grab the oak tree's branch as I hurtle past, and I tear off the edge of a nail as I fight to cling to the rough bark.

Brandon sticks his head out Marcus's window, laughing so hard that his spittle dots my face like drizzle. "Might as well let go, boy. We got what we wanted." He laughs again, and disappears inside the house.

I consider letting go, but it's two stories down with a stony-looking patch of ground to land on. Instead, I monkey climb down the branch and hop onto the grass, too flustered to bother making myself less visible.

Soon as I'm back in my car, I slam closed the door and lock it. I doubt Brandon will come after me, but I'm not taking any chances. The apple certainly didn't fall far from the fruit tree, did it? I'm starting to understand why Marcus is the way he is.

I slam my hands into the steering wheel, a well of red-hot fury burning its way through me. I have all of the answers, except the most important one.

Where in the *fuck* is Marcus Baker?

INDI

"Ready for your play date, Addy?" Marcus says.

I shift on my hard seat, turning to the sound of his voice. Addy lets out a muffled sound of protest before shuffling closer to me. Things crunch and crack under her feet as Marcus brings her closer, and then the heat of her body warms my legs.

"Sit up. There we go. Now put your head in her lap."

A heavy weight rests on my thighs. Addy's body trembles against me, and it's mere seconds before there's a damp spot on my jeans where her tears have wet the fabric.

She moans and shifts as Marcus does something behind her. I sit up straight, straining to see something through the sack over my head.

No, not a sack—it's a pillowcase. If I look down, I can make out the seams. I turn, and glimpse the vaguest suggestion of a big shape to one side.

A wall. Possibly one of those that fell over when the church burned down. It looks monstrous from my seat on the pew, as if it's about to tumble onto my head.

When I look forward, I can almost make out a shape in front of me too, but the light's all wrong, the fabric too dense, my head too sore.

"Shh," Marcus murmurs when Addy starts sobbing.

Something drops to the floor nearby, and I flinch at the sound. Then another.

Shoes.

He's taking off her shoes.

I shift a little and lean forward, resting my head on Addy's—cheek to cheek. I don't know what comfort it will bring her, but at least she's not alone.

At least I won't be alone either…except if he kills her first.

A sob wracks through me at the thought, and then there's nothing I can do to stop the tears.

"Bunch of babies," Marcus says with a laugh in his voice. "Don't be sad. It'll all be over real soon, okay?"

But that only makes me sob harder. Above all else, I know Marcus is a fucking liar.

BRIAR

As I turn the last corner toward my house, my foot slips off the gas. My Mustang grumbles sulkily at the loss of power, and threatens to cut out. I guide her onto the side of the road and shut off the ignition.

Five cop cars with flashing lights line the road outside my house.

Shit!

Even if my father doesn't accuse me outright of stealing his shit, the cops will want to talk to me. And they're not gonna figure out where Indi is any sooner than I can, that's for sure. We'll all just be wasting more time.

More time for Marcus to toy with Indi.

More time for him to kill her…if he hasn't already.

And why are they even here? Just so my father can prove what a delinquent Marcus was? Shouldn't they rather be calling all those clients of his, and letting them know there was a breach? That they should consider moving house.

Because if Marcus knows where they live, Brandon Baker knows where they live.

Christ, of course.

Another piece falls into place. That painting in my father's study, the one with that creepy little goblin. Only now can I finally make sense of the name scrawled in the bottom corner.

Davis. Indi's family home, her mother's maiden surname.

Fuck knows what the initial was, but that scrawl couldn't form any other word, now that the thought's latched in place.

Marcus must have been accessing files on the regular for his dad. Getting me drunk so he could slip into my father's study and get the new client's information, knowing full well of the treasures they were keeping in their homes. That's why Indi's necklace matched that bracelet so perfectly. It was part of the same set her father commissioned mine to make. The one he tried to pay off with his wife's painting.

I almost drop my phone how my hands are shaking. I stab on my father's name and pray to God that just this once he'll answer.

"Please," I murmur, my thumb in my mouth as I tear off a strip of nail.

"Where are you?" Edward answers, voice dangerously low.

"Doesn't matter. Dad, please, just listen."

And through some strange miracle or strange twist of fate, he does.

"I need the address for the client you made that blue bracelet for."

"What?"

"The bracelet and the matching necklace. The one the client

paid for with a painting. The one in front of your safe. I need that address!"

Edward lets out a mirthless laugh. "Why the fuck are you asking me? You already—"

"I wasn't involved, okay? It was all Marcus, Dad. I need that address, okay?"

"Sure son," Dad says casually. "I'll give you the address."

My skin prickles in warning. "Okay," I say through numb lips. "Thanks."

"Soon as the police department's IT guys are done trying to bring my computer back to life."

My heart beats in my throat.

"What?"

"Bit difficult getting anything off the hard drive you two crashed, isn't it?"

CHAPTER FORTY-THREE

INDI

I get myself under control about the same time Marcus is done stripping Addy, which I'm only assuming is the case, based on the sounds I hear and the way Addy's head shifts on my lap. The rip of a knife slicing through fabric.

My wrists are aching from the pressure of the ropes bound so tightly against them, but it's nothing compared with the fluttery uncertainty preying on my nerves.

Especially when I hear a zipper being drawn down.

Addy moans around her gag, and presses against me as if she's trying to get away. Suddenly, it's not just her head on my lap but her entire upper body. I hurriedly straighten when I feel warm air on the back of my neck, and lean back to get away from what must be Marcus's hot breath.

There's a muffled gasp from Addy, a grunt from Marcus. Then the unmistakable sound of two people fucking.

You'd think it would be different. That it wouldn't sound so downright pornographic. But it does. I guess it's still just skin slapping against skin. Breath forced out by every thrust—consensual or not.

"For a whore, you still got a tight little cunt, Addy."

I try to take my mind away, to leave this ungodly moment behind, but I can't. Not with Addy's head bumping into my belly. Not with Marcus's groans filling my ears.

A hand grasps at my breast, and I jerk in surprise at the touch. I try to move away and almost succeed when fingers wrap around my throat and start to squeeze.

I struggle, fighting for breath. Sobs wrack Addy's body as Marcus fucks her harder and harder against me.

My limbs go cold.

Tingles spread into my fingers and toes.

Suddenly, I don't give a fuck about anything anymore. It's black, and so quiet now. There's pain in my chest, my lungs contracting as my body involuntarily heaves for air, but I still have zero fucks to give.

Because it'll all be over real soon

I know he's a liar, but I'm willing to believe him now. I want to believe him. I'm done with this fucking world and my pathetic excuse of a life.

"Ah, fuck, princess," Marcus groans. His fingers tense even more, and a deeper darkness than the one cast by the pillowcase over my head swarms into me.

Through me.

Around me.

I black out a second after Marcus comes, the sickeningly guttural sound he makes echoing in my ears.

BRIAR

Grit crunches under my shoes as I head for my family home. A few cops turn to look my way, but none seem that interested in my presence. Why should they be? My dad's been pissed off at me before. But he protected me before too.

It was probably the only time he ever flew back to Fool's Gold County because I called. And then it wasn't even technically me that made the phone call—it was my lawyer.

I'll never forget the look on his face when he walked into that interrogation room at the local sheriff's office. How his eyes scoured me and my clothing, as if he was utterly disappointed that I wasn't wearing handcuffs and an orange jumpsuit.

Rape.

He hadn't even flinched. But he'd always been good at schooling his emotions, my father.

Except now, looking back, he'd left a trail of clues a freeway wide—I'd just never bothered to question him.

Claim them as yours, son. Claim them and never let anyone else take them from you.

That has been his mantra since I could remember. It was his way of directing his anger at a cheating wife while warning me to make sure my future partner doesn't fuck around.

A cop starts walking toward me—casual like, a spring in his step—when my cellphone vibrates with a new message.

I almost don't look at it. It's not like it could be good news. Either Dylan and Zak finally decided to speak to me again— although their intel would be fucking useless to me now—or someone's just informed me that I qualify for a credit card.

But I have no idea what to say to the cop approaching me, so I buy myself some time by checking my phone.

The phone case creaks between my fingers when I see the name on the screen.

It had never even occurred to me to call Marcus. To just ask him where he was. I guess, deep down inside, I knew he'd never have told me.

How fucking wrong I am.

We're having so much fun without you, but it would be better if you joined. Bring the money. Don't tell the cops. I see anything I don't like, I'll kill them both.

The address below makes my heart skip a fucking beat.

12 Northenden Drive, Lakeview.

I pivot on my heel, ignoring the cop's quizzical, "Hey, are you Prince?"

He could have drawn a gun and shot me right then and I wouldn't have noticed until my head hit the fucking tarmac.

The instant I touch on the address, it opens the map application on my phone.

Five hours, thirty minutes.

I stop in my tracks, and then speed up again. The final yard to my car is a full out sprint.

Five *fucking* hours?

I'm gritting my teeth so hard, the enamel creaks inside my mouth.

INDI

A slap to my cheek hard enough to whip my head to the side rouses me. I cough, splutter, and fight my bonds to escape.

"Relax, princess."

I freeze, my breath getting trapped somewhere deep in my

throat. I lick my lips, and then do it again when I realize the gag isn't in my mouth anymore.

But I still can't see. And this time, it's not because of a pillowcase. There's something over my eyes, something bound tight around my head.

Why, it's a satin blindfold, Indi. Now all you need are some rose petals and champagne.

I laugh before I can stop myself.

Fingers grip my jaw, shaking my head. "What's so funny?"

Marcus almost sounds cheerful. I shift, and realize there's no weight in my lap anymore.

"Where is she?" I croak, and then cough when the words scrape through a dry, rusted throat.

"Who, Addy?" Marcus says, and playfully taps my cheek with his fingertips. "Oh, she was being a drag."

I swallow hard, desperately attempting not to let the full force of his statement sweep me away into madness. "Can I please have some water?"

Because isn't that what you're supposed to do? Remind your captor that you're human, after all.

He already knows my name. He already knows I'll be missed—even if it's just by Briar and my gran.

"So polite," he murmurs, running a knuckle down the center of my nose. "How could I possibly say no?"

He moves away, his shoes crunching over whatever debris is scattered on the ground.

I tip my head to the side and rub my shoulder against my blindfold. It shifts a quarter of an inch, then another, then—

Something strikes my belly hard enough to make me bend over and retch at the impact. While I'm still gasping, saliva threading the space between my mouth and my thighs, Marcus grabs my hair in a fist and wrenches back my head.

Water splashes over my face, and I splutter when a few stray drops go down my windpipe instead of my larynx.

"Had enough?" Marcus snarls. "Or would you like some more?"

Another deluge pours over my mouth. I open my lips and gather as much as I can before closing my mouth and swallowing. It burns, and I get some up *and* down my nose, but it's worth it.

Marcus releases my hair. My head bobs forward before I can stiffen my neck. I cough as quietly as I can, shivering when a breeze cools my now soaked hoody.

Marcus laughs. "You caught me off guard, you know that?"

He pauses, like he's waiting for something, so I shrug a little as I tamper down a last cough.

"First time I saw you," he says. His voice pans left and right as if he's pacing in front of me. I'm itching to see something— any-fucking-thing—but I don't want to suffer another round of punishment for trying to look.

"Scared the living bejesus out of me, I'll be honest." Another laugh, this one a higher octave than the one before. Goosebumps break out on my skin at the manic tone in his voice when he continues.

Just keep him talking, Indi. The more distracted he is, the better chance you have at catching him unaware.

And do what, exactly?

Fuck it, one step at a time.

Step one? Getting loose.

"Why?" I ask, and I'm shocked at how steady my voice is. Deep, rough, but steady.

Guess all that crying helped. I haven't got a shred of terror left in me anymore. I cried it all out. All that's driving me right now is primal instincts. Survival of the fittest style of thing.

Or, in this case, the sanest.

"Weird how that works, isn't it?" Marcus says. "Kids looking like their parents?"

My skin starts to crawl, but I ignore the sensation in favor of focusing on something productive. Like trying to work out the fucking knots Marcus has used to tie me up. They feel complicated as fuck. Overly so.

Arrogant, psychotic prick. Couldn't just have done rabbit ears, could you? Bet you were the despised know-it-all of your fucking Boy Scout club.

"Dad says I look like her. My mother," he adds, as if I'm rocking a single-digit IQ. "But Briar doesn't. Guess he takes after his father then."

Oh my God. He's gone off the edge, hasn't he? How the hell am I supposed to outsmart a lunatic? It's like trying to fit a square peg in a triangular hole. The math just doesn't work out.

"I wouldn't know, of course," Marcus goes on, his voice panning to the left again. "Barely remember her. You know I was six when she fucked off? Back then, we were still living in downtown Lavish, close to the train tracks." He laughs. "Not anymore! Got my dad to thank for that. Picked us up by our fucking bootstraps, he did, after she dumped us."

Mommy issues? I'm not even remotely surprised. By the fact that he has them, *and* that she abandoned him and his father, especially if psychosis runs in the family. And I can't even blame her—I'd also get the fuck out of Dodge.

I find a bit of give by my wrists, and wriggle for all I'm worth, while Marcus goes on talking with his voice aimed away from me.

"But then I saw a photo in Briar's house, and I kinda had to believe pa."

I don't even bother trying to understand. He's still facing away from me, and I've managed to undo a loop in this intricate knot.

"I can really see myself in her," Marcus goes on.

Another loop. There's finally enough give for me to wriggle my hands out of the ropes. I let out a soft sigh, massaging my wrists as discretely as possible behind my back so Marcus won't notice. My fingertips tingle furiously as blood rushes back into them, and I'm rewarded with a flush of bravery that makes me sit up straight in my seat.

"Just like I can see her in you." The angle of his voice changes, and I freeze, willing my heart to slow its furious pounding.

Now he thinks we're related? I can't even.

But I shrug, and drop my chin to my chest in some approximation of meekness, hoping he'll buy it and carry on pacing.

"Who?" I manage, twisting my hands and getting ready to launch myself at him with clawed fingers.

"Chantelle," he says through a laugh.

My body turns to ice. I force a swallow before I can urge myself to speak. "Wh-what?"

"Your mother."

I wrench my blindfold off and stand in a rush. Marcus is a few feet away, his head tilted to one side, hands behind his back. The epitome of a patient teacher. Things start slotting into place almost reluctantly.

My head turns on its own as I force myself to focus on my environment.

The char in the air had me confused. My hard seat. But there's no mistaking it now.

I'm standing in the middle of my gutted house, surrounded by blackened walls and tattered ribbons of yellow police tape.

It wasn't a pew I was sitting on. It was a wooden chest my mother'd kept in her studio. I think she kept spare canvasses in it, but fuck knows.

Marcus steps closer, holds out a hand, and bends a little at the waist. "Shall we dance, while we wait?"

Instead of taking his hands, I press my palms against my belly, trying to still my suddenly twisting stomach. "While we wait for what?" I breathe.

"Briar, of course." Marcus tilts his head again, and steps forward to snatch my hand away from my belly.

He drags me closer. With my ankles still bound, I stumble against him. I don't know if he takes the gesture as me wanting to be close, but his smile certainly makes me believe that he does. When I struggle, he slides an arm around my back and holds me so close I can feel his erection jutting into my tummy.

"I feel bad about what I did last time," Marcus whispers down to me, for all the world like we're conspiring lovers. "I think, this time, he should get to watch."

BRIAR

I don't care about traffic cameras. I fly right through stoplights. They'll have to catch me first. They'll have to have to T-bone me with a truck before I'll slow down or stop.

Fifteen minutes. That's what my GPS tells me. Fuck knows if it adjusts based on my speed. For all I know, Google's already alerted the authorities to a speeding Mustang traveling at breakneck speed down Lakeview's only freeway.

Couldn't. Give. A. Fuck.

Everything up to this point's been a fucking blur. My tank's almost empty, but I care as much about that as I do whether I die or not before I reach Indi's house.

I don't think for a minute Marcus would have kept her alive

just to torture her in front of me. If it's one thing I've recently come to realize about him—he's seriously unbalanced. It took him all of what, one minute, to decide on raping Jessica.

True, he was strung out on drugs, but judging from what he did to Indi's mother, he's only grown bolder since then.

How long did he toy with Indi before ending her?

With Jessica, it took him almost a day to gather the courage to throw her over the bridge at Angel Falls. Indi's mother? A couple of hours.

He's had Indi for five hours, maybe longer.

I don't hold out any hope of seeing Indi alive.

But there's enough furious vengeance flowing through my veins to make up for that. Little does he know I wouldn't even think about involving the cops. All they'd do is arrest him, charge him, send him to jail.

Or, possibly, Mallhaven Mental Institute. I hear it's really fucking cushy over there.

No…I don't plan on handing Marcus over to the cops.

I intend on being his judge, jury, and fucking executioner.

And you know what? I'm gonna make him suffer.

CHAPTER FORTY-FOUR

INDI

I wondered briefly what we would dance to once Marcus had me against him. But then he started humming and it all made sense. At first, I kept stumbling. Then weakly apologizing when he growled at me. Soon, he realized that the best dance partners don't have knots around their ankles. So he got rid of those.

Now we're sweeping around the ruins of my living room, his hand at the small of my back, and my cheek on his chest as he leads me through a surprisingly good waltz. Maybe he had lessons when he was young. You know, in-between torturing animals, setting fires, and wetting his bed?

But I jest.

This shit's fucking serious as hell, and I only wish I could form some kind of plan that didn't involve a random meteorite crashing into the house.

Even now, dancing a crazy waltz through the remnants of my home, I can feel how strong he is. How the muscles along his spine bunch as he moves. How tightly he grasps my hand. The sure-footedness of every step he takes.

Bet you wish you had your switchblade now, don't ya?

Oh, you bet I do!

Then again, I wish for many things right now. Like enough backbone to attempt to seduce him. I could do that. But every time I look up and see that vacant, dreamy look in his eyes, everything inside me shrivels up.

Then all I can do is gently rest my head on his chest and wish myself the fuck away from this place.

But dear God, it's not a fuck working.

It's not *working*.

BRIAR

I slam on the brakes when the signpost for Indi's road comes into view. The car behind me streams past blaring its horn, and the driver even throws me a zap through his passenger-side window.

No fucks given.

I put my Mustang into gear, and cruise around the corner. My GPS tells me I'm a minute away from my destination before I turn her off with a stab of my thumb.

I got this, Siri.

I fucking got this.

I'd wished more than anything that I'd taken the gun from that safe.

Why the fuck didn't I?

Oh, right. Back then, I was still under the impression it was Addy blackmailing me.

I don't think I've ever felt this naive in my fucking life. This…duped.

My best friend and I didn't have a fucking clue. Is it because he was the only one that was ever there for me? The only one who ever insisted on protecting me, even when I didn't need it?

Doesn't matter, of course. What's done is done. I can't change the past, I can only affect change in the present.

And presently, I need Marcus's head on a fucking spike.

INDI

I hear footsteps the same time Marcus does. We both turn to the side. Briar's standing on the threshold of what used to be the entrance hall of my house.

He doesn't look close to as pissed off as he did when he was standing in Addy's living room. In fact, he looks a little taken aback. The flip my stomach just did ends in a fucking belly flop.

What, you never seen a murderer waltzing around with his victim before, Briar?

"Hey, man. What's up?" Marcus releases me, dismisses me, abandons me. Then he's striding up to Briar, a hand outstretched like Briar's just arrived at the football game he's streaming at his house. Late, but instantly forgiven since he brought his own six-pack of Bud.

And instead of lunging forward, tackling him, and busting his head open on the soot-covered tiles of my living room floor…Briar shakes his *motherfucking* hand.

"Long drive," Briar says.

My feet take root. My hands curl into fists.

"Glad you could join us, bro," Marcus says, completely oblivious to the fact that I'm sprinting toward him at full speed.

Briar's eyes go wide, and he barely manages one shake of his head.

Then Marcus turns, catches me, spins me around.

Are we waltzing again? Is this one of those flashy moves that will end with me sliding between his legs?

Nope.

This is Marcus anticipating my every fucking move like a goddamn assassin.

We spin. He throws me away from him. Briar lunges toward him. And then there's suddenly a gun involved in the situation.

I'm on my ass on the floor, but I freeze just as much—if not more—than Briar does.

Marcus makes a show of drawing back the hammer with his thumb.

Briar lifts his hands.

Right now I hate them both equally. Marcus for being a psychotic asshole, Briar for being a cowardly freak.

Where's the cinematic rough and tumble between besties? The well-aimed punch that has Marcus sliding over the tiles, stunning him just long enough to let Briar snatch up the gun?

Nope. They just fucking stare at each other.

Slowly, quietly, *patiently*, I get to my feet.

Fuck this shit.

I'm done being held against my will. I'm done with Marcus's rapey threats.

Done.

Just fucking done.

Lips peeling up into a snarl, I launch myself at Marcus.

BRIAR

What the fuck is she thinking? What in *the fuck* is Indi fucking Virgo thinking?

Wait. She's not. This is all raw adrenaline, and the bone she has to pick with Marcus. I'm guessing she knows about her mom. I'm guessing he's already toyed with her to the point of rousing that infernal fury I'm already so familiar with.

There's nothing left for her now but to dig herself out of an early grave. Guess she's already given up all hope that I'll be the one responsible for rescuing her from the tower, my virgin Rapunzel.

So what then? I get to stand back and watch Marcus shred her apart?

Not a fucking chance.

But I don't get a say in the matter, because when Marcus hears Indi getting closer, he turns and pistol whips her on the side of the head.

I'm two steps closer before he swings back me, Indi crashing to the floor in the background with a yelp of pain that goes through me like an ephemeral whip crack.

"Stop," Marcus says with a shake of his head. "Just stop."

I lift my hands, and do as he says. Behind him, Indi groans and rolls onto her side. Looks as is if she's trying to push herself up, but judging from the trickle of blood running down her face, Marcus got in a solid blow.

"I had such fun shit planned for us," Marcus says. My gaze flashes back to him, my mouth thinning into a grim line. Honest to God, he looks disappointed. Head shaking, his eyes sad. "I was gonna let you have her first, bro. To make up for Jess."

God, I want to charge him so bad. But I have no doubt in my mind that he'll fire. He had no issues torturing Indi's mother and then strangling her to death—what's a bullet between friends?

"Well, maybe some of this is still—" Marcus waves the gun around Indi's burned-out house "—salvageable."

Doubt it. The living room's completely caved in. There is a flight of stairs that look dodgy as shit, and only a quarter of the first floor remains.

I'm pretty sure if this place weren't a crime scene, it would have been condemned.

"Help her up," Marcus says, stepping back and using the gun to wave at Indi. "Come on."

I go over to her, crouch, help her to her feet. She resists until she sees my face and realizes it's me. As I straighten, a shape on the floor catches my eye. I grab Indi and turn her to face Marcus, forcing a hard swallow.

I only saw the back of her, but I know it was Addy. She could have been sleeping, I guess, but no one goes to sleep naked on a singed carpet. Not with their legs that wide. Not with a belt around her neck. And I doubt Indi's seen her—Marcus left her partially hidden behind the blackened lumps of a sofa.

"I have your money," I say, and then cock my head toward the car. "Double what you wanted."

Marcus gives me a cold smile. "You know what? I've had a lot of time to think the past few days." He taps the barrel of the gun against his head. "'Bout you. About me." He points the gun at Indi, and she flinches into me. "About her."

I slide my arms around Indi, holding her tight. She must be terrified, but she's not even shaking. Then again, he has had her for more than five hours. I suppose at some point the fear simmers down.

"And?" I prompt.

Marcus shrugs. "I wanted to disappear." He purses his lips

and looks away. "Thought the money could help me get out, you know. Then I wouldn't have to work with my dad."

Eyes the color of night settle on Indi. His cold smile inches up. "But the more I thought about it, the more I realized I *do* love it, bro."

Marcus's words come back to me then. We were in the pub, talking about his father. About the dodgy shit his dad made him do.

I keep going back and forth—hating it, loving it, hating it.

What if I stop hating it?

"And no one's caught me yet." Marcus shrugs again, and his smile widens enough for me to see his teeth. "So why the fuck should I stop?"

Soot-covered stairs creak alarmingly under my shoes. This is all too surreal, like a nightmare I can't wake up from; the feel of late-afternoon sun on my arms as I'm forced up the stairs of the house I'd lived in for years; the sound of birds, too loud now that the roof's caved in.

How many times have I skinned my knees on these steps as a kid while rushing to get upstairs? Now I'm moving through molasses, every cell in my body protesting.

But what am I supposed to do? There's a gun trained on me —Marcus follows us up the stairs like a predator stalking prey— and I'd break an ankle trying to jump off.

A maimed girl is a dead girl.

Look what happened to Addy.

I realize Briar was trying to protect me earlier, but he shouldn't have bothered. Addy's body is off to one side, in clear view as we head up to the landing.

After I caught sight of her, I nearly threw up. Now I'm keeping my eyes straight ahead.

Not daring to look. Not daring to disobey.

If I'm a good girl, maybe he'll let me go.

If I behave, maybe he'll drop his guard long enough for me or Briar to overpower him.

Chances are slim, but it's all I have.

So up the stairs I go, one foot at a time. By the time I reach the landing, I'm numb with dread anticipation.

There's a gaping doorway ahead.

My room. It's still standing. It's the only thing still standing up here. Some of the wall against the hall has fallen in, but the other three are still there. Blackened, cracked, but still there. Roof's caved in, but there's even a window frame left, a few shards of glass poking out of that wood like teeth.

It's the mattress on the floor, however, that makes me stare.

It's not mine. Mine was a twin. This one's gotta be a queen. And it's completely untouched by the fire, except for a few streaks of soot.

Brand new and bare.

"See?" Marcus says.

I jolt and hurry forward a step, my skin crawling with the realization that he'd been close enough to whisper in my ear.

"Look how nice it looks."

"Just take the money," Briar says. We're standing a few feet apart facing Marcus, who's taking up the doorway to my old room.

Marcus rolls his eyes. "Quit it about the money, already. I told you. I found my calling." He steps inside the room and heads for my dresser. It's pitch black, one leg eaten away by the fire. Marcus takes a phone from his pocket, plays around with it for a second, and then puts it on the slanting surface.

Facing us.

No—facing the mattress.

"Undress her."

Briar shakes his head. Lifts his hands. "I can get more money. Tons more. Just tell me how much—"

"Get her naked!" Marcus yells.

I jerk, my hands closing instinctively into fists. Briar's jaw bunches, but he turns and does as he's told.

Eyes fixed on my throat, he starts undressing me. Every time his fingers graze my skin, I shudder. By the time he's done, I'm full of goosebumps and ice-cold everywhere except my face, which is burning up with shame.

"Good," Marcus says quietly. "Now how about a little foreplay. I'll leave it up to you, but just make sure it's good, yeah?"

Briar looks up at the sky. He takes a visible breath, and then slides his hands over my bare shoulders, pulling me close.

Hiding my nakedness from Marcus.

"Nuh-uh," Marcus says, stepping closer. "I wanna see what you're doing."

He has his gun out again. I'm sure if he came close enough to us, Briar could take it from him. But he keeps at least a yard between us, sometimes more.

"Come on, man," Briar says. "You've made your point. Just let her go." He steps back, lifting up his hands. "You can kill me if you want, but just—"

"You do it, or I will," Marcus growls.

Briar's eyes skip to me, then back again. Oh my god, he's actually considering letting Marcus touch me?

But wait…maybe that's not a bad idea. Marcus would have one hand on me, and only one on the gun. Distracted. Horny as fuck.

I've never in my life wished I had telepathic powers as much as I do right now. We'd have this all worked out, Briar and I.

Marcus would already be lying hogtied on the floor, the cops on their way.

Are the cops on their way? Is Briar playing for time?

Briar's hands close over my breasts and start squeezing. I press my lips into a line, looking up, looking down, looking anywhere but at him.

"Is she getting wet?" Marcus asks.

I squeeze closed my eyes, a shiver chasing down my spine at the leer in Marcus's voice.

"Fuck," Briar mutters angrily, but his hand moves down anyway, skimming over my tummy, my clit. Sinking between my legs.

But he doesn't touch my pussy. Or at least, he doesn't finger me.

"Mmm," he murmurs, looking at Marcus. "A little, but not there yet."

My chest constricts painfully. The fuck does he think he's doing? I step back, throwing an arm over my boobs and cupping a hand over my pussy.

But Briar doesn't even look at me. He's staring at Marcus.

"So…" Briar straightens, leaning his weight to one side. "I saw the video."

My eyes dart to Marcus. Marcus gives Briar a lopsided smile. "Yeah?"

"I liked it," Briar says, nodding a few times. "It cleared things up, you know?"

"Yeah?" Marcus says through a laugh.

The fuck are they talking about?

BRIAR

I have no fucking clue what I'm doing, but I think it's working especially since Marcus doesn't seem that keen to blow my fucking head off anymore. I count that as a win. And I've gotten him to stop thinking about Indi—he's not even looking at her anymore.

Instead, he's fixated on me…like he always is. Suddenly, all those 'bros' we sent back and forth have so much more meaning. Why he always loathed the girls I dated.

I was protecting you, bro.

She wasn't good enough for you, bro.

Time to play on his weaknesses, just like he has every single day.

"You were right." I take another slow step. "You were right every time, bro."

I try to let it sound as natural as possible, but there's suddenly a suspicious gleam in Marcus's eyes. "Yeah," he says quietly, and his eyes move to Indi.

"About her," I say, pointing at Indi. Then I take another step, this one diagonal, cutting off his view of her as if I have something really important to say. "About Addy." I put emphasis on the last word, and Marcus gives me a fierce nod. "Bunch of whores, just like you said."

I try to laugh, but it comes out sounding faker than a three-dollar bill.

"Warned you, bro," Marcus says, and he even has the audacity to waggle his finger at me. "I warned you."

"You did, man, you did. And I didn't listen. I didn't *fucking* listen." I thump my fist into my palm and then drag my hands through my hair. I probably sound like an idiot, but when I glance at Marcus, he's gone stock still. Face expressionless. The hand holding the gun dipping.

Marcus shakes his head, and the gun sinks to his side. "She was a cock tease, that stuck up cunt."

"And the night I'm supposed to pop her cherry," I say, my hands twisting at my side, "I go and fucking pass out."

Marcus lets out a low chuckle that makes my hackles rise. "That's 'cos you drank out the wrong cup, man."

"I…what?" My brow furrows.

Marcus shakes his head, looking up as if he's trying to deal with a difficult kid or something. "Man, I was so fucking careful to keep track, but you got Jess's cup."

I think back to the video, but that couldn't be it.

"Since eleven, I was trying to roofie her." Marcus is grinning openly now. "She either left her drink and fucked off somewhere else, or spilled it. Then you drank it. I was about to give up before I finally got some of that shit in her."

"Well thank God you were there," I say, desperately trying to reign in the conversation. Hoping Indi has the patience and foresight to see what I'm trying to accomplish here. High hopes indeed—I don't think she has a single patient bone in her body.

Marcus cocks his head at me, a calculating twinkle in his eye. "Aren't you mad I set you up?"

"She had it coming, no two ways about it."

Marcus lets out another laugh, but I can see I'm far from convincing him that I'm on his side.

"Where do you think you're going?" Marcus snaps, and the gun lifts so fast I'm already tensing for the impact of the bullet.

But he's not aiming at me. He's talking to Indi, who's snuck out behind me.

"Put it down, Marcus," she snaps. "We both know you're not going to shoot us."

Damn it, Indi!

"Why the fuck wouldn't I?" Marcus growls.

"Because someone will hear and then they'll call the cops. Which means you can't have your fun."

There's no mistaking the venom in Indi's voice. I don't dare look back at her in case she thinks I'm encouraging this stupidity, but I'm a hundred percent positive she's glaring at Marcus.

"Indi," I murmur as quietly as possible, barely moving my lips. "Shut the fuck up."

"What, so you two can go on reminiscing about how you raped Jessica?" Her voice rises into a yell at the end. "I'd rather you shoot me now and get it over with."

"Shut up!" Marcus yells. "Shut! Up!"

Instead, Indi screams at the top of her lungs.

I don't know where my mind is at. I guess I still think my idiotic plan is working. Being chummy with Marcus, at least, had the gun pointed at the floor, not at Indi. Then she intervened.

Stubborn, stubborn!

I slap my hand over her mouth, wrench her around, and throw her to the mattress. I stare for a second as she bounces, and she stares right back at me, shock writ large in her wide eyes and over her trembling mouth.

"Wh-?" is all she gets out before I'm on top of her.

She must have been gagged or blindfolded at some stage, because the cloth used to do it is still hanging around her neck. I rip it off and shove it between her lips. She slaps at my hands and tugs at my wrists, but it's easy enough to tie off the gag since she's obviously not trying that hard to injure me.

In the silence that follows, my breath sounds like that of a wild animal caught in a trap.

"There," I say, leaning back. I widen my eyes at Indi, but she doesn't seem to notice. Her hands go up to the gag, but I grab her wrists and pin them to her stomach. "Now you can't go running off your mouth again."

CHAPTER FORTY-SIX

INDI

If this is part of Briar's plan, then it sucks. Yeah, it kinda looks like the psycho's letting his guard down, but that doesn't explain Briar's need to shove a gag in my mouth.

So I screamed, so what? If I managed to alert someone in the neighborhood to our plight, then all the better. Because I'm sorry, but I'm not staking my life on the off-chance that Briar can talk sense into someone as obviously psychotic as Marcus.

Guess I was back of the line when they were handing out patience.

I glare at Briar above my gag, willing him to read the furious thoughts I'm daggering at him, but he keeps looking back at Marcus.

He's so heavy on my stomach, it feels like all my internal organs are being pulverized.

I buck under him, letting out a muffled shriek.

That gets his attention. He glances down at me, widens and then narrows his eyes like he's trying to Morse code me the detailed steps of this harebrained plan of his.

So kind of you to keep me informed, Briar.

Really. What a champ.

"Perfect," Marcus says.

I turn my head, and focus my glare on him instead. He's standing a yard away from the mattress, his cellphone in one hand and his gun in the other.

"You wanna do her doggy style, like Jess?"

"Nah. Just like this is fine," Briar says.

Cold concrete oozes into my stomach. This is about the video again, isn't it? I don't even *want* to know, but I'm powerless to stop my thoughts going there.

Proof that Briar raped Jess. The one Addy was apparently using to blackmail him. I don't know how much of it's true. Which parts Briar's bluffing about.

In a perfect—if unbelievable—world, Briar would somehow be innocent of all charges. Marcus is obviously a whack job—so why couldn't it all have been him? Everything.

He killed mom.

I squeeze my eyes shut and swallow down a sob. There's been zero time to deal with any of this shit, but this is not the time. Like hell that stops my brain thinking, though.

None of it makes sense, of course. Why the hell would Marcus drive all the way out to Lakeview? Was it all just for the stupid necklace around my neck?

I twist my hands, trying to get them out of Briar's grip. If I could loosen that chain and throw the thing at Marcus, I would. Maybe then he'll go away. Exploding into a plume of smoke.

Briar looks across at Marcus. "You got a good enough angle, bro?"

Seriously, what the fuck is with all the bros?

"Almost," Marcus says, shifting to one side. "Yeah. Ready when you are."

I look back at Briar the same time he looks at me. He gives me a faint smile, but I don't know what to make of it. He leans back, one hand still gripping my wrists together at my sternum, while the other goes around his waist.

Between my legs.

I let out a muffled protest when he touches me, and shift under him, shaking my head.

There's gotta be another way, I yell telepathically at him. *Marcus is close enough for you to fucking storm him. Just do it!*

But all Briar seems inclined to do is stroke my pussy. I close my eyes, wriggling furiously to get away from his fingers.

He leans down in a rush, putting his mouth right by my ear. "Stop moving. You're making me hard."

When he straightens with a strange leer on his face, all I can do is blink at him in astonishment.

This is getting him hard?

My fuck—and here I thought Marcus was the only psycho in the room.

"Come on, bro," Marcus says. I close my eyes again, and force myself to stop wriggling under Briar.

"She's not wet enough," Briar says.

My cheeks go hot. I grip my fingers together like I'm praying, and then I actually *do* pray.

Not to God, but to Briar.

Please, please stop wasting time and do something!

Fingers—enough of them to stretch my walls—slide inside me and dig deep. I flinch, cry out into the gag, and have to force myself to go still again.

"Feels wet as fuck to me," Marcus says, and then laughs. I cringe, and hurriedly swallow down the bile that rushes up my throat. My eyes pop open. I glare up at Briar, and he scowls down at me.

Is he angry with me because I dared move? Fuck him! And if Marcus was so close, why in the hell didn't Briar attack him?

Briar shifts his mouth to the side, grabs my wrists in both hands, and pins them above my head. My hands sink into the mattress as I give Briar another venomous glare.

"Hey, bro?"

Marcus straightens behind Briar, head tilted quizzically. "Yeah?"

"Can you hold her down while I fuck her?"

BRIAR

My heart's thundering in my chest. Marcus was right behind me, and there was fuck all I could do about it. Why?

Because as soon as his fingers touched mine, there between Indi's legs, he pressed the barrel of his gun to the back of my head.

I could still have tried to disarm him, but I couldn't risk getting shot and leaving Indi to fend him off. I'd do anything not to have her end up downstairs beside cold, dead Addy. I'd even die, if that would help. I was the one who got her into this mess in the first place. Taunting her, bullying her. It's my fault she ever got on Marcus's radar.

All because of my selfish need to *own* shit. To claim what's mine. First, the woods by the house. Then her.

Guess I'm finally going to get what I want.

Right here, right now.

I must be as sick as Marcus. Fuck, maybe we do share DNA. Because the thought of defiling her like this is giving me a hard-on. Despite the fact that she's lying motionless under me and scowling a hole through my head. It doesn't matter.

I told her I'd be her first and I plan on keeping my promise, even if it means she's screaming at me the entire time.

I'd rather have her hate me for the rest of my life, than have Marcus take her virginity while I watch.

Marcus crouches on the mattress by my head and puts the gun down, behind and to his right, before taking my wrists from Briar. The touch of Marcus's cold fingers on my wrists, some still slick with my own lubricant, is enough to make me gag. But the savage hunger in Marcus's black eyes makes me want to hurl.

I can smell myself on him, and it's throwing my head into a state of such overwhelming shock I feel a catatonic state coming on. I can't let that happen.

I have to fight this!

But now Marcus is holding me down, not Briar. And when I start bucking and writhing under Briar, yelling at him through my gag to get off me, to stop, to abandon his stupid plan, Marcus leans real close and sinks his teeth into my jaw.

Briar stops with a hand on his zip. I go rigid in shock, and then melt with fear. Marcus pulls back, but from the fierce stinging where his teeth were, I know he broke the skin.

"Christ," Briar breathes.

My eyes fly to him, but his gaze is transfixed on the spot where Marcus bit me.

"What?" Marcus demands. "Bitch wouldn't lay still."

Briar clears his throat, and hurriedly zips down his fly. "That was so fucking hot."

He's bullshitting, of course. I can see the disgust in his eyes. But I guess, just like some relationships force rose-tinted glasses on your nose, Marcus doesn't notice anything but what he wants to.

And his friend just told him it was hot when he bit me.

So he bites me again. This time, right on my breast.

CHAPTER FORTY-EIGHT

BRIAR

Indi thrashes under me, and all I can do is watch. The gun's too far away for me to grab, and Marcus is in the way. I'm one step closer to disabling him, but Indi's a loose cannon. I can't depend on her to stay still and not get herself killed, I just can't.

I'm in some kind of limbo-land. I know I sound like I'm reading lines off a script. My body moves in fits and starts like I'm a stop animation clay model, not a human being.

Marcus is unraveling. Maybe so far gone in this fantasy of his that he's lost touch of reality. I guess, to him, everything is swell. He and his best friend are double-tagging this stuck up virgin, just like he'd planned for us with Jessica.

A plan I'd fucked up when I'd passed out.

"I'll hold her down," Marcus says. "You fuck her."

"Yes," I say woodenly, and climb off Indi's stomach.

Her eyes are shut, and she's whimpering through the gag every time one of us speaks.

I can't imagine what fresh hell this is for her, but I don't think there's any other way either of us gets out of this alive. I'm fully aware, however, that if something goes wrong in the next minute, she might die thinking I caved in and let my black soul take over.

Kneeling beside her waist, I grab her wrists from Marcus and wrap the fingers of my other hand around her neck.

Her eyes fly open. A piece of me dies when I see tears glittering in those lashes, trapped diamonds. It's already too late. She hates me now. She always will. Doesn't matter how this ends. Doesn't matter if you save her or just prolong her suffering.

Indi Virgo will never be mine. Not how I wanted her to be, anyway.

I make sure there's barely any pressure on her neck. Her eyes flit between me and Marcus, where he's forcing open her legs and holding her down.

What can I possibly say to her?

Should I even bother?

I tug loose her gag and kiss her instead. Then she moans into my mouth, shuddering.

"Come on, bro. Fuck her already."

I break off the kiss, and I don't look at Marcus. I can't, because then I'd have to see what he's doing to make her shudder and convulse so. And that would break me.

"I want you to fuck her," I say, not daring to take my eyes off Indi's.

"What?"

"Please, bro. I want to…" My voice fades as hurt bleeds into Indi's eyes. I can't imagine how betrayed she must feel right now. The indignation, the shame? But I force the words out anyway, knowing they'll cut me deeper than any knife ever could.

"I want to watch you fuck her."

Marcus lets out a soft sound, something between a huff and a laugh. "You sure?"

"You said it yourself," I murmur. "You'd love to pop another cherry."

CHAPTER FORTY-NINE

I'm dead inside. Dead, and cold, and crawling with maggots. But my lips are still tingling. I guess they haven't got the message yet. They still think this is all in good fun; a little roughhousing before the main attraction.

If I weren't a corpse, I'd be spewing up everything I've ever eaten. But all I do is lie here with my legs wide as they can go while Marcus positions himself by my pussy.

"You sure she's a virgin?" Marcus says. "Never seen one with a shaved cunt before."

I swallow hard, and wonder if Briar can feel my throat moving under his hand.

"Don't fight this," Briar says. "Just be a good girl, and take it all."

My brain seethes in quiet fury at his words, but it's the only thing still alive in my dead, dead body. I barely feel Marcus's fingers on my folds, opening me up.

"I said don't fight it!" Briar's eyes flicker past me, but return so fast I could have imagined it.

The gun.

He was looking at the gun.

It's a few feet away from me, but still out of reach.

"You holding her down?"

"Yeah. But she's a good girl. She won't fight you."

"She will when I rip this pretty pussy in two," Marcus says through a chuckle.

He touches me, and it's as if something inside my mind snaps. I scream. Briar's hand closes over my mouth. Then I sink my teeth into his fingers. He jerks away his hand with a shout of pain, and that's when I buck with all my might. Marcus sits back, one hand on his cock, the other cupping his balls.

Told you—drop a bomb, and they always go for their nut sacks. I draw in my leg and kick out as fast as I can, slamming Marcus's own hands into his genitals.

He screams as he falls backward, but by then I'm already twisting, arm stretching for the gun.

The metal's ice-cold against my fingers. I drag it close, grab the grip, and twist to face Marcus.

But he's not there anymore.

I sit up in a rush.

Briar and Marcus are on the far edge of the mattress. Briar has both hands around Marcus's neck, and Marcus is trying to wedge open his fingers as his face starts swelling with trapped blood.

The gun bobs and weaves until I slap my one hand over the other.

I've never shot a gun.

I've never even watched enough action movies to have any idea how this thing works.

But I saw Marcus draw back the hammer, so I do that. And I know what a trigger is, so I curl my finger around it.

"Shoot him!" Briar yells.

But I can't. Not yet. I'd probably end up hitting Briar in the back of the head. "Let him go!" I yell. "Then I'll shoot."

"Just fucking shoot him!"

Marcus abandons his attempts at tearing Briar's hands off his throat. Instead, he slams a fist into Briar's groin.

Briar groans and rolls off him, retching.

Marcus twists to the side just as I jerk back on the trigger.

The gun recoils like a jackhammer, and I almost lose my grip on it.

Almost…but not quite.

Briar pushes himself up and lunges for Marcus.

And then I pull the trigger again.

BRIAR

I've never liked the feel of blood. The silky, slightly sticky warmth of it always makes me cringe. And God, have I felt a lot of blood in my life.

The time I slipped and knocked loose my left incisor.

So much blood. In my mouth, down my throat, choking me. But even through the pain and shock, I'd rummaged around in that coppery pool to retrieve my tooth, dimly aware that it would suck ass if I swallowed it.

Football games bled me a lot. Another tooth lost there. A gash out of my left leg. Some cuts deep enough for stitches.

Blood, blood, blood.

My hands are coated in it now. Not quite as much as when I'd knocked out my tooth, but somehow it feels even silkier, even stickier, hot enough to scorch.

I hear Indi's voice, but it's so far away.

"Leave him. Leave him!"

She sounds angry. She shouldn't be; Marcus is my best friend.

I can't let him die.

I keep my hands over the hole in his chest, trying to ignore the way his blood keeps oozing through my fingers. He's pale as a sheet, his body shivering under me like he's got a fever.

"Hey," I say, not even sure if he can hear me. "Where you going?"

Marcus moves his lips, but the only thing that comes out is frothy pink foam.

"Stay here a bit. Help's coming," I tell him.

Indi grabs my arm, tries to tug me away. "Leave him!" she yells.

But I can't. Marcus is my best friend.

I can't let him die.

"Briar, p-please," she sobs, falling to her knees beside me. "Leave him."

But I can't. Marcus is…

Those dark eyes stop blinking. His lips stop moving.

Marcus was my brother.

CHAPTER FIFTY

INDI

I really gotta find out what the hell these guys put in their tranquilizers. I've never felt this relaxed, this zoned out, this…detached.

Not entirely true, I guess.

I was in almost this exact same spot when I last felt this way. Back then it was my mother's body they were wheeling out of the smoking ruins of my house, not Addy's.

Marcus is already in the ambulance. I heard someone say they're taking him to the hospital. Dunno why—psycho fuck was already long dead by the time they pitched up here.

But then Addy disappears into an ambulance and they drive her away too.

Guess Lakeview was all out of mortuary vans tonight. Actually, now that I think about it, I can't remember if they took Mom away in an ambulance or a—

"Indi."

I twist slowly, and tip back my head. It's night time already, but with all the police cars, ambulances, and the firetruck around —whose presence I have to get someone to explain to me before the night is out—Briar looks like a character in one of those cyberpunk movies where the whole city is basically just one big neon sign.

"Briar," I say.

He steps closer, but almost reluctantly. "They want us down at the police station to give our statements." There's a clink from his hands—he's busy toying with his keys. "Want a lift?"

I consider for a while, watching the play of red and blue on his face. Maybe they gave him something for his shock too, because he looks ready to wait all night for my answer.

"Can I drive?" I ask.

"No." He shrugs. "You've been sedated."

"So have you."

"Can barely feel it." Another shrug. "Plus, you're not on my insurance."

I stand, and it takes me forever just to take two steps closer to him. "You just don't want me driving your car."

"Not tonight."

"But someday?"

His eyes lock onto mine. He reaches for me, but I'm too far away. We step forward at the same time, and then I'm in his arms. I wish I could feel it. I'm sure it would be a wonderful moment, full of comfort and bliss.

But I'm still dead inside. Those maggots have stopped moving, but I have a sneaking suspicion that's only because they're sleeping.

I'm not sure if they'll ever wake up again. I'm hoping they won't.

I don't want to think about that. What I want is for this day to be over. I want tomorrow to come.

Briar turns, his arm over my shoulder as he leads me to his Mustang. No one stops us—other than the bump on my head which, apparently didn't give me a concussion—I don't really have any wounds.

Even those two bite marks turned out to be much shallower than I'd imagined. No need for stitches. I did get a tetanus shot, though. Briar must have too. Turns out humans have filthy mouths.

I glance back over my shoulder, my eyes tracing the broken outline of my house. My other hand goes to the necklace that's still hanging from my neck.

All I want to do is go home and sleep, but I know the police need information.

Go to sleep, my girl.

Have pleasant dreams.

Tomorrow is a new day.

This time, when I look ahead, I don't see darkness. Maybe it's the tranquilizers singing through my veins, but there's some kind of numb hope seeping into me as Briar opens the passenger door.

I guess I can wait to go to sleep, because I know this time, Mom's promise will come true. Tomorrow, when I wake, it *will* be a bright new day.

I peek at Briar through my lashes as he turns the ignition and his Mustang rumbles into life.

How do I know? Because Briar will be there.

EPILOGUE

INDI

I've been zoning out to the *clop-clop* of our horses's hooves. When Briar touches my arm, I gasp and wrench myself away.

We stare at each other before he breaks into a wide smile. "I'm gonna have to ask for my money back," he says.

I frown at him.

"They said, and I quote, a 'relaxing, romantic horseback trail'."

I let out a rueful chuckle and shrug at him, facing forward again. "I love it."

"You do?"

"It's perfect, Briar." I glance at him, looking away before our eyes can meet. "Although I still don't know how many palms you had to grease to pull this off."

"What, school?" He snorts. "We've both got B-averages. We've both just gone through a traumatic—"

He cuts off, and when he speaks again, there's no mirth left in his words. "You needed a break."

"So did you."

"Yeah, I'm selfish like that, my little virgin."

I snort this time, and shake my head. "Never grows old, does it?"

He leans over and pokes a finger in my side, making me twist over in my saddle and my horse take a side step as if she thinks she's next.

"Stop it," I snap, scowling at him.

"Only if you promise not to be upset."

My scowl turns into a frown. "Why would I be—?"

His expression turns serious. "Because I lied to you."

Something wriggles around in my guts, and I wonder briefly if the maggots are back. But I shove that thought away before it can latch on.

"About what?" I say, trying to keep my voice airy.

"I don't like you, Indi."

Luckily, my mare is well trained. Even when I stiffen, she just carries on plodding down the forest path at the same pace as before. I, however, almost don't duck in time to avoid being swept away by a low-hanging branch.

"Um…okay," I say, forcing a swallow. "And you had to tell me this during a romantic horse ride through the forest?"

"I couldn't keep living a lie," he says.

If his tone weren't so goddamn serious, I'd be convinced this was all part of a foolishly elaborate prank at my expense. He's never outgrown those, not in the four months we've been dating. Maybe he never will.

"Well, I'm glad it's all out in the open," I say. "So, should we turn around, or do you still want to have that picnic you promised me?"

"Oh, we're having the picnic," he says, sounding almost grumpy. "But don't think I'm gonna enjoy it."

"Pity," I say, lifting my chin. "I was really looking forward to your charming banter while we snacked on some pretzels and warm champagne."

He chuckles low in his throat. "You thought there'd be champagne?"

"There'd better be fucking champagne." I glare at him until he looks at me, and then I intensify it even more. "Else I'm not taking another step."

I reign in my mare, and Briar's gelding plods on a few steps before he brings him to a stop. He looks over his shoulder, clearly exasperated with me. "Fine, there's champagne. But it's definitely warm, and possibly even flat by now."

"I said we could trot." I push my knees into my mare's ribs, and she starts forward. "But nooooo. Briar's a little chicken shit bitch, isn't he?"

"You're gonna pay for that," he murmurs quietly, but also just loud enough for me to hear.

I smirk to myself, shaking my head. We've been riding through this gorgeous forest just south of the Devil's Spine for the last three hours and it truly has been everything Briar said it would be. I'm almost starting to feel like myself again, and that's saying a lot. These past few months have been difficult. Sleeping pills helped, as did the anti-anxiety medication Briar's doctor gave me for the panic attacks I kept having. But there was always that feeling lurking deep inside me, like there was something bad waiting just around the corner. That it would pounce as soon as I let my guard down.

Briar seems to be doing fine, but I can never tell with him. I mean, we're not living together or anything, so I don't know what he's like the times I'm not with him. He's always been one to put on a brave face, so he could be hiding a ton of pain about losing his friend.

And not just a friend. A half-brother. A fact I'm still trying to wrap my head around.

One of many, in fact.

A lot of shit came to light when the police started their investigation. Brandon Baker, Marcus's father, was arrested for multiple jewelry heists and as an accessory to murder. They're also opening a case against him for the possible homicide of Natalie Briar after Brandon started spouting some shit about being glad that he'd dealt with that whoring bitch.

Briar told me it was an accident, and that's what everyone thought. But one of the witness statements mentioned that Natalie's brake lights came on long before she went off the side of the road.

Her car, however, never slowed down.

The wreckage of her vehicle has long since been harvested for scrap metal, but I guess everyone would like to heap as many charges on Brandon's head as judicially possible to make sure the creep never gets out of jail.

One case reopened, another case closed.

And boy, were the police in Lakeview only too happy to archive my mother's homicide file. After the insurance company began pressuring them to take another look at the evidence, an internal investigation revealed that several of the officers working the case had been paid off to screw up the case.

All by Marcus's dad, of course.

Lured with some time knocked off his sentence, Brandon gave a full confession about how he'd forced his son to break into people's homes and steal the jewelry Briar's father had made for them.

Briar told me about the beatings Marcus got. Seems they were very real indeed. Marcus had hospital files thick as an encyclopedia with multiple instances of domestic abuse injuries.

He was just as good as Briar at keeping up appearances. Plus, it seemed he could endure a shit load more pain when he smoked that weed vape of his. Healed faster, too.

With such an extensive history of abuse, I almost feel sorry for Marcus.

Then I remember what it felt like when he bit my breast, and the feeling goes away.

If Marcus had lived, he would have been charged with arson, rape, and first-degree murder. They matched his DNA to hair, skin, and semen samples found on my mother's body.

I feel less sorry for him every day.

"Hungry?"

I snap out of the past and come back to the present feeling a little glum for all my macabre introspection.

Until I see the suggestion of a cabin up ahead.

"Is that…?"

"I don't like picnics," Briar announces like he's in a confessional booth at mass.

I spur my mare into a trot, too eager to see what's ahead to be bothered if Briar's keeping up. As soon as her hooves plod on flagstones, I slide off my mare and absently loop her reign around a nearby tree branch.

This is exactly how I always pictured the grandmother's cabin in Red Riding Hood. From the log walls to the smoke curling from the chimney.

"It's gorgeous," I breathe, hurrying to the front door.

It opens at a push from my fingers, and swings inward without a sound.

I expected a moodily lit interior, but it's bright as noon inside here. Downlights gleam from their studs in a pine ceiling, and peek out from behind furniture.

There's a massive three-seater sofa in the middle of the living area, facing a lit fireplace that crackles as the flames dance for me.

My riding boots echo on wooden floorboards when I move into the space. It's all one open-plan layout, except for a small room tucked behind the kitchen's oven range and backsplash.

It has to be a bathroom, because the west side of the cabin is dominated by a king-sized bed straight out of a fairytale with its elaborately carved mahogany footboard and rich, velvet headboard.

There are rose petals on the sheets. Champagne in a bucket on the nightstand. The entire space is scented with roses and wood smoke.

Hands slither around my waist and draw me back against Briar's warm body.

"Surprise," he murmurs into my ear.

"My fuck," I say, and then instantly regret how my words seem to defile this sanctum.

"There'll be enough time for that later," Briar says. "But first…" He releases me, slips past, and heads toward the fire.

I was expecting a campsite, not a fucking cabin. I had a bag packed and everything.

But this?

"Hang on," I say, crossing my arms over my chest. "You just told me you didn't like me. Why'd you go to all this trouble, then?"

"I thought it would lessen the sting, my little virgin."

My cheeks are suddenly suffused with heat.

Briar turns to look at me, a cheeky smile tugging at his wide mouth.

"Briar…" I want to tell him I'm not ready, because, fuck, that's exactly what it feels like.

I know he's been patient. I know I've been holding back. But he promised me he would wait.

He *promised*.

I open my mouth, but before I can say a word, he lifts a finger to his lips.

"I want to show you something," he says.

My eyebrow quirks up. "What is it?"

He cocks his head at me. "If I told you, it would ruin the surprise."

I inhale a deep, grounding breath, squeezing my arms around me as I give this gorgeous cabin another once-over.

I could live here. I don't give a fuck about TV or wi-fi, or anything else.

I could live here.

But only if Briar was going to live with me.

I look at the floor, closing my eyes as I chastise myself for my own naivety.

This is no place to live. We're both going to university next year. Briar to become a psychologist, me to study microbiology. Or history. Or art. We can maybe make it out here once a quarter, but—

"Open your eyes."

They fly open at his command, and then narrow warily.

Nothing's different. Except…

"What's behind your back?"

He smirks at me. "I meant what I said."

"About what?"

"I don't like you anymore, Indigo Virgo."

I bristle at my full name, but bear it out of sheer curiosity. "Go on…"

Briar's smirk fades, and is replaced with a deadly serious expression.

I know this is all some ruse, but that doesn't stop the flutters blooming in my stomach.

Flutters. Because it's not worms burrowing around down there anymore.

It's butterflies.

Briar drops to one knee, bringing out a deep-blue velvet box and flipping it open all in one smooth motion.

My hands are at my throat, and I don't remember how they

got there. "Did you practice that or something?" I ask weakly.

"Too many times to count." He clears his throat, and his eyes dart to the box.

Which I haven't even looked at. I've been transfixed on his eyes this entire time. But when I look down, my legs cave in, and I sink to the floor in front of him.

"Briar…"

"I don't like you anymore, Indi. Maybe I never did. I fucking love you." He moves the box closer to me, as if I'm not admiring the diamond-encrusted sapphire ring he's holding out for me quite enough for his tastes. "You'd better marry me, or I'll make your life a living hell."

I reach for the ring, but he snaps the box closed before I can take it. My eyes fly up to his, and I scowl deeply at him. "What the fuck?" I snap.

"You don't get the ring until you say yes."

"Well let me see how it looks first."

"You're shitting me," he says through a laugh. "This is all hinging off whether the ring looks good on your finger?"

I shrug, and waggle my left hand in his face. "And if it fits. If it doesn't fit…"

He glares at me, and then flips open the box again. "How do you always manage to make me so fucking mad?"

He takes out the ring, hesitates, and then slides it onto my finger.

Oh my fuck. It's absolutely fucking gorgeous. I sniff, twist my hand around a bit, and go to take it off.

"Nope," I say, shaking my head. "This isn't gonna cut it."

Briar lets out a deep-throated growl. Before I have time to squeal, he scoops me into his arms and charges with me into the bedroom. I bounce hard on the bed, sending rose petals fluttering into the air beside me.

I grab the ring and try to yank it off, but Briar clambers onto the bed and pins me down.

"You'll wear the fucking ring," he says, voice so low it's more of a growl than actual words. "And you'll fucking like it."

"Bastard," I murmur, narrowing my eyes. "Think you can buy my love?"

"I don't need to buy anything." He shoves a hand between my legs and squeezes me through my riding slacks. "I already own you."

I try to laugh him off, but then his mouth is against mine, bruising my lips, his tongue forcing its way inside.

I melt into the bed, every shred of resistance fading. Briar grasps my breasts, squeezes me roughly through my pants, and then sits up and strips off his shirt.

My lips part as I run my hands over his chiseled chest, fingers lingering on some of his scars.

Football injuries, he tells me. Some, rough nights out partying.

I couldn't care if he got them cage fighting in a back alley. He's broken, this brutal prince of mine, and I wouldn't have it any other way.

He swats away my touch, and then yanks open the blouse I am wearing. Buttons ping against the wall and clatter to the floor. I gasp, shocked at his vehemence, but then his lips are on my breastbone, working their way down my belly.

My pants come off next, tossed God knows where. My bra, my panties. Until I'm naked and bare beneath him, nothing but a few crushed rose petals for modesty.

He sinks his fingers into my thighs and wrenches open my legs. I moan, arching my back as he stares hungrily down at my pussy.

"You have any idea how fucking beautiful you are?" he says, his eyes slowly tracing their way up my body. I shiver, and instinctively cover my breasts from his ravenous eyes.

Briar grabs my hands, forcing them back onto the bed. He shifts his grip, using only a single hand to keep me down, and tugs off his pants with the other.

A second later, his hard cock touches the inside of my thigh.

I shift up the bed, trying to close my legs. But Briar's between them now, and I know he won't let me say no again.

He dips his hips down and forward, and I moan when the crown of his dick touches my already soaking folds.

"Are you going to scream for me when I break you?" he murmurs, putting his lips right by my ear.

"Fuck you," I mutter, twisting my hips. "You really think you're that big?"

"I *know* I'm that big." His mouth closes on the side of my neck and works its way down to my collar bone, then my nipple. He rolls it between his teeth until it's a tight bud, and then sucks it as he massages it with his tongue.

God, I feel ready to come and he hasn't even touched my clit yet.

I arch my back, and he takes more of my breast into his mouth. He tightens his grip around my wrists as if reminding me that I don't have a choice in the matter, and then snakes his hand down my tummy.

He taps his fingers over my clit, and I come out of my delicious haze with a yelp.

"Fuck, Briar."

"In a minute, my little virgin." His lips brush mine, and I let out a low moan as he rakes his fingers through my folds. "Gotta make sure you're ready first."

I'm not. I can't be. I don't know why, but I'm terrified. I shouldn't be—it's not that big of a deal...except it is.

It *is*.

I've always wanted my first time to be perfect. Special. Roses and fucking champagne.

I have all that and more.

So why the fuck am I still hesitating?

"Mmm," Briar says, his lips vibrating against mine. "A little wet, but not nearly enough."

Then he's gone. His warmth, the solidity of his body, his whispered promises. Everything.

I barely have time to open my eyes before his mouth closes over my clit.

I groan deep in my throat, my hips arching involuntarily off the bed. Briar pushes me down with his hand on my stomach, and works my clit with his tongue like he's pissed off at it.

Ecstasy washes over me. I lose myself in space and time and float in an endless sea of pleasure.

I'm dimly aware that I have Briar's hair in a death grip, but I don't give a fuck if I pull out every strand by the root.

He makes me come way before I'm ready, and then drinks me down like a shot of tequila.

I'm still shuddering in the aftershock of my orgasm when he rests his entire weight on me and puts his mouth by my ear.

"Now you're wet enough," he murmurs.

Fingers sink into my pussy, stroke my folds, tweak my clit. I barely have enough faculties to moan in protest, although trust me: I do try.

"I love you, my little virgin," Briar says. "But I don't want to keep calling you that."

He shifts around between my legs, and then his fingertips are teasing open the folds covering my entrance. The smooth crown of his cock pushes against me.

I stiffen, whimper, try to back away up the bed. "I can't," I blurt out.

There are tears in my eyes, and I don't know how they got there. The room's starting to spin, my skin crawling like it wants to tear off of my flesh. "Briar, please, I can't—"

"It's me, Indi," he murmurs. He strokes the side of my face. "Look at me, Angel."

I force my eyes open, blinking through a stream of hot tears.

"Do you see me?" he asks.

I nod, and squeeze a few more traitorous tears from my eyes.

"You feel me?" he says as he gently strokes my pussy with the tip of his cock.

I nod again, and bite back a sob.

"I love you, Indi. I'll never hurt you. Hear me?"

I nod again. "I l-love you too," I manage, although my words are so stuttered I don't know if Briar hears a thing.

"Fuck," he groans. "Say it again."

"I love you." This time the words are clear.

"Again."

"I love you, Briar."

"Then let me make you mine," he whispers. He rubs his cock against me, coaxing me. "Let me in."

I let out a long sigh. Relax my thighs,

"Deep breath, Angel," he says. "One deep breath, and it'll all be over."

I inhale.

His cock forces its way past my entrance. My pussy resists, clamping around him like a vice. I burn and itch as slices of pain shoot through me.

I whimper, but then Briar kisses away the pain.

I writhe, but he just keeps going deeper.

"Deep breath."

And I realize I'm still inhaling. My head feels too light, the bed a cloud in the midnight sky.

And then he's inside me, impossibly deep, stretching me impossibly wide. I whimper again, and he eats the sound with hungry lips.

"Christ, you feel so fucking good," he murmurs. "So fucking tight, so fucking hot."

He moves, slowly as first, and then a little bit faster.

Slow, deep pleasure overwhelms those pinpricks of pain inside me. He draws back, and then pushes inside me, so slow I can feel every inch of his cock the deeper he goes.

I moan, my back arching, and grab hold of his shoulders.

"Fuck, you're everything I ever thought you'd be," he says. He fills me up entirely, and then stays lodged deep inside me as he rains kisses over my face. "Say I can fuck you now," he mutters, nipping at my earlobes.

"Wh-what?" I manage breathlessly. "But you're already—"

He cuts me off with a rude laugh. "Oh, Angel, I haven't even started."

My core constricts around him at those words.

"Yes," I whisper. My eyes open, fluttering as he slowly draws out of me again. "Fuck me."

"Your wish is my command."

He sits up, grabs my thighs, and forces my legs wide apart. Then he grabs his cock in a hand, dips his hips, and rams into me.

I hiss with pain, mewl in pleasure. His eyes dart up to my face, then down to my pussy.

I can't imagine what it looks like. To me, all I see is his beautiful body tensing as he starts thrusting into me.

There's still pain, right till the end. But I barely notice it over the bliss.

He pulls out of me before he comes, and before I know what I'm doing, I'm up on my elbows with my mouth open wide, begging to taste him.

He makes the most wicked sound, like I'm tearing apart his fucking soul, and forces his cock between my lips. I feel him tense, shiver, pulse on my tongue, and then a flood of tangy cum fills my mouth. It's horrible, but it's still better than the taste of blood.

Briar grabs the back of my head, forcing his dick so far back I think I'm going to hurl. But I don't. I suck at him and milk him with my tongue, hoping to make him feel a sliver of the pleasure he's shown me.

He pushes me away, and covers me with his heavy body again. I swallow hard, trying not to retch at the taste, and then his lips are on mine.

I don't know how long we lie there for, making out like kids on our first date, but by the time we stop, Briar's cock is jutting into my belly again.

He pushes up onto his elbows, cups his hands on my face, and stares deep into my eyes.

"So?" he says, a light laugh in his voice.

"So, that hurt. A lot."

He shakes his head. "Not that."

"Then what?" I frown at him, feeling like I've just come out of a haze.

"Indi Virgo," he growls. "Will you fucking marry me or not?"

I laugh, and clap my hands over my mouth. "Oh, that."

He scowls at me, and I run my hands down his face, smiling up at him. "Only if you promise to fuck me like that every day for the rest of my life."

He quirks an eyebrow. "Only once a day?"

"Yes."

"But what if I want to fuck you in the morning and the evening?"

I shrug "Then we'll just have to work something out."

He kisses me again, and this time he moves until he's lying on his side. Lifting my leg, he pushes against me until I force myself to unclench.

I moan when he's inside me again.

Then I laugh, but as quietly as I can.

He still hears me, and stops with his dick all the way inside me. "What's so funny, Angel?"

"Nothing," I murmur. I reach down and run my fingers around my entrance where he's stretching me wide as I can go. "Just thinking about what you said that day in Veroza's class."

"Really?" he mutters. "Now?"

"Yeah," I say, twisting so I can look at him over my shoulder. "Guess you were right, Prince Briar."

He pulls out of me, and then eases his way back in. I shudder at the sensation, and moan when he starts massaging my clit.

"I always am." He gives me a suspicious look. "Which specific time are you referring to, though?"

I laugh and shake my head at him. "*Everyone* bows to the prince."

The End

Need more of Indi and Briar in your life? Visit the link below to sign up for my VIP newsletter and I'll send you an EXCLUSIVE bonus scene!

https://authorloganfox.com/brutal-bully-bonus

Can I send you my secret dark romance novella that's never been published…?

Join my VIP newsletter and you'll receive your own exclusive copy of My Darling, and I'll keep you up to date with my new releases and promos!

https://authorloganfox.com/my-darling-signup

MORE BY LOGAN FOX

For more books by this author, reading order, playlists, trigger warnings, socials, and more…please visit:

https://authorloganfox.com

www.ingramcontent.com/pod-product-compliance
Lightning Source LLC
Chambersburg PA
CBHW070149120726
47909CB00001B/42